W9-BMR-254

DEBBIE MACOMBER

One of America's favorite storytellers!

Praise for Debbie and her previous novel,
This Matter of Marriage:

In *This Matter of Marriage*, Debbie Macomber
"retells the parable of women's age-old concerns
with gentle humor and charm."
—*Publishers Weekly*

This Matter of Marriage is "so much fun it may
keep you up till 2 a.m."
—*The Atlanta Journal*

"Debbie Macomber's sparkling sense of humor
infuses [*This Matter of Marriage*] with a
sarcastic wit that will have readers doubled
over with laughter. Absolutely fabulous!"
—*Rendezvous*

"In the vein of *When Harry Met Sally*,
Ms. Macomber will delight. She uses her
unique voice and sense of humor in
[*This Matter of Marriage*] and readers should
rejoice at this 'never leave your house' keeper!"
—*Romantic Times*

"Popular romance writer Macomber has a gift for
evoking the emotions that are at the heart of the
genre's popularity."
—*Publishers Weekly*

AUTHOR'S NOTE

My publishing path has taken many twists and turns over the years. It all started back in the late 1970s with a rented typewriter set up at the kitchen table. Between car pools, Cub Scouts, ballet lessons, teaching Sunday School and analyzing new math, I wrote. Day after day, month after month and year after year. As soon as the kids walked out the door for school, Supermom was magically transformed into the struggling young writer. I make a great case study on how to become an overnight success in twenty years or less!

In those early years all I had to sustain me was my dreams. And dream I did. I'd close my eyes and picture my name on the cover of a book. I could even see the artwork. For someone who had yet to publish a word of fiction, this was heady stuff. But here I am, twenty years and dozens of books later, with the publication of *Montana*—a story I've wanted to write for a very long time.

I have a lot of people to thank for this incredible opportunity, but no one more than my editor, Paula Eykelhof. She's supported this project from inception with energy and enthusiasm. Her insights and editorial skills have helped shape this story from beginning to end. As always, I'm incredibly indebted to Irene Goodman, quite possibly the world's greatest agent. And to my best friend, Linda Lael Miller, who is always there for me. I have to thank Renate Roth, my secretary, for keeping my life organized and sane. Thanks, also, to Geri and Scott Bier, who generously let me call on their ranching expertise. And of course a big kiss to my husband for encouraging me to live my dream. He could complain a great deal more than he does! But mostly, thank you, my loyal readers, for your continued interest and support. Your letters have touched my heart. You can reach me at P.O. Box 1458, Port Orchard, WA 98366.

DEBBIE MACOMBER

MONTANA

MIRA®

ISBN 1-55166-434-8

MONTANA

Copyright © 1997 by Debbie Macomber.

Printed in U.S.A.

Dedicated to my Thursday Morning Breakfast Club:
Janelle Brothers, Lillian Schauer, Diana Letson,
Betty Wojcik and Stephanie Cordall.
Each one is a power woman with a direct
connection to the source of all power.

And dedicated to Barb Dooley, with thanks for
blessing my life with her wisdom and friendship.

One

"I don't know how much longer your grandfather's going to live."

The words hit Molly Cogan with the force of an unexpected blow. Sinking onto a stool beside the kitchen phone, she blocked out the blare of the television and her sons' ongoing argument over whose turn it was to set the table for dinner.

Tom and Clay were at each other's throats, but Molly could only deal with one crisis at a time. "Who is this again, please?"

"Sam Dakota. Listen, I realize this isn't the best time, but I felt I should tell you." He paused, then added, "Walt wouldn't appreciate me calling you, but like I said, you have a right to know his health isn't good."

The unmistakable sound of shattering glass filtered through the television noise as the boys' skirmish escalated.

Placing her hand over the mouthpiece, Molly shouted. "Boys, please! Not now." Something in her voice must have communicated the importance of the call, because both turned and stared at her. A moment later, Tom reached for the broom.

Molly's hand trembled as she lifted the receiver back

to her ear. "How do you know my grandfather, Mr. Dakota?"

"I'm his foreman. Been here about six months."

The fact that Gramps had willingly surrendered control of his ranch to a hired hand—a stranger—told her a great deal. For the past few years, he'd sold off portions of the once-huge spread, until all that remained was a couple of thousand acres, small by Montana standards. He'd managed the Broken Arrow Ranch himself as long as she could remember. Hired hands came and went, depending on the size of the herd, but as far as she knew, he'd always maintained tight control of the day-to-day operations. Over the years his letters had been infrequent, but in the last one—which she'd received after Christmas, four and a half months ago— Molly had sensed something wasn't right with Gramps. She'd put aside the feeling, however, consumed by her own problems.

"Tell me again what happened," she said abruptly, struggling to regain her composure. The man's first words had been such a shock, much of what he'd said afterward had escaped her.

"Like I told you, spring's our busy time, and yesterday your grandfather told me he'd be out to help check on the new calves. When he didn't show, I returned to the house and found him unconscious on the kitchen floor. Heart attack, I figured."

Molly pressed her fingers to her lips to hold in a gasp of dismay. Gramps...in pain. Unable to breathe. Losing consciousness. It frightened her to think of it.

With her mother and half brother living in Australia, Gramps was her only family here. Her only connection with her long-dead father.

"I got him to the clinic in town and Doc Shaver

confirmed what I thought. It *is* his heart. Walt has a pacemaker, but the walls of his heart are old and brittle, and it isn't working as well as Doc had hoped.''

"Gramps has a pacemaker?" Molly cried. "When did this happen?" She raised her hand to the cameo hanging from a gold chain around her neck and clenched it hard. It was the most precious piece of jewelry she owned. Gramps had given it to her the day they buried her grandmother nine years before.

"More than six months ago. First I'd heard of it, too."

"Why didn't he *tell* me?" Molly asked, although she realized Sam Dakota couldn't possibly know. She wished—not for the first time—that San Francisco was closer to Montana. Right now, Sweetgrass seemed a million miles away.

"I can't answer that. I thought you should know Walt's probably not going to live much longer. If you want to see him, I suggest you plan a visit out here soon."

"What exactly is wrong with his heart?" It might have sounded as if she was avoiding the real issue, but she needed to understand Gramps's condition before she could even *begin* to think about anything else. Like her finances. And how she could possibly afford a trip to Montana now.

"Do you know anything about pacemakers?"

"A little." Just enough to understand that they emit an electronic beep, which assists the heart in beating at a steady pace.

"Well, as I said earlier, the walls of your grandfather's heart are brittle and it's difficult to get the pacemaker to function properly. Doc Shaver worked on him a couple of hours, but he couldn't make any guarantees.

Said there's nothing more he can do. It's only a matter of time before his heart gives out completely."

Molly clamped her teeth over her lower lip while she tried to take in what this man was telling her. "I...I appreciate the call. Thank you." With each word, she felt herself more overwhelmed by emotion. *Not Gramps, please dear God, not Gramps. Not yet.*

"Sorry to call with such bad news."

"How...how is he now?" She glanced toward the living room and discovered Tom and Clay standing in the doorway, studying her intently. A smile would have reassured them, but even that was beyond her.

"Better. Will you be coming, then?" the foreman asked.

"I'm not sure." Molly didn't see how she could manage it. With the child-support payments cut off and the financial adjustments they'd already been forced to make in the past year, she couldn't imagine squeezing one more expense into her already stretched budget. Even a short trip would require at least a week away from her job—a contract position without paid holidays. Plus, she'd have the cost of airfare or, more likely, gas and lodging for the drive. She'd have to take the boys; Gramps would want to see them, and they deserved to see him.

"When will you know whether you're coming?"

It might have been her imagination, but she detected a note of censure. This man knew nothing about her—knew nothing about her circumstances or her life. How dared he stand as judge and jury over her decisions?

"If I knew that, I'd have said something sooner!" Leaning the back of her head against the kitchen wall, Molly tried to think clearly, desperate to find a way, a solution—anything that would lighten the burden of her fears. Never one to weep openly, particularly with strangers, she fought the growing constriction in her throat.

"Then I won't keep you any longer," Sam said gruffly.

Molly wanted to shout that he should wait, that she had other questions, but he'd already answered the important ones. What she wanted even more was to hear this stranger tell her Gramps was on the mend.

But he wasn't going to say that.

"Thank you for phoning," she said, feeling guilty about the sharp retort she'd made a moment ago. No one enjoyed delivering bad news, and it was kind of Sam Dakota to make sure she learned of her grandfather's condition. "I'll let you know if we're coming for a visit," she felt obliged to add.

"Fine. Your grandfather should be home in a day or two. I'd consider it a favor if you didn't mention I called."

"I won't. And thank you." Standing up, she replaced the telephone receiver and looked at her sons. Both had their father's deep-set dark brown eyes—and both had been born with the ability to look straight through her. At fourteen Tom was growing by leaps and bounds, a gangly youth with feet too big for his body. He hadn't grown into his height, and had become painfully self-conscious. This was an awkward stage filled with frustrations and raging hormones. They'd once been close, but that had all changed in the past few months. Tom barely talked to her now, no longer sharing confidences the way he used to. Often he was sullen and angry for no apparent reason. His attitude worried Molly; she sensed he was keeping something from her. She tried not to think about it, but every now and then the fear that he was experimenting with drugs or running with the wrong crowd would enter her mind and refuse to go away.

Clay, at eleven, was a younger version of his brother. Neither boy had inherited her auburn hair or clear blue eyes. Both resembled their father's side of the family—dark-haired and dark-eyed. Not that Daniel's family had revealed much interest in her sons. But then, neither had Daniel.

"That was about Dad, wasn't it?" Tom asked, his eyes locked on hers. His shoulders stiffened as though he was bracing himself for her response. The situation with Daniel hadn't been easy on any of them. They'd seen his name in the newspapers and on television night after night for weeks, that whole time the trial was taking place.

"The call wasn't about your father," Molly answered carefully. The kids had been through enough because of Daniel. He'd never been a good father, any more than he'd been a good husband; he had, in fact, left her for another woman. But she'd say one thing for him: until a year ago he'd faithfully paid child support. The payments had stopped when Daniel's troubles had begun. His legal problems had eventually led to financial problems for her and the boys.

"What did Dad do this time?" Tom demanded, his eyes narrowing suspiciously. It was a look Molly recognized, a look that said Tom, with his newly developed teenage cynicism, wasn't about to believe *any* adult. Especially his mother...

"I told you this has nothing to do with your father!" It bothered Molly that her son would assume she'd lie to him. There was nothing she abhorred more than lying. Daniel had taught her and their children more than enough on *that* subject. "I wouldn't lie to you."

"Then what's wrong?" Clay moved into the kitchen and Molly held out her arms to her youngest son. Clay didn't object to an occasional hug, but Tom had let it be known he was much too old for that sort of thing—and much too cool to display affection toward his mother. She respected his wishes, and at the same time longed for the times when they could share a simple hug.

"It's Gramps," she said. Her throat started to close and she couldn't say more.

Clay wrapped his arms tightly around her waist and pressed his head to her shoulder. Molly sighed deeply.

"Is Gramps sick?" Tom asked, shoving his hands in his pockets. He paced restlessly, back and forth across the kitchen floor. It'd become a habit of his lately, a particularly irritating one. Oh, yes, Molly thought, sighing again. The last twelve months had been hard on all of them. Tom seemed to be having the toughest time coping with everything—the public humiliation of his father's trial for fraud, the lack of any extra money and then the move from a spacious three-bedroom house to a cramped two-bedroom apartment. But this place was the best she could do, and his dissatisfaction underscored her own feelings of inadequacy.

"Gramps's heart is giving him trouble," Molly finally answered. She spoke in a low toneless voice.

"Are we going to go see him?"

Molly brushed the hair from Clay's brow and gazed down on his sweet boyish face. "I don't know yet."

"But, Mom, don't you *want* to?" Tom cried.

That hurt. Of course she did. Desperately. If she had

the choice, she'd be on the first plane out. "Oh, Tom, how can you ask me that? I'd give anything to be with Gramps."

"Then let's go. We can leave tonight." Tom headed toward the bedroom he shared with his younger brother, as if the only thing they needed to do was toss a few clothes in a suitcase and walk out the door.

"We can't," she said, shaking her head, disheartened once again by the reality of their situation.

"Why not?" Tom's voice was scornful.

"I don't have enough—"

"Money," her oldest son finished for her. He slammed his fist against the kitchen counter and Molly winced, knowing that the action must have been painful. "I *hate* money! Every time we want to do something or need something, we can't, and all because of money."

Molly pulled out a kitchen chair and sagged into it, her energy gone, her spirits deflated by anger and self-pity.

"It's not Mom's fault," Clay muttered, placing his skinny arm around her shoulders, comforting her.

"I don't know what to do," Molly said, thinking out loud.

"If you wanted to go by yourself," Tom offered with a show of reluctance, "I could baby-sit Clay."

"I don't need a baby-sitter," Clay insisted. "I can take care of myself." He glared at his older brother, challenging Tom to proclaim otherwise.

"I can't leave now, with or without you boys," Molly told them sadly. She had less than twenty dollars in her checking account. It was the all-too-familiar scenario—too much month at the end of her money.

"I remember Gramps," Tom said suddenly. "At least I think I do."

The last time Molly had visited the ranch was shortly after her divorce almost ten years ago. Her grandmother, who'd already been ill at the time with a fast-spreading cancer, had died shortly afterward. Gramps had asked Molly to come live with him, and for a while she'd seriously considered the invitation. She told herself now that if she'd had any sense, she would have taken him up on his offer. She might actually have done it if she'd managed to find work. Fluent in both French and German, Molly was employed on a contract basis by an import agency. Unfortunately there wasn't much call for her skills in the cattle country of western Montana.

During that visit Tom had been four and Clay still in diapers. Whatever memories Tom had were more likely the stories she'd told him about the ranch. Tucked against the foothills of the Bitterroot Mountains, the Broken Arrow was one of the lonely ranches scattered through the Flathead River valley. Molly often talked about it, especially after a letter arrived from Gramps. There weren't many, only two or three a year. Her grandmother had been the one who'd taken care of family correspondence. Molly had discovered that Gramps hated talking on the phone even more than he hated writing letters; nevertheless, he made the effort to keep in touch with her. Each one of his letters was read countless times and treasured. Losing his lifelong love had devastated him, and even now, nine years after her passing, Gramps mentioned his wife in every single letter, every conversation.

Molly always answered his letters and routinely mailed him pictures of the boys. Over the years they'd talked on the phone a number of times but their conversations had obviously been uncomfortable for him. Gramps never had been much of a talker, nor was he like the stereotypical kindly old characters who populated kids' storybooks. Nope, he was actually a bit of a curmudgeon. He yelled into the telephone as if he thought that was necessary in order to be heard and fretted constantly over what the call was costing.

No small man, he stood a good six-two and weighed at least two hundred pounds. Four-year-old Tom had found his appearance so scary that he'd clung to her leg the first few days of their visit. Clay had buried his face in her shoulder and wailed the instant Gramps came into view. Her grandfather didn't have the slightest idea how intimidating he could be to small boys.

Had it really been nine years since she'd last seen him? It seemed impossible, yet she knew it was true.

"He yelled," Tom murmured, lost in his own thoughts.

That was Gramps, all right. He was gruff and impatient and about as subtle as a gun in your face. To really know him was to love him, but he rarely gave anyone the opportunity to get that close. Never afraid to voice his opinions, Gramps went out of his way to make sure folks around him knew what he thought and why; anyone who dared to disagree was called a "danged fool." Usually to his—or her—face.

When Molly's grandmother was alive, she'd smoothed the waters. Her charm and humor had more than compensated for Walt Wheaton's prickly nature. By now, Gramps had probably alienated just about everyone in Sweetgrass.

The foreman who'd phoned said he'd been around

for more than six months. If Gramps had mentioned hiring a foreman in any of his letters, she'd missed it—hard to believe, considering how often she'd read them. But knowing Gramps, he'd rather chew nails than admit he needed help.

Sam Dakota. The name sounded almost familiar. She grinned weakly, allowing herself to be amused for just a moment—maybe she was confusing him with *South* Dakota. Or maybe Gramps had mentioned him, but not in a discussion about hired hands. She was sure of that.

The boys went to bed that evening with a minimum of fuss, for which Molly was grateful. She followed soon after, weary to the bone.

It shouldn't have come as a surprise that she couldn't sleep. Every time she closed her eyes, all she could see was Gramps. All she could think about was the cantankerous old man she loved.

At midnight, Molly gave up the effort and turned on the light. Tossing aside the covers, she went to her desk and sorted through the drawers until she found the last letter she'd received from Gramps. She sat on her bed, legs crossed, and read it slowly.

Dear Molly,
Thanks for the pictures of you and the boys. They sure don't look like they're any relation to us Wheatons, do they? Guess I can't hold it against them that they resemble their father. They aren't to blame for that. The picture of you is another story. Every time I pick it up, it's like seeing my own sweet Molly at your age. Only she wore her hair long.

I don't understand what's with women these days. They cut their hair short like they want to

be men. Ginny Dougherty, the gal who ranches
the spread next to mine, for instance—damn fool
woman thinks she can tend a herd as good as a
man, so she decides to look like one. She might
be a handsome woman if she kept her hair long
and even wore a dress. I tell you, her husband
would turn over in his coffin if he could see what
she's done to herself.

As for the hair business, I'll admit men aren't
much better. Seems a lot of them prefer to wear
it long—like back in the sixties, hippies and all.
But I never thought I'd see grown men—gray-
haired geezers, for Pete's sake!—wearing pony-
tails. Even worse—what do you call them?—those
pigtails. Far as I'm concerned Willie Nelson's got
a lot to answer for.

It isn't just the way people do their hair, either.
More and more strange things are going on in
Sweetgrass. A man doesn't know who to trust any
longer. People talk as if the government was the
enemy. I didn't fight in a world war to hear that
kind of crazy talk, but then folks around here
never have been keen for my opinion. I give it to
them, anyway, whether they want to hear it or not.

The weather's been good and bad. Winter
hasn't been too hard so far—only one blizzard.

The chickens are laying more eggs than I can
use, which means they're content. There's nothing
better than bacon and eggs for breakfast. I hope
you're feeding the boys a decent breakfast every
morning and not that sugar-coated junk.

Now about you. It sounds like Daniel finally got
what he's deserved all along. Imagine cheating
those decent folks out of their hard-earned cash!

I never did understand why you married that smooth talker. I knew the minute I met him he wasn't any good. If you'd asked me before you were foolish enough to go through with the wedding, you might have saved yourself a lot of trouble. Well, at least you have your boys, so something good came out of the marriage.

You're my only grandchild, Molly, and you're all I have left. You know that. I remember the day you were born and your father called to say Joan had given birth to a girl. Your grandmother wept when she learned your parents decided to name you after her. They must have known something even then, because small as you were, you resembled my Molly, and you do so more every year. She was a beautiful woman, and you are, too.

I wish your marriage had been like ours. It was the best thing in my life, Molly. I'm glad you're rid of that no-good Daniel, but I wish you'd marry again. Though I suppose that subject's best saved for another day.

I want to talk to you about something else. I recently celebrated my seventy-sixth birthday, so I decided it was time I got my affairs in order. I had a new will drawn up. When I was in town last week, I stopped off and talked to Russell Letson. He's an attorney who's been around awhile, and his father and I used to be friends. I like Russell well enough, even though I suspect most attorneys are shysters. Anyway, I brought in my old will, and Russell and I talked a bit and he asked me a bunch of questions that got me to thinking.

There's certain things you should know. First off, I've got a safe-deposit box at the bank. I put some medals in there from the war. When the time is right and they appreciate that sort of thing, you can give those medals to my great-grandsons. I suppose I should put your grandmother's wedding band in there, but I never could bring myself to part with it. I got it on the nightstand next to the bed. Nine years she's been gone, and I still miss her.

The ranch will be yours. I wish you'd moved here after Molly died, but I understood why you decided to return to California. For myself, I don't know how you can breathe that foul air—I've seen what San Francisco's like, on television. It can't be good for the boys to be taking in all that smog. I'm hoping that after I'm gone you'll give Sweetgrass another try. Folks here are hardworking and decent. Most years, the ranch should at least break even. And the house is solid. My father built it in 1909, and after he died, Molly and I added electricity and indoor plumbing. As houses go, it isn't fancy, but it's stood all these years and will stand longer.

That pretty well takes care of what I wanted to tell you.

I love you, Molly girl, and those youngsters of yours, too. I'm sure you know that, although I'm not one to say it often. This letter seemed like a good time to do it.

Remember—don't let Daniel give you any more grief. He's getting what he deserves.

Gramps

Molly read the letter a second time and then a third. It all made sense now.

According to what the foreman had told her, Gramps must have written it two months after he got the pacemaker. Her beloved grandfather hadn't said one word about his health problems, and she knew why.

Daniel.

Gramps hadn't wanted to burden her with more worries while she dealt with the publicity and embarrassment of Daniel's trial.

Gramps was right about Daniel; a prison term was exactly what he deserved. As an investment specialist he'd been regularly stealing retirement income from his elderly clients. He'd been clever about it, concocting schemes and falsifying numbers; it had taken several accountants and finance specialists almost a year to uncover the full extent of his crimes. Throughout his entire so-called career, he'd been cheating the very people he was supposed to be helping. He'd lied to his colleagues and clients, lied to the police and the press. He'd even been caught lying under oath. His trial had lasted for weeks, with mobs of angry senior citizens packing the courtroom demanding justice. They didn't get their money back, but they were there to see Daniel sentenced to twenty years.

Because Molly had been so distressed by what was happening to all these people who, like her, had once trusted Daniel, she hadn't paid enough attention to some of the remarks in Gramps's letter. She'd read and reread his words for the comfort they gave her, for the way they brought him close, but she hadn't stopped to question his sudden interest in a will and settling his affairs. Hadn't recognized that he was preparing her for his death. It seemed obvious now that he didn't expect to live much longer.

Besides this letter, she could remember only one

other time Gramps had told her he loved her—the day they buried her grandmother. She had no doubt of his love; he said it loud and clear, but rarely with words. Open displays of emotion embarrassed him, as they did many other men, particularly men of his generation.

This letter wasn't the first time he'd commented on her marrying again. That theme had been a constant one since the divorce. The ink hadn't dried on the legal papers, and Gramps was already trying to introduce her to the bachelor ranchers in the area.

The thought of another relationship still sent chills up Molly's spine. As she liked to tell her friends, she'd done the marriage thing and wasn't interested in repeating it.

Tucking the letter back in the envelope, she lay down, not expecting to sleep. But she must have drifted off because the next thing she knew, the alarm was buzzing. Gramps's letter was clutched in her hand, held close to her heart.

It was clear to her then. So clear she should've figured it out months ago. The answer had always been there, but she'd been too blind, too stubborn, too willful to see it. It'd taken nearly losing her grandfather to show her what she had to do.

The small conference room off the principal's office was the last place Tom wanted to be. Referred to as "the holding cell" at Ewell Junior High, the room was cold even during the hottest weather, and it had an unpleasant odor that reminded him of a dentist's office.

Eddie Ries sat in the hard wooden chair beside him. Eddie's mother was on her way to the school. Tom hadn't heard when his own mother would arrive. All he knew was that when she did, she wouldn't be happy.

Suspended for three days. That was supposed to be punishment? Tom almost laughed out loud. Time away from classes was practically a *reward* for screwing up! Personally Tom was sick of school. Sick of a lot of things he couldn't change. His no-good dad for one, and the way the kids had looked at him when they learned the guy in the news was his father. He was sick of feeling helpless and frustrated—which was why he'd become involved in something he'd never thought he would.

He wasn't friends with Eddie. Didn't even like him. Eddie went searching for trouble; it made him feel big. Made him look like somebody to the homies. A big man on campus when in reality he'd never fit in. Tom wasn't sure he did anymore, either; maybe that was what had made him do something so stupid.

While he didn't regret the suspension, Tom hated adding to his mother's worries. He could see how this news about his great-grandfather's health had depressed her. All through dinner the night before, she'd barely said a word; she hadn't eaten much, either.

Tom hadn't had much of an appetite himself. He couldn't stop thinking about Gramps. He wasn't sure if he remembered the old man or not, but he let Clay think he did, mainly because he was the oldest and *should* remember. Clay had been a baby that time they were in Montana.

On his twelfth birthday—and the two birthdays after that—Tom had gotten a personal letter from Gramps and a check for twenty bucks. Before that, Gramps had always mailed his mother money and then she'd go shopping and pick something out for him. These last birthdays, the check was made out to him.

In his first letter Gramps had said a boy of twelve

was old enough to know what he wanted. Old enough to go out and buy it, too. Tom never forgot the feeling that had come over him with that letter. For the first time in his life he'd felt like a man. He might not remember what Gramps looked like, but Tom loved him the same way his mother did.

His mother was worried. She worried about a lot of things. Tom could always tell when problems got her down. Work, his father, money. Now Gramps. Over the years, he'd come to recognize the symptoms. She'd grow quiet and then three small vertical lines would form in the center of her forehead. It hurt to see those lines and know there wasn't a damn thing he could do to help her. Those were the times he went to his room, put on his earphones and played music so loud his head pounded afterward. The music helped him not to think, because when he did, his stomach ached.

Tom *wanted* to help his mother. When he was a kid, he'd planned to become a magician and make all the bad things in life disappear with one flamboyant wave of a wand. He used to imagine doing that sometimes. With a flick of his wrist every problem would magically disappear.

The door to the conference room burst open, and Tom sat up straighter as his mother stormed in, her eyes blazing with anger.

Tom lowered his own eyes. He toyed with the idea of greeting her, then decided against it. She didn't look like she was all that happy to see him.

"Gang symbols, Tom?" she said through clenched teeth, hands on her hips. "You painted *gang symbols* on the gym wall?"

"Outside wall," he corrected, and regretted it immediately.

"Do you think it matters *which* wall?" she asked in a tone that told him the three-day suspension from school was the least of his worries.

Mr. Boone, the principal, walked briskly into the room, looking far too satisfied with himself—like he'd accomplished what he'd set out to do. Tom had never had strong feelings about the man, but he was inclined to dislike him now—simply for the smug way he smiled, knowing Tom was in major trouble at home.

"As I explained earlier, Mrs. Cogan," the principal said, "this school has a zero-tolerance policy with regard to gang activities. While I don't really believe Tom's involved in a gang, there are plenty of wanna-bes. I'd like to believe Tom's smarter than that, but after today I'm not sure."

"Get your things, Tom. I'm taking you home," his mother instructed. He could tell from her voice that said she had plenty more to say later.

Nevertheless, Tom nearly leaped off the chair in his eagerness to escape. He grabbed his jacket and followed his mother outside.

"Of all the stupid brainless things for you to do," she said as they headed out to the parking lot. Her steps were so fast he had trouble keeping up.

Yeah, well, he wasn't especially proud of himself, either.

They climbed in the car and he thought she was going to take rubber off the tires the way she squealed across the lot. She missed the Stop sign and zoomed into the street, almost hitting another car.

"Mom!" Tom shouted, holding on to the edge of the seat as he was thrown against the passenger door. "It's not a good idea for you to drive when you're this mad."

"Mad isn't the half of it."

"Okay, okay, so I made a mistake."

"A *mistake?* Gangs, Tom?"

"I'm not in any gang!"

She tossed him a look that assured him she knew otherwise. "Then why spray-paint their symbols?" Without inhaling she added, "You're going to repaint that wall all by yourself, young man."

"Hey, I wasn't the only one who painted it." Talk about unfair!

"You're going back to school first thing tomorrow morning to do it."

"What about Eddie?"

His mother sent him a sidelong glance sharp enough to cut glass. "I don't have any say over him, but I have all kinds of say over you."

She liked to *think* she did. But this didn't seem the appropriate time to discuss it. "According to what Mr. Boone said, I'm not supposed to be on school property," he told her. One of them had to keep a cool head, and it was obvious his mother had already lost hers.

"Don't concern yourself—I already asked Mr. Boone and he's willing to make an exception."

"That isn't fair! How come I have to come back and paint the wall? Eddie should be there, too." The anger was brewing inside him, and he tightened his jaw, knowing it would do neither of them any good to vent it now.

"Eddie's parents can see to his punishment."

Which meant Eddie was off the hook. Eddie's mother drank too much, and even Eddie didn't know where his father was. Tom certainly knew the where-abouts of his own father—and so did everyone else.

"Can't I paint the wall *after* the suspension?" he asked, thinking he'd prefer to do it during the weekend. Having the entire school watch him suffer such humiliation held little appeal.

"No," came her emphatic reply.

"Why not?" he demanded, clenching his fists.

"Because I need you for other things."

"What things?"

"Packing."

That captured Tom's attention. He waited a moment, then asked, "Are we going somewhere?"

"Montana."

His heart nearly burst with excitement. She'd found a way. His mother was taking them to Montana. This was good news, better than anything he'd anticipated. "We're visiting Gramps?"

She didn't answer him right away. Tom watched as her hands tensed on the steering wheel. "Not exactly. I handed in my two weeks' notice this morning. We're moving."

Two

Sam Dakota bolted upright out of a sound sleep. His heart slammed against his rib cage with a punch almost powerful enough to hurt. Cold sweat dampened his forehead and clung to his bare chest. One ragged breath followed another as his body heaved in a near-desperate effort to drag oxygen into his burning lungs.

The dream always woke him. Whenever he had it, he would feel that panic again, the fear as vivid and real as the first day the prison door had clanged shut behind him. It had echoed against the concrete walls, reverberating in his ears. Twenty-four months into freedom, and he still heard that terrible sound. It invaded his sleep, tortured him, reminded him constantly that he was a living, breathing failure. Thankfully he didn't have the dream often anymore—not since he'd started working for old man Wheaton.

Closing his eyes, Sam lay back down, his head nestled in the feather pillow. He swallowed and flexed his hands, trying to ease the tension from his body, forcing himself to relax.

It was over. Over.

Prison was behind him, and so was the life he used to live. Yet at one time he'd been a rodeo star, riding bulls, flirting with fame. Fame and women. He'd had his own following, groupies who chased after him.

They stroked his ego, cheered for him, drank with him, slept with him and, on more than one occasion, fought over him.

The groupies were gone, the way everything that had once been important to him was gone. In his rodeo career and after his accident, he'd faced danger, injury, death, and he'd done it without a trace of fear.

Riding the wave of success, he'd achieved everything he'd ever wanted. That was at the rodeo championships in Vegas, six years earlier. But the silver buckle that proclaimed him the best of the best had been pawned to help an old man hold on to his ranch. These days Sam stayed out of trouble, kept his nose clean, minded his own business. When the urge hit him, he moved on.

Sam didn't like to dwell on his rodeo days. That was all in the past, finished. The doctors had warned him of the risks of ever competing again. Another fall like the one that had ended his career could cripple him for life. Or kill him. It was that simple. The money, what little of it he'd managed to save, had been swallowed whole by doctor and hospital bills.

Friends had stuck by him for a time, but he'd driven them away with his anger and frustration. Even his parents didn't know his whereabouts, which was just as well. Pride had prevented him from ever letting them know he'd landed in a Washington-state prison for second-degree assault. After two years of silence it hadn't seemed worth his trouble to write and fabricate an account of where he'd been and why he'd stayed away.

It'd been a few years now since his last contact with family, and as the months went on, he thought about them less and less.

Until he ended up at the Broken Arrow Ranch, Sam

had drifted across three or four states, depressed, miserable and mad as hell. The restlessness inside him refused to die.

He'd lasted longer here in Sweetgrass than anywhere else.

Mostly because of the old man. Walt was as mean as a grizzly bear and as demanding as a drill sergeant, but that didn't keep Sam from admiring him. Six months earlier Sam had arrived in this backwoods Montana town; six minutes after that he'd crossed the sheriff. He hadn't been looking for trouble, but trouble always seemed to find him. All he'd meant to do was help a lady in a difficult situation, a lady who was being bothered by a drunk, and in the process he'd stepped on the wrong toes. It turned out the drunk was a friend of the sheriff's. Before he knew it, the sheriff had learned about his prison record and Sam was headed for jail, charged with unlawful conduct and disturbing the peace. The other guy—the man who'd been beating up on the woman—had walked away scot-free. Then, for no reason he could understand, Walt Wheaton had stepped in, paid his bail and offered him a job. Eventually the charges were dropped, thanks to some negotiating by Walt's attorney.

Sam could deal with just about anything. Pain, disappointment, the reversal of fortune. But he'd discovered that he was unprepared to handle kindness. It embarrassed him. Made him feel uneasy. Indebted. The only reason he'd agreed to accept the foreman's job was that he owed the old coot. The pay wasn't much, but Walt had given him a small house on the property, rent free. It was the original foreman's place—rundown but livable.

The minute Sam set foot on the ranch, he realized

Walt was in dire straits. The Broken Arrow was in deplorable condition. No sooner had Sam started work when a series of mysterious and seemingly unrelated events began to occur. Pranks and vandalism, nothing serious, but a nuisance all the same.

Walt was an exacting employer, but never unreasonable. Sam worked hard and at the end of every day he felt good, better than he had in years. Partly because there was a sense of accomplishment in restoring order to the deteriorating ranch. And partly because the old man needed him. It was as simple as that.

He'd been working for Walt about six weeks when out of the blue the old man invited him to come for dinner one night. That was the first time he'd seen the photograph of Walt's granddaughter, Molly. Set in a gold frame on top of the television, the snapshot had caught her in what he could only describe as a *natural* moment. She stood with an arm around each of her sons; one of them, the younger boy, grinned up at her, while the older one half scowled. The wind tossed her hair as she smiled shyly into the camera. What Sam noticed was her eyes. He didn't think he'd ever seen eyes that blue. He might have suspected she wore colored contacts if not for the photo of Walt and his wife. The other Molly. This Molly's eyes were the identical shade of cobalt blue. Her hair was the same rich shade of auburn. Walt's granddaughter was pretty, in an ordinary sort of way. Attractive but not beautiful. Sam had known plenty of women who could run circles around her in the beauty department, but he liked her picture. There was something about her that appealed to him. And he knew Walt cared deeply for her and his two great-grandsons.

Since his brief conversation with Walt's granddaughter, Sam had found her drifting into his mind at the oddest times. Like now. Actually, it was easy enough to figure out why. He'd been celibate for too long. What he really needed was to drive into town one Friday night and let some sweet young thing take him home. But he couldn't seem to dredge up the necessary enthusiasm.

In his rodeo days he'd enjoyed the occasional one-night stand, but over the years, he'd lost interest in sex for the sake of sex. When he crawled into bed with a woman, he didn't want to worry about remembering her name in the morning. Besides, remembering names was a minor concern these days when it came to one's bed partners. If he chose to self-destruct, Sam preferred to do it on the back of a bad-tempered bull, not in some bed with a lumpy mattress and a faceless woman moaning in his ear.

After that first invitation to share dinner, Walt and Sam began eating all their meals together. The old man routinely plied him with questions. Some he answered. Some he ignored. Walt depended on him, trusted him, and Sam tried to live up to the rancher's faith in him.

The Broken Arrow was a good spread, with plenty of grass and a fine herd. If Sam ever considered settling down, it'd be on a place like this. Not that he could afford it. Some days he struggled against bitterness. If not for the accident, he might have had it all: fame, money, a good life. A demon bull had put an end to those hopes and expectations. But he'd endured.

In the process Sam had learned something about himself. He was a survivor. Fate might sucker-punch him again, only next time he'd be prepared. All he had to do was make sure he didn't give a damn about anything—or anyone. Because if he did, he was vulnerable. It occurred to him that he was already becoming too attached to the old man, and that worried him.

By the time he'd sorted out his thoughts and calmed his raging heart, the alarm was ready to sound.

He climbed out of bed, put on a pot of coffee and dressed as the sun peeked over the Rockies, streaking the sky with translucent shafts of pink and gold. It'd become habit to check on Walt before he headed out for the day. He half expected to arrive some morning and find the old man had died in his sleep. He didn't look forward to that, but as the rancher said, he'd lived a good life and suffered few regrets. That was the way Sam wanted it to be when his own time came.

The kitchen light was on when he stepped onto Walt's back porch. Walt was rarely up this early anymore. With his heart as weak as it was, he spent half the day napping.

"Coffee's ready," Walt said when Sam let himself into the kitchen.

The old man seemed downright chipper, Sam noted, a pleasant contrast to his lethargic manner lately.

Walt gestured toward the coffeepot with his own mug.

"No thanks, I've already had a cup." Sam had never been much for talk in the morning. A grunt now and then usually sufficed.

"I got a call from Molly last night." Walt's crooked grin took up half his face. "Looks like you're going to meet her and the boys, after all."

"She's coming out?" Sam hoped to hell she was smart enough not to mention his phone call. As he'd told her, Walt wouldn't appreciate his interference.

"Better than that." Walt cupped the steaming mug

between his callused hands. His eyes fairly glowed with happiness.

"How long is she staying?"

"For good," Walt snapped as if it should have been obvious. "She's finally come to her senses and sold what she could, packed everything else in a U-Haul and she's driving on out. Should be here week after next."

Sam lowered himself slowly into a chair. This was something he hadn't expected. He folded his hands, resting them on the scarred pine table, as the old man's words sank in.

"The ranch is hers," Walt announced cheerfully. "There's no one else. I just pray she'll be strong enough to hold on to the place when I'm gone."

Sam had done some thinking about the ranch and what would become of it after Walt died. He'd always known Molly would inherit the Broken Arrow. He'd even toyed with the idea of forming a partnership with her, running the ranch himself and sharing the profits. He'd make sure the arrangement was lucrative for them both, even if it meant working twenty-four hours a day. Eventually he could, maybe, save up enough to buy the spread himself.

His plans were still vague, but this was the first thought he'd given to the future in a hell of a long time. All that would change now. The last thing Walt's granddaughter would want was an ex-con hanging around the place. In light of this news, it'd be best if he sought other employment. He'd write a letter or two that night, send out a few feelers now his confidence was back. He'd enjoyed working the Broken Arrow Ranch almost as much as he'd enjoyed the feisty old man who'd given him a chance.

"Don't you have something to say?" Walt asked, glaring at him. Then he laughed, and the sound was like a sick calf choking.

This was probably the first time Sam had heard Walt laugh. "What's so funny?"

"You." Walt's mirth died slowly. "I wish you could've seen your face when I said Molly was coming. Just wait till you see her in person. If she's anything like her grandmother—and she is—you'll be walking around with your tongue hangin' out. That photo on the television doesn't do her justice. She's a real beauty."

"Don't get any ideas," Sam warned. Walt had misread the look, but Sam wasn't inclined to correct him. He'd let the old coot have his fun.

"Ideas about what?" Walt was obviously playing dumb.

"Me getting together with your granddaughter."

"You should be so lucky."

Sam didn't want to be rude, but he wasn't up to this conversation. "It isn't going to happen."

Walt's smile faded and he narrowed his pale eyes on Sam with an intensity that would have made a lesser man squirm. "I doubt she'd have you."

Sam couldn't fault him there. "I doubt she would, either," he agreed. Grabbing his hat from the peg on the porch, he headed out the kitchen door.

The sun broke over the horizon like the golden arm of God, ushering in another perfect California morning. Tom sulked in the bucket seat beside Molly, his arms folded defiantly across his chest. His posture told her that nothing she said or did would placate him for the grave injustice of moving him away from his friends.

Clay, on the other hand, bounced like a rubber ball in the back seat, unable to sit still. His excitement, however, did not appear to be contagious.

Because she wasn't able to see out her rearview mirror, Molly checked the side one to make sure the trailer was all right. She wasn't accustomed to hauling anything and the U-Haul was packed tight. Everything she'd managed to accumulate in the past thirty-four years—everything she hadn't sold, donated to charity or given to friends—was jammed in it.

Although she was deeply concerned about her grandfather, Molly hoped the drive to Sweetgrass would be something the three of them could enjoy. A trip that would "make a memory," as her grandmother used to say. She thought about her childhood summer visits and how her grandmother had let her name the calves and explore the ranch and gather eggs....

The last year had precious few happy memories for her and the boys. This was a new beginning for them all. A challenge, too—building a new life, a new home. Few people were given this kind of opportunity. Molly fully intended to make the best of it.

"Are we there yet?" Clay asked, his head bobbing in the rearview mirror.

"Clay," his brother groaned. "We haven't even left California."

"We haven't?"

"Unfortunately, no," Molly concurred.

Clay's head disappeared as he sank down on the seat. His small shoulders slumped forward. "How long's it going to take?"

"Days," Tom said grimly.

Molly resisted the urge to jab him. From the first, her older son's attitude about the move had been less than enthusiastic—although he'd approved of *visiting* Montana to go and see Gramps. But not to stay there forever, as he'd told her repeatedly this past week. He'd barely uttered a word from the time they started out a couple of hours earlier. As far as she could tell, he continued to blame her for making him repaint the gym wall. Molly didn't know why *she* should feel guilty when he was the one who'd sprayed it with gang symbols.

If she needed confirmation that she'd made the right decision, Tom had provided it. The mere thought of her son involved in a gang turned her blood cold. She was terrified of the attraction a gang might hold for him—for *any* confused angry fatherless boy. Gangs weren't an issue in Sweetgrass. The people were decent and hardworking, and she wouldn't need to worry about big-city influences.

"Did I tell you about the Broken Arrow?" she asked in an attempt at conversation. If she displayed a positive attitude, perhaps Tom would start to think that way himself.

"About a thousand times," he muttered, his face turned away from her as he stared out the side window. The scenery rolled past, huge redwoods and lush green forests, so unlike the fertile river valley of Montana.

"There's horses, too," Molly added. As she recalled, Gramps always had a number on hand. These were strong sturdy horses, kept for work, not pleasure or show.

Tom yawned. "How many?"

Molly lifted one shoulder, her gaze trained on the road. *Interest.* Even this little bit was more than Tom had shown from the moment she'd announced her plans.

"What about my report card?" Clay asked, launching himself against the front seat, thrusting his head between Molly and Tom.

"The school promised to mail it." Molly decided not to remind her son that she'd answered the same question no less than ten times. They'd miss the last couple of weeks of school, but had finished all their assignments beforehand. Molly had feared even a two-week delay might be too long, considering her grandfather's condition.

"You could've asked if I wanted to move." Tom leaned his head against the back of the seat and glared at her. Apparently holding his head up demanded more energy than he could muster.

"Yes," Molly admitted reluctantly, "you're right, I should have." This was a sore point with Tom. A transgression he seemed unwilling to forgive.

"But you *didn't* ask me."

"No, I didn't. Gramps needs us right now and I didn't feel we could refuse." Perhaps she'd made a mistake; it wasn't her first one and certainly wouldn't be her last. Molly felt she'd had few options. Besides removing Tom from involvement in a gang, she had to get to Gramps as soon as possible, to be with him during his remaining days. And since she would inherit the ranch, the more she learned about the management of it now, the better.

"You're taking us away from our friends."

"Like Eddie Ries?"

It was clear to Molly that Tom needed a better class of companions. She worried incessantly about her son and wondered what had happened to the good-natured helpful boy he used to be. The transformation had come virtually overnight. He'd grown sullen, ill-tempered and moody.

In the beginning she feared he might have started using drugs. She'd gone so far as to call a drug hot line. She'd learned that the best way to figure out if her son was experimenting with illegal drugs wasn't to dig through his backpack or his room for evidence. Kids were experts at hiding paraphernalia, and even better at convincing family they were innocent of anything so dangerous or devious. She suspected that was because parents didn't want to believe their children were caught up in something so destructive and therefore chose to believe whatever the kids told them. Facing the truth was far too painful—and would demand action.

The true test, according to the pamphlet she'd read, was knowing your children's friends. One look at the type of friends your son or daughter associated with was usually enough.

Until last fall Tom's friends had been good kids, from good homes, who made good grades. She felt relatively reassured until he started hanging around with Eddie Ries. Even then it was difficult to gauge the truth.

According to Mr. Boone, the school principal, Tom's friendship with Eddie had been a recent development. Molly hoped that was true.

"Will Gramps teach me to ride?" Clay asked, straining forward in his seat.

"Probably not," Molly said with a renewed sense of sadness. "Remember, he isn't well. I don't think he rides anymore."

"This is gonna be a bust," Clay said, slumping against the window.

Molly shook her head in wonder. "What in heaven's name is the matter with you two?"

"We don't have any friends in Montana," Tom said sulkily.

"You'll make new ones." That was one thing she could say about her boys. Not more than a week after moving into the apartment they'd met every kid within a five-block radius. Neither Tom nor Clay had any problem forming new friendships. The ranch kids would be eager to learn what they could about the big city, and before long Tom and Clay would be heroes.

"Let me tell you about the ranch," she tried again.

"Yeah!" Clay said eagerly.

"I'm not interested," Tom muttered.

One yes. One no. "What's it to be?" she asked cheerfully. "Do I get the deciding vote?"

"No fair!" Tom cried.

"Plug your ears," Clay said, snickering.

Tom grumbled and looked away, wearing the mask of a tormented martyr. He had brooding down to an art form, one he practiced often. Molly couldn't remember her own adolescence being nearly this traumatic, and Tom was only fourteen. She hated to think of all the high-scale drama the coming years held in store.

"Originally the Broken Arrow was over 15,000 acres," Molly began. She said this with pride, knowing how difficult it had been for Gramps to sell off portions of his land. All that remained of the original homestead was 2,500 acres.

"How come the ranch is named the Broken Arrow?" Clay asked.

"Because they found a broken arrow on it, stupid."

"Tom!"

"Well, it's true, isn't it?"

"Yes, but it wasn't a stupid question. If I remember correctly, Tom, you asked me the same one."

"Yeah, but that was when I was a little kid."

"About Clay's age, as I recall." She recalled no such thing, but it served him right for belittling his younger brother.

"What about his foreman?" Clay asked next.

Gramps's foreman. Molly had nothing to tell. All she knew about him was his name and the fact that he was apparently devoted to Gramps. Devoted enough to make sure she knew of Gramps's ill health.

She'd reviewed their short conversation a number of times in the two weeks since his phone call, afraid she might have missed something important. She wondered if there'd been something else he'd wanted to tell her, a hidden message beneath his words. She'd sensed his urgency, accepted the gravity of the situation. Yet when she'd phoned Gramps the next night, he'd sounded quite healthy. He'd been thrilled with her news, and she'd hung up equally excited.

Molly's thoughts turned from Sam Dakota to employment possibilities. Eventually she'd need to find a job in Sweetgrass. While there might not be much demand for a translator, she wondered if the high school needed a French or German teacher. If all else failed, she could try getting long-distance freelance assignments. Perhaps she could tutor or give private lessons. Several of the upmarket preschools in San Francisco were beginning to offer foreign-language lessons to their three- and four-year-old clients. Hey—she could start a trend in Montana!

Molly sighed. She didn't want to think about the dismal state of her finances. She'd sold everything she could—furniture, dishes, household appliances. She wasn't carting away fistfuls of dollars from her moving sale, but with her meager savings and her last paycheck, she'd have funds enough to see her through the next couple of months. After that—

"Mom," Clay said, breaking into her thoughts, "I asked you about Gramps's foreman."

"What about him?"

"Do you think he'll teach me to ride?"

"I...I don't know, sweetheart."

"Why should he?" Tom asked, and rolled his eyes as if he could barely stand being in the same car with anyone so stupid.

"I can ask, can't I?" Clay whined.

"Of course," Molly answered, attempting to divert a shouting match.

After repeated warnings, Clay finally secured his seat belt and fell asleep, his head cocked to one side. Because the car's air conditioner didn't work, Molly had hoped to avoid the heat as much as possible by leaving before six that morning. Already both boys were tired and cranky. Not long after Clay dozed off, Tom braced his head against the window and closed his eyes.

The silence was a blessed relief after two hours of almost continual bickering. Molly was grateful for the quiet, grateful for her grandfather—and grateful to Sam Dakota for calling her when he had.

She hadn't met the man and already he'd changed her life.

A cooling breeze came from the north. Walter Wheaton sat on his rocker on the front porch and enjoyed the fresh sweet morning air. He was weak, but even his bad heart couldn't curtail his excitement.

Molly and the boys were on their way. They'd been on the road two days and by his best estimate would arrive around noon. He was already imagining how they'd turn from the highway and onto the meandering dirt road that led to the ranch. When they did, he wanted to be sitting right here on the porch waiting for them. Damn, but it'd be good to see Molly again. Good to see those young ones of hers, too. She hadn't said so, but he knew she worried about being a good mother. The world was a different place now, compared to when he'd grown up, but love and discipline still worked wonders.

The older boy had a sassy mouth; Walt had heard it himself when he'd talked to her on the phone. And the younger one was like a puppy, making a mess wherever he went. In time they'd learn, though. Tom might require a little help adjusting his attitude, but Walt felt up to the task. What that boy needed was a man's influence, a man's guiding hand. That and a switch taken to his backside when he deserved it!

In the big city someone was liable to report him for suggesting the rod. Child abuse they'd call it and probably toss him in the clinker. Walt believed that child abuse was ignoring your children, neglecting them, not giving them guidance or a good example. Those things hurt kids far more than an occasional smack on the rear. What was the matter with people these days? he wondered.

A plume of dust showed at the end of the driveway. Molly. He hadn't expected her quite this early. His Molly and her boys.

Walter stood carefully, taking his time so as not to overtax his heart. My, oh my, he was looking forward to seeing his family. Thank goodness Molly had mailed all those pictures! Without them, he wouldn't recognize the boys.

His eyes weren't what they used to be and it took Walt far longer than it should have to realize it was a truck that barreled toward him and not a car pulling a trailer. Another minute passed before he recognized his neighbor, Ginny Dougherty. The woman didn't have the sense God gave a rock chuck.

Walt grunted in annoyance. Ginny was a damn fool. The widow simply didn't know her limitations; she was crazy trying to run a ranch on her own. Fred, her bachelor cousin—aged at least sixty—lived with her and helped out on the place. In Walt's opinion, the two of them were like the blind leading the blind. And he'd told her so, too. Frequently.

Ginny's truck squealed to a halt, kicking up dust. The door opened and she leaped out so fast you'd think the seat was on fire.

"Before you start shouting," she began, "I suggest you hear me out."

Walt didn't have the strength to yell much these days, but he wasn't letting Ginny know that. "What do you want this time?" he demanded. He wrapped his arm around the post and casually leaned against it, so she wouldn't realize how weak he was.

Ginny stood with her hands on her hips. Walt looked her up and down, then shook his head. A woman her age had no business wearing dungarees; he was firm on that.

"Someone knocked down your mailbox," she told him, her chin angled stubbornly toward him. "The way the tire tracks went, it looks deliberate."

Vandals had been wreaking havoc the past few

months. Walt didn't understand it. "Who'd do such a thing?"

"Anyone who knows you, Walt Wheaton. You've gone out of your way to make yourself the most unpopular man in town."

"Are you going to stand on my property and insult me, woman?" He forgot about conserving his strength. Ginny always did have a way of getting his dander up. He suspected she did it on purpose, and if the truth be known, he often enjoyed their verbal skirmishes.

"I'm not insulting you. I'm telling you the truth."

"I don't...have to...take this," he said, then slowly lowered himself into the rocker.

Ginny frowned. "Are you okay?"

"Of course I'm okay." He closed his eyes, and his breath came in shallow gasps. It always happened like this; without warning, he'd be unable to catch his breath. No feeling on earth could be worse. It felt as though someone's hands had closed around his throat.

"Walt?"

He dismissed her with a flick of his hand.

"Walt?" She sounded much closer now.

"Pills," he managed between gasps. He patted his shirt pocket. His head slumped to one side and he felt Ginny's hand searching around for the small brown bottle. The entire time, she was talking. Leave it to a woman to chatter at a time like this. If his heart didn't kill him, Ginny's tongue would.

An eternity passed before she managed to get the pill under his tongue. A couple of minutes later, it took effect. Walt managed to remain conscious, but only by sheer force of will. He refused to pass out; otherwise Sam was sure to haul him back to the medical clinic.

If a man wasn't sick when he walked in there, he would be by the time he walked out.

Dr. Shaver had damn near killed him while Sam sat there watching. Walt had fired Sam three times in the next few days, but Sam had ignored his orders. The problem was, his foreman could be as stubborn as Walt himself.

"Drink this." Ginny thrust a glass under his nose.

"What's in it? Arsenic?"

"Water, you old fool."

When he didn't obey her fast enough, Ginny grabbed it back and gulped it down herself.

"I thought you said that was for me," he grumbled.

"I needed it more than you."

Ginny collapsed in the rocker next to his own. Molly's rocker. For forty years she'd sat on the front porch with him each night. She'd darned socks, crocheted, knitted. His wife hadn't believed in idle hands. Every now and again he'd find a way to steal a kiss. It had never ceased to amaze him that a woman as beautiful and talented as Molly MacDougal would marry the likes of him. Her one regret was that she'd only been able to give him one son.

Now they were both gone. Adam killed by a drunk driver while still in his twenties and then, later, his Molly. He'd be joining them soon. But not right away. There was work that had to be done. Affairs settled. Arrangements made. He wanted time with Molly and her boys first. God would grant him that much, Walt was sure. The good Lord had seen fit to take Adam and Molly early in life, and as far as Walt was concerned God owed him this additional time.

"You gave me the scare of my life!" Ginny cried.

She was rocking so fast she damn near stirred up a dust devil.

"What'd you do with my mail?" he demanded, hoping to change the subject.

Ginny glared at him, her dark eyes burning holes straight through him. "I saved your life and all you care about is your stupid mail?"

"You've got it, haven't you? Suppose you read it, too."

"I most certainly did not."

He snorted in disbelief.

"How about thanking me?" Ginny muttered. "If it wasn't for me, you could be dead by now."

Walt made a disgusted sound. "If I'd known you were going to nag like this, death would've been a blessing."

Three

"It's probably the biggest, most beautiful home I've ever seen," Molly told her boys wistfully as they sped along the two-lane highway. Eager to reach Sweetgrass, she drove fifteen miles above the speed limit. They hadn't seen another car in more than half an hour, and she figured the state patrol had better things to do than worry about an old country road.

"How many rooms does it have?" Clay asked.

"More than I could count," Molly said, smiling to herself. As a child, she'd considered her grandparents' home a mansion. It had taken her two entire summers to explore all three floors. The original house had been built just after the turn of the century, a grand home for its time, with a turret dominating the right-hand side of the wooden structure. There was a wide sweeping porch along the front of the house, added in later years; it looked out over the rolling green paddock where the horses grazed. A narrow dirt drive snaked in from a marked entry off the highway.

"I can have my own room, then?" Tom asked, showing some life for the first time since lunch.

"There must be four, possibly five bedrooms not in use now."

"I'd sleep in the attic without electricity if it meant I wouldn't have to share a room with Clay."

For Tom, that had been the most difficult aspect of their move into the apartment. He'd been tolerant about it for a while, but living in such close proximity to his younger brother had quickly become a problem.

"My grandmother kept the house in meticulous condition," Molly said. During her last visit, the month following her grandmother's death, she'd marveled at how clean and neatly organized the house still was. Molly Wheaton had regularly waxed the wooden floors and washed the walls. She'd line-dried all the clothes, ironed and crisply folded almost everything. Even the dish towels.

Out of respect for his wife, Gramps had removed his shoes before stepping into the house, to avoid tracking mud across the spotless floors. Every room had smelled of sunshine, with the faint underlying scent of lemon or pine. Molly could almost smell it now.

"How big's the barn?"

"Huge."

"That's what you said about the house."

"I named you right, son," she said, reaching over and mussing his hair. "Doubting Thomas."

Tom slapped at her hand, and she laughed, in too good a mood to let his surly attitude distress her.

They were within an hour of Sweetgrass, and Molly felt a keen sense of homecoming. It was an excitement that reminded her of childhood and warm summer days, a joy that wanted to burst forth. After the long hard months of Daniel's trial, months of struggle and embarrassment while their names were dragged through the media, this was a new beginning for them all. At last they could set aside the troubles of the past and move forward.

"There's a weeping willow beside the house,"

Molly said. "When I was a girl, I used to hide behind its branches. Gramps would come looking for me and pretend he couldn't find me." The remembrance made her laugh softly. Her grandfather might be crusty on the outside, but inside he was as kind and loving as a man could be. While her grandmother fussed over her only grandchild, coddled and pampered her, Gramps had growled and snorted about sparing the rod and spoiling the child.

But it had been her grandfather who'd built her a dollhouse and hand-carved each small piece of furniture. It'd taken him a whole winter to complete the project. Instead of giving it to her, he'd placed it in the attic for her to find, letting her think it'd been there for years.

Her grandmother had never allowed any of the dogs or cats in the house, but it was her grandfather who'd smuggled in a kitten to sleep with her the first night she was away from her parents, when she was six. Molly wasn't supposed to have known, but she'd seen him tiptoe up the stairs, carting the kitten in a woven basket.

All the memories wrapped themselves around her like the sun's warmth, comforting and lovely beyond description.

"Does Gramps have a dog?" Clay asked excitedly.

"Three or four, I imagine." Gramps had named his dogs after cartoon characters. Molly remembered Mr. McGoo and Mighty Mouse. Yogi and Boo Boo had been two of her favorites. She wondered if he'd continued the practice with more recent dogs.

"That's it!" she said, pointing at two tall timbers. A board with BROKEN ARROW RANCH burned in large capital letters swung from a chain between them. The brand was seared on either side of the ranch name.

"I don't see the house," Clay muttered.

"You will soon," she promised. Molly took a deep breath. They'd been on the road for two days and it felt ten times that long. Her heart was ready for sight of the house, ready to absorb the wealth of emotion that stirred her whenever she remembered those childhood summers.

Her ten-year-old Taurus crested the first hill, and she gazed intently ahead, knowing it was here that the house came into view for the first time. She could hardly wait for her sons' reaction. Could hardly wait for them to suck in their breaths with awe and appreciation. Could hardly wait to show them the home that would now be theirs.

It wasn't Tom or Clay who gasped, but Molly herself. The house, at least the outside, was nothing like she remembered. It sat forlornly, revealing years of neglect and abuse. Most of the shutters were gone, and those that remained hung askew, dangling by a couple of nails. The paint had blistered and peeled, leaving behind large patches of sun-parched wood. Two of the posts along the porch had rotted away, and the railing around the front showed gaping holes as unsightly as missing teeth. A turquoise tarp was spread across the roof over what had once been her bedroom, presumably to stop a leak.

"Are you sure this is the same house?" The question came from Tom.

"This isn't it…is it?" Clay's words seemed to stick in his throat.

"The Addams family would love this place," Tom said sarcastically.

Molly felt her sons' scrutiny, but was speechless, not knowing what to say.

"Are we just going to stay parked here?" Clay asked.

Molly hadn't realized she'd stopped. She squared her shoulders and forced herself to swallow the disappointment. All right, so the house wasn't exactly the way she'd recalled it. She'd personally see to the repairs and the upkeep; it was her responsibility now. Her hands squeezed the steering wheel as a new thought struck her. If the outside was this bad, she could only imagine what had happened to the inside.

"We need to remember Gramps is ill," she said more for her own benefit than her children's. "He hasn't been able to take care of things. That's why we're here, remember?"

"This place is a dump."

"Thomas, stop!" She would hear none of this. None of it! "This is our home."

"We were better off in the apartment."

Molly's fingers ached from her death grip on the steering wheel. "It'll be just as beautiful as ever in no time," she said forcefully, defying the boys to contradict her.

Either they recognized the determination in her voice or were too tired to argue.

Molly had half expected Gramps to be on the porch waiting for her when she arrived and was disappointed when he wasn't. She pulled the car around to the back of the house, close to the barn where Gramps generally parked his vehicles. Two dogs, one of them hugely pregnant, began barking furiously.

She turned off the engine and a man stepped out of the shadows from inside the barn. He removed his hat and wiped his forearm across his brow, then paused to study her.

This could only be Sam Dakota. Her grandfather's foreman. The boys scrambled out of the car, eager to escape its confines. They were obviously anxious to explore, but stayed close to the Taurus, waiting for her. The instant he was out the door, Clay squatted down and petted the pregnant dog, lavishing her with affection. The other dog continued his high-pitched barking.

Molly worried when she still didn't see Gramps. Her immediate fear was that she'd arrived too late and her grandfather was already dead. Sam would've had no way of contacting her while she was on the road. It'd been foolish not to phone from the hotel, just in case... As quickly as the idea entered her head, she pushed it away, refusing to believe anything could have happened to Gramps. Not yet! She opened her car door and stepped into the early-afternoon sunshine.

Sam walked toward her, which gave Molly ample opportunity to evaluate his looks. After that first glimpse, when he'd briefly removed his Stetson, she couldn't see much of his facial features, which were hidden beneath the shadowed rim of his hat. The impression of starkly etched features lingered in her mind, his face strong and defined. He was tall and whipcord-lean.

If his clothes were any indication, he didn't shy away from hard work. His jeans were old, faded by repeated washings. The brightly colored shirt with the sleeves rolled past his elbows had seen better days. He pulled off his right glove, and even from a distance Molly could see that those gloves had been broken in long ago.

"You must be Sam Dakota," she said, taking the

initiative. She walked forward and offered him her hand; he shook it firmly—and released it quickly. "I'm Molly Cogan and these are my boys, Tom and Clay. Where's Gramps?"

"Resting. He thought you'd arrive earlier. He waited half the morning for you." The censure in his gruff voice was unmistakable.

Involuntarily Molly stiffened. Clay moved next to her and she slid her arm around his neck, pressing him close. "How's Gramps feeling?" she asked, choosing to ignore the foreman's tone.

"Not good. He had another bad spell this morning."

Molly frowned in concern. "Did you take him to the clinic? Shouldn't he be in the hospital?"

"That'd be my guess, but Walt won't hear of it. It would've taken twenty mules to budge that stubborn butt of his."

Molly smiled faintly. "My grandmother was the only person who could get him to change his mind, and that was only because he loved her so much."

An answering smile flashed from his eyes. "Unfortunately he holds no such tenderness for me," he murmured, then turned his attention to Tom and Clay. "Are you boys thirsty? There's a pitcher of lemonade in the fridge." Without waiting for a response, he led the way into the house.

With a mixture of joy and dread, Molly followed. She paused as she stepped into the kitchen—it was even worse than she'd feared. The once-spotless room was cluttered and dirty. A week's worth of dirty dishes was stacked in the sink. The countertops, at least what was visible beneath the stacks of old newspapers, mail and just about everything else, looked as if they hadn't been cleared in weeks. The windows were filthy—

Molly could tell they hadn't been washed in years—and the sun-bleached curtains were as thin as tissue paper.

Molly wasn't nearly as meticulous a housekeeper as her grandmother had been; as a working mother, she didn't have the time for more than once-a-week cleaning. Nevertheless she had her standards and this house fell far short of them.

"Is lemonade all you got?" Tom asked when Sam took three glasses from the cupboard. Molly was surprised there were any clean dishes left. "What about a Pepsi? A Coke? Anything?" Tom whined.

"Water," Sam suggested, then winked at Clay, who had no problem accepting the homemade offering.

Tom tossed his mother a look of disgust and snatched up the glass of lemonade as if he was doing them all a favor.

"Your grandfather's asleep in the living room," Sam said, motioning toward it.

Molly didn't need directions, but she said nothing. Not wanting to startle Gramps, she tiptoed into the room. She stood there for a moment watching him. He leaned back in his recliner, feet up, snoring softly. Even asleep, he looked old and frail, nothing like the robust man he'd been only ten years ago.

It demanded both determination and pride to keep her eyes from filling with tears. Her heart swelled with love for this man who was her last link to the father she barely remembered. She'd been so young when her father died. A child of six. Her entire world had fallen apart that day of the car accident; she missed him still. Her mother had remarried less than a year later, and Molly had a baby brother the year after that. And the summer she graduated from high school, her mother, stepfather and half brother had immigrated to Australia.

Kneeling beside the recliner, Molly gently brushed the white hair from Gramps's brow. Needing to touch him, needing to feel a physical connection, she let her hand linger.

"Gramps," she whispered, so softly she could hardly hear her own voice.

No response.

Tenderly Molly placed her hand over his. "We're here, Gramps."

His eyes flickered open. "Molly girl," he whispered, reaching out to caress the side of her face. "You're here at last. To stay?"

"I'm here to stay," she assured him.

His smile made it to his eyes long before it reached his mouth. "What kept you so damn long?" he asked in his familiar brusque tone.

"Stubbornness. Pride," she said, and kissed his weathered cheek. "I can't imagine where I got that."

Gramps chuckled, looking past her. "Where are those young'uns of yours? I've been waitin' all day for this, and none too patiently, either."

Tom and Clay stepped into the room. Tom had his arms folded and a scowl on his face. He lagged behind Clay, who was grinning and energetic, unable to hold still. "Hi, Gramps!" Clay's exuberant greeting was echoed by Tom's reluctant "Hi."

Gramps studied her sons for what seemed like minutes before he nodded. It was then that Molly saw the sheen of tears in his tired eyes. He sat up and braced both hands on his knees.

"You've done a fine job raising these boys of yours, Molly. A fine, fine job."

* * *

"That her?" Lance whispered, staring out from the alley between the café and hardware store. He motioned with his head toward Molly Cogan.

She walked out of the Sweetgrass bank, glancing up at the man beside her. He wore a Stetson and walked like a cowboy.

Monroe's gaze followed his fellow Loyalist's to the other side of the street. It surprised him that a cantankerous old guy like Wheaton would have a granddaughter this attractive. From what he understood, she'd been divorced a number of years. A woman who'd been that long without a husband might appreciate some attention from the right kind of man. He'd heard redheads could be real wild women in the sack.

He quickly banished the thought from his mind. It'd be a mistake to mix business with pleasure. And it could end up being a costly mistake. Once this matter of getting hold of the ranch was settled, he'd show her the difference between a Montana man and a city boy.

Oh, yeah. Monroe had heard all about those men in California, especially in the San Francisco area. Those gay boys sure didn't know what to do with a woman. Seemed they were stuck on each other, if you could imagine that! The whole damn country was going to hell in a handbasket—but not if he could help it. That's what the Loyalists were all about. They were a militia group—been around for ten years or so. At their last meeting, more than a hundred men had crammed the secret meeting place to show their support for the changes he and the other Loyalists were planing to bring about. Of course some folks who didn't know any better took exception to the cause. Walt Wheaton, for one. The old cuss was as stubborn as they came. Monroe had done everything in his power to convince the rancher to sell out. Subtly of course. Guarding his own identity and his position of power in the organization was crucial. Only Loyalists knew him as Monroe, and although he'd attended the last meeting, no one in Sweetgrass had any idea how deeply involved he was with the militia. His cover was useful and too important for Loyalist purposes to break.

After a careful study of possible sites for their training grounds, the group had decided old man Wheaton's property was the ideal location. But Walt Wheaton had remained inflexible. As his banker, Dave Burns was in a position to put the pinch on him, but it hadn't worked. When things hadn't fallen into place, the head of the Loyalists had sent Lance to help them along. Monroe didn't think much of Lance, but he kept his opinions to himself.

In a last-ditch effort to keep violence out of the picture—not that he was opposed to using force, if necessary—he'd convinced the powers-that-be to give him one last chance to reason with the old rancher. He hated like hell to see a hothead like that fool Lance get credit for obtaining the property when he might finesse the deal himself—with a little assistance.

That was when he put the pressure on a third cousin of his to make the old man an offer he couldn't refuse. Now that Walt's granddaughter was in town, they might finally make some headway. The ranch was on its last legs, Burns had seen to that, refusing Wheaton any more loans and calling in the ones he already had.

"How much longer is the old guy gonna live?" Lance asked, cutting into his thoughts.

"Not long," Monroe said under his breath. If necessary he'd let Lance give Wheaton a good shove into the hereafter, but he'd prefer to avoid that. Too messy.

And the last thing the Loyalists needed was a passel of state cops and reporters looking in their direction.

"Who's that with her?"

"Sam Dakota." Monroe snickered softly, disliking the protective stance the foreman took with the woman. He could see the lay of the land with those two. Sam wanted her for himself, but Monroe wasn't going to let that happen. Dakota was a jailbird and once old man Wheaton found out, he'd send the foreman packing. Right quick, too, if he knew Walt Wheaton.

"Will he make trouble?"

"Unlikely." Dakota wouldn't know the meaning of the word "trouble" until he tangled with the Loyalists. The foreman was admittedly a problem, but Monroe didn't expect Sam to stay around much longer.

"I thought you said we'd have the Wheaton land soon," Lance grumbled.

Monroe frowned. "Takes time."

"You're sure the old man doesn't know?"

"I'm sure." Monroe's patience was growing thin. It wasn't the younger man's place to question him, and he let it be known he didn't appreciate it by glaring at him fiercely.

"I could convince him to sell in a week if you'd let me," Lance muttered.

"We'll do this my way," Monroe said from between clenched teeth. The necessity of maintaining a low profile was key to the group's survival. The government, especially the FBI, would go to great lengths to stop the militia movement. All you had to do was look at Ruby Ridge and Waco and you'd realize just how corrupt the feds had become. Well, that was all about to change.

"I'm not going to do anything stupid," Lance assured him.

"Good." Against his better judgment, Monroe found himself staring at Molly Cogan again. Her jeans stretched nicely across her butt. Not so tight as to invite a look and not so loose that they disguised the fact she was a woman. And just the way she walked proved she was a Wheaton, all right. Proud as the day was long, and if she was anything like her grandfather, stubborn, too.

"She's pretty, I'll say that for her."

"Don't get any ideas," Monroe said, struggling to hold on to his temper. "We've already got more complications than we need."

"All right, all right, but let me visit one of the girls soon. I'm a growing boy, if you catch my drift."

The kid might think he was clever, but Monroe failed to be amused. A large part of the Loyalists' financial support came from a prostitution ring that covered the entire state. The money they brought in was the lifeblood of the organization, but there wouldn't be enough with young bucks like Lance and his friend Travis helping themselves to the goods. He was guilty of taking advantage himself, but then he considered Pearl and a couple of the others his fringe benefits. He figured *he* was a hell of a lot more entitled to them than Lance.

"Stay out of town unless I tell you different," Monroe instructed the other man.

Lance frowned.

"You heard what I said, didn't you?" He knew Lance had been sneaking into town behind his back. That boy better realize he had ways of learning about whatever went on here.

"I said I would," Lance mumbled.

"Good." Monroe sent Lance off and waited long enough to be sure he'd taken the road out of Sweetgrass. Then he climbed into his car; it was as hot as a brick oven. He was hot in other ways, too, and blamed the Wheaton woman for that. It was time to pay Pearl a visit—she'd probably missed him. He drove down several streets and stopped next to the community park. No need to announce where he was headed by leaving his car in front of her house.

He cut through the alley and walked across Pearl's backyard, then let himself in by the door off the kitchen. He didn't bother to knock.

Still in her housecoat, Pearl stepped out of the hallway. She looked shocked to see him. Noon, and she wasn't dressed yet. Not that he was complaining. It saved time.

"What are you doing here?" she demanded, placing her hands on her hips. The action tugged open the front of her robe and offered him a tantalizing peek at her breasts.

"Guess," he said with a snicker. He loosened his belt buckle, in no mood to play games.

Her bravado quickly disappeared and she backed away from him. "Our agreement was once a month."

"That's not the way I remember it."

Pearl might have been pretty at one time, but too many years of making her living on her back had spoiled whatever had been attractive about her. Her makeup was applied with a heavy hand—not like Molly Cogan's. Monroe frowned as he thought about the old bastard's granddaughter.

"I...I don't want you to tie me up this time." Pearl's voice trembled a little. He liked that. Just the right amount of fear, enough to make her willing to do things she might not do for her other customers. But then he wasn't like the others. The Loyalists owned Pearl, and she did what he damn well pleased, whether she wanted to or not.

Gramps had insisted Sam accompany Molly into Sweetgrass, and although she couldn't see the sense of it, she hadn't made a fuss. The boys were far too interested in exploring the house and unpacking their belongings to be bothered with errands. So Molly had left them with Gramps.

Actually she'd hoped to use the time alone with Sam to find out what she could about her grandfather's health. The old man seemed pale and listless this morning, although he'd tried to hide it from her.

Gramps's old pickup had to be at least twenty-five years old. Molly could remember it from when she was a child. The floorboard on the passenger side had rusted through, and she had to be careful where she set her feet.

The ride started off in a companionable enough silence. Every now and then she'd look at Sam, but he kept his gaze carefully trained on the road ahead.

She'd spoken first. "Are you from around here?"

"No."

"Montana?"

"Nope."

"Where else have you been a foreman?" she'd asked, trying a different tack.

"I haven't been."

"Never?" she asked.

"Never," he repeated.

That was how their entire conversation had gone. In

the forty minutes it took to drive into Sweetgrass, Sam didn't respond once in words of more than two syllables. Stringing together more than a couple of words appeared to be beyond his capabilities.

Molly had hoped to ease into her conversation, get to know him before she dug for answers concerning her grandfather's condition. But no matter how she approached him, Sam Dakota remained tight-lipped and uncooperative.

Molly gave up the effort when the town came into view.

"Oh, my," she whispered.

If the Broken Arrow Ranch had changed in nine years, Sweetgrass hadn't. Main Street seemed trapped in a time warp. Foley's Five and Dime with its faded red sign still sat on the corner of Main and Maple. Her grandmother had often taken Molly there as a child so she could watch the tropical fish swim in the big aquarium. The hamsters, racing about in their cages, had intrigued her, as well. In addition to pets, the store sold knickknacks and tacky souvenirs to any unsuspecting tourist who had the misfortune of dropping by. Not that there'd ever been many tourists. In retrospect, Molly decided it must be the bulk candy displayed behind the glass counter that kept Foley's in business.

The bank's reader board, which alternately flashed the time and the temperature, was directly across the street from Foley's. Sweetgrass Pharmacy and the barbershop were next to the bank. Molly wondered if the singing barber had retired. As she recalled, he'd done a fairly good imitation of Elvis.

The ice-cream parlor with its white wire chairs was exactly as she remembered.

Sam glanced at her.

"Everything's the same," she told him.

"Everything changes," he said without emotion. "Looks can be deceiving, so don't be fooled." He eased the truck into an empty parking space and turned off the engine.

"I need to stop at the bank," she said, looking over at the large redbrick structure. From there she'd go to the Safeway and buy groceries. The Safeway was at the other end of town, about six blocks away. A stoplight swayed gently in the breeze at Main and Chestnut. For a while it had been the only one in the entire county. But five years ago Jordanville, forty miles east, had its first traffic light installed, stealing Sweetgrass's claim to distinction. Gramps had taken the news hard; he'd written her a letter complaining bitterly about the changes in Montana. Too damn many people, he'd grumbled.

Without looking at her, Sam added, "I've got some supplies to pick up."

Sam wasn't unfriendly, but he hadn't gone out of his way to make her feel welcome, either. Molly had no idea what she'd done or hadn't done to create such... coolness in his attitude. This morning he'd seemed neutral, but neutral had definitely become cool.

"I'll meet you at the bank when I'm finished," he said.

Molly climbed down from the truck and hooked the strap of her purse over her shoulder. Sam walked close beside her until they reached the bank, then he crossed the street. As she opened the heavy glass doors, she caught a glimpse of him studying her. It was an uncomfortable feeling.

While the outside of the bank was relatively unchanged, the inside had been updated. The polished wood counters were gone, and except for the lobby with its marble tiles, the floor was now carpeted.

Molly moved toward the desk with a sign that stated: New Accounts.

"Hello," she said, and slipped into the chair.

"Hi." The woman, whose nameplate read Cheryl Ripple, greeted her with a cordial smile.

"I'm Molly Cogan," she said, introducing herself. "Walter Wheaton's my grandfather."

Cheryl's smile faded and she stood up abruptly. Almost as if she couldn't get away fast enough, Molly thought.

"Excuse me a moment, please," the woman said. She hurried toward the branch manager's office, and a moment later, a distinguished-looking middle-aged man appeared.

"Ms. Cogan?" he said, coming over to her, hands tightly clenched. "I'm David Burns. Is there a problem?"

Molly blinked at him, taking in his well-tailored suit and polished shoes. "No, should there be?"

David Burns's laugh held a nervous edge. "Not exactly. It's just that your grandfather has…shall we say, challenged the integrity of this banking institution on a number of occasions. I came to be sure there wasn't any problem with his account. Again."

"None that I know of," Molly said, wondering what her grandfather had said or done to raise such concern. On second thought she didn't want to know. "Actually I came to open my own account."

"Your own?" His relief was evident. "That's great."

"I'm moving in with my grandfather."

"I see. Welcome to Sweetgrass. Cheryl will be more

than happy to assist you.'' He took a couple of steps backward before turning toward his office.

Within ten minutes Molly had signed the necessary documents and chosen a check design. As she got ready to leave, she noticed a tall attractive man standing in the lobby, watching her. When he saw Molly, he smiled and nodded as if she should know him. She didn't. A moment later he approached her.

''Molly Cogan?''

She nodded, frowning, certain she didn't recognize him. His was a face she would have remembered, too. Appealing, boyish, blue-eyed. His blond hair was tousled as if he'd forgotten to comb it. He stood well over six feet.

''I'm Russell Letson,'' he said, stepping toward her, his hand extended. No wedding ring, she automatically noticed. His eyes darted away from her and she realized he was actually rather shy. This was something she didn't expect from the rough, tough cowboy types she generally associated with Montana.

They exchanged handshakes as Molly mulled over where she'd heard the name before.

''I'm your grandfather's attorney,'' he added.

Gramps's letter. That was why the name was familiar. Her grandfather had mentioned him when he'd told her about having his will updated.

''Would you have time for a cup of coffee?'' he asked, glancing at his watch. ''I've got an hour before my next appointment and there's a matter I'd like to discuss with you.'' He seemed slightly ill at ease about this.

Molly wondered what he could possibly have to say to her; she couldn't help being curious and, to her surprise, tempted. Russell Letson was one of the best-looking men she'd seen in a while, and what amazed her was that he didn't seem to know it.

Russell added, "It won't take long."

Just when Molly was about to agree, Sam walked into the bank, and she experienced a twinge of disappointment. "I'm afraid I can't today."

"Dinner then?" he suggested. "Tomorrow night, if that's agreeable?"

"I…" Too stunned to respond, Molly stood in the middle of the bank with her mouth hanging half-open while she struggled for an answer. A date. She couldn't remember the last time a man—an attractive single man—had asked her to dinner.

"I don't know if Walter's told you, but there's a decent steak house in Sweetgrass now. We could talk there."

"Sure," she said, before she could find a convenient excuse. "That'd be great."

He set a time for dinner and promised to pick her up at the ranch, although it was well out of his way. Handsome and a gentleman, besides. She could grow to like Russell Letson, Molly decided. He was a pleasant contrast to the surly foreman who'd driven her into town.

"I'll see you tomorrow evening, then," Russell said, giving her a small salute before walking out of the bank.

It had happened so fast Molly's head was spinning. She walked over to Sam, who leaned against the lobby wall, waiting for her.

"What was that about?" he asked with a scowl.

After the silent treatment he'd given her all the way into town, she wasn't inclined to answer him. "Nothing much."

"You're letting Letson take you to dinner."

If he already knew, why had he asked her? "As a matter of fact, I am," she returned, and enjoyed the rush of satisfaction she felt at letting him know she had a date.

Four

It felt good sitting on the porch, rocking and whittling, Walt Wheaton mused. Molly's boys sat on the top step, sanding a couple of carvings he'd fashioned from canary wood. The yellowish wood was one of his favorites. He hadn't worked on his carvings for at least six months. Molly and the boys had renewed his energy. Gladdened his heart. He might not always remember what day of the week it was anymore, but that didn't matter. Not now, with Molly and the boys here where they belonged.

It wouldn't take much to imagine it was his own Adam sitting on that step, forty or so years back, with a school friend. Or to imagine his Molly in the kitchen getting dinner ready to put on the table.

Walt's fingers skillfully moved the sharp knife over the wood, removing a sliver at a time, cutting away everything that wasn't the bear. He'd chosen oak for this piece, and the black bear would stand about ten inches high on his hind legs. He'd give it to Tom. The boy reminded him of a young bear, struggling to prove his manhood, all legs and arms and feet. He remembered himself at that age, when his voice had danced between two octaves. He'd been tall and thin like Tom, with legs like beanpoles and no chest to speak of.

Walt toyed with the idea of saying something to his

great-grandson. He wanted to assure Tom he'd fill out soon enough, but he didn't want to embarrass the boy.

The three worked in comfortable silence. Walt yearned to share stories of his youth with the two brothers, but talking drained his energy. The hell with it, he decided. God had given him the opportunity to spend time with these young ones and he was going to use it.

"Bears eat trees, you know," he stated matter-of-factly.

Tom glanced up. "Trees? Are you sure, Gramps?"

The older of Molly's two boys had a skeptical nature; Walt approved. He didn't like the idea of his kin accepting anyone or anything at face value. He suspected his granddaughter might be more easily swayed, but her son wouldn't be. It reassured him that the boy revealed some good old-fashioned common sense, a virtue in shockingly short supply these days. Take that local militia group, for example. He'd butted heads with them more than once in the past few years. While Walt didn't necessarily agree with everything the government did, he sure didn't believe the militia's wild claims of foreign troops planning to invade the country with the assistance of the federal government. That was as ludicrous as their other ideas, like computer chips surgically implanted in peoples' brains so the government could control their activities. He'd never heard such nonsense in all his days and cringed every time he thought about decent folks believing such craziness.

"Gramps?"

Tom's voice shook him out of his thoughts. He had trouble keeping his mind on track these days.

"What is it, son?"

"Is that true?"

He frowned. What was the boy talking about? The militia's paranoid ideas, he guessed. Wasn't that what they'd been discussing? "Of course it's not true," he barked. This computer-chip nonsense was as asinine as the supposed sightings of black helicopters swooping down and spraying bullets from the sky. "Question everything, son, you hear me?"

Tom nodded and returned to his sanding.

With his heart as weak as it was, Walt didn't know how much longer he'd be around on this earth. He liked to think there'd be time to tell Tom and Clay about life during the Great Depression. And the war. Children these days didn't know the meaning of hardship, not like his generation.

"Gramps?" Clay stared at him expectantly. "But you *said* bears ate trees. So don't they really?"

Oh, yeah. That was it—*that* was what he'd said. About bears. "They eat the bark," he explained, his mind traveling the winding twisting byways of time long since passed. He shelved the depression stories in order to explain what he knew of bears. "They scrape off the bark with their claws. Without the bark, the tree dies. So, yeah, you could say bears eat trees. Next time you're in the forest, take a gander at a dying tree. If it isn't some disease, my guess is that a bear's been clawing on it."

"Is that why you're carving a bear?" the older boy asked. "Because they eat trees?" He ran the sandpaper lightly over the carving of the owl. Watching him reminded Walt that he didn't see many of the northern saw-whet owls these days. The saw-whet was small as owls went, only seven inches high, and weighed less than four ounces.

He didn't get much opportunity to study nature the

way he once had. He missed his walks, missed a lot of things, but that was all part of growing old.

"Gramps?" It was Tom again.

"What is it, son?"

"Clay asked you about the bear. Why you're carving it."

"Oh, yes…the bear. It nearly got me, it did at that."

Both boys stared up at him, and he grinned, recalling the adventures of his youth. "I happened upon her clawing up a conifer. I was just a kid at the time, but old enough to know better than to do something stupid—like get too close to a bear," he added, muttering to himself. "Neither my horse nor I saw her until it was too late. The mama bear had two cubs and she was in no mood for company. She reared onto her hind legs and scared my horse so badly he tossed me clean off. I thought I was a goner for sure."

Both boys listened intently. "What happened next?" Tom asked.

"Happened?" Walt chuckled, remembering the incident as vividly now as that day almost seventy years ago. He smiled and continued whittling as his mind filled with the details of that fateful afternoon. "Once I recovered enough to stand, I took off running, screaming at the top of my lungs." He shook his head, grinning again.

"How old were you, Gramps?"

"Ten or so," Walt answered. "My legs were good and strong."

"So you ran?" Clay's hands went idle.

"I didn't figure on hanging around there and letting that bear eat me for dinner." This reminded him of another lesson Molly's boys needed, a lesson only a man would think to teach them. Women didn't take to fighting much; they didn't understand a man's need for confrontation. What was important, however, was knowing when to fight and why. Knowing what was worth fighting for. And yet there were times when all the questions might have the right answers and still the best thing to do was walk away. He'd turned his back on a fight or two, and it had taken far more courage to back down than it had to stand his ground.

"She didn't catch you, did she?" Clay asked.

"Damn near, but my pappy saved me." To this day Walt remembered the surge of relief he'd experienced when his father burst into the clearing, his horse at full gallop. He'd raced toward Walt and it was hard to figure who'd reach him first, his father or the bear.

"My pappy saved me," he said again. "He galloped up, grabbed me by the arm and swung me over his horse's back."

Even with his eyes so tired and faded, Walt saw the awe in the boys' faces. He nodded slowly. It did his heart good to spend time with Adam's grandsons. They needed a man in their lives, someone to take the place of their useless father. He *wanted* to teach these boys, but he didn't have much time left....

The screen door creaked and Molly stepped onto the porch, holding the door open. "Dinner'll be ready in ten minutes," she announced. "Time to put your tools away and wash your hands."

Almost from the minute they'd arrived, Molly had been scrubbing and cleaning that kitchen. It comforted him, somehow, to see her put the house to rights. His own sweet Molly would've thoroughly disapproved of his housekeeping methods. He probably should have hired one of the women from town to take a scrub brush to the place, at least before his granddaughter arrived to find such a mess.

He'd always intended to hire a housekeeper, but had yet to meet anyone he wanted in his home for longer than five minutes. Nor did he like the idea of a stranger touching his Molly's things. Maybe Ginny, but she didn't keep her own house too well, and he'd wager she'd be insulted if he suggested she clean his, even if he was willing to pay her.

Tom and Clay didn't need to be told twice about dinner. They were inside the house quicker than two jackrabbits. Walt wasn't as fast on his feet. He heaved himself up, grateful that the boys had put away his carvings and tools. That Tom might have a smart mouth on him, but at heart he was a considerate kid. Walt took a deep breath, inhaling the aroma of something delectable. He didn't know what his granddaughter had cooked, but the tantalizing smells wafting from the kitchen told him he was in for a treat. Preparing meals had become an onerous chore; more and more of late Sam had been seeing to his dinner.

Walt trusted Sam, and that trust hadn't been given lightly. It was why he'd asked his foreman to drive Molly into town earlier in the day. When they returned, Sam had silently carried in the groceries and left immediately afterward. Walt smiled to himself, amused at the way Sam was keeping his distance since Molly's arrival.

Walt headed for the kitchen, moving at his own pace. Although Sam hadn't said anything, he probably wasn't too keen on Molly dating Russell Letson. It surprised Walt that she'd agreed to have dinner with that puppy of an attorney. The boy hadn't let any moss grow under his feet, that was for sure.

Letson was a good man, shy and kind of quiet. Nothing like his father, who'd been outspoken and opinionated. His son seemed to keep to himself. He wondered why Russell hadn't married. Of course there weren't a lot of marriageable women around Sweetgrass.

Now that Molly was here, Walt suspected plenty of young men would be dropping by the ranch. Once they got a good look at his granddaughter they'd find excuses to visit. Pretty as a picture, Molly was. Smart, too, and a fine cook. Given time, she'd make a good rancher's wife.

He believed that Molly needed a man, although he was sure she'd disagree with him. He'd like to see her get married again. She was still young and if she remarried, she'd probably have more children. It saddened him to realize he wouldn't be around to know and love them, but he refused to think about that. He was determined to enjoy what time he had with her and the boys and let the future take care of itself.

He paused in the doorway leading to the kitchen. He barely recognized the room. The walls shone because Molly had washed them, the floor boards gleamed with wax, and the windows sparkled behind new gingham curtains Molly had sewn on her grandmother's old Singer. She'd found a length of cotton up in the attic; his Molly must have bought it shortly before her death. As the boys hurried about setting serving dishes on the table, Walt marveled at the change in the room. So it took him longer than it should have to realize the table was only set for four.

"What about Sam?" he asked, surprised that Molly had excluded the foreman.

Molly's chin came up slightly, as if she was affronted by the question. "I invited him over, but he said he had other plans."

That was interesting. Walt watched his granddaughter as she brought a platter of chicken from the counter to the table. Her lips had thinned slightly when she mentioned Sam. Now that Walt thought about it, he'd sensed a bit of tension between the two.

"What other plans?" Walt pressed.

"He didn't say."

And Walt figured she hadn't asked, either. Grinning, he glanced out the kitchen window to the small foreman's house where Sam lived. Beyond that stood the old bunkhouse; the run-down structure was a reminder of the Broken Arrow's glory days, when the spread had been large enough to justify hiring on several hands. Now there was only Sam. His battered truck was parked the same place as before, which meant he hadn't left the ranch.

"Isn't he hungry?" Walt demanded. The man had too much pride for his own good. His stubbornness was cheating him out of the best damn meal he was likely to get. Not that there was any point in telling him. Might as well argue with a tree stump.

Clay put a green salad on the table with a bottle of no-fat dressing.

Walt frowned. He preferred his own brand and he didn't care if it was loaded down with fat. A man could only be asked to sacrifice so much. As it was, he already had one foot in the grave. His cholesterol count was the least of his worries.

"Do you want me to invite Sam again?" Molly asked, standing stiffly behind the kitchen chair.

Although she'd made the offer, Walt could see she had no desire to do so.

"If he doesn't want to eat with us, fine. The choice is his."

She nodded. "My thought exactly."

Sam hardly knew Russell Letson, and he wasn't sure why he was so angry with the guy. Except for that incident his first day in Sweetgrass, he and Russell had very little to do with each other. Which was fine with Sam. It occurred to him, as he pitched a forkful of hay into Sinbad's stall, that he couldn't think of a single reason to dislike the man—other than the fact that Letson had invited Molly to dinner. True, Sam had an innate distrust of lawyers, but he had no personal reason to feel wary of Russell Letson. And, of course, what Molly chose to do was none of his business.

Then why did it bother him so much?

The muscles across Sam's shoulders tightened. He'd mucked out the stalls and put down fresh straw—although it wasn't really necessary—simply because he felt the need to keep moving. If he worked hard enough and long enough, maybe his thoughts would leave him alone.

Not only did Sam dislike Letson, he wasn't sure he liked Molly Cogan, either. Not that anyone was asking his opinion. Nor was he offering it.

An endless series of questions buzzed around his head like pesky flies. But Sam decided he wasn't going to concern himself with the answers. He wasn't willing to waste time analyzing his feelings about Molly. First and foremost, why should *he* care who she dated? He didn't dammit!

Perhaps he should think about moving on. He'd worked on the Broken Arrow Ranch longer than anywhere, and he wasn't the kind of man who was comfortable staying in any one place. When he was in town that afternoon, he'd gotten the addresses of a number of large ranches in the state. This was as good a time as any to inquire about jobs. He'd been here too long, and he'd grown restless. At least that was what he told himself.

But he realized almost immediately that it was a lie.

Working for Walt Wheaton had given him a sense of satisfaction. The old man had needed him, and Sam had definitely needed a job. And more. He'd needed a home, needed some respect, needed to be *useful*. He was willing to admit that now, although it wasn't easy. The last six months had given him perspective.

The bitter taste of his anger was gone and he was able to look back on his time in prison with a sort of...acceptance. He'd been drunk and stupid, raging over the loss of his career and every dime he'd saved. He'd been looking for trouble that night—almost four years ago now. The fight had been his fault, and he'd paid the price for his stupidity.

Sam had *thought* he'd learned his lesson, but he hadn't been in Sweetgrass more than a few minutes when he made the same mistake. He'd gone into Willie's for a beer; all he'd wanted was to quench his thirst. Everyone in the bar had been content to ignore the quarrelling couple. Sam, too. Until the drunk started slapping the woman around. That was when he'd stepped in. The fight had spilled into the street, where Walt Wheaton was standing, talking with a couple of old cronies. Before long, the sheriff was on the scene and Sam had been hauled away. Walt had seen the whole thing....

Sam was grateful to Walt for hiring him without asking endless questions about his past. He didn't understand what had prompted the old man to bail him out. All the rancher cared about was Sam's skill in running the ranch, and once assured he knew his way around a herd, Walt had offered him the job.

Unless someone else had told him, Walt didn't know Sam had served a two-year sentence in a Washington-state prison. Sam didn't figure it was relevant; besides, being an ex-con wasn't something he was proud of. And it wasn't something he liked to talk about.

Sam still wondered why this sick old man had trusted him. It'd been a long time since anyone had willingly placed faith in him. That was why Sam had stayed, why he'd worked himself to the point of exhaustion, month after month. Sam would rather have died than disappoint Walt Wheaton.

It'd been a long time, too, since he'd allowed himself to care about anyone. Feelings were a luxury a man on the move couldn't afford. They'd always made Sam uncomfortable, for more reasons than he wanted to examine.

Over the weeks and months he'd worked the Broken Arrow, he'd become fond of the crotchety old man. On some level they'd connected. He owed Walt, in a way he'd never owed anyone before. He also saw Walt's despair over the deterioration of his ranch, and he was determined to salvage as much as he could. In an effort to prove himself worthy of Walt's faith, Sam had struggled to build up the herd. He'd ridden the land so often he was familiar with damn near every square inch of it.

And he'd made a mistake. A big mistake. He'd started to dream.

Once in a while he'd find an excuse to ride up to

the crest of the hill that overlooked the valley and dream that this land was his.

He supposed it was because he carried the sole responsibility for this ranch now. He'd started to feel he *belonged* here. And that was dangerous.

At night, it had become his habit to walk among the outbuildings and check everything one last time before he turned in. All too often his thoughts grew fanciful and he'd pretend that inside the house a woman was waiting for him. His wife. He'd pretend that his children slept upstairs, tucked securely in their beds, loved beyond measure.

It was never meant to be. When Walt died, the Broken Arrow would pass to Molly and her two boys. Then she'd find herself a new husband, who'd send him on his way.

He grimaced. His dreams were downright laughable, and the sooner he put them out of his mind, the easier it would be to pack his bags and move on. With this experience under his belt, he'd apply elsewhere and await the replies. No point in lingering when he could read the writing on the wall. He'd be out of a job by the end of the year.

All of a sudden Sam realized he was no longer alone. He turned and found Tom, the older of Molly's two sons, standing just inside the barn. The boy looked hesitant, glancing about as if he wasn't sure he should be there.

"Do you need something?" Sam asked gruffly, sounding more unfriendly than he'd intended. Actually he liked Tom. The boy reminded him a little of what he'd been like at that age.

"No. I...thought I'd feed the horses."

Sam noticed the boy had one hand behind his back. "And what do you think you'll feed them?"

Tom brought his arm forward and revealed a handful of carrots.

"Have you been around horses much?"

Tom shook his head.

"Then let me give you a few guidelines." The last thing the old man needed was the shock of having one of his great-grandkids bitten by a horse. Or kicked in the gut.

Hearing voices, Sinbad arched his sleek black neck over the edge of the stall. The gelding was friendly, just right for a boy about Tom's age. Gus, Walt's Morgan horse, wasn't opposed to a bit of attention himself, but Sam would rather steer the kid toward the more reliable Sinbad.

"You like to ride?" Sam asked, while he showed Tom the proper way to hold a carrot without risking the loss of a couple of fingers.

"I never have," the boy admitted.

"You're going to have to learn, then, aren't you?" If his mother decided to keep the ranch, Tom would probably be riding the herd himself, taking on some serious responsibilities.

"I'd like to know how to ride." Tom shot a look at Sam, as if to suggest he'd need someone to teach him, and Sam was the obvious choice.

"You feel you're man enough?" Sam asked bluntly.

"Yes." The boy's voice sounded confident.

Sam grinned. "That's what I thought." Opening the bottom half of Sinbad's stall door, Sam grasped the horse's halter and led him out. "He's about fifteen hands high," Sam explained, running his palm down the gelding's neck. "Which means you'll be about four feet off the ground." He glanced at the boy to gauge his interest. "I gotta tell you, the air's just a little bit sweeter when you're sitting tall in the saddle."

Tom's grin stretched all the way across his face.

"I always feel everything in life is much clearer when I'm on a horse. There's a good feeling in my gut. When I'm riding, I'm happy and it's the type of happiness I've never found anywhere else."

Tom was mesmerized and, with such a willing audience, Sam could have talked all night. Riding was more than just a means of getting from one place to another. It involved a relationship with another creature. You depended on your horse; you and your horse had to trust and respect each other. This inner wisdom was as important as any technique Sam could share with the boy.

"If you ask me, spring's about the best time of year for riding. Especially after a downpour, when the wind's in your face and the scent of sweetgrass floats up to meet you. It's even better when you're riding a horse with heart." Nothing was more exhilarating than a smooth steady gallop across acres of grassland. But it was the silence Sam loved best, a silence broken only by the rhythm of the horse's hooves.

"Sinbad's a working horse," Sam went on to say, in case Tom believed that any one of these animals was bred for fun and games. Gramps and Sam shared the same opinion when it came to animals. They worked for their keep. The dogs, too. Gramps might have given them cutesy names, but every last one of them worked as long and hard as he did himself.

"What do you mean by 'working horse'?"

The question was sincere and Sam answered it the same way. "He's a cow pony. He's been cutting cows, trailing cattle and rounding up steers all his life. A cowboy is only as good as his horse, and Sinbad's a damn good horse.''

Tom tentatively raised his hand to the gelding's neck. Sam could tell he didn't want to show he was intimidated by the large animal. He didn't blame the kid for feeling a bit scared. In an effort to put him at ease, distract him from his nervousness, Sam continued to speak.

''Sinbad's a quarter horse, which is an American breed. All that means is they were used at one time to compete in quarter-mile races. Far as I'm concerned, a quarter horse is the perfect horse for ranch work.''

Tom's interest sharpened and he moved closer. His stroking of the horse's neck was more confident now, and it seemed he'd forgotten his fears. ''Is that one a quarter horse?'' the boy asked, looking at Gus, who'd stuck his head over the stall door.

''Gus is a Morgan,'' Sam explained. ''It's an excellent breed, as well, especially for a ranch. They can outwalk or outrun every other kind of horse around. Did you know that the only survivor of the Battle of the Little Big Horn was a Morgan? Go ahead and touch him. He's pretty gentle.''

''Hi, Gus,'' Tom said. He smiled broadly and walked over to rub the Morgan's velvety nose.

''When can I start learning to ride?'' Tom's voice was filled with eagerness. ''How about right now? I've got time.''

''Hadn't you better talk to your mother first?'' Sam resisted the temptation to discreetly inquire about the boy's father. He knew Molly was divorced, but little else.

At the mention of his mother, the excitement slowly

drained from Tom's dark brown eyes. "She won't care."

"You'd better ask her first."

"Ask me what?" Molly said. She had just entered the barn. The open door spilled sunlight into the dim interior. Bathed as she was in the light, wreathed in the soft glow of early evening. Molly Cogan was breathtakingly beautiful.

No wonder Russell Letson had asked her out to dinner. It demanded every bit of concentration Sam could muster to drag his eyes away from her.

"Sam's going to teach me to ride!" Tom burst out excitedly. "He's been telling me all kinds of things about horses. Did you know—" He would've chattered on endlessly, Sam felt, if Molly hadn't interrupted him.

"Teach you to ride a *horse?*" Molly asked.

"Duh! What did you think? It isn't like I could hop on the back of a rooster!" The boy's enthusiasm cut away his sarcasm. "Sam says we can start tonight. We can, can't we?"

Molly's gaze pinned Sam to the wall. "I'll need to discuss it with Mr. Dakota first."

Mr. Dakota. Sam nearly laughed out loud. The last time anyone had called him that, he'd been flat on his back in a hospital emergency room in pain so bad even morphine couldn't kill it.

"Mom…" Tom sensed trouble and it showed in the nervous glance he sent Sam.

"I didn't come outside to argue with you," Molly said, her voice cool. "I need you to go back in the house. Upstairs."

"Upstairs?" Tom cried indignantly. "You're treating me like a little kid. It's still daylight out! You aren't sending me to bed, are you?"

"No. Your grandfather has some things he wants you to get for him, and they're upstairs. He can't make the climb any longer."

"I'll get them," Sam offered. If Tom didn't recognize an escape when he heard one, Sam did. With Tom out of earshot, Molly was sure to lay into him for what he'd done—agreeing to teach her son to ride.

"Tom can do it," Molly said pointedly.

So he wasn't going to be able to dodge that bullet. Taking Sinbad's halter, Sam led the gelding back into his stall and closed the gate.

"I can come back, can't I?" Tom asked his mother.

"If...if Sam agrees."

Tom swiveled to look at Sam, his heart in his eyes. Sam couldn't disappoint him. "Sure. We'll start by learning about the tack, then once you're familiar with that, I'll show you how to saddle Sinbad and we'll go from there."

"You're doing all of this tonight?" The question came from Molly.

"I'll stick with the tack lesson for now," he assured her.

Taking small steps backward, Tom was clearly reluctant to leave.

"It'll be fine," Sam said, hoping the boy understood his message.

Tom nodded once, gravely, then turned and raced out of the barn.

The moment they were alone, Molly let him have it.

"Tom is my son and I'm responsible for his safety," she began. "I'd apreciate if you'd discuss this sort of thing with me first."

Sam removed his hat. If he was going to apologize,

might as well do a good job of it. "You're right. This won't happen again."

His apology apparently disarmed her because she fell silent. Still, she lingered. Walking over to Sinbad's stall, she stroked his neck, weaving her fingers through his long coarse mane. "Was there something I said earlier that offended you?" she said unexpectedly. Her voice was softer now, unsure. "Perhaps this afternoon while we were in town?"

"You think I was offended?" he asked, surprised.

She slowly turned and looked at him. Sam had never seen a woman with more striking blue eyes; it was all he could do to avert his gaze.

"Gramps was concerned when you didn't join us for dinner."

He wasn't sure how to put his feelings into words. The simplest way, he decided, was to tell her the truth. "You're family. I'm not."

"It's silly for you to cook for yourself when I've already made dinner."

"I don't mind."

"I do," she insisted, her voice flaring with anger. She tamed it quickly by inhaling and holding her breath. "Both Gramps and I would like you to join us for meals." She paused. "It'd mean a lot to Gramps."

"What about you? Would it mean anything to you?" Sam had no idea what had prompted the question. He was practically inviting her to stomp all over his ego!

"It just makes more sense," she said. "But—" she took another breath "—whether you come or not is up to you."

So that was it, Sam reasoned. She'd done her duty. No doubt Walt had asked her to issue the invitation.

"Will you?" she asked, then added, "I need to know how much to cook."

"I haven't decided yet."

"Don't do me any favors, all right?"

What Sam did next was born of pure instinct. It was what he'd been thinking of doing from the moment he first set eyes on her. What he'd wanted to do the instant he heard Russell Letson invite her to dinner.

Without judging the wisdom—or the reasons—he stepped forward, clasped her shoulders and lowered his mouth to hers.

Their lips met briefly, the contact so light Sam wasn't sure they'd actually touched until he felt her stiffen. Taking advantage of her shock, he parted his lips and was about to wrap his arms around her when she pressed her hands against his chest and pushed him away.

"Don't ever do that again!" She wiped the back of her hand across her mouth. "How dare you!"

Sam wondered the same thing.

"Gramps would fire you in a heartbeat if I told him about this."

"Tell him," Sam urged. He didn't know why he'd done anything so stupid, and he wasn't proud of himself for giving in to the impulse. But he'd be selling snow cones in hell before he'd let her know that.

"I *should* tell him—it'd serve you right!"

"Then by all means mention it." What Sam should do was apologize—again—and let it go at that, but the same craziness that had induced him to kiss Molly goaded him now. He might have continued with his flippant responses if not for the pain and uncertainty he read in her eyes.

"I'd like your word of honor that it won't happen again."

Without meaning to, he laughed outright. Honor? Ex-cons weren't exactly known for their *honor*.

"You find this humorous, Mr. Dakota?" Her eyes narrowed and her voice rose in a quavery crescendo.

If he hadn't riled her earlier, he sure had now. Unintentionally. She whirled around and marched out of the barn. Sam sighed, leaned against the center post and rubbed one hand over his face, still wondering why he'd kissed her.

Then again, maybe he knew. He didn't like the idea of her dating Letson. His dislike of lawyers was instinctive, following the less than fair treatment he'd received from his own defense attorney. Which, to be honest, wasn't Letson's fault. In any case, it was more than that.

Sam had seen the way Letson looked at Molly—like a little boy in a candy store, his mouth watering for lemon drops. Letson would take Molly to dinner and afterward he'd kiss her. And when he did, Sam wanted Molly's thoughts to be clouded with the memory of *his* kiss. The memory of *his* touch.

Why, though? He reminded himself that he didn't even *like* Molly all that much. So why was he competing with Letson?

Damned if he knew.

And which kiss would Molly prefer—his or Letson's? Sam groaned at the thought.

If he were a betting man, he'd wager it wouldn't be his.

Five

Russell Letson was by far the most attractive man Molly had ever dated. When it came to looks, Sam Dakota took a distant second. Actually, she told herself, he wasn't even in the running. Nowhere close.

If she was interested in remarrying—which she wasn't—Molly wanted a man like her grandfather. While Gramps was no Mr. Personality, he was solid and strong in all the ways that mattered. The world needed more men like him. His body had deteriorated with age, but in his prime he'd been a man who inspired others. He was honest and good and fair, and he'd loved her grandmother to distraction. Just as her grandmother had loved him.

From her conversation with the bank manager and from the infrequent letters Gramps had sent her, Molly realized that over the past few years, he'd alienated a number of people. When her grandmother was alive, she'd smoothed over quarrels and difficulties, but with her gone, Gramps had turned cantankerous and unfriendly. Molly hoped all that would change now that she'd moved in with him. And while he had his faults, Gramps was her knight, her compass, her guiding light. Molly couldn't imagine life without him.

At least Gramps seemed to approve of Russell—and

Russell had gone out of his way to make this a special evening.

The restaurant was everything he'd claimed. The interior was elegant, the booths upholstered in a plush rust red velvet, and the lights low. There was a small dance floor and a live band every Friday and Saturday night, according to the sign outside. Molly was surprised a town the size of Sweetgrass could support an upscale restaurant like The Cattle Baron.

"I'm delighted you could see me on such short notice," Russell said as he closed his menu. His smile was cordial and Molly smiled back.

She'd gone to some lengths with her appearance. Even Gramps had noticed how long she spent fixing her hair and applying her makeup.

The move to Montana offered a long-overdue opportunity for a social life. Molly was ready to set aside the mistakes of the past and look to the future. As a member of the Sweetgrass community, she wanted to meet and mingle with other adults, and this dinner date was a step in that direction. Marriage didn't interest her, but a social life did.

When she lived in San Francisco, she'd rarely dated. She wasn't opposed to meeting men and never had been. But it was difficult to find a man who understood the responsibilities of single parenthood and shared her values. Even if she'd actually met someone interesting, squeezing in time for a relationship between her family and her job—well, there just weren't enough hours in the day.

Excuses. All excuses.

She hadn't been ready then, but she was now. The difference was her willingness to take a risk. Maybe it was because, with Gramps close at hand, she felt safer, more secure. He obviously liked and trusted Russell. And Sam...

"I hear you've created quite a stir among the fellows in town," Russell said, looking at her and blushing slightly.

"Me? I caused a stir?"

"There aren't many single women your age in Sweetgrass. There's been plenty of talk—you know, interest." Russell seemed a bit flustered as if he'd said more than he should. Not a trait she would have expected in a lawyer, but it made him all the more endearing. She liked him already.

"I'm sure you've had plenty of phone calls." This sounded more like a question.

"Some." A lady from the local Baptist church and a return call from the school-district office, but that was it. Men weren't exactly pounding down her door, but it didn't hurt her ego any that Russell assumed otherwise.

The waiter, a staid older man, delivered their wine, and after Russell had tasted it, filled their goblets. Russell had chosen well, Molly determined after her first sip. The California merlot was excellent.

She finished her glass and allowed Russell to refill it. A relaxing evening out was just what Molly needed, especially after the long week she'd endured. She'd driven from California to Montana, carting all her worldly belongings. She'd refereed her sons' battles across several states, dealt with the realities of Gramps's health and had begun to improve the appalling condition of the ranch house. It was a week to remember.

After ordering dinner, they chatted amicably. Russell had charming manners and Molly was soon enjoying herself. She couldn't remember the last time she'd spent a quiet evening in the company of an attractive man.

The band arrived, and around nine o'clock, the music started. Not the country-and-western tunes Molly expected, but the mellow sound of light rock. The music was an accompaniment, not an intrusion into their conversation. A few couples got up to dance, and Molly glanced enviously toward the small hardwood floor.

"Would you like to take a spin?" Russell asked, and held out his hand. His eyes twinkled as if he'd been waiting for her cue. A woman could get used to a man this sensitive, she mused.

Not until Russell had placed his arms around her waist and brought her close did she experience a sense of disappointment. It took her a couple of anxious moments to understand what was happening.

The last man to hold her close was Sam Dakota. His hands on her shoulders had been strong and forceful; his touch had rocked her, but his kiss had been gentle. The contrast had been…shocking. Memorable. Twenty-four hours later, and that memory was still potent.

Molly closed her eyes in an effort to banish Sam Dakota from her mind. Russell was handsome and well educated. Polite. Successful. Exactly the type of man she'd hoped to meet. Sam, though, was hard and lean and rough as rawhide. A hired hand. She knew almost nothing about his past, nothing about his future.

It exasperated her that she could be in the arms of a perfectly good dinner date and her mind was full of another man. The *wrong* man!

Despite her determination to put Sam out of her

thoughts, Molly found it difficult. She was grateful when their meal arrived and she could sit across from Russell and talk.

"You might remember there was something I needed to discuss with you," Russell said. He smoothed the napkin onto his lap and sipped his wine.

Molly had the impression he wanted to get this matter, whatever it was, settled now. Immediately. From the way he nervously toyed with his wineglass, she guessed this wasn't a discussion he'd been looking forward to.

"I imagine you're curious as to what I wanted to ask you," he began, gripping his goblet with both hands.

Until he'd mentioned it, Molly had actually forgotten the reason behind this dinner invitation. "Naturally," she responded, pretending she'd been breathlessly awaiting their discussion.

"I realize this is a bit premature," he said. "Personally I'd prefer to wait, but my client is anxious, which is understandable." His eyes darkened with sincerity. "Forgive me, Molly, if this offends you."

"Offends me?" Client. He was talking to her on behalf of a client? None of this made sense. She'd assumed they'd gone out primarily to get to know each other and enjoy each other's company—and perhaps to discuss some trivial matter in regard to her grandfather's will.

"This has to do with the Broken Arrow Ranch," Russell continued.

She tensed. "What about the ranch?"

He frowned as if this was distasteful to him, something he'd prefer not to do. "My client wants to know your intentions after your grandfather dies."

Molly put down her knife and fork, and clenched her hands in her lap. "My intentions to *what?*" she asked, her voice low. The evening was ruined, her illusions shattered. This was no dinner date; this was some kind of business negotiation.

"I've been asked to approach you with the idea of selling out. Naturally my client is prepared to wait until the appropriate time."

Until Gramps is dead and buried, that is. But not long enough for his body to grow cold. For an instant her anger was blinding. Her chest tightened and her breathing went shallow.

"This is a sick joke, right?" It wasn't, deep down she knew that, but she had to ask.

Russell's apology was instantaneous. "I'm sorry, Molly, really I am. Like I told you, I felt the timing with this was wrong, but my client insisted. I didn't want to approach you about it now, not so soon, but my client's afraid someone else is going to contact you first. I'm sure once you think all this through, you'll recognize his request as reasonable."

Her grandfather wasn't dead yet, and already the vultures were circling overhead. "You can tell your...client, whoever he is, that I won't be selling the ranch."

"You're not serious, are you?" Russell's eyes widened. "What do you plan to do with it?"

Molly hadn't made any decisions yet. Her one overwhelming concern had been to reach her grandfather before the unthinkable happened. The move from California to Montana had absorbed all her time and energy, dominated every waking moment. She wasn't prepared to answer Russell, nor did she feel any obligation to do so.

"Who hired you?" she demanded. "Who would be so cold and unfeeling—offering to buy the ranch before Gramps is gone? And doing it like this—through a lawyer. Who would do such a thing?"

Russell avoided her eyes. She knew he'd dreaded this and understood now why he'd invited her to dinner. He'd been hoping to smooth the way—and soften the blow.

"I can't answer that, Molly. My client has requested anonymity."

She laughed shortly. "That's understandable, isn't it?" She sighed and glanced at the ceiling while she collected her thoughts. "If you must know, I'll be working the ranch myself."

"You," Russell said slowly. He'd begun to frown again.

"You make it sound as if you don't think I'm capable of doing it."

"How much experience have you had?" he asked matter-of-factly.

"Experience," she repeated, feigning a laugh. "I'll learn as I go."

Russell's frown deepened. "Molly, I realize this whole subject is…unpleasant. Trust me, I wasn't looking forward to broaching it with you so soon. If it'd been up to me—well, never mind, that isn't important. The fact is, a woman alone with two school-age boys isn't going to be able to manage a ranch on her own. Not in these times. Not in this current market."

"Why not? According to Gramps, Sam Dakota is an excellent foreman."

Russell crumpled the linen napkin and set it on the table beside his plate, his appetite apparently gone.

Molly's had vanished, too. "The foreman's another question. How well do you know this man?"

Molly mulled over her response, but no ready answer came to mind. "Gramps hired Sam and that's good enough for me," she said. There simply hadn't been enough time to find out much about him or assess his character. She knew she found him somewhat disturbing. But she also knew that Sam cared about her grandfather, and had, in fact, saved Gramps's life. If for nothing else, his devotion to Gramps had earned him her gratitude. And her loyalty.

Once again Russell appeared hesitant. "If Dakota does agree to stay on as foreman, will you be able to continue paying his wages?"

"Wages?" Something else that had never occurred to her.

"You'll remember I was the one who drew up Walter's will, so I'm well aware of the state of his financial affairs. Molly, I have to be honest with you. They're dismal. Even if you were able to strike some kind of financial agreement with Dakota, there's no guarantee you'd be able to make a go of ranching.

"Cattle prices are down. Many long-established ranches are experiencing financial difficulties. There are fewer and fewer independent ranches left. Fewer and fewer true cowboys. Conglomerates are moving in and buying financially strapped spreads at prices well below market value. Ranchers often have no option but to sell, and they're left with nothing to show after a lifetime of effort. I don't want to see you lose your inheritance like that."

"Thanks for your vote of confidence."

"It isn't easy saying these things to you," Russell murmured. "But I feel it's my duty. In six months, when the ranch is on the auction block, I don't want you to look at me and ask why I didn't warn you.''

Molly inhaled a deep stabilizing breath. In time she knew she'd need to make these decisions, but she hadn't expected to be confronted with them her first week in Montana. On a dinner date, yet.

"Molly," he said, and stretched his hand across the table to grip hers firmly. "I realize this is upsetting—hell, it would distress anyone. But you need to give the matter of selling your consideration *now*. When Walter does die, it'll be the worst time emotionally for you to make this type of decision. All I want you to do is think ahead a few weeks or months, or however long Walt lives.''

Molly knew Russell was right, but she didn't want to face this question yet. She propped her elbows on the table and leaned her head on her hands. "The land has been in the family for four generations." Gramps and her own father had been born in the very house in which she and her sons now lived.

For all those years the family had stuck together. Survived. During two world wars, the Wheatons had held on to the land; they'd struggled through the long lean years of the Great Depression. Through it all, cattle prices had plummeted and then risen, over and over, like a wild roller-coaster ride, and through it all, the Wheatons had managed. They would again, God willing.

The ranch was Molly's heritage from her grandfather and from the father she barely remembered. One day it would belong to her sons. Briefly she closed her eyes. As angry as the offer made her, Russell had done her a favor by forcing her to acknowledge her responsibilities to her grandfather and the ranch.

"This is very difficult," she whispered, "but…"

Russell relaxed and smiled as if to say he knew he could count on her to be reasonable. "Then you'll consider the offer?"

Molly stared at him dumbfounded. He'd misunderstood completely.

"Let me assure you right now the money is good," he told her warmly. "Damn good. You won't need to worry about finances for a very long time."

"I'm not selling, Russell," she announced flatly. "Not while I live and draw breath. I'll do whatever needs to be done in order to hold on to the ranch."

Russell was right about one thing—she would definitely need help. If that meant swallowing her pride and asking Sam Dakota for his expertise, then she'd do it. Pride, even female pride, had its limits.

"How are you planning to do this? Who's going to help you?" Russell demanded. His face had contorted slightly, masking his striking good looks.

"Sam Dakota, for one." There'd be others too, Molly knew. Gramps had lived in this community all his life. She didn't doubt for an instant that, when the time came and she needed help, someone would step forward and lend a willing hand.

Russell settled back in the booth and held her eyes for a long moment. He seemed to be carefully gauging his words. "I wasn't going to say anything, but now I realize I must. Molly, exactly how well do you know Sam Dakota?" he asked.

"This is the second time you've mentioned Sam. Gramps hired him and he's—"

"Don't let your judgment be clouded by your grandfather's relationship with him. You need to form your own opinion."

"I only met him a few days ago." Molly was beginning to wonder if she *should* trust her instincts regarding Sam. They'd been muddled, confused by his kiss. Confused by a lot of things that had nothing to do with her grandfather or how good a foreman Sam was.

Russell nodded thoughtfully. "Sam Dakota is a stranger, a drifter. No one knows exactly where he came from or anything about him. He showed up in town one day, down on his luck."

"There's nothing wrong with that."

"True enough, but it's what happened afterward that's cause for concern."

"What?" she asked, not entirely certain she wanted to hear this.

"Trouble, Molly, lots of trouble. He wasn't in town more than an hour before he became involved in a...an altercation at Willie's tavern and—" He stopped. "I'll leave it at that."

"What do you mean?"

"I think it would be best if you asked Sam yourself."

She hesitated, watching Russell intently.

"Molly, listen to me, please. I'm not sure you should trust him."

"Don't be ridiculous!"

"You think that's what I'm being?" The attorney was obviously uncomfortable. "All I ask is that you be damned careful, understand?" His face was somber, concerned—as if it was all he could do not to divulge further information.

"Oh, no, you don't." Molly wasn't about to let it go at that. If Russell knew something she didn't, she had every intention of getting the facts, even if it took half the night. "Tell me what you know, Russell. I have a right to know the truth."

"I can't, Molly. I'm stepping out of line as it is." He looked away before slowly releasing his breath. "Let me put it this way. Wherever Dakota goes, trouble follows. There've been a number of unexplained incidents around the area recently. Strange incidents. Has Walt mentioned them?"

Molly shook her head.

"None of this started until after Sam Dakota arrived."

"What are these incidents?"

"Ask your grandfather. I'm not a distrustful person, but I'd find it mighty coincidental if Sam wasn't involved."

"Involved in *what?*" Her immediate concern was for her children. With Gramps at the ranch they were probably safe, but he was feeble and in ill health. She couldn't imagine what Russell was trying to tell her.

"I can't say, Molly. I probably shouldn't have said anything at all, but I felt it was my duty to warn you."

"Strange, you said. What is it? You're blaming Sam for some mysterious alien sightings?" The suggestion was enough to make her laugh.

"It isn't that kind of strange," Russell was quick to inform her. "Ginny Dougherty and her cousin were in town not more than two days ago and reported a case of vandalism. Apparently someone knocked over Walter's mailbox. It's the third time this month. She's had trouble herself."

Molly could vaguely recall Gramps saying something about the box being vandalized.

"That isn't all."

"What else has happened?"

"Ask Ginny Dougherty," he said.

"Ginny?"

"I've said more than I should have already." He pinched his lips together and Molly could see it would take a crowbar to pry any more information out of him.

That evening Tom sat on the front porch with a dog by his side. Natasha, the pregnant collie. Sighing, he stroked her silky ears. He'd heard about people experiencing withdrawal, but he never thought he'd have to deal with it himself. Only he wasn't on drugs. No way—he wasn't *that* dumb. What he missed to the point of wanting to scream was television. Good old-fashioned color television with a remote control and a twenty-three-inch screen.

Gramps got one channel on an old black-and-white set. Tom was surprised to learn there were still black-and-white televisions left in the United States. What irked him most was that Gramps refused to buy a dish or bring in cable, and the only station his tinfoil-wrapped rabbit ears delivered was from somewhere up in Canada. An educational channel! If he wanted to learn something, he'd go to school. Even sadder was that Gramps didn't have a clue what he was missing. The old man didn't know what MTV was, and furthermore he didn't care.

Gramps was asleep on the recliner now, with the television on Mute, the picture fuzzy. What Tom could make out convinced him he wouldn't want to watch it even if the picture came in clear.

Sweetgrass's lone radio station was just as bad. Every morning at ten-thirty the entire town apparently went into a frenzy for radio bingo. Tom knew certain people enjoyed playing bingo. In San Francisco the

Catholic church down the street had bingo nights twice a week, but he'd never heard of anyone playing it over the *radio*.

And if that wasn't enough, Tom had been subjected to a litany of farm prices from about noon on. He hated to disappoint Gramps, but he didn't really care about the price of pork bellies. Then the extension agent would come on and talk about the fall fair and something called 4-H. Mostly his little discussions had to do with how to grow vegetables and groom cows. Tom didn't know what an extension agent was or what he did, other than talk about animal grooming. And when the radio station actually played some music, it was this horrible stuff from the 1940s and 1950s. Stuff that was around before his mother was even born!

Now she was off on some hot date. His mother dating? Tom wasn't sure he liked that idea, but had decided he'd be mature about it. Still, he thought, if she was interested in an evening on the town, she should check out Sam.

Tom liked Sam. Clay did, too. Neither of them knew anything about Russell Letson. They'd met him when he'd come to pick Mom up, and Tom didn't have feelings toward him one way or the other. Letson was all right, he guessed. Sam, however, was terrific.

Okay, so the foreman wasn't as good-looking as the lawyer, but Sam had the advantage of knowing everything there was to know about horses. The attorney looked clueless, on *that* subject, anyway.

For the past two nights, Sam had spent time with Tom after dinner, teaching him about horses. He'd seemed distracted this evening, though. Maybe it was Clay's fault. Clay had been a pest, but Tom was used to his younger brother making a nuisance of himself. Sam wasn't.

He would say one thing about Gramps's foreman—Sam hadn't once talked down to either him or Clay. He spoke to them both as if they were regular guys.

Clay was sound asleep, but Tom had come downstairs and sat in the dark, waiting for his mother's return. He'd heard about mothers waiting up for their kids to come home from a date. He'd never thought *he'd* be the one sitting there killing time until *she* showed up. But with Gramps asleep, someone needed to keep an eye on the clock.

Headlights appeared in the distance. Tom knew the car could be miles away. He'd never known anyplace to get darker than Montana. In California in the middle of the night, no matter where he was, Tom could look out the window and find a light. Somewhere.

Not in Montana. When night came, it settled over the land like…like black ink. It covered everything. Except for the moon and the stars, he couldn't see a thing. The first night when he looked out the window, he'd been astounded. At the darkness. And the quiet. It was enough to unnerve anyone.

The headlights missed him as the car took a sharp turn and followed the road around the back by the outbuildings. Tom almost made the mistake of walking into the house, but he didn't want to stumble on his mother and her lawyer friend kissing. That would embarrass everyone. Besides, Tom wasn't sure how he'd feel if he saw the attorney with a lip lock on his mother. He might do something stupid, like punch him out.

Tom returned his gaze to the heavens. Away from the city lights, the night sky was ablaze with stars. He'd had no idea there were that many. Suddenly he noticed that the car was leaving, its lights stretching out toward the highway. Well. That hadn't taken long.

"Gramps, are you awake?" Tom heard his mother ask from inside the house.

He stiffened. His mother's voice was agitated. Letson had tried something and she was telling Gramps. Damn. Tom knew he should have gone inside, but it was too late now.

"Gramps, I hate to wake you, but I have a few questions."

The urgency in his mother's voice brought Tom up short. Letson would be sorry by the time Tom was finished with him. No one messed with his mother!

"Molly, darlin'," Gramps said and Tom heard the old man yawn. "Did you enjoy yourself?"

"Gramps, we need to talk."

"Talk?"

From his position on the porch, Tom could look into the living room through the screen door and not be seen. Gramps was on the recliner and his mother sat on the ottoman in front of him. She learned forward and folded her arms around her knees.

"What do you know about Sam Dakota?" she asked abruptly.

"Sam?" Gramps scratched the side of his head. "You went to dinner with Letson and discussed Sam?"

"Tell me what you know about him."

"Why?" The word was a challenge.

"Because...I need to know if we should trust him."

Tom wasn't sure he liked the tone of his mother's voice or her questions, but he wanted to hear what she said even more than he wanted to run in and defend Sam.

"Why are you asking me such a thing?"

His mother threw back her head and stared at the ceiling as if counting to ten. She did that sometimes when she wanted to keep her cool.

"Did you check his references?" she asked quietly.

Gramps rubbed the sleep from his face. "I don't recall that he provided any."

"Then why'd you hire him?" Her voice rose slightly.

"'Cause I needed help."

Gramps seemed to think that was all the explaining necessary. But Tom knew his mother wasn't about to let it drop. No, she'd hang on until she got what she wanted. All mothers weren't like that, but his was. Stubborn, and she wouldn't let you get away with changing the subject.

"Sam Dakota is a good man, Molly."

"But you don't know that for sure, do you?"

"I didn't need a piece of paper with a bunch of people's names to tell me what two hours on the range said a whole lot better."

"Okay, so Sam's good on the back of a horse." She made that sound like a small thing.

"He handles cattle like a pro," Gramps added. "He's one of the best cattleman I've worked with in years. Now tell me why all the questions. You're not makin' a lick of sense, girl."

She hesitated, then shrugged. "Russell Letson said there were a number of unexplained incidents that've happened since Sam arrived. He said people in town talk about him." Her voice rose again and she leaned forward.

"I'm not a man who listens to rumors. You disappoint me, Molly, if you do."

"But Gramps, Sam spends time with my boys."

"You've been taken in by that silver-tongued devil of an attorney."

"But I thought you liked him! He's your attorney!"

"I should fire him, that's what I should do! I don't want him filling your head with doubts."

"How do you know he's not telling the truth?" Molly demanded. "What did Russell mean by 'incidents'? Why didn't you tell me? Is it true, Gramps?"

"Fiddlesticks."

"Gramps, please. Listen to reason. Everything is fine and then Sam Dakota arrives and stirs up the town…"

"It needed a little stirring up. Whole damn place has gone to seed. I don't know how it happened, but overnight the population of Sweetgrass has turned into a bunch of fanatics. I'm telling you right now that fight wasn't Sam's fault. I saw it happen. I'd have done the same damn thing myself."

"Tell me about this fight. Russell mentioned it, too, but he didn't give me any details."

Apparently his mother didn't know everything. Tom was interested in the particulars himself. Sam might not be as big as some, but he was strong. And Tom knew he wasn't a man inclined to walk away from a challenge, either.

"There's nothing you need to know about it, other than what I already told you."

"Gramps, I'd rather—"

"You're forgetting something, Molly girl," Gramps interrupted. "If it wasn't for Sam Dakota, I'd be a dead man now."

A moment of silence followed his words.

"Oh, Gramps…"

Tom watched as his mother took one of Gramps's

hands and pressed it to her cheek. She closed her eyes and Tom knew how grateful she felt that he was alive. He had to admit he felt pretty grateful, too.

"One more thing I'm gonna tell you," Gramps said gruffly. "Sam was a champion rodeo rider—one of the best till he had a bad accident. He knows about hard work, and the value of a dream. Not only that, he's managed to keep this ranch going. So if you've got anything to say to the man, I suggest you start with thank-you."

Six

It was more out of habit than necessity that Sam stopped by the house each morning. With family around Walt didn't need Sam checking up on him. His visits had become courtesy calls—first he would inquire about the old man's health, then he'd list his plans for the day.

Although Sam's title was foreman, he'd taken on just about all the responsibilities of what bigger ranches would call a general manager. He did the paperwork, ordered supplies, hired and fired temporary hands when they needed extra help and organized the work. And he dealt with any problems that arose, of which there never appeared to be a shortage.

Toward the end of Molly's second week at the ranch, he walked into the kitchen one morning and found her in her bathrobe, standing barefoot in front of the coffeepot. His reaction at the sight of her—looking warm and sleepy, her hair tousled—surprised even him. It felt as if...as if someone had kicked him in the stomach.

"Mornin'," he said, aware that he sounded flustered. In a gesture of respect he touched the tip of his hat.

"Sam...hi." Seeing him had obviously unnerved her, too. Sam watched as she tugged the robe more securely about her waist and rubbed one bare foot against the other.

They'd been avoiding each other for almost a week. Kissing her that night hadn't been one of his most brilliant moves, but try as he might Sam couldn't make himself regret it. Seeing her now, her hair mussed and her face bare of makeup, he thought Molly Cogan was lovely—much lovelier than he'd realized before. It was difficult not to stare. He pulled his gaze away and wondered if her appeal had something to do with getting to know her and the boys. He enjoyed Molly, the small things she did to make every day special. Not a night went by without her adding an extra little touch to the evening meal. Sometimes it was a bouquet of wildflowers placed in the center of the table; other times a low-fat dessert made especially for her grandfather. Without further discussion, Sam had joined the family for supper on Sunday night and every night since.

He and Molly didn't speak or meet each other's eyes, but he found himself listening for the contagious sound of her laughter. It always made him smile, no matter what his mood. The gentleness she displayed toward her grandfather touched him. And he sensed that she was a good mother, too. Not only that, he was impressed with the improvements she'd made around the place. Molly and her boys had already done a number of small repairs that he'd been putting off for lack of time. Fixing the porch steps. Painting the front door. Things like that.

"Do you want coffee?" she asked, breaking into his thoughts. She opened the cupboard and reached for an extra mug.

"Thanks, but no, I've already had my fill." He'd been working the better part of two hours and had downed half a pot before sunup. Sam's routine was to

rise around four in order to sort through an accumu-
lation of paperwork, then head out to the barn.

Last week he'd hired two hands, high-school kids
who worked cheap and were grateful for the jobs. They
arrived early in the morning and returned home at the
end of the day. Pete could shoe horses, mend fences
and fix machinery. Charlie would work half the time
as a hand and the other half as a wrangler; his particular
responsibility was caring for the horses.

Some ranchers used all-terrain vehicles, instead of
horses, but Walt would have none of that. A horse was
the original ATV, he said, and while his opinion might
be outdated, Sam tended to agree with him. He wasn't
opposed to taking the pickup onto the range and often
did, but nothing beat riding. Nothing compared to the
feeling of exhilaration and freedom he experienced on
horseback. During his darkest days in prison, this was
what he'd thought about, how he'd escaped the hell he
was trapped in.

Sam forced his mind back to the matters at hand.
Charlie worked well with the horses, but Sam guessed
that by this time next year Tom would be knowledge-
able enough to tackle the job.

Molly's older son possessed horse sense. It was
something you either had or you didn't. For Tom, it
seemed to come naturally. The boy had a real affinity
for animals, especially horses, and he was a fast
learner. He frequently reminded Sam of what *he'd* been
like at that age—eager to prove himself, looking for
ways to establish his manhood. Nothing better than
ranch work for doing that.

Both Molly's boys were good kids. Sam would have
liked to tell her, but hesitated because the tension be-

tween them remained so strong. Probably because of that damn kiss.

Sam started into the living room where Walt was resting. He knew it was hell on the old man to sit idle, something he had to do more and more lately. That was one reason Sam made a point of visiting Walt every morning, consulting with him and seeking his advice, although he rarely needed it.

"Sam." Molly stopped him as he left to find Walt. He turned around.

"I—there's a question I'd like to ask if you don't mind," she said without meeting his eyes.

Ever since Saturday night, when she'd gone to dinner with Letson, he'd noticed a change in her attitude. He'd assumed it had something to do with the kiss; now he wasn't sure.

"Gramps said you didn't offer any references when he hired you," she said, holding her coffee mug with both hands. "Why was that?"

"He didn't want any." He squared his shoulders in challenge. "Are you asking for them now?"

"Gramps doesn't seem to feel he needs them." A dubious quality in her voice told him she didn't agree.

If he hadn't demonstrated his ability and his commitment by this time, Sam doubted he ever would. He was about to tell her exactly that when she asked another question.

"I've heard there've been a number of... unexplained incidents around the ranch since you started here."

"Unexplained incidents?" There had been, but they'd begun *before* he was hired; Walt had told him that. He wondered who'd mentioned it to Molly. Letson, no doubt. Any problems Sam encountered he'd dealt with promptly and efficiently. For the most part he didn't see any need to worry Walt, so he hadn't brought up any of the recent incidents. The old man knew about the mailbox being knocked over three times, but only because Ginny Dougherty had said something. The damaged fence posts, strewn garbage and rotten eggs thrown against the side of the barn were more a nuisance than a hazard.

The most dangerous incident had happened earlier in the week. A windmill used to pump drinking water for the cattle had been toppled. At first Sam suspected that wind and time had been the culprits, but on closer inspection, he'd discovered the damage was deliberate. It'd taken half a day for two men to repair it.

Molly's right hand clasped the front of her robe. "Gramps suggested if I was concerned about any of this, I should ask you. He's right—you should have the opportunity to defend yourself."

Sam's hackles instantly went up. "Defend myself?" His narrowed gaze locked onto hers as his anger simmered just beneath the surface. "Are you suggesting *I'm* the one responsible?"

"That's not what I said." The hesitation before she answered implied something else. "What I want is the truth. I can deal with anything but lies. If there's some hidden agenda here, then I'd rather you told me about it now."

"Hidden agenda?" He worked his fingers, clenching and unclenching his hands. "In other words you're asking me if I'm causing these problems. That doesn't make much sense to me. Why would I bite the hand that feeds me?"

"To prove how valuable you are." She'd apparently given the matter some thought. "I don't have to make more work for myself to prove how much I'm needed around this place. Look around you—the ranch is in terrible shape! I can't keep up with everything that needs to be done as it is. Trust me, the last thing I'd do is add to my own workload.''

She studied him as if to gauge the truth of his words. After a moment she nodded. ''Thank you, Sam. I apologize if I offended you.''

''No problem.'' She *had* angered him, but he admired her for having the courage to confront him directly. Most folks wouldn't, and he'd be dismissed without ever knowing why. ''Now if you don't mind, I'm going to talk to your grandfather for a while.''

Walt looked pale and drawn when Sam finally entered the living room. Just sitting up seemed to drain him of strength. ''Mornin', Sam.''

''Walt.'' Sam removed his hat and took the seat across from the old man.

''My granddaughter givin' you trouble?''

Sam laughed softly. ''None that I can't handle.''

''Good.'' Walt let his head fall back against the sofa cushion and closed his eyes. ''Were you able to get the Stetson?''

''Yeah, I picked one up in town yesterday.'' He didn't mention that it had cost almost a hundred dollars—or that he'd paid for it himself.

Walt's smile was full, rare even at the best of times. ''Tom will be surprised, won't he?''

''I expect he will.'' Delighted, too.

''Good.''

It was time to get on with the business of the day. ''I'm sending Pete and Charlie out to Lonesome Valley and I'll have them check the—''

''Fine, fine, whatever you think.'' Walt cut him off

with a flick of his hand. "How are Tom and Clay doing? Molly told me they follow you around like shadows."

The boys had taken up the role of sidekicks, asking questions and trailing after him, but Sam didn't mind. Much of the time they were actually a help—Tom especially—doing small chores like cleaning tack and sweeping out stalls. He could always use a couple of extra hands.

"Tom's doing well with his riding lessons," Sam said. "I'd like to take him out on the range."

Walt's mouth quivered with a half smile. "Whatever you think," he said again. "What about the younger boy?"

"Not yet. He's too nervous. Needs his confidence built up first."

Walt showed his agreement with an abrupt nod. "Didn't you tell me Natasha recently delivered her pups?"

"A couple of days ago now." Sam grinned. "Clay's been spending his days baby-sitting them—when his mom hasn't got him painting shutters or nailing down steps."

"Good. Let the boy choose one of those pups for his own."

The old man was wise; giving the younger boy a puppy was the perfect thing. "I'll see to it."

"And—" A clamor arose outside, followed by a shout.

Sam recognized Ginny's frantic voice and knew it meant trouble. He leaped to his feet and raced through the kitchen, nearly colliding with Molly in his rush.

Stepping away to avoid him, she lost her balance. Sam instinctively reached for her shoulders to steady her. He wasn't sure how it happened, but his hand grazed her breast. The briefest of contacts, completely unintentional, and yet he felt a jolt of desire so potent it was as if someone had pounded a stake right through him.

Molly felt it, too, light as the touch had been, and her startled gaze flew to his.

He opened his mouth to apologize, but she shook her head, wordlessly conveying that an apology wasn't necessary. She understood. He had more important matters to attend to.

"Sam." Ginny's Appaloosa pranced about the yard, his neck lathered from the long gallop. "I was out checking my herd and saw that your fence is down. You've got a hundred head or more making straight for the river."

Sam slapped his hat against his thigh and swore. He'd already sent Pete and Charlie out for the day. First he'd need to find them, and then the cattle. He just prayed none of the herd was injured or managed to get lost before he found them. That wasn't all he had to worry about, either. He'd recently planted seventy-five acres of alfalfa; those cattle could destroy the entire crop in ten minutes.

"Thanks for letting me know, Ginny." He was already running toward the truck.

"What is it, woman?" Walt hollered from the doorway, his eyes flashing with more life than Sam had seen in a week.

Sam stopped abruptly and turned toward them. "There's a fence down," he explained.

Walt's reaction was identical to his own.

"That's not the worst of it," Ginny muttered.

"There's more?" Walt cried. "Dammit, woman, can't you bring any news except bad?"

"It isn't my fault, old man! If you'd gone out of your way to create friends instead of enemies, you might not be in this predicament."

"Would you two stop bickering?" Sam shouted. He didn't have time to stand around while they exchanged insults. If there was more trouble, he needed to hear what it was so he could deal with it as quickly as possible.

Ginny's gaze traveled from Walt to him. "It was deliberate, Sam. Someone cut the wires."

This time Walt and Sam swore in two-part harmony.

Molly didn't understand the full significance of what had happened; all she knew was that she didn't see Sam for three days.

She'd phoned the sheriff's office to report the damage but heard nothing back. She wondered if this kind of thing was considered a routine crime in Montana—the way police in San Francisco viewed car break-ins.

Meals were hurried affairs during those days of crisis. Either Charlie or Pete would take something out to Sam, but he never showed up himself. Molly wasn't sure when he slept. Almost against her will, as she worked on the garden she'd begun to plant, she caught herself watching for him, worrying about him. She was constantly aware of his absence.

Gramps was anxious, too, grilling her with questions, repeating the same ones over and over until her patience was gone. He fretted and stewed, and Molly knew it couldn't be good for his heart. She worried about leaving him even for a short time, but Gramps hated her fussing over him. The atmosphere in the house seemed to crackle with tension. Molly gardened obsessively to escape it.

The boys were nervous and at loose ends, and Molly didn't object when they started spending most of their time hanging around the barn. That was their way of coping with anxiety, as gardening was hers.

Saturday evening, the third day, just as the sun was about to sink into the horizon, Tom spotted Sam riding slowly toward the house.

"Mom! Mom!" Tom raced over to her, his thin legs kicking up dust. Molly set aside the hoe and rubbed her arm across her sweat-dampened forehead. She still wasn't accustomed to seeing Tom in a cowboy hat. Not a cheap imitation, either, but a felt one that must have cost the earth. He'd found it on his bed the day they learned the fence had been cut. The only person who could've put it there was Sam. Why, she couldn't guess. Not that it mattered to Tom. He'd placed it on his head and hadn't removed it since, except to sleep.

"I see him, honey," Molly said, looking out at the horse and rider. Their shape was silhouetted against the pink sky of sunset.

Despite herself, Molly felt her breath catch. The scene was classically, beautifully Western. *Return of the Cowboy.*

But this cowboy had barely slept for two nights. He'd eaten on the run. And he'd worked long back-breaking days.

Molly's hand crept to her throat. Sam was slouched over the saddle; it looked as if he barely had the strength to stay on his horse. As he drew near the yard and saw Molly and the boys, he straightened.

Tom and Clay gathered around her. Sam rode still

closer, and she searched his face for signs of trouble, fearing he'd come with more bad news.

Unsure what she intended to say, Molly hurried toward him when he stopped. There'd been so many things she wanted to tell him, had thought about over the past three days. Not a single one came to mind now.

"Hi." That sounded incredibly stupid. Juvenile. She wanted to grab the word back the instant she'd said it.

"Hi, yourself," he said. He grinned. It was the lazy tired smile of a man who'd been too long away from home. A man who'd finally returned and found someone waiting for him there. His gaze held hers an extra moment, then moved to her oldest son. His grin broadened. "Nice-looking Stetson, son."

Son. The word slipped effortlessly from his lips, and Molly watched Tom's reaction. It seemed he stood a little straighter, a little taller.

The tension between Molly's shoulder blades eased. "Did you find all the cattle?"

"Think so. The last two were trapped in a bog hole, up to their knees in mud. I had a hell of a time freeing them. Are Pete and Charlie back?"

Tom answered. "Came back about an hour ago."

"Good."

For the first time Molly noticed that Sam was wearing some of the bog hole. His clothes were caked with dried mud. The hem of his jeans was thick with it, as were his sleeves. His face was splattered. Funny she hadn't realized it earlier.

"I'll take Thunder for you," Tom offered. "I'll give him a good rubdown and some extra oats—he deserves it."

"Charlie should do that. It's what we're paying him for."

"Charlie and Pete have gone home now," Molly said.

Sam's eyes flared briefly before he sighed. "Can't say I blame them. I don't think they figured they'd be working this hard on a summer job."

"I don't think *anyone* figured they would," Molly added.

Holding on to the saddle horn, Sam slid heavily from Thunder's back. The leather creaked and for a moment he braced himself against the horse. "I need a shower, something to eat and my bed, in that order."

"There's plenty of leftovers from dinner," Molly assured him.

Tom took the gelding's reins and led him into the barn. "Don't worry about Thunder," he said, not hiding his pleasure at helping Sam.

"I'm sure Gramps is going to want to talk to you, too," Molly said. She hated to burden Sam with any more demands, but with the state Gramps had been in these past few days...

"I'll give him a report as soon as I've finished eating," Sam promised.

Molly wondered if Gramps would be able to wait that long.

Tom and Clay were still in the barn tending to Thunder when Sam entered the kitchen fresh from his shower. In a clean set of clothes, his hair wet and just combed, he made a striking figure. Trying hard not to stare, Molly turned the thick slice of ham sizzling in the pan while she warmed mashed potatoes and peas in another skillet.

Sam closed his eyes and for a wild moment Molly feared he was about to collapse. It turned out he was just inhaling the aroma of a home-cooked meal. "I swear I could eat a horse."

"Don't let Thunder hear you say that," she joked.

Sam pulled out a kitchen chair and sat at the table. "Or Tom," he muttered with a laugh.

Molly brought him his meal, along with a letter that had arrived for him. He glanced up expectantly when she set the envelope on the table, then stuck it inside his shirt pocket, unopened. Not without a sense of guilt, Molly had studied that envelope long and hard. The return address was a well-known ranch on the other side of the state.

He was halfway through his meal when Gramps wandered into the kitchen. "So you're back."

"I'm back," Sam agreed.

"Didn't hear you come in," Gramps said. "Fell asleep." He pulled out a chair and sat across the table from Sam, who didn't so much as pause in his appreciation of the meal. He reached for a second buttermilk biscuit and slathered butter across the warm top.

"You've had a few rough days."

Sam nodded, biting into his biscuit with a look of pure contentment.

Molly brought Gramps a cup of coffee, then sat down beside him.

"Molly's been hard at work herself," Gramps said next. "She's put in a garden. Exactly the same place my Molly used to have hers. That woman had a way with plants." He shook his head wonderingly. "My guess is her granddaughter has the same green thumb."

Only days ago, the spot where her grandmother had cultivated one of the finest gardens Molly had ever seen was covered with blackberry vines and weeds. With the boys' help, she'd cleared the space, roto-tilled and enriched the earth, then planted vegetables and—she couldn't resist—flowers. Low-maintenance flowers, like nasturtiums and impatiens. The work had been physically demanding and her body ached everywhere.

"We'll have to wait and see about that green thumb, Gramps." He embarrassed her with his praise. She'd weeded her grandmother's garden during her childhood summers, but she'd never created one of her own. It would be an experience, especially planting as late as she had.

Gramps frowned. "I had to stop Molly from climbing up on the roof, though. Fool woman seems to think she can patch a leak, too." He shook his head. "She's beginning to act like Ginny—thinks she can do everything herself."

"I've been meaning to get to that roof myself," Sam said, and his face darkened briefly. "It's just one of those things I've put off."

"You have enough to do as it is," Molly protested. She wasn't entirely helpless, and she wanted both her grandfather and Sam to know that she intended to do her part. While she didn't relish the thought of maneuvering her way across the steeply pitched roof, it had to be fixed before the fall rains started.

"Your grandfather's right—you shouldn't be on that roof," Sam told her. "If I don't get to the repairs within the next week, I'll have someone else work on it." He looked straight at her until she met his eyes. "Understand?"

"Yes," she grumbled, but she had to admit it felt good to hand the responsibility over to him. Other than during the first few years of Tom's life, there hadn't been a man around to help her with things like that.

She'd had to learn to handle small repairs and fix what needed fixing—knowledge that came in handy now.

A short silence followed. ''There was a call for you this afternoon,'' Gramps muttered.

Something about her grandfather's voice told her this was more than a casual comment.

''For me?'' Sam's head jerked up.

''Curly Q Ranch outside of Laramie. Ever heard of it?''

His expression decidedly uncomfortable, Sam shifted in the chair. ''What'd they want?''

Molly glanced from one man to the other, puzzled by the undercurrent of tension. Now that she thought about it, Gramps had been agitated since answering the phone, muttering under his breath and asking about Sam again and again.

''The foreman said he'd gotten a job inquiry from you. Is it true?'' Walt demanded.

Sam slapped the biscuit down on the edge of his plate. ''Yeah, it's true.''

''I'm not dead yet!'' Gramps barked, his voice shaking.

''Maybe not, but Molly's going to sell out. All I'm doing is protecting my interests.'' Sam pushed his plate aside, his appetite apparently satisfied—or ruined, she didn't know which.

''I'm not selling the ranch,'' she insisted, wanting that clearly understood.

Sam's expression said otherwise.

''You may not think so now, but when the offers—''

''I've already turned down one offer,'' she interrupted. Her anger seared each word. Sam was like everyone else. He could see the vultures circling overhead and he was going to bail out at his earliest convenience. What struck Molly hardest was the thought of running the ranch without him. She was a novice at this, a greenhorn, and without his help and guidance she'd be at a terrible loss. If Sam left, she might not have any choice but to sell.

Both Gramps and Sam were staring at her.

Molly blinked. "What?"

"You've already had an offer for the ranch?" Gramps asked. "Who from?"

"I'm not exactly sure who Russell's client is. He never said."

"Letson brought you the offer?" To Molly's alarm, Gramps's face turned a deep red, and he let loose a string of swearwords—some of which she'd never heard before.

"Gramps!" She was grateful the boys weren't around.

"That son of a bitch is not to be trusted." Closing his eyes, Gramps took several deep breaths, apparently hoping to calm himself.

"I'm not selling the Broken Arrow," Molly repeated, directing the comment at Sam. It felt as if the foundation of everything she'd planned was cracking. Without Sam to manage the ranch for her, to sell off cattle and teach her what she needed to know, she'd be hopelessly in trouble within days. There was no one else she could ask. The hands he'd hired were only high-school boys, and they'd be back in school soon.

"I apologize if I disappointed you, Walt," Sam said, and he did sound contrite, "but I've got to look out for myself. You and I both know that I'll stay as long as *you* need me."

Molly didn't miss the emphasis. He was saying his loyalty belonged to Gramps and not to her or the boys.

The foundation of her future had not only cracked, the entire structure was about to crumble at her feet. But pride had carried her a long way, and she wasn't about to let this...this fickle foreman know how badly he'd let her down.

"He's right, Gramps," she stated breezily, as if Sam's defection was of little concern. "It would be unreasonable to expect Sam to stay on any longer than necessary. He's got his own life to worry about." Even as she spoke, her blood heated at the thought that this man she'd chosen to trust—against her better judgment, dammit!—would do anything so underhand. It'd been a mistake to put her faith in him, to believe he'd care enough about the ranch, care enough about anyone here other than Gramps, to want to stay on.

She'd begun to lower her guard with Sam and so had her boys, who admired and trusted him implicitly. That had been a mistake, all right.

She stood abruptly and grabbed the dirty dishes from the table, clattering cutlery onto the plate.

"Molly."

"It's all right, Gramps." Thankfully something in her voice revealed that she was in no mood to discuss this further. With her back to the two men, she slammed the plate into the sinkful of hot water and scrubbed it forcefully enough to remove the floral pattern.

She heard Sam leave and her grandfather shuffle into the living room again. She closed her eyes in gratitude that they'd both left her in peace. Bracing her hands on the edge of the sink, she inhaled a deep breath and continued washing the pans, fighting back the emotion that threatened to choke her.

Men were not to be trusted; Molly had learned that

painful lesson years earlier. But Sam Dakota, with his gruff gentleness toward her grandfather and his patient encouragement to her sons, had somehow worked his way into her stubborn heart. She hadn't wanted that to happen! Then there was that kiss in the barn.... It mortified her to remember how she'd worried about him the past three days, waited for him, even missed him.

Sam wasn't the problem, she decided, as she banged the frying pan onto the drainer. *She* was. Her hand trembled, and she paused, closing her eyes once again.

After cleaning up the kitchen, Molly headed back outside to work. It was already dark, but the yard light was turned on. Hard physical labor might help her deal with her anger.

In all honesty, she had to acknowledge that Sam had no reason to continue working on the ranch without Gramps. She'd *assumed* he'd be willing to stay on— but then, that was the way of assumptions.

The hoe was where she'd left it, and she picked it up and started hacking away at the base of the wild blackberry vines that had tangled in the lower limbs of the apple trees. Her grandmother's six-tree orchard sported two each of plum, pear and apple. The orchard was as badly run-down as the garden had been.

Venting her frustration as she chopped at the stubborn vines and yanked them away with gloved hands, Molly realized that the letter addressed to Sam must have been a response to a job inquiry.

Not that it mattered. Not really. Why should Sam Dakota be any different from Daniel or any other man she'd ever known? With the exception of Gramps, of course. She ignored the small faint voice that said maybe she wasn't being fair. This was her reward for giving a damn, she raged. This was her reward for allowing herself to hope and care! What hurt most was that she'd actually started to *like* Sam. He'd shown more interest in her boys in the past two weeks than their father had their whole lives.

He'd made friends with her children, and all the while he'd been planning to leave, to walk out on them. It was heartless and cruel. Dammit, he'd made her believe he cared—cared not only about Gramps but about the ranch...and the boys. Despite Russell Letson's warnings, she'd given him her trust.

"Mom! Mom!" Clay came racing out of the barn, screeching with excitement.

Molly leaned against the hoe.

Clay carried a small bundle in his arms. "Look!" he cried, holding out the puppy for her to examine.

The brown-and-black collie was so young his eyes had yet to open.

"Remember I told you Natasha had her litter? Well, guess what?" Clay could barely contain himself. "Sam says I can pick one of them as my own! I've never had a dog before, and now I can choose one myself. Sam says I'll need to train him and take care of him and everything. Sam says—"

One more *Sam says* and Molly swore she was going to explode. "He gave you the puppy?" she cut in sharply.

Clay nodded. The excitement emptied from her son's dark eyes, replaced with the sober look of a child knowing he was about to hear something disappointing. He held the tiny newborn pup tight against his middle, as though he feared she was about to jerk it from his arms.

Molly threw down the hoe and with quick steps headed toward the barn. She wanted to confront Sam now. She wouldn't rest, wouldn't sleep, until she'd settled this.

"Mom...Mom, what are you gonna do?" Clay asked, catching up with her. "I'm old enough to take care of a puppy, honest I am! I'll do everything, I promise. I'll feed him and brush his coat and train him to work with the cattle the same way Natasha does."

Of all the nerve. Sam had given Clay the puppy without asking her first. He'd promised he wouldn't do things like that! Not only was he abandoning her and the children, he was complicating her life before he left. She'd had enough.

Tired though he was, Sam hadn't gone directly to bed the way he probably should have. He met her outside the barn, and his posture, his very stance, spoke of defiance.

"I warned you about this sort of thing before," she snapped.

"Warned me?"

"I specifically asked you to check with me first before doing anything like this again."

Sam stared at her as if he didn't know what she was talking about. "Listen, Molly, if you're talking about the puppy—"

"What else could it be?" Even as she spoke, she realized her reaction was out of all proportion, but she couldn't help herself. Anger and resentment fused in her mind.

"Mom, I'm old enough. I am!" Clay insisted, close to tears. "I'll take good care of him, I promise." His pleas were breaking her heart.

"This isn't about the puppy, and you know it," Sam said quietly.

He was right.

"This is about the phone call Walt took for me, isn't it? And that letter." He wiped his hand across his brow. "A man needs to eat, Molly."

"You might have asked me what I plan to do with the ranch first!"

He frowned. "Perhaps, but at the time the situation didn't look all that promising."

"Mom, Mom." Clay tugged at her shirttail in an effort to get her attention.

She glanced guiltily down at her son. "You can keep him," she said softly, feeling wretched for the way she'd treated him. Before she could say another word, she heard Gramps calling her and Sam. She turned to see him standing on the top step leading from the house.

Thinking something might be wrong, Molly raced toward her grandfather. Sam was right behind her.

Gramps leaned weakly against the doorjamb. "I need to talk to you both," he said.

"Now might not be the best time," Molly advised. Sam was exhausted, and she…so was she. Emotionally and physically exhausted.

"Now seems as good a time as any," Gramps said. Without waiting for an argument, he led the way back to the kitchen, giving them no choice but to follow.

"I've come up with a solution," Gramps announced, grinning broadly.

"Solution to *what?*" Sam asked. He sounded as impatient as Molly felt.

"You two and the ranch," Gramps explained. His smile grew even wider as he gazed first at his granddaughter and then at Sam. He chuckled in real amusement. "You two already squabble like you're married What I figure is, you should make it official."

Seven

Pearl was tired. It'd been a busy night and her regular clients had been more demanding than usual. She found it increasingly difficult to dredge up enthusiasm—or the pretense of it—for her trade. She was good. One of the best. Guys had been telling her that since she was sixteen years old. She'd never had a chance to be like normal teenagers. Her uncle had stolen her virginity when she was barely old enough to know what had happened, and later he'd introduced her to his friends. By the time she was in high school she'd learned how to use her body to get anything she wanted. Every emotion was expressed through sex. Happiness. Grief. Pain. Anger. It was all she knew. The ever-present need to be needed, loved. Used.

She'd never intended to become a prostitute, but pleasing men in bed was the only talent she possessed that earned her a decent wage. In the beginning, when she was young and still pretty enough to attract a lot of attention, it'd actually been fun. It hadn't been just sex back then. There were restaurant dinners and bottles of champagne, and for a few hours she could make believe she was on a date. The pretending had come a lot easier, too. The soft sighs and shallow pants had been effortless, and when her john was finished, she clung to him and smiled secretly to herself. Each one laid claim to her body, which she gave for a fee, but no one had ever touched her heart.

Until Russell.

With him it was different. It'd always been different. The first time he'd visited her he'd been nervous and even a little shy. Surprisingly, a lot of men were. Some sought her out because they had certain "problems" and felt she might help. Others were nervous because they feared discovery—although the fear often heightened their pleasure.

Pearl controlled these eager but reluctant lovers, tempted them and teased them and encouraged their fears. Just when they were ready to turn tail and run, she'd calm them, satisfying their every need. Inevitably they returned. The fear brought them back. The fear and the pleasure.

Then Russell had walked into her life. She was his birthday gift, and the instructions Monroe gave her had been specific. She was Russell's reward for doing a favor and she was to keep him happy all night. In exchange for her services she would be handsomely reimbursed. Pearl had willingly accepted the offer. Keep one man content for the night and she'd earn more than she normally would with five or six.

When he'd first arrived, Pearl had been surprised. She'd anticipated a man who had trouble attracting women, but that clearly wasn't the case. Russell was good-looking enough to have any woman he wanted. He certainly didn't need her when plenty of women would eagerly have slept with him for free.

Because he was nervous and struggling not to show it, and because she had plenty of time to fill, Pearl had suggested they have a glass of wine first. Russell had started talking to fill the awkward silence. He spoke to her as if she were a friend, as if she were a real date. Not a hooker. More importantly he treated her with respect.

They quickly learned they enjoyed the same movies and listened to the same kind of music, New Orleans-style jazz. Normally she was the one responsible for putting a client at ease, but it was Russell who'd gotten her to lower her guard and relax.

Soon she was laughing and joking with him as though she'd known him all her life. Russell was wonderful, with his interesting conversation and dry sense of humor. After a while he'd removed his shoes and propped his feet on her coffee table. Next he loosened his tie. He hadn't eaten dinner and suggested they order pizza. It was the first time a customer had dinner delivered to her house.

While they ate, he'd found the listing for a favorite movie and asked if he could turn on the television. They'd cuddled on the sofa like high-school sweethearts, and Pearl had rested her head against his shoulder.

She'd never experienced this kind of tenderness as a teenager. She'd never sat on a sofa with a man and not had his hands crawling all over her. Not until that first night with Russell.

The ironic thing was that she'd been paid more to entertain him than to service a bachelor party, and in the end all they'd done was kiss. Gently. Slowly. And with such sweetness it brought tears to her eyes every time she thought about it. He could have taken her at any time and she would have welcomed his body. But he hadn't.

If she'd told anyone what had happened that night—or more precisely, *hadn't* happened—she knew people would get the wrong idea about him. Some would suggest he was gay. Or that he was impotent. Or asexual. But he wasn't any of those. Pearl had a sixth sense about such things, and she knew better. He was all man, but more than that, Russell Letson was a gentleman.

Sweetgrass being a small town, it didn't take her long to inadvertently run into him again. She'd been in the grocery store, and her heart, the one she'd assumed had shriveled up and died, had nearly leaped out of her chest when she saw him. A hooker, however, knew her place, and one thing she never did was greet a customer in public.

Avoiding eye contact, she'd walked past him without a word. It was one of the hardest things she'd ever done. By the time she was in the parking lot she wanted to cry. But whores didn't cry. It was the first rule. Never care. Never reveal any genuine feeling. The mind was hollow, and the body was…something to be used.

Russell had followed her out of the Safeway store, and she'd explained that it wasn't a good idea for him to be seen with her. People would talk. He insisted he didn't care. He wanted to see her again, even if it meant paying for her services. For the first time in her life Pearl turned down a paying customer.

But Russell wouldn't leave it at that. Because she was afraid of hurting his reputation, she refused to let him visit her. It was then that Russell told her about his cabin on Lake Giles, fifty miles outside town. He simply set a time on Sunday afternoon and gave her directions.

Pearl couldn't have stayed away to save her soul. When she arrived, he'd stepped onto the porch and smiled as if her coming meant more to him than anything in the world. After that she drove out to Russell's cabin every Sunday, and with each visit Pearl changed a little more. When she was with him, she didn't need makeup or sexy clothes. He loved her best with her hair pulled back in a ponytail, wearing tight jeans and a loose cotton shirt.

Eventually, because she trusted him, Pearl told him her most shameful secret—that she'd never learned to read. Pearl had never written a check, never become engrossed in a good book or followed a recipe. She'd wept and hidden her face after he learned the truth. Unlike others who'd snickered and called her stupid, Russell had kissed away her tears and said he'd teach her himself. That was the day her entire world changed.

They had become lovers, but not right away. Not for several weeks. He was a considerate lover, passionate and caring. It was with him that Pearl *made love* for the first time in her life. Afterward she wept in his arms and he'd held her against him and wept with her.

They never talked about what she did at night. The subject was as taboo as the future.

Pearl didn't know if this was love. All she knew was that she felt something for Russell she'd never felt for anyone else. She lived for Sundays, for their time together. Although she'd never been much of a housekeeper, she discovered how much she enjoyed cooking. Each week she tried out new recipes, cooking and serving him gourmet meals. Pearl liked to pretend this was her real life, these few stolen hours away from Sweetgrass, and everything else a bad dream from which she would eventually awake.

Two a.m. Friday, after she'd finished for the night, Pearl heard the back door open. Adrenaline shot through her blood, and she stiffened. Only one person had a key to her back door; only one person would dare to come to her this late. The man she hated. Monroe, Russell's cousin. How could any two men be less alike? Monroe controlled her and a dozen other women in a number of small towns across northwestern Montana. He kept her customers in line, supplied her with condoms at a discount and made frequent use of her body himself.

"Pearl." He slurred her name, his voice demanding and impatient.

She closed her eyes and cringed. He'd been drinking. Sometimes he was a mean drunk, and it often took a week for the bruises to fade. Other times he was like a child. A few months earlier, when he'd been drunk, he'd tied her to the bed, and by the time he'd finished with her, she'd been frantic, certain he intended to kill her.

"Pearl." He called for her again, sounding now like a little boy who'd had his toy taken away. A little boy in need of his mother. Pearl's shoulders sagged with relief. The little boy she could handle; the mean drunk frightened her.

"I'm here, baby," she replied softly, slipping into character.

She heard him make his way down the dark hallway and forced herself to smile when he stood in her doorway looking lost and forlorn in the soft haze of her bedside lamp.

"Do you want Mama to make it all better for you?" she murmured sympathetically.

He unhitched his belt buckle and nodded.

"I've been waiting all night for you." She said the well-practiced line as she untied the sash to her silk robe. "You know how very special you are to me. Come to Mama, and let me make it all better for you."

"That's why I'm here. Make it better, Pearl. Make it better."

She managed a smile—more of a grimace—as he crossed the room and fell on top of her, crushing her with his weight. He smelled of hard liquor and cigarettes. She barely had time to fit him with a condom before he was gasping and moaning, his head thrown back and his teeth clenched.

Pearl closed her eyes and turned her head away, praying he'd finish soon. With her eyes shut she could dream of the day she'd be free of him and all the other men like him.

Walt smiled slightly at the identical looks of shock on Molly's face and Sam's. If he hadn't been serious, he might have laughed outright. But the suggestion that they get married made sense to him. A lot of sense. To be fair it had only occurred to him recently, so he couldn't blame Molly or Sam for overlooking the obvious when the idea was almost as new to him as it was to them.

Sam stared at Walt in a way that implied there was more wrong with him than a bum heart. Molly's eyes were the most telling; they snapped like fire on wood too green to burn properly.

"Gramps."

"Walt."

"Let's sit on the porch a spell," Walt said. He'd always loved the peacefulness of a summer evening. He liked to imagine his Molly rocking at his side, and in a spiritual way he believed she'd never really left him. He felt her presence far more than her absence these days, and suspected that was because he'd be joining her soon. No doctor needed to tell him his days were numbered. Walt felt it himself, and difficult as it was to leave his granddaughter and her boys, he was ready to go.

Easing himself into the rocking chair, he waited for one or other of the pair to raise the first objection. He chuckled softly when he realized they were still too dumbfounded to speak.

"You think this is funny, old man?" Sam asked in a hard voice.

His foreman generally didn't use that tone with him, but Walt forgave him, considering that Sam had spent most of the past three days in the saddle, chasing cattle.

"Gramps, I don't think you understand what you're saying," Molly offered next in gentler tones.

"You think I'm senile, girl, is that what you mean? I realize this is something of a shock, but let's be realistic. I'm not going to be around much longer and—"

"Don't say that," Molly interrupted, more comfortable with her denials than facing her fears.

A sigh rumbled through Sam's chest. "You're talking nonsense, old man."

Walt's amusement didn't fade. He hadn't expected either of them to take to his idea right off. The first time it had popped into his mind he'd immediately assumed it wouldn't work, either; on closer examination, however, the wisdom of it became apparent. He sincerely hoped these two had enough common sense to recognize that. To see the advantages.

"You takin' that job offer?" Walt asked, pinning Sam with narrowed eyes.

"I already explained. I don't hand out charity and I

don't expect any, either." Sam's expression was as unyielding as his voice.

"Molly can't manage this place on her own," Walt continued. "What I'm asking you, Sam, is this: are you planning on walking out on her and the boys the minute I'm six feet under?"

Sam didn't respond, not that Walt blamed him.

"I don't need him," Molly said defiantly.

"That pride of yours is going to get you into nothing but trouble, girl," Walt said. "Without the right kind of help you'd lose the ranch inside a month. Are you ready to wipe out four generations of history because you're too damn proud to admit you need Sam?"

"I need someone to manage the place, I'll admit that, but a *husband* I can live without."

"I'm not looking for a wife, either," Sam snarled. He crossed his arms, leaned against the porch railing and stared down at the newly painted wood-plank floor.

"It wouldn't be a *real* marriage," Gramps said. He'd mulled this part over, and he figured that if they weren't interested in a normal marriage, a business arrangement might be the best solution. Although he suspected that this marriage of convenience wouldn't remain merely a convenience for long....

In the months since Sam had come to work for him, Walt had grown fond of him. His own son was long dead, and because he loved Molly, he worried about her future and that of his great-grandsons. In his view, she needed a man, and he could think of no better man for her than Sam Dakota.

"You're talking about a marriage of convenience?" Molly asked, folding her arms. "You mean to say people actually agree to that sort of thing in this day and age?"

"It makes sense," Gramps said mildly.

"Not to me, it doesn't," Sam muttered. "When and if I marry, it isn't going to be any business arrangement. My wife will share my life *and* my bed."

Molly's chin rose a defiant notch at the mention of his bed. "This entire thing is out of the question."

"If you'd both quit being so damn stubborn and hear me out, then maybe you'd learn something." Walt knew his strength was limited, and he didn't want to waste it arguing with two stubborn fools. He inhaled deeply and started again. "First of all, Sam, you should be able to appreciate Molly's concern. For all either one of us knows, you'll hire out somewhere else. You've already started looking."

"Exactly." Molly glared at Sam as if to say she doubted she'd ever be able to trust him; Sam frowned back at her. Walt shook his head, but he understood their need for defenses far better than they realized.

Sam's mouth thinned. "Walt, what makes you think marrying Molly would help?"

"Because you'd have a vested interest in keeping this ranch in the black."

"Are you suggesting I'm not giving one hundred percent right now?"

The fact that he was nearly dead on his feet said more about his commitment to the ranch than any statement he could have made. "It's because you *have* worked hard that I'm prepared to make you this offer," Gramps replied quietly.

"Offer?" Molly exclaimed. "Exactly what is it you're suggesting?"

Walt liked how she drove straight to the point. His own Molly had been like that, but her ways were more subtle. The hard edge around his granddaughter's heart was because of the divorce. She'd made one mistake in judgment and intended to punish herself for the rest of her life. Yes, the more he thought about it, this marriage would be good for her. Good for Sam, too.

Walt loved Molly, loved Tom and Clay. His blood flowed in their veins. They were all he had left in this world, other than the land his father had handed down to him. Persuading them to go along with this marriage might be the last thing he could do for her. The last way he had of protecting her future. And dammit, that was important.

"I was thinking…" Gramps's voice was almost a whisper, so depleted was his energy. It was a task to find the right words. "I'd feel better leaving your care in the hands of someone I trust."

"I already told you, Gramps—I don't need someone to take care of me! And I don't need a husband." She glanced at him sharply. "Gramps, you're tired!" When he shook his head, she sighed. "Look," she began, "let's say we were to agree to this preposterous idea. There's nothing to prevent Sam from walking out on me after we're married."

"Not if he's got something of value at stake."

"Like what?" Sam asked. He uncrossed his arms and rested his hands on the railing, leaning forward slightly.

"Five hundred acres and fifty head of cattle."

Molly gasped and her face turned a deep shade of red. "You're offering him land and cattle to marry me? A dowry? Now, I *know* they don't still do *that*."

"I'm offering Sam what he's always wanted," Gramps explained. No use wrapping it up in a silk bow. It was the truth, as plain and simple as he could make it. "A man will fight to the death for land and cattle."

"And dump a wife and family in a heartbeat!"

"You appear to hold a low opinion of men," Sam stated matter-of-factly, revealing none of the emotion Walt knew simmered below the surface. Molly was at a disadvantage; she hadn't known Sam nearly as long as he had. The adage "still waters run deep" had been coined for men like him.

Sam hadn't said much about his background, but Walt trusted him. Completely. He'd handed over the management of his ranch, and when it would have been easy to steal from him or cheat him, Sam hadn't. Not by so much as a penny. He worked hard, and Walt couldn't ask for more than that.

Only, he *was* asking. He wanted Sam to marry Molly. To be a father to Molly's sons. Walt yearned to know that when they carried him to his grave his family and his land would be in the hands of a man who'd take care of them.

"What you make of the marriage is up to you," Gramps said, glancing from one to the other. Weary now, he closed his eyes. He almost wished he could be around to see the battle. Molly would put up a good fight and so would Sam, but he'd wager a year's income that it wouldn't be long before they fell in love.

His biggest regret was that he wouldn't know their children or hold them close to his heart.

"Walt?" Sam's voice caused his eyes to flutter open.

"You *are* tired." Molly spoke softly. She sounded so much like his Molly that Walt was confused for a second.

"Let's help him inside," Sam was saying.

Molly must have agreed, because the next thing Walt knew the two of them had escorted him into his bedroom. It was the only one on the main floor; the other five were upstairs. "Get out of here," he said, using the small reservoir of strength that remained. "I can undress myself. You two go talk." He aimed his look in Molly's direction. He felt that of the two, she was the one who needed convincing most.

"Talk some sense into her, boy," Walt advised.

"I think you're both crazy!" Molly cried. "Get this straight right now, Sam Dakota. I'm not marrying you. I'd be a fool to agree to anything so...so..."

"Ridiculous," Sam supplied.

Molly's mouth sagged open and she nodded. "That's exactly the word I was searching for. It *is* ridiculous. That my own flesh and blood would suggest such a thing..."

"Perhaps we should let Walt rest now," Sam said as if fed up with the subject.

It would take an extraordinary man—a strong and honest man—to handle his granddaughter, Walt decided. He was convinced Sam was that man.

Now all he had to do was convince Molly.

If he hadn't heard it with his own ears, Sam would never have believed that Walt had actually suggested he and Molly get married.

Molly appeared none too pleased with the idea, either. "I want you to know up front that nothing you say is going to change my mind," she said the minute she walked out of her grandfather's bedroom.

"I didn't say I was interested in marrying you," Sam returned.

"You didn't have to." She marched into the kitchen, grabbed the kettle and stuck it under the faucet. "It's nothing personal, but I have no desire to marry again."

"Fine." He wasn't in any mood to argue with her, although in all honesty the sound of those five hundred acres and fifty head of cattle appealed to him. He'd be a liar if he claimed otherwise.

But if he'd wanted to get married, he'd have done so long before now. Still might. But like he'd told Walt, he wouldn't enter into any marriage of convenience; he and his wife would sleep in the same bed.

He had to admit it, though—for a moment insanity had taken hold and he'd been tempted. Damn tempted. Land and cattle were a hell of an incentive.

Feeling wearier than he'd ever been in his life, he headed out the door. It banged shut behind him, the sound echoing in the silence of the night. Tom met him halfway across the yard, followed by Boris, the father of Natasha's litter. The Stetson was a good fit, shading his youthful face. Tom hitched his thumbs in the waistband of his jeans the way Sam did and walked with a stride that suggested a swagger. A cowboy stride.

"What'd Gramps have to say?" the boy asked.

"He, uh, had an idea."

"For what?"

Sam grinned, wondering what Tom would say if he knew. Well, damned if *he* was going to be the one to tell him. "Ask your mother."

"I know she won't tell me, but I was thinking you might."

"Really?"

"Yeah." Tom walked up to the corral and braced his right foot on the bottom rail.

Sam stood beside him and experienced a sort of twinge. A strange feeling. One he had difficulty defining. The tiredness had seeped into his bones, and he was ready to call it a night. But he lingered, looking out over the property. He could see it clearly, despite the darkness and the wan moonlight. And he knew that without him, without someone like him, it would all come to nothing.

A coyote cried in the distance, and Sam's gaze returned to the boy at his side.

Sam had wasted a lot of years on the rodeo circuit, chasing an empty dream. Killing himself one bull ride at a time. In the end all he had to show for it was a bad back, a pretty belt buckle and a broken-down truck. It wasn't long before he'd added a prison sentence to his list of accomplishments.

Tom looked up at him and grinned. "It doesn't get any better than this, does it?"

Sam laughed. "You've been watching too much television, kid."

Tom's face fell, and Sam could see he'd offended him. He cut his laughter short and patted Tom's shoulder. "It's late. I'll see you in the morning."

"Okay." The boy's eagerness was undisguised, and Sam was relieved his thoughtless amusement hadn't damaged their relationship. As Tom loped off, Sam glanced over his shoulder and grinned at him.

"I would've been proud to call you son," he murmured.

The light on the porch behind him suddenly came on, and he turned to see Molly standing there, watching him. She was a fine-looking woman, too stubborn for her own good, but then he was far from perfect himself.

In time he suspected she'd remarry. Probably someone like that attorney. Well, no denying it, Russell Letson would make her a hell of a better husband than *he* ever would.

* * *

For the life of her Molly couldn't sleep. She'd tossed and turned so many times that the sheet had wrapped itself around her legs, binding her at the knees.

Groaning, she reached for the lamp on the nightstand and switched it on. Light flooded the room, and Molly squinted until her eyes adjusted, then glanced at the clock radio.

Three a.m.

She wouldn't do it. That was all there was to it. Marriage was never intended to be a business arrangement. It still irked her, the way Sam's eyes had lit up at the mention of land and cattle. Gramps hadn't a clue how badly he'd insulted her! He would never intentionally hurt her, of that Molly was certain. But his suggestion had opened her eyes to the truth.

Gramps was right to worry about her, she thought wryly. Sam was no solution; he'd stick around the Broken Arrow until he had a better offer. Because of his fondness for Gramps, she doubted he'd leave until after her grandfather was dead and buried.

She could hardly breathe when she realized where her thoughts had taken her. Gramps was dying. Much as she wanted to reject the evidence, it was unmistakable. In the few weeks she'd been in Montana, she'd witnessed his physical and mental decline. Each day he seemed a little weaker, a little frailer. Even his memory was going. Twice now he'd thought she was his Molly.

Gramps tried, but he couldn't hide how ill he was. As an adult, she needed to face the reality of the situation; she knew that, but it didn't make things easier. She owed it to Gramps to provide some reassurance, to show him she could look after herself and her boys. And the ranch. That was what all the marriage-of-convenience nonsense had been about.

Right after breakfast, she'd call the local newspaper and place an ad for a foreman. Naturally she'd talk it over with Gramps first, get his approval. Sam was already seeking greener pastures, so to speak. Not that she blamed him—at least, not entirely. But she had to accept that he'd eventually be leaving, which meant it was time she took control.

That decided, Molly leaned over and turned off the lamp. Gazing up, she watched the moonlight make patterns on the ceiling.

She wasn't sure what time she fell asleep; it must have been close to dawn, but even then her sleep had been fitful.

She awoke at six, hearing sounds in the kitchen. Bolting upright, she reached for her robe and raced down the stairs to discover Gramps sitting at the table. Tom and Clay were busy fixing him breakfast. Dry cereal littered the tabletop and there was a small puddle of milk beside an empty bowl.

Standing in her bare feet, Molly yawned.

"We think you should do it," Tom said eagerly, his eyes bright and happy.

Molly blinked, afraid to ask what he was talking about. Gramps *wouldn't* have. He couldn't have. If he'd mentioned anything about her marrying Sam to the boys, she didn't know *how* she'd respond.

"Do what?" she asked uneasily. Her gaze slowly traveled to Gramps, who looked far too pleased.

"Learn to ride," Clay answered. "Sam can teach you."

"I could teach you, too," Tom said confidently.

She hoped her relief wasn't evident. "I...I think that's a good idea," she said.

The back door opened and Sam walked in. His eyes

immediately went to her, and self-conscious, Molly gripped the lapels of her robe together. This was the second time he'd come upon her in her nightclothes. She didn't imagine herself as any beauty, not with her hair plastered to the side of her head and her eyes red from sleeplessness.

"Morning, Sam," Tom greeted him.

"Mornin'." He removed his hat and set it carefully on the counter. "I've got a list of supplies I need," he said, unfolding the sheet. "But I don't have time to run into town."

"I'll go," Molly offered before he had the opportunity to ask.

His smile told her he appreciated it. Nodding once, he handed her the list. Molly read it over and it might as well have been Greek for all the sense it made. Sam must have noticed her confusion because he took the time to explain each item to her, making small notes in the margins.

When he'd finished, Molly realized they were alone. She'd heard Gramps and the boys leave but she'd been busy concentrating on what Sam was telling her, and had paid it no mind. The supply list was important if she intended to learn how to manage a ranch.

"Did you sleep well?" Sam asked, the question catching her unprepared.

"Like a log," she lied, brushing the hair away from her face. She didn't want him to know how restless her night had been. Or how often she'd reviewed the conversation they'd had after taking Gramps to his room.

Sam hadn't appeared too eager to marry her, either. Although if he *had* revealed any enthusiasm, she'd have to credit it to the offer of cattle and land.

Judging by his smile, he knew she'd lied about sleeping well.

"I was awake most of the night," she admitted, lifting her hand to her forehead and running it through her uncombed curls. "What about you?"

"I certainly didn't have any trouble falling asleep," he said, "but I woke up early."

"I slept late."

"So I see," he said, eyeing her robe and bare feet.

Turning away, he helped himself to a cup of coffee, took his first sip and grimaced. "I take it you didn't brew this?"

She smiled and shook her head. He offered her some, but she declined. "I've tasted Tom's efforts before. He can't seem to understand it's only one scoop of grounds and not five." Molly wasn't sure when Sam moved closer, but suddenly he had. Scant inches separated them. His gaze burned into hers as he set the coffee aside.

Molly held her breath. She knew what he wanted and realized she wanted it, too. She was tempted to close her eyes and offer him her lips—but that would be wrong. They'd made their decision, both of them. Marriage was marriage and not to be mocked. Neither one of them was interested in a business arrangement; he'd assured her he wasn't, and she'd told him the same thing.

Sam didn't move. Nor did she. Molly began to wonder if they'd both stopped breathing.

"I...I did a lot of thinking last night," she whispered, lowering her gaze. He deserved her honesty if nothing else. "I can't see it working with you and me." She seemed to have difficulty shaping the words. "Following through with Gramps's idea, I mean."

His face moved a fraction of an inch closer to hers.

Hardly aware of what she was doing, Molly let her tongue moisten her lips. A quick movement—but that was all it took for Sam to accept her unspoken invitation. His warm moist mouth settled over hers.

The kiss was gentle, unhurried. Pleasurable. Even more than that first kiss, in the barn. Not satisfied to keep it simple, Sam stroked her lips with the tip of his tongue, sweetening the contact. She shivered and grabbed hold of his upper arms.

She wasn't sure which of them moaned. Then Sam wrapped his arms around her waist and pressed her body to his as he devoured her mouth with his own.

Her mind screamed that this had to stop, while her body responded to him totally, almost involuntarily. The kiss went on, slow and soft, until he trapped her bottom lip between his teeth and introduced his tongue, coaxing and enticing her own.

A sharp discordant sound shattered the moment. They broke apart like teenagers caught necking in the school hallway.

Molly reeled back, her chest heaving. The sound, whatever it was, was gone. It took her a moment to register that Gramps had turned on the radio in the living room.

Sam moved behind her and nuzzled the side of her neck. "You okay?"

She couldn't have spoken to save her life, so she nodded.

"Good."

Still he lingered, his warm breath fanning her neck. "I'm glad we got that settled," he murmured.

"Settled? What…"

"I've got to get back to Pete and Charlie." His reluctance to leave her was as apparent as her unwillingness to let him go.

"Sam!" she cried, stopping him before he walked out the door.

He turned back, his eyes darker and more intense than she could ever remember seeing them. "What...what did we settle?"

He placed the hat back on his head. His gaze held hers for a long moment. "You figure it out."

Eight

"**B**ingo!" Clay yelled. He leaped up and danced a triumphant jig about the living room. The puppy, who'd been asleep on the couch, barely raised his head at the commotion.

"Hurry and phone in before someone claims your three bucks," Gramps said, pointing to the telephone. Radio bingo was one of the few pleasures he could still enjoy. Molly had agreed to collect the bingo sheets every week from the sponsoring merchants in town, and Walt listened at eight and ten-thirty each weekday morning for the announcer to read off the numbers. The big jackpot was up to $385, but to win that, you had to bingo within the first five numbers. He'd come close several times. Close but no cigar.

"The line's busy," Clay said, beginning to pout.

"Then someone beat you to the punch, boy," he said. This was one of life's lessons, Walt believed, and Clay would be wise to learn it now while he was young. Act fast. Don't delay. Take a risk once in a while. Walt wished Molly had learned that lesson a little more thoroughly, that she was more of a risk-taker. Then this marriage business might be resolved. As things stood, his granddaughter stubbornly refused to marry Sam.

"But I had a bingo," Clay argued. "I should be able to get my prize."

"You need to be the first one to phone in with the correct numbers," Gramps said. "I told you that when we started. Someone else got bingo, too, and they beat you to the phone."

The three-dollar prize money wasn't much, but Clay would have had bragging rights. Walt had an inkling that was what concerned him most.

Molly strolled into the living room, holding Sam's shirt. Walt seemed to remember that she'd offered to mend it for him. "What's all the commotion?" she asked.

"I had a bingo, but I didn't call in fast enough." Clay's shoulders sagged, as if this were a tragedy of biblical proportions.

"I haven't had bingo in three weeks," Walt complained. If he didn't know better, he'd think the game was rigged. He placed the bingo sheets inside an old greeting-card box and set it down beside him on the end table. Normally he kept the sheets on his desk, but it was crowded with bills and invoices and bank statements, a lot of them in unopened envelopes. He felt a surge of guilt every time he thought about adding the paperwork to Sam's already heavy workload.

Working all hours of the day and night, Sam had no time for dealing with the piles of business-related documents and correspondence, so Molly had recently taken it on. She'd just begun to study the books, to get a grasp of the situation. Walt tried to answer her questions, but his mind wasn't always clear. He was afraid he might be doing more harm than good, confusing her rather than explaining things properly.

Their finances weren't in good shape, he knew. Cattle prices were down and had been for a number of years, dipping lower and lower each season. To say money was tight was an understatement. Walt had barely scraped by the past few years. Paying bills only depressed him, so it was a task he tended to avoid. Molly hadn't said anything yet, and he wondered if she was aware how poorly the ranch was doing.

"The Millers are having a moving sale Friday, Saturday and Sunday at 204 Walnut from eight to five all three days," the radio announcer said.

Molly looked astonished. "They're advertising a garage sale on the radio?"

Gramps reached over and turned the knob. "They do every weekday. It's part of the community programming."

"I remember the Millers," Molly said thoughtfully. "They ran one of the service stations."

"They've been around here nearly as long as the Wheatons," Walt told her, shaking his head sadly. "They sold out." It bothered him that Brady Miller had given in to outside pressures. Brady said it was because of financial problems, that the business wasn't making a profit, but Walt was convinced those damn fanatics had something to do with it. They wanted *his* land, too, but Walt had refused to sell.

"I never heard a radio station that plays hardly any music until we moved to Montana," Clay said. He cradled the puppy against his shoulder like a mother carrying her newborn babe.

Walt figured the dog had been one of his better ideas. Clay was learning about responsibility, about caring for another creature. And when Bullwinkle was about four months old, they'd start his training. The dog would earn his keep, the same way Boris and Natasha did.

"This is a small-town radio station," Gramps heard Molly explain.

"But all they do is talk," Clay said. "The bingo's fun, but the rest of it's all about how much alfalfa costs and stuff like that. What about rap? What about grunge?"

"They play that for a couple of hours at night," Walt explained. "Kid stuff." It wasn't real music, in his opinion. Tom had been listening to some hideous tape one night recently, and it sounded more like a barnful of sick calves crying for their mothers than anything associated with musical instruments. It'd bothered Walt so much that he'd wadded up tissue and stuck it in both ears. Molly had taken one look at him and burst out laughing, but hell, a man needed to protect his hearing.

Walt hadn't appreciated being the source of Molly's amusement. Dammit, a man could go deaf listening to what his great-grandsons considered music. He'd told them both exactly what he thought of it, too.

"You're going into town later?" he asked Molly, "'Cause I need razor blades."

"I'll make sure I pick some up while I'm there."

He nodded and raised his hand to his jaw. His Molly had asked one thing of him shortly after their marriage, and it was that he shave every night. It seemed a small thing, so he'd complied, willing to do whatever it took to make his sweetheart happy. A lifetime habit was hard to break. Even now, all these years after her death, he rarely went to bed without shaving.

"I've got a list going," she said. "Do you need anything else?"

Walt shook his head. He watched her as she returned to the kitchen and the sewing machine she'd set up on the table. He'd been worried about her and Sam. A week had come and gone since he'd made his suggestion, with no result. Walt studied the two of them every chance he got, hoping to read their thoughts, but it was impossible to decipher what either one of them was thinking.

Especially when they worked so hard at avoiding each other. Sam rarely joined the family for supper these days, although Molly always set out a plate for him. Generally, he reheated what she'd left and ate alone, often out on the porch, surrounded by dogs. Some nights he didn't get to the ranch house until well after dark. Walt didn't know if he purposely stayed away or if he was doing the work of two men. Probably both.

"You napping, Gramps?" Clay asked softly.

"Just resting my eyes, boy." Walt's afternoon naps came earlier and earlier these days. He'd only been awake a couple of hours and already he was so tired he couldn't keep his eyes open. The doc had wanted him to make another appointment, but Walt couldn't see where it would do any good. It cost money he couldn't spare. Not only that, the price of medicine these days was outrageous. Highway robbery. No government handouts for him, either. Walt Wheaton paid his own way or he went without. True, he'd let the government help him with the cost of his pacemaker, but that was as far as it went. That was all the charity he was willing to accept.

"Sam's taking us to the Fourth of July parade," Clay said, sitting down on the ottoman with the puppy. The kid would be the ruin of that dog yet, but Walt was secretly delighted that there was such a strong bond between those two. A boy needed a dog—and vice versa.

"Good." He liked the idea of Sam spending time with Molly and the kids. Walt himself couldn't handle standing in the hot sun to watch a bunch of youngsters walking down the street pulling little red wagons. He'd never been fond of parades, although he'd attended plenty in his time because his wife had enjoyed them. He'd have done anything for his Molly. *A man does that when he's in love.*

"Sam...said he wanted to come along?" This news appeared to surprise Molly.

Walt peeked at his granddaughter who'd come to stand in the doorway. He saw that this information had flustered her considerably. Good. Maybe, just maybe, the idea of marriage wasn't a lost cause, after all. Holding back a grin was damn near impossible as Walt leaned his head against the recliner and dreamed of Molly's future with Sam.

In all her life Molly had never washed clothes this dirty. Mud crusted the knees of her boys' jeans, dirt they'd accumulated following Sam around the ranch. Tom spent the majority of his time with him. That wasn't all; her son was beginning to sound like him and to walk like him, and even to imitate his gestures.

If that wasn't bad enough, Tom constantly talked about him, too. It was *Sam this* and *Sam that* until Molly felt like covering her ears and demanding he stop.

She stuffed three pairs of jeans into the washer. As the water churned, a thick layer of mud and scum formed on the surface. She'd have to run this load through the wash cycle twice, which meant keeping a close eye on the timer.

Sam. The harder she tried to push him from her mind, the more difficult it became. Twice he'd kissed her and twice he'd left her…confused.

I'm glad we got that settled.

He'd said that to her after the most recent kiss, almost a week ago, and when she'd asked what he meant, he'd told her to figure it out herself. Molly was still so angry she could barely look at the man.

Her only conclusion—and it didn't settle anything—was that she was a woman with normal needs and desires. It'd been years since a man had kissed her the way Sam had. Years since her dormant senses had been stirred awake. Well, she didn't like the feeling. Didn't enjoy being vulnerable. His kisses embarrassed her, and consequently she'd avoided him all week.

And he'd avoided her, too. Why, she could only speculate. Perhaps he regretted the kissing incident as much as she did. Somehow, though, she knew that wasn't the real reason he'd kept his distance.

He was giving her space. Enough space to flounder in. She wanted to hate him, but she couldn't. Not when he was so good to Gramps and her boys.

That was what made everything so damned difficult. Gramps didn't need to tell her how pleased Tom and Clay would be if she married Sam and how devastated they'd be when he left. Especially Tom, who worshiped the ground Sam Dakota walked on.

That hurt a little. No, actually it hurt quite a bit. Not for a second did Molly begrudge her son a mentor, but she missed the closeness she and Tom used to have—until a year ago, when he'd become so moody and difficult.

She should be thrilled that Tom's attitude had completely changed. And she was. What she found hard to take was the fact that the positive influence on her son had been Sam's. Not hers. Only Sam's. She supposed it was natural enough, but...

The tears that brimmed in her eyes came as a surprise. She blinked several times, trying to keep them at bay.

Sam would marry her, she thought grimly. All she had to do was say the word. He'd be a fool not to, seeing that Gramps had offered him what amounted to a dowry. The memory of that conversation—five hundred acres and fifty head of cattle—was enough to make her want to stomp her foot with outrage. Gramps had actually tried to bribe his foreman to marry her! It was absolutely mortifying.

More than once in the past week she'd felt Sam watching her. His eyes were like a warm caress and left her all too aware of what he wanted. What she wanted, too. What distressed Molly the most was her own response. Idiot that she was, she'd have welcomed his touch—and he knew it.

When she'd restarted the wash cycle, she picked up the shirt she'd mended for him. Folding it she left the laundry room to return it to Sam's place.

Still angry with herself, she crossed the yard to the small house where he lived. She knew so little about him; he revealed so little of himself. Russell Letson had suggested Sam wasn't trustworthy and implied that he had information he couldn't or wouldn't share. Gramps had been furious that she'd listened to such gossip and had defended Sam as if he were his own flesh and blood.

While her instincts told her Sam *was* trustworthy,

Molly reminded herself she'd once had complete faith in Daniel, too. By the time she'd discovered the truth, it was too late. To be fair, she'd been younger then, less experienced, more naive. Nevertheless, she didn't want to repeat her mistake.

Molly had been in Sam's living quarters, mostly to drop off laundry, a number of times. His bedroom was small and cramped. But although the accommodations were modest, he kept them in decent order.

She placed the mended shirt on his bed and turned to leave then paused in the doorway and looked around, seeing the room with fresh eyes. Sam had slept in this room for more than seven months. Not a single picture was displayed. No family photographs. Nothing to indicate there was anyone important in his life.

The letter that had arrived a week or so earlier—the letter from the other ranch—was the only piece of personal mail he'd received in all the time she'd been here. Suddenly she saw the ticket, tucked in the corner of his mirror. She shouldn't have read it, should simply have walked away, but she couldn't seem to stop herself from crossing the room and looking.

The ticket was from the Sweetgrass Pawnshop. Sam's name was printed on it, along with the article he'd pawned. A silver buckle. Sam had pawned a silver buckle and going by the amount of cash given him, this wasn't any ordinary buckle. A rodeo buckle? She couldn't imagine why he'd pawn it, since it must have held real significance for him.

She knew from Gramps that Sam had been a rodeo cowboy, a successful one, and that he'd had an accident of some kind. She found herself wondering what had happened and how he'd felt, seeing his career come to an end like that. And pawning the buckle... He'd obviously needed the money.

Stepping away from the mirror, she decided to put the matter out of her mind. This was Sam's business, not hers, but it made her suspicious. Once again she recognized that he was a man who had nothing to lose and everything to gain should she agree to marry him.

With her hand on the doorknob, she glanced around one last time. Her thoughts skittered crazily about—from rodeos and prize money to the ranch and its bills. Every evening this past week had been spent going over the financial records. Gramps's bookkeeping left much to be desired. The books were a mess; despite that, she could tell almost immediately that the Broken Arrow's finances were in dismal shape. She'd been paying for groceries and supplies from her own limited savings, but with no money coming in, those dollars would quickly disappear. Then what? Molly didn't want to think about the answer.

Of one thing she was sure: when the money ran out, so would Sam. He'd as much as said it himself. Unless he had a reason to stay, a reason like five hundred acres and fifty head of cattle, Sam would be moving on. The reality of their situation terrified her. There had been no response to her ad for a new foreman, and the hands would be gone by the end of the summer.

Completely lost in thought, Molly closed his door, turned around—and walked smack into Sam.

"What are you doing sneaking up on me like that?" she demanded, furious that she'd been caught gazing into his bedroom.

"I came to tell you there's been a small accident—Tom cut his hand on a piece of wire. I couldn't find you at the house, so..."

Molly sucked in her breath. It must be serious if Sam had brought her son in from the range. "Does he need stitches?" she asked, her heart pounding in her ears. "Should I drive him into town?"

"He's fine," Sam assured her, gripping one of her shoulders. His touch calmed her immediately. Calmed and somehow reassured her. "The cut's nasty, but he's going to be fine."

"Stitches?" she repeated.

"No."

"What about a bandage?"

"I already did that."

"Oh." She'd always looked after things like this. Cuts and bruises. Hugs and healing. She was Tom's mother, after all, and Sam was the mentor. Couldn't he at least keep their roles straight? She knew she was being petulant, but she couldn't help it. "I would've preferred to do it myself," she said in a tight voice.

"I'm sure you'll want to clean it and rewrap it," he said. His hands, free of gloves, stroked her upper arms. A warm sensation settled in the pit of her stomach and refused to go away.

He understood what she felt. His eyes told her so. Told her that, and more. Without words he said he'd been watching her the same way she'd been watching him.

He wanted her. His longing was unconcealed. He tensed, and she knew he was fighting back the sharp pungent taste of desire. Then abruptly he removed his hands.

"Where's...where's my son?" she asked.

"In the house."

"I'd...I'd better find him."

Sam nodded and stepped aside.

Molly raced toward the house, grateful to be away from Sam's influence. It was growing stronger every minute of every day. She began to feel panicky. Soon it would be impossible to escape him. Soon she'd be just like her boys, completely in his power. Unless she took measures to keep it from happening, she'd risk trusting another man. Risk saying yes to Sam Dakota.

The cut was on the fleshy part of Tom's palm. Although it looked mean, it wasn't terribly deep. Her son was more angry than hurt.

"Sam hasn't left yet, has he?" he asked, squirming as she reapplied the bandage.

"I wouldn't know," she said, gritting her teeth at his eagerness to get back to the foreman.

"He didn't need to bring me here. I would've been all right."

"Maybe he was worried about blood on the saddle," she said frivolously.

"Sam sees blood all the time," Tom argued, frowning at her for suggesting anything so silly. "He didn't want you to be mad at him."

"Me?"

"Yeah," her son explained patiently. "You're a mother. He said mothers worry and that you'd be furious with him if he let me work all day without taking care of this stupid cut first."

"Well, he was right about that. You could've ended up with an infection if you'd waited until you were done for the day."

"Mo-om," he groaned, rolling his eyes. "Hurry up, please. Sam's waiting for me!"

She finished with the bandage and Tom roared to his feet like a roped calf suddenly set free. He was out the door before she could stop him.

Molly followed, but by the time she got outside, Tom and Sam were both back in the saddle and headed south. Standing on the top step, she watched them ride off, like John Wayne and his sidekick in some dumb Western.

When she returned to the kitchen, Molly found Gramps sitting at the table. "Sheriff Maynard phoned while you were out," he announced.

Molly flicked a stray hair from her face, hoping Gramps could read none of her frustration. "What'd he say?" She'd called the sheriff shortly after the fence had been purposely cut, and the man had taken his own sweet time responding.

"Not much. Just that there's been a series of such things happening the past few months." A scowl darkened Gramps's face, telling Molly he hadn't revealed all of the conversation.

"What is it?" she asked.

Looking disgruntled, Gramps shook his head.

"I'll need to hear it sooner or later." She pulled out a chair and sat across the table from him.

"Damn fool sheriff suggested we ask Sam about it."

"Sam? That's ridiculous." She might have had her suspicions about him earlier, but no longer. Sam had spent almost seventy-two hours rounding up the lost cattle. No one in his right mind would create that kind of work for himself.

"That's what I said." Gramps's gaze held hers; the approval in his eyes made it clear that he was pleased by her quick defense of Sam.

"What reason did the sheriff give for suggesting it?"

"All he'd say was that Sam's a stranger." Gramps's voice was gruff. "Far as I'm concerned, he's more than proved himself. I don't consider him a stranger. And I trust him enough to hope he'll marry my only grand-child."

Molly froze; she didn't want to discuss this with Gramps.

"Are you going to do it, girl?" he asked.

Inhaling deeply, she mulled over her answer, knowing Gramps would argue with her. "Probably not."

Gramps went quiet, then muttered, "That's a shame."

"It's my life, Gramps. I make my own decisions."

"And your own mistakes."

"Those, too." She couldn't argue with him there.

"Molly girl," he said softly, his disappointment obvious, "you need a man. For lots of reasons. Especially living on this ranch. If not Sam, who?"

"Gramps, you're way behind the times." It was difficult for Molly not to laugh. Or cry. Her heart ached just thinking about what would happen to Tom and Clay when Sam walked out on them.

As if reading her mind, Gramps added, "All right, you insist you don't want a husband. But what about the boys? Look at the change in them since you got here. You might not want to marry Sam, and that's your choice, but both Tom and Clay have made him a substitute father."

Molly swallowed tightly, unable to deny it. She'd been thinking about this very thing.

"They're desperate for—whaddaya call it?—a role model," Gramps went on. "It would have been an easy thing to ignore them, but Sam didn't do that. I'll tell you what, Molly girl, he's been more father to them than Daniel ever was or ever will be."

"I'm leaving for town now," she said, reaching for

the list Sam had given her that morning. Talking to Gramps was impossible, she decided. Just impossible.

It was well past the supper hour—and just before the storm broke—when Sam and Tom arrived back at the ranch. Pete and Charlie had already returned and left for the day. Thick gray clouds had followed them in from the range, and the scent of rain was heavy in the air. The day had been busy but productive. They'd moved the herd from one pasture to another, the second such move that summer. Each time, they brought the herd closer to the house and the road, so when it came time to sell the cattle, they'd be nearby and easier to transport. Rotating pastures was good for the land, as well.

Boris had put in a hard day's work. When Sam dismounted, he stopped to pet the dog. For every mile he went, Boris had gone two. Later on, Bullwinkle would be good with the cattle, too, especially with his father to learn from.

Thunder crashed close enough to shake the barn roof. "We beat the storm," Tom said proudly as he opened the door and led Sinbad toward his stall.

The boy didn't understand that storms came and went; they struck when they damn well pleased and left without rhyme or reason, often just as quickly.

Rain beat against the barn roof, echoing through the building. Tom looked up. "Wow, that's some storm." He slipped the saddle from Sinbad's back and carried it to the tack room. "I wonder what Mom's cooking for supper. I'm hungry."

"Me, too."

"I bet she made chili. It's one of my favorite dinners, with corn bread hot from the oven so the butter melts as soon as you put it on. Yum.''

The kid was making Sam hungry just talking about it. Sam had been staying away from the house at suppertime, preferring to give Molly a chance to think, consider her options. He didn't want to influence her one way or the other. In a matter as serious as marriage, he wanted her to be sure. He'd marry her, if she agreed, but not for love—and he'd be honest about that. He intended to be a good husband, though, and a father to her boys. What interested him was the promise of that land and the herd. It represented a second chance, and second chances didn't come along every day.

"You go on in and wash up," Sam told the boy. "I'll finish out here."

Tom hesitated. "You mean it?"

"I always mean what I say." Sam didn't want Tom ever to question that. A hundred times in the past week he'd stopped himself from talking to Molly. He wanted to assure her that given the chance, he'd prove himself to her and the boys. Even though it wouldn't be a love match, he *liked* her, dammit. And he was attracted to her. Another thing—if they got married, they'd be man and wife, and none of this sleeping-apart business. The couple of times they'd kissed should tell her they were compatible sexually. A lot of marriages started out with less.

Tom set his hat lower on his head as he opened the barn door and raced across the yard. Sam saw a jagged flash of lightning cut across the sky. As his stepfather used to say, the night wasn't fit for man or beast. That memory brought with it an unexpected ache, a desire to reconnect with his own family. Someday, he would, he promised himself. Later. When he was ready.

Taking the brush, he rubbed down his gelding, hands working at a steady pace while he thought about marriage. Marriage to Molly. He knew next to nothing about her ex-husband. The boys hardly ever mentioned their father. From what he'd gathered, Daniel Cogan hadn't spent much time with his sons. His loss, Sam decided. Walt hadn't said much about Molly's ex-husband, either, only that he was a damn fool, and without even having met the man, Sam agreed. Anyone who'd walk away from a woman like Molly and those boys didn't have a lick of sense. As for Molly herself, it was plain the breakup of her marriage had soured her.

Sam let his mind drift back to his own family. He'd learned—from a hometown newspaper—that his stepfather had died a couple of years earlier. Sam's heart ached each time he realized he'd never had the chance to thank Michael Dakota for being a father to him. His mother had been a teenager when she'd gotten pregnant with Sam. Three years had passed before she married Michael, who'd adopted Sam as his own son, loved him and raised him. When he'd reached his teens, Sam had rebelled and brought nothing but trouble and grief to the family. Michael had reacted with patience, but it was Sam who'd rejected him. Sam had allowed his stubborn immature pride to hurt his family.

At the time all he'd wanted, needed, was the opportunity to compete in the rodeo. He found it painful to admit now, but those years had been a waste. A selfish indulgence that had cost him more than he wanted to think about.

The barn door flew open and, assuming it was the wind, Sam hurried over to close it.

"Mom isn't back!" Rain pouring off the brim of his

hat, his eyes filled with panic, Tom burst into the barn. "She left for town a little after twelve and she isn't back. Gramps expected her home around three."

Sam checked his watch. Seven-fifteen.

"I thought she might've decided to wait out the storm, but she would've phoned. I know she would." The boy was trying to stay calm, but it was an obvious struggle.

"Which vehicle did she take?"

"Gramps's truck."

Sam handed Tom his brush and headed outside. Walt's vehicle was on its last legs. She shouldn't be driving it at all! Then he realized that she was probably picking up the shingles and drainage pipe he'd ordered—which would never have fit in her car.

"Where are you going?" Tom asked, racing after him.

"Where else, boy? After your mother."

"But she could be anywhere."

"True." But it made no difference. "You won't see me again until I've found her, understand?" No one would rest easy until Molly was back, safe and sound. He'd find her, and he wouldn't return until he had.

Five minutes later Sam was on the road that led to town. The windshield wipers slapped the rain from side to side, and visibility was practically zero. The rain streamed down in torrents that quickly filled the gullies and washed across the roadway. Driving was hazardous and it took Sam's full concentration to keep his truck on the road.

Wherever Molly was, Sam prayed she'd be smart enough to seek shelter. If the truck had broken down, the worst thing she could do would be to leave it. Anyone from the country would know that, but Molly was a city girl.

As he carefully steered down the highway, going no faster than ten miles an hour, he shuddered, trying not to think beyond the moment. If anything had happened to Molly, it'd kill the old man. She was the only thing that kept him alive. She and her boys. And what about Tom and Clay? What if they lost their mother?

What if *he* lost Molly? Without ever really knowing her. Without ever having the chance to see if they could build a life together.

Sam saw a vehicle in the distance parked by the side of the road. He squinted through the furious beating of the windshield wipers and tried to make out the type and color.

It didn't take him long to recognize the vehicle as Walt's run-down truck. The Chevy was in about the same shape as the old man's heart.

He pulled over and left the headlights on, facing the other vehicle. Through the pounding rain it was impossible to tell if she was inside the cab or not.

He opened his door and leaped out. Hunching his shoulders against the storm, he ran, slipping and sliding, to the other truck. With both hands, he shielded his face and peered through the passenger window.

She wasn't there.

He cursed and turned around, looking frantically up and down the road. His biggest fear was that she'd decided to walk to the ranch, fallen into a gully and drowned.

"Molly!" he shouted.

Nothing.

He'd told Tom he wouldn't return without her, and he'd meant it. He tried to think where she'd go, what she might have been thinking. Logic would've told anyone with half a brain to stay in the truck, dammit.

Lightning briefly lit up the sky, and in that second he saw a flash of color huddled against the trunk of a massive oak tree. It stood across a field planted with alfalfa.

"Molly?" He couldn't understand why she'd be sitting next to a tree with the rain pouring down on her when she could be warm and dry inside the truck.

It wasn't until he drew closer that he realized Molly wasn't sitting.

She was lying facedown in the mud.

Nine

"Molly! Molly!"

Her name seemed to echo, ringing in her ears. It was giving her a headache. No, she already had a headache. She struggled to sit up but couldn't. When she tried to raise her arm and investigate what was wrong, she found herself unable to move.

The sound of her name was clearer now. Sam? What was he doing here? For that matter, where the hell *was* she? Molly moved her hand and black mud oozed between her fingers. Slowly, painfully, she used what strength she possessed to raise her head.

"Molly." The relief in Sam's voice was unmistakable.

She felt herself being lifted and turned, and all she could see was Sam Dakota against a backdrop of dark sky. Rain hit her face and she blinked. There was a blinding streak of lightning, and she squinted at the brightness and the instant pain it produced.

"Are you all right?" Sam demanded fiercely. He sounded worried—and angry. He was rubbing a cloth across her face, smearing the mud.

Molly shook her head in order to avoid this punishment, but it did little good and only served to make the pain worse. "Don't, please…don't…don't." But he ignored her pleas.

"What happened?" He brushed the hair from her brow, and when he drew his hand away she thought she saw blood. She hoped it wasn't hers.

"Is that blood?" she asked. "And is it mine or yours?" Her mouth felt so dry she had trouble speaking.

Apparently he didn't hear her or more likely didn't want to answer. His attention seemed to focus on her forehead. "What are you looking for now?" she asked irritably, her voice gaining strength. "The mark of the beast?"

The merest hint of a smile flashed in his eyes, but his mouth remained drawn. "You must have fallen and hit your head."

His words prompted Molly's memory. On her way back from town, the truck had suddenly died. Although she'd never been mechanically inclined, she could certainly read a gauge. Gas wasn't the problem, and the battery had been fine earlier. Nonetheless, the truck had sputtered and stalled, and after a few gasping coughs stopped altogether. Not knowing what else to do, she'd waited for help.

After several hours, with no other vehicles on that road, the storm had come. The rain had pounded the truck, vicious and unrelenting. Any hope she'd had of rescue disappeared. She realized she'd have to wait out the storm. But after thirty minutes, when it showed no sign of lessening, she'd ventured from the safety of the cab to be sure she wasn't in danger of floating away.

"While I was out there, I saw a light," she told him. "So I was sure there must be a farmhouse close by." She avoided meeting his eyes, knowing he thought her every kind of fool, and she didn't blame him. It had been stupid to leave the truck in a storm, but the light hadn't seemed far away, and she'd assumed she could walk there.

"Didn't you stop and think about...?" Sam didn't bother to finish his question.

"Crossing the field didn't look all that daunting, and I figured I'd rather deal with a little mud than leave Gramps and the boys worrying. It seemed like the right thing to do at the time."

"What happened then?"

"I'd only gone a short ways and the mud was up to my ankles. I...tripped and the next thing I remember was you bending over me."

"Hasn't anyone ever told you that..." With what appeared to be considerable effort, he bit off whatever else he intended to say. Molly was grateful; she wasn't up to hearing a lecture right now.

"Don't scold me—I know what I did was stupid." She was drenched to the bone, her temple throbbed something fierce, and she was covered head to toe in black ooze. Worse, she'd made a world-class fool of herself—and naturally Sam had been the one to find her.

At least the rain had slowed to a drizzle.

Sliding his arm around her waist, he helped her stand. Rainwater ran from her hair down her neck and back. Once she was upright, the alfalfa field began to spin and she had to lean against Sam. He tightened his arm while she struggled to regain her equilibrium.

After a moment, in which the world still reeled, Sam cursed under his breath and hoisted her into his arms.

"Put me down," she insisted, closing her eyes at the sudden jarring pain. "I can walk—just give me a couple of minutes and I'll be as good as new."

"The hell with it! You can't even stand." He started

toward the truck, taking slow careful steps. He was having as much difficulty as she'd had earlier, with the mud pulling his boots deeper and deeper. Each time he lifted his foot the ground made a sucking sound of protest.

"How much do you weigh, anyhow?" he growled when they'd covered about half the distance.

"I'll have you know I've lost five pounds since June."

"Right now, I wish it'd been ten."

Feeling as wretched as she did, she could do without the insults. "Put me down this instant." Molly figured he'd welcome the opportunity to dump her right then and there; she steeled herself to being dropped butt-first in the muck. But he ignored her and continued the long arduous trek back to the road.

Every couple of steps he'd mutter something she was glad she couldn't understand. Her head hurt, throbbing in unison with her pulse. After the first few minutes she closed her eyes and pressed her temple against his shoulder. She was cold and miserable, yet she felt secure in Sam's arms, secure enough to be thankful he'd found her—despite his anger. And her embarrassment. Soon they'd be home....

"Molly, wake up."

Her eyes flew open. "What?"

"Don't go to sleep. You've probably got a concussion."

"Okay." But despite her efforts, her eyelids drooped.

"Dammit, Molly," he said, "this is difficult enough."

It was so hard to keep her eyes open. So very hard. "I...I'm sorry. I never meant for this to happen."

Sam's labored breathing slowed once he reached the road. He carried her to his truck, opened the passenger door and helped her inside, settling her on the seat with surprising gentleness. She glanced at her reflection in the side mirror and gasped. Her wet hair was plastered to her head, and the stringy tendrils trickled water against her shoulders. A large bump protruded from her forehead, along with a nasty-looking gash at her hair-line. It didn't seem too deep or in need of stitches. Mud was smeared across her cheeks. Her clothes dripped with thick black muck.

"I've seen cattle with more sense than you," Sam said between clenched teeth as he climbed into the driver's seat.

Molly turned and stared out the side window, shaking with cold and feeling more wretched by the moment. The brief illusion of security she'd felt in Sam's arms was gone. Perhaps the best thing would be to contact Russell Letson and tell him she'd had a change of heart and she'd sell the ranch, after all. No. She couldn't do that to Gramps. It was just her misery talking.

Silently she waited, expecting Sam to turn on the ignition. Nothing happened for so long that curiosity got the better of her. She looked over to find him sitting with his arms outstretched, hands clutching the steering wheel. He seemed to be staring at something directly in front of them.

He must have sensed her scrutiny because he gave a deep sigh. "I apologize, Molly. I shouldn't have said that."

"I…I don't blame you. I deserved it—and your other insults, too. It was stupid to leave the truck." Even wearier now than before, she laid her head against the window and managed a weak smile. "Can we go home now? All I want is a hot bath and about a hundred tablets of extra-strength aspirin."

"Home." He repeated the word as though it was some kind of magical incantation, and in that instant she realized that the Broken Arrow Ranch *was* home. Hers—and his? Somehow she'd find a way to keep this property. He'd be welcome to stay. But with or without Sam Dakota, she was going to do her damnedest to hold on to her heritage.

Tom had pretended he had no real interest in participating in the Fourth of July celebrations. But in truth he was excited about it. He just didn't want anyone to know. Back in San Francisco his friends bought illegal fire crackers and set them off to annoy people. Stupid. This was going to be different. He couldn't remember the last time his family had gone on a real picnic or watched a parade.

To admit he was looking forward to the holiday might give his mother the wrong impression, though. He wasn't a kid anymore, but a man. Or almost one. He worked alongside Sam, who'd assured him he was a real help. Tom felt good about that. He'd never expected to like Montana, but found he enjoyed life on the ranch and the challenge of each new day.

And his little brother—well, Clay was as excited about this picnic as that silly puppy of his. He ran back and forth from the house, loading up the car with stuff from the kitchen. His mother sure knew how to pack a picnic basket. There was enough food to last them a week—which suited Tom just fine. He kind of wondered if she'd gone to so much effort to impress Sam.

The foreman was driving into town with them. Ever

since they'd come here, Tom hadn't seen Sam take a single day off. Not a whole day, anyway. Man, if anyone deserved a holiday, it was Sam! Better yet, Sam would be with his mother. Not that this was a real date or anything, but close enough to maybe get them talking. Tom wished they *would* talk.

Ever since Sam had gone looking for his mother in the storm, things had been better between them. Before that, he'd noticed how stiff and polite they were, as if they were afraid to say what they really meant. Like everything was on the surface, not from their hearts. Tom had his own suspicions—his own hopes—about what their hearts might want to say.

The goose egg on his mother's forehead wasn't as big anymore, and with that powder stuff she put on her face, the bruise was barely noticeable. She'd been in bad shape when Sam brought her home. Although he was cold and wet himself, he'd insisted she take a hot shower right away, and while she was doing that, he'd reassured Gramps there was nothing to worry about. He'd phoned Doc Shaver, telling Gramps it was just a precaution. Then he'd called a garage in town to arrange a tow for the truck. Sam's clothes had dried before he ever got a chance to shower.

The afternoon his mother had gone missing hadn't been an easy one for Tom. He hadn't wanted to say anything to Clay, but he'd been worried. Real worried. His stomach had cramped, and every time he thought about what might have happened, he felt like he had to go to the bathroom. What had helped most was remembering Sam's words about not coming back without her.

Every few minutes he'd looked out the window,

hoping to see headlights, but it'd been hours before Sam finally pulled into the yard.

Gramps was relieved, too. He'd been just as concerned, but kept it hidden, the way Tom had. They'd exchanged worried glances, but neither of them had said anything.

"You ready, cowboy?" His mother stood at the foot of the stairs and called up to him.

"I guess." Although his voice didn't reveal any enthusiasm, he raced downstairs and nearly collided with Clay.

"I'm taking my pillow," his brother said as he slipped past Tom and bounded up the stairs.

"I didn't know you still took naps," Tom said. He enjoyed riling his little brother.

"I don't," protested Clay as he ran downstairs clutching his pillow. "But when the fireworks start, I want to lie back and watch them."

"Sweetgrass isn't going to have any fireworks," Tom muttered, amazed at how disappointed he felt. A town only big enough for a weekly newspaper wasn't going to come up with the money to afford real fireworks.

Either Clay didn't hear him or wasn't in the mood to argue, because his little brother let the comment slide.

"What car we taking?" Tom asked, slouching in the kitchen chair as if this was all too much effort.

"Ours," his mother answered, tucking a jar of pickles into a cardboard box.

"Your mother trusts me enough to drive," Sam said, and held up the car keys. "Before long you'll be doing the honors."

"He's only fourteen," Molly said, adding a can of insect repellant to the box.

"He'll be at the wheel before you know it," Sam told her. He caught Tom's eye and winked.

Tom hid a smile. What his mother didn't know wouldn't hurt her. Sam had been giving him lessons for a couple of weeks now. His legs were just long enough to reach the clutch and the gas pedal. At first he was sure he'd never be able to do it, but Sam had assured him everyone had trouble in the beginning. Before long he'd gotten the hang of it and was confident enough to drive Sam's truck for short distances.

Molly ran her fingers through her hair. "Gramps," she said, "are you sure we can't talk you into coming with us?"

Gramps shook his head and grumbled something about a parade being a waste of taxpayers' money. He left it at that.

"Guess that means he's not interested," Sam said, picking up the cardboard box. "It's your loss, old man."

Gramps stood in the doorway, as they piled into the car. Tom climbed into the back seat with his brother, although he almost always sat next to his mother up front. He didn't mind—but only because it was Sam who sat beside her. With anyone else, he might not have been so generous. On the way into town his mother sang. Little kids' songs, for crying out loud— they were the only ones she knew all the words to.

She only did that when she was happy.

They arrived in Sweetgrass early enough to get prime seats for viewing the parade. They found a vacant bench at the edge of the park, and the four of them sat facing the street, eating flavored snow cones while they waited.

Sam teased Tom and Clay, telling silly jokes that made them both laugh. Tom noticed when Sam stretched his arm across the back of the bench and placed it around his mother's shoulders. He encouraged the foreman with a wink, but if Sam saw it, he didn't respond.

Just as the parade was about to begin, something happened. Tom didn't understand exactly what it meant—only that it changed the course of their day. Sam had been laughing when all at once he went quiet.

Tom looked up to find Sheriff Maynard standing directly in front of Sam, blocking his view of the street. The sheriff was a big man with a belly that hung over his belt. But he wasn't soft, Tom could see that. He stood with his feet apart and glared down at the four of them. The way he scowled at Sam made Tom angry. And it really bugged him that the sheriff was checking out his mother like...like she was some bimbo in a bikini.

"Dakota," the sheriff drawled.

"Sheriff."

"Come to enjoy the festivities?"

Although the words were friendly enough, Tom had the impression the sheriff would have welcomed a reason to ask Sam to leave or, better yet, arrest him. Tom glanced from one man to the other.

"I understand there's been some trouble at the Broken Arrow," the sheriff remarked next. Just the way he said it irked Tom. He knew Sam was angry, too, because he saw a small muscle jumping in his jaw.

"Nothing I can't handle," Sam returned after a moment, and there seemed to be a hidden meaning in his words. His eyes had narrowed and there was a hardness in his face.

Tom studied the lawman and decided Sheriff Maynard looked like he ate too many doughnuts. His hands were huge, too. Tom wondered what Sam had done to get on the bad side of the authorities. It didn't take much; he'd learned that himself back in San Francisco.

The sheriff left as soon as the parade started, but he might as well have stayed, because all the fun had vanished. Both his mother and Sam were subdued. They tried, everyone did, but to little avail.

Later, when they ate at a picnic table in the park, Tom wondered why everything had changed. He watched his mother and Sam. In the past the idea of his mother remarrying had bothered him. It wasn't that he didn't want her to be happy, but things were good with just the three of them. She didn't need anyone else. Every now and then she'd dated when they lived in California, but there'd never been anyone Tom would want for a stepfather.

He wouldn't mind if Sam married his mother. That might be cool. And he wouldn't have to worry about Sam moving away, either.

Russell had given up counting the number of excuses he'd invented to get out of attending the town's Fourth of July celebration.

Carrying a tall glass of iced tea onto the cabin's deck, he gazed out at the valley below. He'd bought the place a couple of years earlier as an investment. He wasn't really the outdoor type. He'd always figured he'd leave the adventures of back-to-the-wilderness living to those who appreciated that sort of thing.

He'd never guessed the cabin would become his love

nest. *Love nest*. Silly term. Kind of old-fashioned. It made him smile. Sitting down, he arranged the chess pieces on the board and waited for Pearl to join him. She wasn't long.

"I'm after revenge," he announced, grinning up at her. Pearl claimed she hadn't known how to play chess until he'd taught her. After the first few games he found that hard to believe. Her skill was amazing. It wasn't only chess that she was good at, either. She had an incisive logical mind and grasped ideas quickly. Because of her reading difficulties, she'd assumed she was stupid when in reality the opposite was true. He marveled at her almost photographic memory. That, together with her wit, made an intriguing combination. She fascinated and challenged him. The Sundays he spent with her had become the highlight of his week.

He'd asked her about IQ tests in high school, and she had told him she'd dropped out before ever taking any. Then, when she confessed she couldn't read, he'd decided to teach her. She picked it up with astonishing ease. He loved her reaction, the excitement and giddiness she didn't try to hide. She was never without a book these days, and he was impressed by her insights into character and theme.

Ironic. Pearl had been his birthday present. An evening with a prostitute. He'd felt sordid, at first, going to her—as sordid as he'd always considered his older cousin. But what his cousin didn't understand was that knowing her, loving her, was perhaps the greatest gift he'd ever received.

The one question that had hounded him for months was how she'd become involved in this life. Despite his curiosity, he'd never questioned her. Fear was the main reason for keeping his questions to himself. He'd recognized immediately that the subject of her career, for lack of a better word, was strictly off-limits. The one time he'd mentioned it, she'd refused to speak and had nearly run away. He couldn't, wouldn't, risk it again.

What most concerned him was the question of her pimp. She had one. Almost every hooker did. But Russell had never had the courage to ask who it was. So he had to pretend things were different. Pretend they had a normal relationship.

Either he was the biggest fool who'd ever lived or her love for him was as real as his law degree. As real as she said it was. He chose to believe her. It was as if there were two Pearls. One of them was the brazen cold-eyed hooker he'd met on his birthday. The woman who was a consummate actress, using soft baby talk with him and behaving in an almost subservient way as she offered tantalizing glimpses of her wares.

Then there was the other Pearl. The real Pearl.

He wasn't sure why he'd suggested they talk first that night. Probably because he'd been nervous and on edge. His cousin had made a big deal of this evening, and while it had embarrassed and even disgusted Russell, he'd reluctantly gone along.

He'd never intended to go to bed with her, never intended to visit her again. But their first evening together had been…so wonderful. So unexpected. He discovered he could be himself with her, whereas with other women he felt self-conscious and shy. He knew women considered him attractive; nevertheless he'd never found it easy to talk with them.

Later his cousin had interrogated him about his gift. Pried him with questions. Russell had lied, saying as little as possible. His cousin had given him a congratulatory slap on the back, then lowered his voice and asked if he'd sampled Pearl's specialty. It was all Russell could do not to slam his fist down the other man's throat as he relayed in profane detail what kept Pearl's customers coming back again and again.

Then Russell had stumbled on her in the grocery store, and they'd started meeting at his cabin. He was fairly sure no one knew, which was undoubtedly for the best. Their secrecy protected his reputation and, she'd once implied, her safety. And there was the fact that she wasn't exactly the type of woman a man introduced to his mother. Yet Russell would gladly have married her. He'd asked her to be his wife a dozen times; he'd stopped only because he could see how much it hurt her to turn him down. Tears would fill her eyes and she'd whisper that he didn't know what he was asking. Russell *did* know. But he'd let the matter rest and went about proving how much he loved her, even when it meant turning a blind eye to how she made her living.

Looking at her now, no one would ever guess her occupation. Her hair was tied back in pigtails and her baggy T-shirt disguised the fullness of her breasts and just about every other feminine attribute.

"Your move," she said, glancing up and beaming him a wide triumphant smile.

It was difficult to stop gazing at her long enough to examine the chessboard. Once he did, he frowned. The obvious move would put him in check; any other move would place his queen in jeopardy. He reconstructed her moves and saw that there was no hope for it. She'd won. They could play to the end, if she insisted, but the outcome was inevitable. She'd outsmarted him again.

He looked at her and grinned. "Come here," he whispered.

"Russell?"

He held out his hand to her. She knew what he wanted and blushed. The first time he'd seen that tinge of color on her cheeks he was convinced it was a trick. This woman knew everything there was to know about sex. But over time Russell had come to trust that everything between them was as new and fresh for her as it was for him. Like him, she was in love for the first time in her life.

"You can get out of that," she said, pointing at the chessboard.

But Russell already had his next move planned, and it didn't involve chess.

Pearl giggled, sounding like a teenager. She exhaled the softest of sighs, then gently placed her hand in his. Russell pulled her close.

Out here he could forget that this never should have happened. That he'd fallen head over heels in love with a whore.

On Friday morning Molly and Gramps received news from Sam that one of the water holes had been poisoned. The carcass of a calf had been dumped in the largest cow pond in the new pasture. Every indication was that this had been done deliberately.

Ten cattle were already dead and another thirty head were sick. Between the vet bills and the loss of cattle, this was one more disaster they didn't need.

"We've got to do something, Gramps!" Molly cried in outrage as she stormed about the kitchen. She wasn't sure how she expected him to respond. She'd thought it over countless times, and her conclusions were always the same. The record books told her they were already in financial trouble. Any more would cripple them. It was clear to her that someone wanted the ranch to fail. "Who would do this to us?" she muttered. "Who?"

"If I knew who'd do such a thing, Molly girl, I wouldn't be sitting here stewing." He'd played solitaire for the past hour, slapping the cards against the table and just as quickly snatching them up again.

"But why?"

Gramps slowly shook his head. "I wish to hell I knew."

"Isn't it obvious someone wants us to bail out?" Surely he hadn't forgotten the offer Russell Letson had brought her a few days after her arrival. That seemed the perfect place to start looking. "Maybe we should ask Letson who his client is."

"Sam already did that."

"He did?" That the two men would exclude her didn't sit well with Molly, but this was an issue she'd take up with Sam, not Gramps.

"Now, don't go gettin' your dander up," her grandfather muttered. "It was a logical decision. You'd just arrived and we couldn't see any need to drag you into something you knew nothing about."

"So do you know who made the offer?" she asked.

"It wasn't someone local, if that's what you're asking. No one from Sweetgrass would want this land so bad he'd be willing to hurt us in order to get it,' Gramps told her.

"Who is it, then?"

Gramps scratched the side of his head. "My guess is it's one of those movie-star types outta Hollywood. I hear that's quite common now. These people think they're gonna turn back time and have bison on the land again. Romantic malarkey.'' The old man rolled his eyes. ''Sam talked to Letson for quite a while. Letson couldn't tell him who made the offer, but he didn't say no when Sam mentioned the movie-star idea. So we don't know for sure, but that's who we think it is. Some actor. Most folks around here won't sell to a movie star, so he must've hired Letson.'' Gramps paused. ''Can't see one of those Hollywood pretty boys comin' out here to knock down mailboxes and poison our cattle, though.''

Molly agreed. But she was going to ask Sam about it. In the meantime she wanted to clear the air about something else. Something she'd put off since the Fourth of July.

''What exactly do you know about Sam?'' she asked in what she hoped was a conversational tone.

''Sam?'' Gramps's eyes narrowed suspiciously. ''Not that again! Why're you asking *this* time?''

''Sheriff Maynard stopped by for a chat with us before the parade last week.''

''Oh?''

''He wasn't particularly...pleasant.''

''Oh.''

''He seems to know something about Sam that we don't.''

''Oh?''

The *oh*'s were beginning to irritate her. ''Gramps, I know you like Sam. I do, too, and so do the boys. But something's not right. Why would Sheriff Maynard want to make trouble for Sam? And even more important, why did Sam clam up afterward?''

''You'll have to ask him.''

Gramps was hiding something from her. Molly was

convinced of that, and it angered her. She was his flesh and blood. His granddaughter. And apparently he didn't trust her enough to tell her the whole truth about a hired hand.

"Fine. I *will* ask him." She was going to have so many questions for Sam she'd have to start a list. "The man responsible for keeping the law in this county looks at Sam as if he isn't to be trusted and you're pushing me to *marry* him. What kind of message does that give me, Gramps?" She didn't allow him an opportunity to answer. "It says you're so desperate to see me married off that you're willing to throw me to anyone. Even a man you hardly—"

"Enough!" Gramps pushed the deck of cards aside. "You ask me what I know about Sam Dakota. I know he's decent and honest. I know he cares for those boys of yours and he'd make you a damn good husband. That's what I know. As for his trouble with the sheriff, you can think what you will, but it was nothing Sam did."

"All Sam's interested in is the land you offered," she said. It still offended her that Gramps had dangled part of *her* inheritance as an inducement.

"Did Sam tell you himself that he'd only marry you if I threw in the land and cattle?" Gramps asked.

"No," she admitted. "But he didn't have to say it," she added sarcastically. His attitude had said it all.

"Do you honestly believe I'd suggest you marry a man I don't trust?" Gramps asked her quietly.

"Why him?" she cried. "Do you think I'm incapable of finding my own husband? What if Sam marries me, sucks the ranch dry and then leaves me?"

Gramps shook his head. "I told you before, Molly, that isn't going to happen."

"How can you be so sure?"

He sighed deeply and looked away. "Without Sam, I would have lost the ranch last winter."

"Any hired hand would have saved the ranch," she argued. "Sam was there when you needed him, but it could have been anyone."

Again Gramps shook his head. "No. For one thing, he got the cattle sold off in time to pay my bank loan. I'll grant you another foreman might've managed that for me. But the other thing he did…" Gramps rubbed at his eyes. "He pawned his silver buckle to pay back taxes. Those things are worth a lot, Molly. Remember I told you he was a world-champion rodeo rider until his accident? It was his prize that he hawked for the ranch. He didn't tell me about it right away, either. I found out when I went in to the assessor's office to ask for some extra time. That was when I discovered Sam had already been in and paid the bill. The only reason he told me was I pressured him into it."

Sam had done that? Molly felt a sudden need to sit down.

"I'd been having a bit of a problem with money," Gramps said, and Molly understood how difficult it was for her grandfather to admit this. "I put off thinking about it as long as I could, but when the dunning letters started coming in, I knew it was time I faced the music."

"You told Sam?"

"No!" This was said with vehemence; she realized it hurt his pride to talk about his financial failures. "Sam was the one who brought in the mail. He saw the final-notice envelope himself."

"How much was it?"

Gramps named a substantial figure. "He hawked the

most precious thing he owned to help me. Despite what you think, Sam Dakota is a good man. Give him a chance to prove himself, Molly girl. You might be surprised.'' Gramps hesitated and his voice grew gentle. ''You should have seen him when he first arrived. He was mad as hell and the chip on his shoulder was the size of an oak. But after a while, when he got to working the land, he changed. The land will heal you, too, Molly. If you let it.''

Molly *wanted* the land to heal her. She wanted the contentment of a life lived close to the earth. She wanted the sense of accomplishing something real.

''Sam paid the taxes without telling me what he'd done,'' Gramps whispered. ''He's that kind of man. You won't go wrong marrying him. He'll be good to you, Molly, and a decent father to your sons. I won't be with you much longer.'' He held up his hand to stop her when she started to protest. ''Think about marrying him. I promise you, you won't be sorry.''

Molly spent the evening doing just that. Thinking. Much later, while the house slept, she was still wide awake. Worrying. Wondering. What would she do without Sam? Who could she trust? Was it *right* to marry him?

Staring out at the moonless night, she felt alone and afraid. Someone was trying to frighten her off her land. Hurt her family. If ever there was a time she needed a strong ally, it was now.

Was that enough for a marriage, being allies?

The house was quiet and dark as she hurried downstairs. The clock on the stove said it was after midnight. She wasn't sure what prompted her to look out the kitchen window, but she did, and the first thing she noticed was that Sam's light was on.

Before she could lose her nerve, she pulled on a sweater and a pair of boots and made her away across the yard.

She knocked twice before he answered.

"Yeah? What is it?" He raked back disheveled hair as he opened the door.

"I...I thought you were up," Molly apologized.

"I must have dozed off in front of the television." He didn't invite her in, which was just as well. She'd say what she had to say quickly and be done with it.

"Two things." She straightened holding her head high, and forced her voice to remain calm and unemotional. "First, I've decided to approach you about Gramps's suggestion."

He didn't say anything for perhaps a minute. Just stared at her. "You're willing for us to get married?" he finally asked. He didn't sound like he believed her.

"Yes," she said, and nodded once for emphasis. "Are *you* willing?"

"I'm willing." No ands, ifs or buts. No questions or hesitations, but then she'd doubted there would be.

"All right. We can get the license later this week." He nodded. "You said two things."

"The next one is a question. Please be honest. Would you have agreed to marry me without Gramps's offer of the cattle and land?"

"No," he said, steadily meeting her gaze.

If nothing else, she appreciated his honesty. "That's what I thought."

Ten

Sam was sitting at the kitchen table when Molly came downstairs the following morning. The coffee was made, and she glanced his way before helping herself to a cup. His silence grated on her nerves. The night had been miserable. She'd slept, but only intermittently. Her dreams had been full of strange fearful scenarios. She remembered one in which she was at her wedding—except that the groom turned out to be Daniel and the preacher Sheriff Maynard.

Judging from the dark shadows beneath Sam's eyes, he hadn't slept any better. Neither spoke, although Molly knew he was as aware of her as she was of him. For two people who'd agreed to marry, they didn't appear to have much to say to each other.

She noticed that he waited until she'd had time to drink half her coffee before he spoke. "Have you changed your mind?"

Molly's gaze flew across the room. "Have you?"

"I asked you first."

If he was trying to make her feel like a fool, he was definitely succeeding. "No. I'm willing to go through with a wedding if you are, but—"

"I am," he interrupted, not giving her a chance to finish. He stood and reached for his hat.

"*But,*" she continued as though he hadn't spoken,

"I'd prefer the marriage to be strictly a business arrangement."

Sam's eyes narrowed. "You already know my answer to that. We'll be man and wife in every sense of the word, or the whole thing's off."

"But you said...you admitted you'd never have agreed to the marriage if it wasn't for Gramps's offer."

"Think of that as my guarantee."

"*Your* guarantee?" she flared. *She* needed a guarantee if anyone did. This was no love match, after all. Even if her husband-to-be thought they were going to share a bed. That issue wasn't resolved yet, as far as she was concerned. "Your guarantee?" she repeated. "Of what?"

"Who's to say that a couple of years down the road, after I've worked my fingers to the bone, you won't file for divorce and kick me off the place?" Sam asked coolly.

"Who's to say you won't sell off the cattle and abscond with the profits?" she threw back.

They glared at each other across the room.

Sam was the one to break the tense silence. "It would help, don't you think, if we could agree to trust each other? The only person who's shown any confidence in our ability to make a go of this marriage is Walt. For his sake—if not our own—let's put aside our doubts and agree to make the best of it. Can we do that?"

This was more difficult than she'd thought it would be. Faith and trust didn't came easily. "All right," she whispered at last.

He relaxed then. "Good. I'll get Pete and Charlie set for the day and then we can drive into town and apply for the license."

"Already?" she gasped.

"Is there a reason to wait?"

No one knew about this yet, not even Gramps or the boys. Molly needed time to discuss it with her children. It wasn't fair just to spring a stepfather on them. They had the right to express their opinions and concerns first. Not that either boy was likely to object.

"I have to tell my family. Phone my mother in Australia." Molly nervously brushed the hair from her face. "But other than that I don't suppose there's any reason to wait."

"We'll both need a blood test."

She tightened the belt on her dressing gown.

"I thought we could have the test done, get the license and make an appointment with a justice of the peace for tomorrow afternoon."

Molly inhaled sharply. A justice of the peace made the entire proceeding sound so...calculated. This might not be a love match, but she still wanted her wedding to take place in a church.

"What's wrong?"

"What about having a minister marry us?"

"Seeing that we aren't getting married for the normal reasons, saying our vows before a man of God seems somewhat hypocritical, don't you think?"

He was right of course, and Molly was unable to come up with an adequate justification for a church wedding—although she still wanted one. She nodded unhappily.

"Smile, Molly," Sam said with sudden amusement. "It could be worse."

Molly wasn't sure that was true. She was about to pledge her life to a man who didn't love her, who openly admitted he was only marrying her for five hun-

dred acres and fifty head of cattle. Worse, she was going into the marriage for selfish reasons of her own.
She needed his help, to run the ranch and to *keep* the
ranch.

Truly what you'd describe as a marriage of convenience.

With such odds against them, it seemed doubtful
they'd manage to stay married for more than six
months, Molly thought with sudden pessimism.

"It's a business agreement—and more," Sam clar-
ified, and waited for her to agree.

"And more," she concurred reluctantly.

Sam left after that, while she lingered over her coffee
in the kitchen and prayed she was doing the right thing.

Tom and Clay wandered down for breakfast a few
minutes later. Molly gave them time to fill their bowls
with cereal and sit down at the table. "What would
you say if I told you I was thinking about getting married again?" she asked, avoiding eye contact.

"Who?" Tom asked suspiciously.

"Yeah, who do you want to marry?" Clay echoed.

Molly drew in a deep breath. "Sam."

Tom grinned and punched a fist into the air. "Yes!"
He nodded. "I figured it had to be."

"Cool, Mom!"

"Neither one of you objects?" Although it seemed
pointless to ask.

"I *like* Sam," Clay said without hesitation.

Molly looked to her oldest. Tom was still grinning
widely. "If I'd handpicked a new dad, it would've been
Sam."

"I see." Molly could hardly claim to be surprised.
And, of course, Sam's closeness to her boys was one
of the reasons she'd agreed to this.

"What's all the shouting about in here?" Gramps asked as he slowly made his way into the room.

"Mom's marrying Sam!" Clay burst out.

Gramps went silent as if he wasn't sure he should believe it. "Is that true, Molly girl?"

She nodded.

"Praise be to God." Gramps clasped his hands together. "I haven't heard better news in fifteen years. You won't be sorry, Molly, I promise you," he said again.

What she didn't tell her grandfather was that she already had regrets. An uneasiness in the pit of her stomach refused to go away. Despite the reasons that had led to the decision—sound *convenient* reasons—Molly couldn't shake the feeling she was making a terrible mistake. She still knew next to nothing about Sam, and he barely knew her.

Well, she was committed now. She'd given her word. She'd just have to make sure they learned a little more about each other. And soon.

An hour later, when Sam returned to the house, Molly was dressed and ready for the drive to town.

"I've got to stop off for some supplies," he announced as if that was the main reason for this trip into Sweetgrass. Anything else, he seemed to imply, was just a trifling errand. Or worse, an annoyance.

Once in his truck, she barely had the seat belt snapped before Sam took off down the driveway. He drove as if he couldn't get this whole thing over with fast enough. They bumped over potholes and rocks at a speed well above what Molly considered safe.

"Stop!" she shouted just before they hit the paved highway.

He slammed on the brakes. "What for?" he demanded.

The seat belt was all that kept her from pitching forward into the windshield.

Sam's arms remained on the steering wheel. He waited for her to speak.

"Why are you so angry?" she asked.

"I'm not."

"Is there some logical reason you're driving like a wild man?"

Her question seemed to bring him up short. "I'd like to get this done as quickly as possible so I can get back to work."

Molly had the almost irresistible urge to cover her face and weep. "I realize we're not in love," she said, surprised by how small her voice sounded. "But I'd like us both to treat this wedding as something more than a business agreement. Since you insist you eventually want a real marriage—with a shared bed—then I insist on something, too." Her voice gained confidence as she spoke. "I agree to your stipulation." Molly stared straight ahead of her. She *did* agree; she'd come to a decision about it. She *would* sleep with him. Maybe not right away, but when they felt more comfortable with each other. She'd do anything she could to make the marriage work. "But," she went on, "I have a stipulation of my own."

"All right, what is it?"

"A real wedding."

He went stock-still. "You want a wedding?"

"Yes. One that's more than a five-minute civil ceremony."

"So, what exactly do you want?"

"I want a minister to perform the wedding."

"All right. But I don't know any ministers."

"I'll find one." She could tell he wasn't thrilled with her request; nevertheless he was willing to agree to her terms, just as she'd agreed to his.

"Okay." He glanced at her. "Can I drive again now?"

"No." She had to tell him about Daniel; he deserved to know that much. But she found it excruciatingly difficult.

"No?"

"I have to tell you something." She clenched both hands. "My first marriage wasn't a good one."

"So I gather."

"You know about Daniel? The boys told you?" It made sense when she thought about it. The boys had probably told him. That was fine. She wanted him to understand her fears—that her inability to judge character had scared her to the point of being afraid to marry again.

"Yes," he said. Then, "What were they supposed to tell me?"

They hadn't. Molly stared out the side window. "He's...in prison."

Sam was silent so long she wondered if he'd heard her. "What's he in for?"

"Fraud. He cheated a lot of people out of their retirement income. Especially older people. Pensioners."

"Bastard." Sam grimaced. "What's his sentence?"

"He got twenty years with no possibility of parole," she said. "The trial went on for weeks. People can be so cruel. They asked the boys questions. Kids taunted them."

"I'm sorry, Molly."

"Yeah, well, it's all water under the bridge now. But

I thought you should know." It amazed her how much better she felt for having told him. At least it was out in the open and they could discuss it.

"Are you okay now?" he asked.

"Uh-huh." And she was. For the first time since this morning, she felt good about their decision. Not just resigned but genuinely optimistic. Perhaps, with a bit of compromise and a lot of hard work they could make a success of this marriage.

Sam did drive more sensibly after that, but he remained silent. So did she. Twice she caught Sam shifting his attention from the road to her. As they neared town, he slowed the truck down to well below the speed limit. For someone in a hurry, he suddenly seemed to have plenty of time on his hands.

He tapped his index finger against the steering wheel; she could tell he had something on his mind.

"Before we apply for the license," he began, then hesitated.

"Yes?"

"I've lived damn near thirty-six years on my own," he said, as though this was new information.

"I realize that." She didn't mention that other than a four-year marriage, she'd been on her own, too.

"I've lived a...varied life, Molly. For a long time I followed the rodeo circuit."

Although she knew that, it was the first time he'd mentioned it.

"There were plenty of women in those days, and—"

So this was confession time. Frankly Molly didn't want to hear about his groupies and all the women he'd loved. Or slept with. It would be just one more piece of baggage in a marriage that would be burdened with enough.

"Don't tell me," she said, stopping him.

He pulled his gaze off the road long enough to look at her. His brow knit in a puzzled frown. "What do you mean?"

"I don't want to hear it."

"But there're things about me you should know—things that could change your mind about this marriage business. I haven't lived the life of a saint."

"Neither have I."

He ignored that. "I'm not proud of my past, and as my wife you have a right to know what you're getting in the husband department."

"It doesn't matter."

"Some of it does," he said. The stiffness in his back and shoulders made her wonder what that might be.

"Are you healthy? Are there children you're supporting? A common-law wife?" Those were the important issues.

"Yes to the first question—I had enough blood tests in the hospital to be sure of that. And no to the others. To the best of my knowledge I've never fathered a child and I've never had a wife, common-law or otherwise, but my past—"

"Is past," she interrupted. "Confession might be good for the soul, but in this instance...I think not. Let's start with a clean slate, shall we? What's in your past has nothing to do with the future, and the same applies to me."

He was quiet for a moment. "You're sure about this?"

"Very sure." She smiled. "There's lots I want to hear about your life—your family and your childhood, your glory days in the rodeo, where you've worked since. But anything you feel guilty about, you can keep to yourself. Okay?''

He reached for her hand and squeezed it. ''I intend to be a good husband, Molly. I realize these circumstances aren't the best, but if we both try, we can make this a good marriage.''

Was it possible? Molly didn't have an answer to that, but she was beginning to feel real hope.

Three days later at five o'clock in the afternoon Sam stood with Molly in the office of Reverend Ackerly at Sweetgrass Baptist Church. Tom, Clay and Walt crowded around them. Sam couldn't help smiling at Walt's attempt to appear suitably solemn—as befitted a member of the wedding. He and Mrs. Ackerly had agreed to be their witnesses.

Molly wore a floor-length dress in a pretty shade of pink with big buttons and a wide belt. She wore the cameo that had once belonged to her grandmother and pearl earrings. Her auburn hair was freshly cut and curly. Sam had never seen her look so pretty and had difficulty not staring at her. Although he hadn't said anything, it pleased him that she'd wanted to make something special of this wedding. It boded well for their marriage.

What *didn't* help was that she knew nothing about his prison record. He'd tried to tell her, but had backed down when she'd insisted she didn't want to know about his past scandals. Her insistence had relieved him, because he was afraid that once she heard the truth, she'd change her mind. Not that he'd blame her. She sure wasn't getting any bargain.

Someday, he promised himself, he'd tell her about that part of his past. But not now. When the trust between them was firmly established, then and only then would he feel safe enough to reveal the darkest shadows of his own life.

Before the wedding ceremony they'd stopped at the jeweler's and purchased simple gold bands, but Sam's gaze had wandered over the diamonds. A year or two from now, when he could afford it, he'd buy Molly the diamond she deserved. Maybe by then he'd be the husband she deserved, too.

He quickly reined in his thoughts. Although they both wanted the marriage to work, fooling himself into believing this was a love match would only lead to trouble. He wasn't stupid. He knew why Molly had developed this sudden desire for a husband. She was scared and, frankly, he understood that. Especially when someone—some unknown person—was after the ranch and willing to go to just about any lengths to obtain it.

Sam didn't mean to be so distracted by these problems in the middle of his own wedding, but the worry was there. When it came time to say his vows, he had a few of his own he intended to silently add. He would protect Walt, Molly and the boys or die trying.

On the minister's instructions, he spoke his vows. His voice was strong, firm, clear. The words came directly from his heart. It'd taken him thirty-six years to marry, and he only intended to do it once.

He didn't know if what he felt for Molly was love. He did know he genuinely cared for her and her children. He knew he wanted her in his life and longed to be part of hers.

Molly repeated her vows in a voice just as strong and confident as his. Sam instinctively recognized it as bravado and admired her for it. He respected this woman for a number of reasons. Her love for her grandfather. Her courage in coming to Montana—and in marrying him. The fact that she loved her children and worked hard to be a good mother. His own mother had been a teenager when he was born, little more than a child herself. Her husband, Michael Dakota, had adopted Sam as his own son. Through the years, his stepfather hadn't played favorites among the children, and neither would Sam. If sometime in the future Tom, Clay and Molly were willing, he'd like to look into adopting her boys. He only hoped he could be as good a stepfather as his own had been.

He thought about Michael with renewed sorrow and genuine regret. He wondered about his mother and the rest of his family. He'd call or write them soon....

Then the ceremony was over, and they signed the documents, witnessed by Gramps and Mrs. Ackerly. When they finished, Gramps shook Sam's hand and said he'd have Letson draw up the paperwork on their agreement.

"What about dinner?" Gramps said as they walked out of Pastor Ackerly's study. "My treat." The old man looked pleased with himself, as well he should. Sam suspected that Walt had planned this wedding for quite some time.

"What do you say, Mrs. Dakota?" Gramps asked, smiling at Molly.

Mrs. Dakota. They'd discussed the possibility of her keeping the name Cogan, if for no other reason than it was the name she shared with the boys. Molly had declined. This was Montana, and while it was common practice for women to keep their surnames in other parts of the country, it wasn't here. Besides, she had no loyalty to Daniel or his family.

Mr. and Mrs. Sam Dakota.

Not only did Sam have a wife and two stepsons, but he was a husband now. The unencumbered life was forever behind him. And Sam was glad of it. He felt nothing but gratitude to an old man who'd had the insight to suggest this marriage—and the shrewdness to offer him the right incentive.

Gramps chose the restaurant, claiming he wanted to eat at the new steak house. Sam smiled at the way Clay eyed the dessert platter the minute they entered the place. The hostess greeted them warmly. "Congratulations, you two!" she said. "We'll be bringing you some complimentary champagne and appetizers."

"Thank you," Molly murmured, then cast Sam a puzzled look.

"How'd she know?" Sam asked once they were all seated.

Gramps cleared his throat, looking spry and happy. "I called the radio station and they announced it."

"Gramps!" Molly groaned, and Sam watched the color brighten her cheeks.

"It isn't every day my granddaughter snares herself a husband. I wanted folks to hear the news."

Actually it didn't bother Sam one bit that the town knew he'd married Molly.

"They talk about weddings on the radio?" Tom asked, shaking his head in wonder.

"Between the beef prices and the garage sales," Gramps said with a chuckle. "And after bingo."

That launched a conversation about Clay's most recent bingo success; he'd gotten to the phone fast enough this time and won himself a big five dollars.

"I suspected I'd find you in here," Ginny Dougherty called out as she made her way across the restaurant.

She wore clean blue jeans and a red plaid shirt. "So how's the happy couple?"

"Married," Walt answered on their behalf. "I imagine you're looking for an invitation to join us. Damn snoopy neighbors," he grumbled.

It was all for show, Sam realized with a grin. He caught a glimpse of Molly's twinkling eyes. Every time he looked in her direction it was hard to pull his gaze away.

The waitress returned with a bottle of champagne and four glasses.

Walt peered at the label. "Where's it from?" he asked as though he was some kind of connoisseur. Sam hid a smile.

"You never could see worth a damn without your glasses," Ginny said, pulling out a chair and making herself at home. "It's domestic—from California." She took Molly's discarded menu and read through it.

"My eyesight's good enough to know you're an interfering old woman," Walt complained.

"Gramps!"

"Well, she is. No one invited her to dinner."

"I did," Molly said.

"When?"

"Just now. Please join us, Ginny. I apologize for my cantankerous ill-mannered grandfather."

"You'll do no such thing," Walt growled.

"I brought a wedding present. From Fred and me," Ginny said, changing the subject before a full-blown argument broke out, which it often did when Ginny and Walt were together. Sam used to wonder why these two fought so much, but over the months, he'd come to realize they enjoyed sparring with each other. He had to admit Walt showed more life when Ginny was around than any other time.

"A present?" Molly sounded delighted.

Sam wanted to kick himself. He should have bought Molly something. Not that he could afford much, but he should've picked out some little gift just to reassure her that he wasn't a heartless cold-blooded bastard marrying her for a piece of land.

"I figured," Ginny said, "neither Walt nor Sam would've done anything about a honeymoon."

"We couldn't afford one," Molly explained, making it sound as if they'd carefully weighed the decision. In reality, not a word had been uttered by either of them.

Once again Sam felt lacking. He hadn't been a husband more than an hour and already he'd failed Molly. Not once, but twice!

"Well, you're gonna have a honeymoon now," Ginny said, grinning sheepishly. She reached into her jeans pocket and pulled out a key. Holding it up, she let it swing a couple of times before handing it to Sam.

"What's that?" Walt asked, frowning.

"The key to a hotel room, what else? I booked the best room available, so Molly and Sam can celebrate their wedding night in *private*."

Gramps glared at his neighbor. "I wasn't planning on making a video recording of it, if that's what you're implying."

"Gramps!"

"All right, all right," he muttered, looking none too pleased.

"It was a very thoughtful thing to do," Molly said. When she realized Sam was watching her, she lowered her gaze.

Sam wondered if anyone else noticed how the tips

of her ears turned as red as her hair. So she was a bit hesitant. That was fair; he had a few qualms of his own. It'd been a long stretch since he'd last made love.

Just then the waitress brought the promised platter of appetizers—tiny ones, no more than one bite each, in Sam's opinion. Things with shrimp and smoked salmon and a white substance that was apparently goat's cheese. Molly and Ginny loved them, Gramps complained about the size and what he considered odd ingredients, and the boys wolfed down a bunch, surprisingly without comment. Sam ate a couple, finding he wasn't all that hungry.

"Can I order the lobster?" Clay asked once the appetizers were gone.

"Not now," Gramps answered. "You can order it when Sam's buying, not me."

Clay closed the menu. "I don't see anything else I'd like."

"I'm sure there's something," Molly said and read off a number of entrées Clay had apparently enjoyed in the past.

The boy repeatedly shook his head. "Can I have chocolate cake and cherry pie, instead?"

"Sure," Sam answered.

"You most certainly may not," Molly said at the same time.

Clay frowned. "Can I or can't I?"

"You'd better not," Sam answered.

"I suppose it wouldn't hurt you this one time," was Molly's response.

Again they'd spoken simultaneously.

Sam looked at her and she at him, and they both laughed. It felt good. As far as he was concerned, laughter was something this family could use.

The meal was ordered and the champagne was drunk. With great fanfare Gramps asked for a second bottle to accompany their entrées. He proposed a toast that brought tears to Molly's eyes, wishing his grand-daughter and her husband a marriage as happy as his own had been.

Ginny wasn't the only one who came to offer con-gratulations. Twice during the meal, businessmen stopped by their table to shake Sam's hand and to offer their best wishes. The Wheaton name had been part of the Sweetgrass community for a lot of years. In other circumstances Sam might have resented the intrusions, but not now. He was being welcomed. He'd become part of the community, no longer a drifter, a man with-out roots. This marriage made people feel differently about him; he understood that. It meant he'd made a commitment not only to Molly but to a vision of the future. Sweetgrass was where he belonged and where he intended to stay.

A sense of well-being filled him. In one twenty-four-hour period, he'd gained a wife and family and found a home. A man couldn't ask for much more than that.

By the time they returned to the ranch it was after nine. Sam quickly changed out of his jacket, dress shirt and string tie into a comfortable pair of jeans and West-ern-style shirt. First thing in the morning, he'd move his things out of the small house and into Molly's bed-room upstairs in the ranch house. Molly might think she'd gotten a reprieve, but he had news for her. She was his wife and he wasn't planning to sleep alone ever again.

For their night in the hotel, Sam packed his shaving kit and little else. When he'd finished, he got the truck and went to pick up Molly. She was ready, a suitcase in her hand. Walt hugged her goodbye and she clung to him.

She lingered over both her children before walking down the porch steps to the truck, where Sam waited patiently. Her eyes shyly met his as he leaned across the seat and opened the passenger door.

In minutes they were on the road again.

Sam toyed with the idea of initiating a conversation, but there was only one subject on his mind and he didn't figure talking about it would help.

As they neared town, he slowed down so that he was driving well within the legal limit. Wouldn't Sheriff Maynard just welcome the opportunity to throw his butt in jail on his wedding night? Sam didn't plan to give him the chance.

The hotel was on the outskirts of town. The neon sign was old, and the *V* in vacancy had burned out. Molly waited in the truck while he went inside to sign the register.

"Well, hello there," Bob Jenkins greeted him from behind the counter. "I hear congratulations are in order."

"That's right," Sam said. Although he had the key, Ginny had explained he'd need to check in before going up to the room.

"The missus put a bottle of champagne on ice for you and the new wife," Bob said.

"That's great." Although Sam figured they'd probably had enough champagne. "Thank you from us both."

"Don't worry none about neighbors, either. Business has been kinda slow lately and I'll make sure whoever checks in won't be anywhere near your room."

Sam nodded, pleased to know they'd have a lot of privacy. He signed his name with a flourish and hurried back to Molly. She was huddled against the passenger door.

He started the engine. "You aren't nervous, are you?"

"No," she said quickly. Perhaps too quickly.

"Good."

"I...I'm relieved we decided to do the intelligent thing and wait before entering into the, uh, physical aspect of this marriage."

Sam frowned, recalling no such agreement. "Wait? You and me? This is a joke, right?"

"But we agreed...I assumed we had, anyway. When we spoke in the car—the day we applied for the license... You don't actually think we're going to make love tonight, do you? We barely know each other!"

Now Sam was worried. "That's not the way I understood it."

"It isn't?"

"I told you up front that I fully expect this to be more than a business agreement, and you agreed. Not with a lot of enthusiasm, perhaps, but you did agree to become my wife in every sense of the word."

"Yes, I know—but not right away. I thought...I believed you understood that. I wanted us to become... familiar with each other first."

He clenched the steering wheel with a ferocity that whitened his knuckles.

"Molly, I want to make love to you tonight."

"No matter how I feel? You said yourself you don't love me."

"But I like you and respect you. We're attracted to each other—our kisses tell me that much. Isn't that enough?"

She took a long time answering. "No...it's not."

Eleven

Pearl wondered if wives realized how much business she enjoyed because they refused to make love with their husbands. More than one miserable man had sought her out because of his wife's recurring "headaches." As a rule a married man went to his wife first and Pearl second. She was convinced half her clientele would rather have stayed home with their wives, if only the women had been a bit more accommodating.

The man sitting at the bar was a prime example. He looked like he was about to cry in his beer. Pearl read the signs like the pro she was. The gold band on his finger told her he was married. The scenarios ran pretty much alike: husband and wife would argue and he'd leave the house, needing time away to cool down. These couples had forgotten that making up should be fun and it should happen in bed. A few of the men went to Pearl to restore their damaged egos. Some visited her on impulse. Others craved a little tenderness even if they had to pay for it. Then there were the angry men, looking for someone on whom they could take out their rage. Those were the ones Pearl avoided.

It was difficult to tell which category the cowboy at the bar fell into. She walked over to where he sat and slipped onto the stool next to him.

"Hello, there," she said in a husky provocative voice. "You're looking lonely."

He ignored her.

Pearl was accustomed to the cold shoulder, but she knew how to work her way around that. "Is there anything I can help you with?"

No response.

"Al, I'll take a bloody Mary," she called. The bartender acknowledged her order with a nod and she winked. Pearl rarely drank mixed drinks, and Al knew to make hers a virgin.

"Problems at home, cowboy?" she asked gently.

He glanced in her direction—an encouraging sign. She smiled prettily and, without being too obvious about it, made sure he got a good view of her assets. He downed his drink in short order, and Pearl noted the way his hand shook as he lowered the glass. Her guess was the argument he'd had with his wife had to do with sex. This guy was so damned hot, she could feel the heat radiating off him.

"Do you want to talk about it?" she asked, and leaned forward to suck on the colored straw.

"No."

Ever so lightly Pearl placed her long nails on his forearm. "Want to *do* something about it?"

She had his full attention now. In no hurry, she ran the tip of her tongue over her lips, cold now from the iced drink and reddened from the spicy tomato juice. The cowboy didn't seem able to stop looking at her mouth.

"Nobody can take care of you better than Pearl," she promised, and took a long exaggerated suck from the straw.

He shut his eyes.

The battle was half-won. Pearl smiled to herself.

To her surprise he slapped his money on the bar and started to leave. He hadn't taken more than two or three steps before he hesitated.

Pearl sensed that he was weakening and followed him outside. This wouldn't take long. Johns like this cowboy were ready to explode before she had a chance to remove her underwear. She considered them easy money.

"My place is right around the corner," she told him, tucking her hands in her jacket pockets.

"I'm not interested."

"Don't be so hasty. I'm good, cowboy, and I can help you forget whatever's troubling you. Come on, let Pearl make it better."

"Just how good are you, Pearl?" he asked, standing outside his truck, his hand on the door.

It wasn't a question she was often asked. Generally, all men cared about was a willing body. Any sexual finesse was lost on them.

"Good enough to satisfy you, cowboy."

He laughed once, abruptly.

She held her arms open to him. "Pearl will take care of you. Satisfaction guaranteed."

He rubbed his face with a shaking hand. "Are you good enough to satisfy a bridegroom on his wedding night?"

She'd heard some good lines in her time, but this was a new one. "Sure, honey, whatever you need. Let Pearl take the ache away. I promise to do the job a whole lot better than a couple of aspirin." She slipped her arms around his waist and moved suggestively against him, letting him feel the lush fullness of her breasts and inhale the scent of her perfume. She refused to use cheap perfume.

"Sorry. Like I said, I'm not interested." He spoke slowly, thoughtfully, and put his hands on her shoulders, gently pushing her away.

The regret and disappointment she heard in him tugged at her heart. Pearl hadn't really known she possessed a heart until Russell. Although she was grateful for everything he'd done for her, she didn't want to care or have feelings when it came to dealing with her customers. She provided a service, one devoid of emotion or sentiment. She was a businesswoman who appreciated her own value. Repeat business was her staple, and once she'd given a man a satisfactory experience, she encouraged him to set up a regular time with her, even offering a discount program. Monroe didn't know anything about that, not that he would've cared. All that concerned him was the money he collected from her and the other girls.

This cowboy had the potential to become the kind of customer she liked best. She could persuade him; she felt sure of it. She'd persuaded men like him before. Yet she hesitated. He was an emotional wreck. While she offered a temporary solution, sex with her wouldn't help him if his bride found out.

"Do you love her?" Pearl asked softly, barely knowing where the question came from.

The cowboy didn't answer right away. "I guess I must, otherwise that skirt you're wearing would be over your head by now."

"Then go back."

He shook his head. "She doesn't want me touching her. She's not interested."

Pearl laughed. "Listen, I don't pretend to know a

lot about human nature, but if she married you, trust me, she's interested.''

The cowboy wanted to believe her. Pearl saw it in the fierce way his eyes held hers. ''This isn't a normal marriage,'' he said, shaking his head.

''What marriage is?'' Pearl wrapped her hand around his forearm, letting her long painted nails gently scrape the inside of his elbow. ''Listen to me, cowboy, I don't care what led up to your marriage—she wants you.''

''That's not what she's saying.''

''I'll tell you what. You go back, and if you can't settle this with her, find me and I'll give you one on the house.'' Pearl had never before made that type of offer. But if his bride wasn't a born idiot, she'd appreciate the good man she'd married and count her blessings.

The cowboy looked like he was in grave danger of smiling. ''You honestly think it'd help if I went back?''

''I do.''

He gave a deep, shuddering sigh. ''Then I will.'' He opened the truck and bounded inside. As the engine fired to life, he glanced at her. ''Thanks.''

''Not a problem.'' But it was. Loving Russell had changed her, and she stood at a crossroads. Either she continued on with the only life she'd ever known or she changed. Russell had repeatedly asked her to marry him. He didn't understand what she was really involved in. Nor did he understand that if they were seen together, he'd be in danger. So would she. He continually told her how smart she was, but it wasn't true. If she was even half as smart as he believed, she'd find a way to marry the only man she'd ever loved.

* * *

The ice cooling the champagne had long since melted. Molly sat on the edge of the bed, more miserable than she could remember being since the judge had declared her divorce from Daniel final. A second marriage was quite possibly the only thing that could drag her this low.

For the past few days she'd actually looked forward to marrying Sam, but this evening, as the time for their so-called honeymoon arrived, she'd started to worry. Being alone in a hotel room hadn't been part of the plan. Not *her* plan, anyway. She would have preferred their first night together to be in the comfort and familiarity of the ranch. But then Ginny and Fred had given them this honeymoon night, and Molly didn't have the heart to disappoint them.

The problem was with herself, Molly realized, and her fear of letting anyone get close, even the man she'd married just hours before. Intimacy terrified her, and because she'd been afraid, because the thought of allowing Sam to touch her and hold her had frightened her, she'd sent him away.

Panic had set in when they reached the hotel. Sam had been quick to remind her of her promise to him, and an argument had immediately ensued. Molly couldn't remember everything she'd said, but whatever it was, she regretted it. Sam had dropped her off and driven away, tires squealing. And so Molly had been left to fret and wonder where he was and what he was doing.

With her arms folded around her middle, she paced the floor, feeling wretched and defeated.

For a while she convinced herself she didn't even *want* to know where he'd gone.

Like hell she didn't. This was her wedding night,

and she was minus a bridegroom. Minus her pride and dignity. Every doubt she'd harbored after divorcing Daniel returned full force. He'd left her for someone else and claimed she'd driven him away. She'd protested the accusation loud and long, yet she was driving her second husband away in what appeared to be record time. It'd taken all of four years for Daniel to leave her and less than four hours for Sam to walk out.

Although it was useless to try to sleep, she made the effort, slipping between the cool sheets and hugging a pillow to her breast. The shadows from the broken neon light danced against the wall, making her desolate, reminding her what a failure she was.

She must have fallen asleep because her eyes flew open when she heard Sam. He inserted the key into the lock, opened the door and walked silently into the room. A flood of relief and gratitude washed over her. It was all she could do to keep from scrambling out of bed, throwing herself in his arms and begging his forgiveness. Nothing had gone the way she'd planned. Instead of talking about her fears, instead of reasoning everything out, she'd become defensive and unrealistic.

Sam stood uncertainly in the middle of the dark room.

"Sam," she whispered, and sat up in bed.

"Yeah?"

Her chest hurt from holding her breath. "I'm sorry." She heard his sigh. "Me, too."

"I don't blame you for leaving…" She let the rest fade, fearing her emotion would embarrass them both.

Sam crossed the room and sat on the bed. "I'm afraid you got the short end of the stick in the husband department, Molly. I don't blame you for—"

"It isn't me who's been cheated, it's you."

He turned and stared at her in the darkness. The only light came from the neon sign outside, but it was enough to see the puzzled frown on his face.

Molly owed him the truth. "I'm afraid."

"Of what?"

It hurt to voice her doubts aloud, to confess her flaws, knowing that his rejection now would devastate her. "Of getting hurt again. Of being vulnerable—so many things. I don't think I realized myself how frightened I was until we arrived at the hotel."

"Do you still feel that way?"

"Yes, but not as much."

He lifted his hand as if to touch her face, then hesitated. "Are you willing to try? You can set the pace. If you want to stop, we can."

"Are you willing to give me a second chance?" she asked.

"More than willing," he assured her, leaning forward to gently press his mouth to hers.

Molly's eyes fluttered closed and she slid her hands against his wide shoulders. This wasn't Daniel, she reminded herself, but Sam. He'd married her, wanted her as his wife, needed her.

When they kissed again, it was Molly who initiated the contact. She knelt on the bed and wrapped her arms around his neck. This was good. Better than good. They were both quiet when the kiss ended.

Sam chuckled and got to his feet, then began to unsnap his shirt with hurried movements. "She was right."

"Who?"

"I met someone tonight at Willie's place."

"The tavern?"

"Yeah. First time I've been there since the fight. I

guess that tells you how bad I was feeling. Anyway, I talked to this woman for a bit and she urged me to come back."

Whoever the woman was, Molly owed her a debt of gratitude.

Sam removed his boots, which landed with a thump on the floor. "I need you, Molly. I don't claim to be any prize as a husband, but I'll try." He pulled off his jeans and got beneath the covers.

"It's...it's been a long time for me, Sam."

"It has been for me, too." He moved closer to her. "You're wearing far too many clothes for a bride on her wedding night."

Molly rested her head on his bare shoulder and placed her hand on his lean hard chest. She could feel his heart hammering against her palm. "You think so?"

"I know so." He kissed her with a pent-up hunger that nearly devoured her. Molly's response was immediate and just as heated, surprising even her. The kiss was wild and wonderful, and their hands moved frantically, touching, arousing, exciting.

Molly let her fingers creep up his chest, enjoying the smooth feel of his skin, appreciating the man in her arms. Nothing mattered right now except their fierce physical craving for each other.

Molly linked her fingers behind his neck and drew his mouth to hers. The kisses that followed were hot and urgent. When he positioned himself above her, she shifted her body to accommodate his. Raising her head from the pillow, Molly kissed him, barely allowing their lips to touch. The kiss was more breath than contact.

"Molly." He said her name in a pain-filled groan,

then caught her hips, holding her still against the mattress. Sweat glistened on his upper lip and forehead.

Panting beneath him, her arms stretched out at her sides, Molly dragged a harsh breath through her lungs. She lifted her head just enough to touch the tight cords in his neck with her tongue. He tasted of salt and man and smelled faintly of roses.

He made love to her, filled her body with his own, until they reached a wild exhaustive crescendo that left her utterly drained.

There was no sound but their breathing, harsh and rapid. Neither spoke. For her part Molly felt incapable of saying a single word. Sam's breathing steadied first and he smiled at her, then spread soft kisses over her face.

"How do you feel?" he whispered, holding her in the crook of his arm.

"Wonderful."

Sam kissed the crown of her head. "Me, too."

"I want to be a good wife, Sam...I know I started this night off all wrong, and I regret—"

He silenced her with a finger to her lips. "Don't apologize. It isn't necessary. Just promise me that from now on we'll talk everything out. It's the only chance we have. This marriage can be a good one if we're both willing to work at it."

She nodded. "I promise."

Happier than she could remember being in a very long while, Molly hugged him close. If they shared nothing more than incredible sex in this marriage, it would be enough.

She'd been in love once and the love hadn't even lasted the length of her marriage. She was afraid to count on it again. She cared for Sam, respected him, needed him. But loving him would be dangerous. Loving him meant risking more than she could afford to lose. She had too much at stake to let her heart get in the way.

This unbridled feeling of happiness couldn't last. Molly was sure of it. The two weeks following her wedding were the best days of her life. Her boys were content. Each had adjusted in his own way to the change from their lives in California to life here in Montana. Tom spent his days riding with Sam, learning all he could about horses and ranching. He displayed a natural talent that Sam fostered and encouraged. Sam's approval and the attention he paid Tom did wonders for the boy's self-esteem; the changes in him were dramatic. In two months he'd gone from a moody adolescent to a hardworking responsible young man.

Clay stuck close to the ranch house with Molly and Gramps. Her younger son worked countless hours training Bullwinkle. The boy and his puppy were inseparable. Sometimes Clay helped Molly in the garden or with work around the house.

Clay also spent a lot of time with Gramps playing cribbage. Or he'd sit contentedly on the porch with the old man, whittling away at his block of wood, inordinately proud of his masterpiece. He and Gramps had grown very close.

Gramps seemed happy, too—although his health had declined to the point that he spent most of the day in his chair or listening to the radio. It seemed he had found serenity, a quiet peace.

Molly saw her husband off each morning, then counted the hours until he returned. It wasn't that she didn't keep busy; with the house and the garden she had more than enough to fill her days. Every evening she'd wait for him. He and Tom would ride in, exhausted, and the three of them would walk to the barn. Any outward display of affection between husband and wife was reserved for the privacy of their bedroom.

In two weeks' time their eagerness for each other hadn't dissipated. Always, after they made love, he held her in his arms and they talked. He told her about his years with the rodeo and the accident that had cost him his career. She kissed his scars and her eyes filled with tears at the pain each one must have caused him.

One such night she asked Sam, "Are you happy?"

He went very still at the question and she wondered if she'd unwittingly stepped over the line of what they could openly discuss. Perhaps he thought she was asking him to declare his love for her. She wasn't. If he did love her, he'd tell her in his own good time.

"Yes, I'm happy."

It wasn't the words but his voice. The way he said it. With honesty, looking directly into her eyes. With gratitude, as if she, and only she, had done this. Made him happy.

"I am, too," she whispered.

"No regrets?"

She slid her fingers through the dusting of dark curly hair on his chest. "Not recently," she teased, and was rewarded with a playful swat on the backside.

As she occasionally did, she responded in French, telling him that she'd like to have another child some day. With him.

"Are you going to tell me what you just said?"

"Oh, sometime."

"I understood one word."

"My, my, and what would that be?"

"Baby." His eyes were serious. "Molly, is there a possibility you could be…"

"Don't worry," she assured him. With money tight and the problems around the ranch still unsolved, no one needed to tell her that now wasn't the best time to have a child. Later, though, she'd bring up the subject again.

It was midnight before Molly fell asleep. She wasn't sure what woke her two hours later. The full moon shone like a beacon into the bedroom. Sitting up, she experienced the oddest sensation that something wasn't right.

After a moment, Sam, too, stirred and sat up.

"What is it?" he asked, his voice groggy with sleep. She shrugged. "I don't know."

"Did you hear something?"

"No. It's just…" She couldn't put it into words.

Sam sat on the edge of the bed and reached for his pants.

Molly threw on her housecoat and followed him downstairs. The first thing she noticed was that the front door was open.

On the hottest days of summer Gramps usually left it open to allow a breeze between his bedroom and the living room. But the evening had been cool with the promise of a rainstorm. The winds had come and then just as quickly shifted north.

As she went to close the door she saw him. Gramps had fallen asleep in his rocking chair. Sam stepped into the kitchen and turned off the light, then hurried through the house to check the other doors.

"Gramps," Molly said softly, sitting in the rocker beside him. "Wake up. It's time to go inside."

He looked so peaceful. Chatting with him, she

waited for Sam's return so her husband could help her guide Gramps to his bedroom.

"I love Sam. You knew I would, didn't you?" She rocked contentedly and glanced up at the full moon, now obscured by clouds. "You were so right."

She glanced over at Gramps and could have sworn she saw him smile in his sleep.

"Molly?" Sam called.

"Out here," she said softly. "Gramps fell asleep on the porch."

Sam joined her and gently shook Gramps, trying to wake him. After a moment he turned away and clutched one of the porch railings.

"Sam?"

He turned back and knelt in front of her, taking both her hands in his. "Molly." He kissed her fingertips and held her hands against his lips. "My love. Gramps isn't asleep. I'm afraid he's gone."

Twelve

Molly didn't sleep the rest of the night. She didn't even try. Instead, she sat on the porch holding the cameo Gramps had given her. His Molly's cameo. The one she'd worn at her own wedding. It seemed so unfair that he should die now. Her mind filled with a thousand regrets, begrudging every day she'd wasted before moving to Montana. If only she'd known sooner. The words echoed in her heart. *If only, if only, if only...* But her tears hadn't come yet.

To Molly's gratitude, Sam made the necessary phone calls as soon as the day began to lighten. The coroner was the first to arrive. He'd spoken briefly to Sam and asked her a couple of questions, but afterward she didn't remember either the questions or her responses. Later Mr. Farley from Ross Memorial stopped by to discuss the burial. Gramps had made his preferences clear in a letter he'd mailed to Ross Memorial a few months earlier. Mr. Farley had brought it with him. Gramps had stated that he didn't want money wasted on a funeral, and as for a service, if there was to be one, he wanted it private. Just his immediate family. Then, like an afterthought, he'd granted permission for Ginny to attend if she wanted, but no one else.

Once again Molly was glad to let Sam handle things.

When the burial had been arranged, Mr. Farley left with the promise that he'd be in touch shortly.

By far the most difficult task of the day was telling the boys. It astonished Molly that they'd both slept through the commotion that followed her discovery. Rather than wake Tom and Clay, she'd let them sleep. In the morning Clay came downstairs first, took one look at her and knew something was terribly wrong.

"What's going on?" he asked, standing in the middle of the kitchen, socks and sneakers dangling from one hand.

"It's Gramps," Molly said gently. "I'm afraid he's gone. He died last night."

Clay's face showed shock and disbelief. "He *can't* be dead!" her son insisted. "He was all right when I went to bed. We were on the porch together, and he was fine then."

Molly bit her lower lip to keep it from trembling. "I'm sorry, sweetheart, but it's true."

"It can't be!" Clay screamed. "Make her tell me it isn't true," he cried, turning to Sam. "He can't be—he told me about D-day and Normandy and the Battle of the Bulge. He lived through the war." Clay's face tightened with desire as he gazed at Sam, begging him to tell a different truth.

"I'm sorry, son." Sam shook his head.

With that Clay burst into tears and buried his face against Molly, sobbing so hard his entire body shook. She wrapped her arms around his thin shoulders, blinking back her own burning tears as the emotion seared through her, as fresh and painful as the moment Sam first told her.

"What's wrong?" Tom asked as he stepped into the kitchen. Sleep blurred his eyes, and his hair was uncombed and wild-looking. He paused, glancing from his brother to Sam and then her, his eyes filled with question.

Molly told him.

Once he realized Gramps was dead, Tom exploded out of the house, leaving the screen door to slam in his wake. He was gone for more than an hour, and when he returned he joined Molly on the porch, silently slipping into the empty rocker at her side. She longed for words to ease his pain, but could find none, so she remained quiet. It didn't matter. She knew he just needed to be close to her.

After about fifteen minutes he stood, his eyes red and puffy. Voice breaking, he said, "I was *proud* to be related to a man like Gramps."

Molly wasn't sure how Tom felt about being embraced just then, but she pretended not to remember that he was too cool to be hugged by his mother. She held out her arms to him and he bent down to hug her, hard. When he left, she watched him rub his forearm across his eyes. Molly cried then, uncontrollably. Cried till she thought she had no tears left.

She sat on the porch all day. Without asking, Sam brought her food and coffee every few hours. She drank the coffee but barely ate. Activity continued around her. Sam kept the boys occupied, granting her the opportunity to seek her own solace. By evening she'd found a certain peace. An acceptance of sorts.

She clung to that and kept it close to her heart, wanting to celebrate Gramps's life, not concentrate on his death. She refused to get swallowed up in the grief of his passing. It was what he would have wanted, and knowing that helped soothe the terrible ache of his loss.

Gramps had never been religious, but he was a man

of faith. Many an evening, he'd sat on this very porch with his worn Bible spread open in his lap, reading from the book of Psalms.

One night, shortly after the incident of the downed fence, Molly had found Gramps with his Bible. He'd looked up. "King David was a man who knew trouble," he'd told her. "Real trouble, and he said we aren't to lean unto our own understanding."

Molly wasn't sure what that meant, but it was the only time she could remember him commenting on anything the Bible had to say.

That night at dinnertime—their first at the ranch without Gramps—Molly made an effort to put a meal on the table. Her own appetite was still nonexistent. Picking fresh greens from the garden, she made a huge taco salad and set it in the middle of the table, instructing the boys to help themselves.

"Aren't you going to eat, Mom?" Clay asked.

"I will later when Sam returns," she said, but she wouldn't. Couldn't. Everything hurt just then. Her head. Her heart. Even her stomach.

Sam had run into town, for what she couldn't remember now. In fact, she could remember almost nothing of what had happened that day. Knowing Gramps's death was inevitable, Molly had prepared herself for it. Or so she'd believed. But now that the reality of it was upon her, she realized that it was impossible to ever feel ready for death, the death of someone you loved. Grief still came unabated. No matter how certain or even welcomed death might be, it was always a shock.

"You okay, Mom?" Tom asked, joining her on the porch after the sun had set. He sat on the top step, turning so he could study her. Clay came with him, silent and sullen, and held the puppy in his lap. Boris and Natasha curled up on the rug outside the door as if they, too, had come to give their farewells to Gramps.

She nodded. "I'd hoped we'd have more time with him."

"Me, too," Tom said.

"I wish you both could have known him better. He was a wonderful man." It hurt to talk and her fingers clenched and unclenched on the wooden chair arms.

"I'm glad for the time we had."

Her fourteen-year-old son's wisdom touched her heart. Tom focused on what he could be grateful for, instead of all he'd lost. He, too, had achieved a hard-won acceptance. He counted his blessings.

"He taught me to whittle and I can play cribbage now," Clay said.

Gramps had taught her the same things when she was about the same age.

"Last night he talked more about the war," Tom told her. "He told us about men dying even before they made it to land, their bodies bloating in the water."

Molly's hand reached for the cameo and gripped it hard. He'd called it his good-luck charm. He'd carried the cameo into battle with him, taking a small tangible piece of the love he shared with his wife. For protection. As a token of faith in the future.

"He talked quite a bit about dying and how it was nothing to fear," Tom added, as if remembering this for the first time. "He said that with some folks death can be a friend."

"A friend?" Molly knew what he meant but had never heard such talk from her grandfather.

"For those who'd made their peace with God," Clay said. "That's what he said. I think Gramps was ready."

"He talked about a lot of things last night," Tom said. "But mainly it was about the war and about your dad and his Molly."

The tears came again, unwanted. Molly hadn't meant to cry, not in front of her sons. She didn't want to upset them further.

"Mom…"

"I know, honey, I'm sorry. I can't seem to stop. I'm going to miss him so much." At least she wasn't alone anymore. At first Gramps's suggestion that she marry Sam had seemed an interference, an insult, but she knew this terrible void inside her would be ten times deeper if it wasn't for her husband. She accepted that Gramps was gone, but she would always miss him.

She held a handkerchief to her eyes. So many tears had been shed that her eyes ached and her nose was red and sore from blowing.

"I liked him," Clay said quietly. "He might have been old, but he knew a lot of stuff and he never treated me like a kid. Even when I made mistakes in cribbage, he never made me think I was dumb."

The burial service was held three days later. Afterward Sam, Molly and the boys stood at one side of the grave and Ginny stood across from them as the casket was lowered into the ground. The minister who'd married her and Sam said a prayer, then briefly hugged Molly and exchanged handshakes with Sam and the boys. Molly lingered, as did Ginny Dougherty, who repeatedly dabbed a tissue to her eyes.

"I'm gonna miss that crotchety old coot," Ginny said, and blew her nose loudly.

"We'll all miss him," Sam said. His arm rested across Molly's back, and she was grateful for his comfort and support. Molly didn't know what she would have done without him these past few days. He'd given her strength.

"We were neighbors for thirty years," Ginny continued, weeping softly now. "Walt and Molly stood with me when I buried Hank." She rubbed her eyes with one hand and took a couple of moments to compose herself. "Walt and me might not have agreed on a lot of things, but I knew if I ever needed a helping hand, he'd be there."

Ginny's tears came in earnest then, and she raised both hands to her face. "Damn, but I'm gonna miss him."

Molly stepped away from Sam and put her arms around the other woman. "It's going to be mighty lonely without Gramps around," she said, "especially with the boys starting school next week. Do you think you could stop by for tea one day? It'd be good to have a friend."

Ginny nodded and hugged Molly fiercely. "I never had children, you know. If I had, I would've wanted a daughter like you."

Molly savored the compliment. The older woman was a lot like Gramps—just as ornery and just as honest. And just as lonely.

"Would you like to come back to the ranch with us for dinner?" Molly asked.

Ginny shook her head. "No thanks, I've got to get back. Fred's on his own." She kissed Molly's cheek, then hurried to her truck, parked near the cemetery entrance.

As they left the graveyard, Molly realized that Ginny had been sweet on Gramps. She should've guessed it earlier. All the years they'd lived next to each other, watched out for each other, fought, argued and battled. And loved. Silently. Without ever saying a word to each other. Without ever a touch. They'd been the best of friends and the best of enemies.

The shadow-filled alley behind Willie's was deserted now that the tavern had closed for the night. Monroe sat in his car with the lights off and waited for Lance to show. He didn't trust his fellow Loyalist and considered him a loose cannon. In the past couple of months, Lance had grown even more unpredictable, impatient. It grated on Monroe's nerves. He wanted Lance gone, but Burns wouldn't hear of it.

The car door opened and Lance climbed into the front seat.

"You're late," Munroe muttered. He glanced at his watch, letting the man know he begrudged every one of those five minutes.

Not only was Lance out of uniform, he'd grown lazy. Any discipline had vanished from his personal hygiene and his attitude. His face bristled with a two-day beard and his fatigues were rank with body odor. His boots were unpolished, one of the laces broken. Monroe suspected he'd snuck off to attend another rodeo.

"I take it the old man's dead and buried?" Lance said.

"The service was this afternoon," Monroe confirmed.

"Did that lawyer cousin of yours convince his granddaughter to sell yet?"

Monroe wished to hell it was that easy. "Unfortunately, no, and now that she's married Dakota, we're forced to tighten the screws."

"You got any ideas?"

This was supposed to be Lance's area of expertise. The Loyalists had imported him from Idaho, reasoning that it was better if an outsider handled the dirty work, sparing Monroe any hint of suspicion. Other than to make contact with Monroe, Lance wasn't supposed to venture into town. The less seen of him the better. Only, he'd grown bored living in his wilderness camp and started hanging out with another Loyalist, playing pool and getting drunk.

"I thought you were supposed to be the idea man," Monroe snapped.

"I am. All I need to know is how far you want me to go."

Monroe gritted his teeth, trying to control his irritation. "Do what you have to do and don't bother me with the details, understand? And stay out of town."

"No need to lose your cool," Lance muttered, opening the car door.

The interior light came on, illuminating a section of the alleyway. Suddenly Monroe caught a movement out of the corner of his eye and jerked his head around. It took him a moment to locate the source.

Pearl. She'd crouched down behind the garbage dump in an attempt to hide. He wondered what she'd been doing there, but it went without saying that she was up to no damn good. The bitch needed to be taught a lesson. He'd make sure she kept her nose out of his business from now on. Before the night was over she'd be begging his forgiveness; anticipating that scene excited him. He hadn't seen near enough of Pearl lately, and obviously she'd forgotten some of the lessons he'd given her earlier. This was the type of work he relished best—putting a woman in her place. By the time he was through with her, she wouldn't be sneaking around and listening in on his conversations anymore.

"Who did this to you?" Russell demanded, studying Pearl's battered face. Fierce anger consumed him until he barely recognized the sound of his own voice. By God, whoever beat her would pay for this. She sat before him with both eyes swollen so badly he wondered how she could see out of them. The corner of her mouth had a jagged cut.

"Russell—"

"Tell me, dammit! I want to know." He paced her living room, too furious to sit still.

"It's not so bad," she said in an obvious effort to brush off his concern. It didn't work.

"Who?" he shouted again, his hands in tight fists at his sides. Russell had never been a violent man, but the rage he experienced now led him to believe that he was capable of brutality. Capable of anything.

Pearl lowered her head. "Please, it isn't important."

"It is to me."

He'd known something was wrong when she didn't show up at the cabin Sunday morning. He'd waited an hour and then gone searching for her, assuming her car must have broken down along the way. The cabin was a good fifty miles out of town, and on that isolated road, she could wait hours before someone came by. But he didn't find her, nor did he see her rattletrap of a car.

When he returned to the cabin, the message light was flashing on his answering machine. It was Pearl, telling him she wouldn't be able to come that Sunday and probably not the next one, either. Her voice had sounded odd, and after playing the message a second time, he was sure something was wrong.

Unconcerned about his reputation, he drove directly to Pearl's house. She hadn't wanted to let him in and did so only after he raised a fuss loud enough to call attention to his being there. Reluctantly she unlatched the door and he'd found her beaten and bloody.

"Russell, please, just go," Pearl said now. "I'll be fine, and in a couple of weeks, you won't even know I was hurt. I'll...we can continue just like before. Okay?" She tried to usher him to the door, but he'd have none of it. Again and again he'd asked her to marry him, and each time she'd refused. He couldn't understand it, couldn't fathom that she would choose this kind of life over the love they shared.

"I'm not leaving until we have this out," he insisted.

He could see that talking was painful for her. And her bruised swollen eyes—he could hardly stand looking at them. By all that was right she should be in a doctor's office, perhaps even a hospital.

"Please..."

"I can't pretend this didn't happen," Russell said, and continued his pacing. He rammed his fingers through his hair hard enough to tug painfully at the roots.

"Please...you're making me dizzy. Sit down." She gestured toward the sofa.

He sagged onto the ottoman, but couldn't look at her. Every time he did his stomach churned and he felt like vomiting.

She held a washcloth to the edge of her mouth, dabbing gingerly at the cut. "There's no reason to carry on like this," she said, dismissing her own pain. "These things happen now and then. It isn't pleasant, it isn't fun, but it's a fact of life. An occupational hazard, so to speak. I'm sorry it upsets you—I wish you hadn't come.''

She moved slightly, and her robe opened, exposing ugly bruises high on her shoulders. Dangerously close to her throat. It was almost as if her client had attempted to strangle her.

Russell's blood ran cold at the thought.

He loved her more than he'd realized. For months he'd pushed the reality of her occupation from his mind. It was easier to ignore the way she made her living than to face it, especially since Pearl steadfastly refused to discuss it. Instead, he'd concentrated on the time they shared every Sunday. But he couldn't ignore the truth any longer.

Drawing in a ragged breath, he looked at her, looked hard at the bruises and other injuries. ''We're getting married.'' He wasn't asking this time, he was telling her. He wasn't going to let Pearl put her life on the line again.

Her first reaction was to physically pull away. Her back went against the cushion, and slowly, one movement at a time, she seemed to become smaller and smaller, shrinking into herself. First she tucked her bare feet beneath her and drew her robe together, holding it closed. Then she wrapped her free arm about her waist.

''Did you hear me?'' Russell asked.

She turned her head away.

''Well?'' He watched her, waiting, wondering. Hoping.

When she did speak, her voice was almost inaudible. ''Men like you don't marry women like me.''

''*I* do.''

Her chin came up slightly and her words gained conviction. "Let me put it another way, then. Women like me don't marry, period."

"What is this? A rule of some kind?"

She refused to answer.

The silence seemed to last forever, but when she spoke again, he sensed a new resolve in her. The woman could be stubborn, he'd say that for her. "We've already been through this," she finally said. "I can't… I'm so sorry, but it just isn't possible."

"Why isn't it? Look at yourself, Pearl! Your face has been beaten to a pulp. You can't ask me to sit by and do nothing. If you won't tell me who hurt you, then at least let me offer you the protection of my name."

She gave him a small crooked smile and grimaced at the pain it caused her. Russell's gut tightened and the bile rose in his throat as he witnessed her discomfort. Feeling the other person's pain—this was what love did.

Slowly she shook her head. "I can't."

His frustration was nearly overwhelming. "Then explain it to me. At least help me understand. I love you and you love me. Marriage is what happens when people feel about each other the way we do."

"In case you haven't noticed, I'm not like other women." She looked him straight in the eye, and it was the hard-edged look of the woman he'd met all those months ago. "I'm a whore."

He could think of only one way to reach her, to get her to listen to reason, to trust him. With the truth. "I love you, Pearl—you know that. I have for months. I live for Sundays when I know I'll be spending time with you. You're all I think about. Okay, you're right, you're not like other women, but I don't *care.* I don't want anyone but you.''

She glanced away and he knew from the way her eyes glazed with tears that his words had touched her. She stiffened her shoulders and smiled slightly. ''I'm afraid you've confused great sex with love, Russell.''

''We met for weeks before we ever slept together,'' he reminded her. He knelt down in front of her and reached for her hand. She tried to snatch it away, and it was then that he noticed the large welt on her wrist. He grabbed her other hand and saw a similar welt. The son of a bitch had tied her up.

It hurt him to look at her injuries. ''Who did this to you?'' he begged again. He experienced the highly embarrassing urge to weep. She must have heard it in his voice, because she took hold of his shoulder and squeezed hard.

''Listen to me, please, and hear me this time. *It doesn't matter.*''

''I'm calling the sheriff.''

Pearl laughed out loud. ''Oh, please! Do you think he gives a damn about a hooker with an overfriendly john?'' she asked mockingly.

Russell glared at the ceiling and forcefully expelled his breath. ''I care. I can't do this. I can't sit back and see this happen to you. I can't love you like I do and not worry about the fact that you're being abused. I've looked the other way for too long.''

''Just forget about this, please. I'm all right. Really.'' Her eyes pleaded with him to drop his concern, along with his marriage proposal. In the past Russell had given in to her pleadings, but no more. Not when her life was at stake. Not when all she had to do was agree to marry him and let him love and protect her.

"I can't forget." He turned over her hand and kissed the inside of her wrist. The welt was red and ugly, and he felt the heat of it against his lips.

Pearl closed her eyes. "Please," she begged.

"I've never asked another woman to share my life. I'm asking you. I can understand that it might be uncomfortable for us in Sweetgrass. We'll move, and I'll set up a practice in another state. We'll start over, just the two of us."

She shook her head and seemed about to weep. "No. It just isn't possible."

"You can't make me believe this is the kind of life you want. I know better."

She raised her hand to her face, apparently forgetting that her eyes were bruised, and winced at the flash of unexpected pain. "This is something men have never been able to understand about women like me," she said in a half whisper. "I love what I do."

He knew she was lying.

"You might disagree," she went on, "but I provide a valuable service, and if it gets a little rough occasionally—well, that just comes with the territory. I take the beatings, along with the bonuses. You, Russell, were an unexpected bonus, so you see it all evens out in the end."

"I don't want to listen to any more of this." Especially when he knew she was lying. They were too close, too intimate, for him not to recognize that.

She clamped her hand around his wrist. Her grip was hard and relentless. "Listen, and listen carefully, because what you fail to understand, what most men like you can't accept, is that I do this by choice."

Russell yanked his wrist free of her grasp and bolted upright, angered by her lies and her attitude.

"I have a specialty, you know—then again perhaps you don't." She moistened her lips. "A lot of women are averse to it, but—"

"I've heard all about your specialty," Russell interrupted between clenched teeth.

She laughed as if his anger amused her. "You do? That surprises me because you've never asked for it."

"It's different with us."

"Is it? Are you completely convinced of that, or is there a tiny shred of doubt?"

"Pearl, this tactic isn't going to work. No matter how crude you are, it isn't going to convince me that you don't love me. I know how you feel."

"Because I gave you my body gratis," she said, and laughed. "It isn't often a girl like me gets to laze away a Sunday afternoon in a private getaway. Even a call girl needs time to breathe once in a while, and if all it costs is a freebie, then why not? You're pleasant company, and you were nice enough to teach me to read. You can't blame me if you got a little too...involved, can you? A girl like me is—"

"Stop!" he shouted. "Don't cheapen what we shared."

"Then don't make more of it than it was!" she snapped back.

His skin felt clammy even as a chill raced through his blood. He had to get away. Escape. Otherwise he was in danger of making an even bigger fool of himself. Not looking at her, he headed for the door.

"Someday you'll thank me for this," she whispered.

He could hear the regret in her words. It was enough to make him pause. Enough to give him hope. Frozen, he stood with his hand grasping her doorknob, his back to her.

"I learned my lesson with you," she called, her voice filled with pain. "I'm not handing out any more freebies."

Russell jerked open the door and walked out.

He managed to stay away from Pearl for all of two weeks, hoping each day that she'd have a change of heart, that she'd call him. She didn't. He reviewed their conversation over and over, and while he was certain she'd lied, her words had left ugly scars.

For the first time he doubted their love, and as the days passed and she didn't call him, those doubts grew into a feeling of bitterness. By the end of the second week he'd convinced himself that Pearl had played him for the fool he was. She couldn't possibly hold any tenderness for him and stay away this long.

Soon his pain turned to anger. Each morning when he gazed at his reflection in the mirror, he called himself a fool. His anger fed on itself and spread, became even larger.

When he could tolerate it no longer, he had his cousin set the appointment for him—the same way he had that first time. He was prompt, ringing her doorbell at precisely the arranged hour.

It did his ego good to see the surprise in her eyes when she opened the door. "Don't worry, I'm not going to make trouble with your john," he muttered, "because we're one and the same."

Her eyes were only a little puffy now and the bruises had faded. The gash on her lip had healed or, if it hadn't, was cleverly disguised with bright lipstick. She wore black hose and a sexy leather skirt that rode halfway up her thighs. The spike heels added a good four inches to her height. Her breasts spilled out of the halter top, which had to be two sizes too small.

She looked as if she wasn't sure what to do, as if the shock was too much for her.

"I decided to take you up on your offer."

She cast him a puzzled glance. "Offer?"

"I'm here for your specialty," he announced.

Her eyes widened as though he'd slapped her. A stunned silence followed his words.

"I—"

He pulled out his wallet and extracted a one-hundred-dollar bill. "My money's good, isn't it?" He'd practiced what he'd wanted to say for days, but now that the time had come, he realized he couldn't do it, couldn't humiliate and degrade her, because in doing so, he degraded himself.

He stuffed the bill back into his wallet. "Forget it," he whispered.

"Russell…"

Not wanting to hear what she had to say, he pushed past her and escaped, accompanied by the sound of her sobs.

Cleaning out Gramps's bedroom was like reliving the night of his death. Molly knew she had to do it; it was part of coping with grief. And she and Sam had decided to move into Gramps's downstairs bedroom; somehow the prospect was a comforting one.

Each drawer Molly opened revealed more evidence of his love for her and the children. She discovered her letters tucked away inside books and shirt pockets, reread so many times the edges had frayed.

Pictures of her and of Tom and Clay in various stages of their childhood were all over his room. He'd saved everything she'd ever mailed him. Every photo, every note, every drawing the boys had made. But it was reading his journal that tore her apart.

From the day his Molly had been laid to rest, he'd written his journal as a series of letters to his dead wife. He'd poured out his heart, described his loneliness, his hopes and his doubts. He wrote about how much he loved Molly and her boys, and his fear that his love might suffocate her if she decided to live with him. He spelled out his pain when she decided to stay in California.

Sitting on the edge of the bed, she started to weep and couldn't seem to stop. She wept over the wasted years, when all she'd done was write, instead of making the effort to visit. Not once had he chastised her. Not once had he asked her to come. He'd loved her unselfishly, completely. She broke into renewed sobbing as she realized that his run-down ranch and his one granddaughter were all he had to show for seventy-five years of living. His granddaughter and her sons.

"Mom." Tom walked into the bedroom.

She shook her head, telling him without words that she needed to be alone.

"Are you all right?"

She covered her mouth with her hand and nodded.

Tom hesitated, then took off at a run, hollering, "Sam! Sam, come quick!"

Knowing that her husband would be equally unnerved by this sudden attack of emotion, Molly made a concerted effort to curtail her sobs—and discovered it was impossible.

"She's gonna be sick if she doesn't stop crying," Tom said when Sam came rushing in through the living room.

Sam entered the bedroom slowly. "She'll be all right," he said as he sat down next to Molly. He gathered her in his arms, and she rested her face against his shoulder, letting him absorb her pain and loss.

"It's all right, honey, let it out." Gently he patted her back. "You've been holding it inside for two weeks now. Have a good cry."

Tom looked worried. "Should I get her something?"

"Like what?" Sam asked.

"I don't know. Tissue? Aspirin? If she doesn't stop soon, you're gonna need a dry shirt."

"Will you two kindly shut up?" Molly said through her tears.

"Gramps wouldn't want you to cry like this, Mom."

"Then he shouldn't have left his journal for me to read," she blubbered, scrubbing her cheeks with both hands.

"What's for dinner?" Clay said, walking into the room. He stopped abruptly and looked at his older brother. "Are Mom and Sam kissing again?"

"Of course not," Molly said, straightening. She drew in several deep breaths and squared her shoulders. "I'm all right now."

"Then what's for dinner?" Clay asked again.

"Food," Tom said, and ushered his brother out of the bedroom.

Molly gazed up at her husband, knowing her love shone from her eyes. She no longer felt she had to hide it. In a way, Sam was Gramps's final gift to her, and she knew without question that she loved him.

"When did Clay find us kissing?" he asked.

She blushed. "Probably the other morning." The first day of school, and her youngest son had awakened early. He'd stumbled into the kitchen to find Molly sitting in Sam's lap, the two them deeply involved in each other. Muttering under his breath, Clay had ignored them and popped bread in the toaster.

Sam had headed for the barn almost immediately afterward, but he'd snuck back into the house before he rode out for the day and stolen one last kiss. He was more openly affectionate these days, as they grew more comfortable with each other.

Sam followed her into the kitchen now. "I've got something to ask you, Clay," he said, clearing his throat. "Do you have a problem with me kissing your mother?"

Clay shrugged. "Not really."

"You, Tom?"

"It doesn't bother me. You can kiss her all you like. You're the one who married her."

Her son certainly had an eloquent way of putting things, Molly thought, rolling her eyes.

"When you asked us how we felt about you marrying Mom, you said, you know…" Clay looked from Molly to Sam, then back to Molly.

"You talked to the boys before we got married?" Molly asked him after dinner. Tom had cleared the table and Sam was helping her put leftovers away.

"Yeah. I figured they should have some say about me being their stepfather."

"Really. And how did they answer you?"

Sam chuckled and reached for the dish towel. "Tom said he was grateful someone was willing to marry you. He'd about given up hope."

Molly didn't believe him for a minute. Lifting her hands out of the soapy water, she flicked suds at him and laughed when they landed square in the middle of his chest.

He was about to retaliate when the phone rang. Sam glanced regretfully at the wall, then grabbed the receiver. "Hello," he said, still laughing as he flung the suds in Molly's direction.

Molly watched as the laughter abruptly left his eyes and he slammed the receiver back on the hook.

"Who was that?" she asked.

Sam was already halfway out the door. He turned toward her, his jaw taut. "Ginny. We've got a grass fire," he said. "We could lose everything. Get the boys and follow me."

Thirteen

Molly wondered what had started the fire—until Sam found a discarded gas can by the side of the road. He was convinced it had been deliberately set. From what he could determine, the blaze had started in some dry grass and spread within minutes. Thankfully, a shift in the wind had saved the house and barn from certain disaster. Using the tractor and shovels and beating out the flames with blankets, Sam, Molly, Ginny, Fred and the boys, plus members of the volunteer fire department, had stopped it before it roared toward the pasture where the herd grazed.

Exhausted from fighting the fire, smelling of smoke, her clothes and skin covered with soot and ashes, Molly trudged back to the house. The boys followed, too tired to squabble, and dragged their shovels behind them. The volunteer firefighters had already left, and so had Ginny and her cousin. The family had stayed in the field, checking to make sure there were no smoldering patches. When they reached the yard, Sam jumped down from the tractor, and placed his arm around her shoulder.

"You okay?" he asked, searching her face.

His concern and love gave her the energy to smile and offer him the reassurance he needed.

"I think it's time you called the sheriff, don't you?"

Molly asked as they sat at the kitchen table. The fire had frightened her. She'd thought…hoped…that they'd seen the end of this harassment. The other so-called incidents, while disastrous, hadn't been life-threatening. A fire was serious business, and as far as she was concerned it was time to bring in the authorities.

"Fine," Sam said. His mouth tightened. "Not that I expect Maynard to do anything."

"Why not?" Molly knew that for some reason the two men disliked each other, but she didn't want to believe the sheriff would allow his personal feelings to interfere with law enforcement.

"I just don't," was all Sam would say.

After they'd showered and changed clothes, Sam made the call.

Sheriff Maynard was apparently out of town on business; he didn't show up until the following evening. Molly was standing at the sink, washing the supper dishes, when she heard his car. She hurried over to hold open the screen door for him. "Thank you for coming, Sheriff."

"So you had some trouble out here yesterday?"

"We did. Clay, get Sam for me, would you?"

Her son nodded and hurried toward the barn.

"I took the liberty of contacting Chief Layman of the fire department. He'll want to question you and your…husband himself."

He hesitated over the word *husband* in a manner that suggested disapproval. Molly pretended not to notice. "Could I get you a cup of coffee while we talk?" she offered.

"That'd be real nice." He followed her to the

kitchen, sat down at the table and took a small notepad from his shirt pocket.

When Sam came into the house, he chose to lean against the counter, rather than sit at the table with Sheriff Maynard. They eyed each other malevolently.

Molly poured three mugs of coffee and carried the first two to Sam and the sheriff. Both men continued to stare each other down, behaving like junkyard dogs looking for an excuse to fight.

To his credit Sheriff Maynard remained civil. Molly couldn't say the same for Sam.

"You suspect the fire was purposely started?" the sheriff asked, directing the question to Molly.

Sam responded. "I don't think. I know."

"How's that?"

Sam folded his arms. "It doesn't take a genius to figure it out, seeing that it started at the road."

"It could've been an accident," Sheriff Maynard said. "People can be thoughtless and stupid. Someone could have tossed a cigarette out the window. What makes you think this was intentional? I find that hard to believe."

"Believe what you want," Sam returned stiffly, "but the fire wasn't started by any cigarette. Whoever did this left behind a gas can."

The sheriff made a notation on the pad. "No real harm done, though, was there?"

"As a matter of fact there was." Sam's voice grew harder. "I'm getting ready to sell off my herd. If the winds hadn't shifted when they did, we could have lost everything. So I'm telling you right now—"

"Don't raise your voice to me, Dakota, because it wouldn't take much for me to haul your sorry ass to jail." The threat was as shocking as it was real.

"What Sam means, Sheriff," Molly said, intervening quickly, "is that yesterday wasn't the first time something like this has happened. The fire is the latest in a series of such incidents."

"Have you reported everything else that happened?"

Sam looked away, his eyes as dark as a thundercloud.

"I phoned about the cut fence lines," Molly answered.

Sheriff Maynard nodded, studying Sam, regarding him with the same cautious distrust he might give a rattlesnake. When he spoke again, it was directly to Sam. "As I explained to your wife, Dakota, Chief Layman will be out to ask a few questions in the morning. I'll take the evidence back with me for possible prints."

"Whoever did this wouldn't be stupid enough to leave fingerprints. He left the can so we'd know the fire was deliberate."

"As I said, Chief Layman will look things over in the morning. I'm sorry about the fire, but let's just be grateful no one was hurt." The sheriff took a last swallow of coffee and stood, pushing his chair away from the table.

With no thank-you or word of farewell, Sam reached for his hat and headed out the back door. It slammed in his wake.

Molly resisted the urge to apologize for Sam's behavior. She didn't particularly like Sheriff Maynard, either, but he represented the law. Despite personality differences he was a professional, duly elected, and probably a good lawman.

Molly followed him out to his patrol car. "I'm sorry you and my husband don't see eye to eye," she said.

The sheriff opened his door and paused. "Sam and I seem to have gotten off on the wrong foot."

"Do you mind telling me why?" Sam was a lot of things, but unreasonable wasn't usually one of them. And she had to assume that Sheriff Maynard was a rational man, too.

"I think you'd best discuss that with your husband. I can tell you it started the day he arrived in Sweetgrass looking for a fight. With an attitude like that it didn't take him long to find one." He appeared to regret having said this much. "Molly, I wish you'd never married a—" He snapped his mouth closed. "I beg your pardon, it's none of my business."

A *what?*

"Sheriff, please, I need to hear this." Whatever he had to say might help her understand the animosity between the two men. If Sam was going to be part of the Sweetgrass community, he had to learn to put aside differences and make an effort to get along with everyone. The longer she was married, the more Sam reminded her of her grandfather, with his frequently uncompromising beliefs.

"Gramps was fond of Sam, you know," she felt obliged to tell him. "He was delighted when Sam and I got married."

Sheriff Maynard frowned. "That makes me wonder if Walter was aware of all the facts."

"What facts?"

The sheriff studied her long and hard before he spoke again. "Dakota didn't tell you, did he?"

"Tell me what?"

"That son of a bitch," the sheriff snarled.

"Sheriff, whatever it is, tell me!"

He hesitated long enough for her to know this wasn't going to be good news. "It'd be better if your husband had the common decency to tell you this himself before he married you. But seeing that he didn't, I don't trust him to tell you now, so..."

Molly braced herself.

Sheriff Maynard's eyes avoided hers. "Your husband has a prison record, Mrs. Dakota. He served two years in a Washington-state prison for second-degree assault, and left the state as soon as he was released from parole."

A gasp of shock slid involuntarily from the back of her throat. Molly reached blindly for something to support her.

"I'm terribly sorry, Molly. I don't know if Walt ever knew."

Her knees felt as if they were melting. She had to find somewhere to sit before they completely gave out on her.

"Thank you for telling me." Somehow she managed to get the words out.

"Are you going to be all right?" He placed a supportive hand at her elbow.

"Fine. I'm fine." Turning around, she slowly climbed the steps, feeling exhausted by the time she reached the door. She stumbled into the house and sank into a chair at the table, gripping the edge with both hands.

She'd been married twice. The first marriage had nearly destroyed her, and the second was threatening to do the same. Two husbands, years apart, and somehow she'd managed to marry two...criminals.

* * *

The anger and resentment toward Sheriff Maynard galvanized Sam. Sweat poured down his forehead as he pitched hay into the stall, working hard, ignoring his aching muscles.

When Molly suggested they phone the sheriff, Sam knew he was making a mistake. With another man, Sam might have put forth some effort to clear the air. But once Maynard made up his mind about someone, his opinion didn't change.

Sam realized his own anger was a form of self-defense. Sheriff Maynard didn't like or trust him, so Sam was unwilling to offer the hand of friendship. Sure as hell, the lawman would slap a handcuff around it.

The interview had gone poorly, and Sam wasn't sure who to blame. The sheriff appeared to be suggesting that the entire episode with the fire was accidental when anyone with a lick of sense could tell it wasn't. Even asking about the earlier incidents, he didn't reveal any real interest. Nor had he bothered to write down pertinent details, other than what Sam had told him about finding the gas can.

The poisoned water hole could have resulted in disaster; so could the damaged windmill. The pasture near Custer Hills was without a running stream, and the windmill pumped drinking water for the herd. Which was no small thing. Luckily Sam had been able to repair it quickly. He didn't want to consider what would have happened if he hadn't discovered it when he did. There'd been too many incidents like this over the summer. Too many not to believe foul play wasn't involved. The fact that there was already a buyer for the land on the off chance Molly wanted to sell made him even more suspicious.

The old man had been smarter than he realized in

deeding Sam those five hundred acres. His section sat squarely in the middle of the property. Not until after the funeral did Russell Letson get the final papers to Sam, and only then did he realize what Walt had done. Molly could sell the land, if worse came to worst, but her two sides of the property would be cut off from each other unless his land was included in the sale. Come hell or high water, Sam wouldn't relinquish those acres. In any event, he was prohibited from doing so by the terms of the agreement.

Setting the pitchfork aside, he left the barn and headed back to the house, fully expecting to get an earful from Molly. He wasn't blind to the looks she'd sent him when they'd spoken to Sheriff Maynard. She hadn't been pleased by his attitude. Well, he wasn't going to apologize. The sheriff was equally at fault.

Halfway between the barn and the house, Sam paused. He stood in the middle of the yard and surveyed the grounds, and even in the waning light he saw that the grass was charred and black. He shuddered; he could only be grateful that this latest disaster had passed them by.

He'd purposely delayed going back into the house, giving Molly time to cool down before he showed his face. The burns on his hands still throbbed, his back ached, and he wanted to be with his wife.

When Gramps had first suggested the marriage, Sam had been interested. The promise of land and cattle was one hell of an inducement. Molly could have resembled one of Cinderella's stepsisters and he still would've been tempted. What he hadn't understood at the time was how damn much he'd enjoy married life.

Sometimes when he woke in the middle of the night with Molly lying at his side, he was overcome with a sense of humility. Much of his life had been hard, devoid of tenderness. He'd served time in prison, although he tried to push that memory to the farthest reaches of his mind. In the years since, he'd drifted from one town to the next. One job to the next, until one ranch had looked much like another.

Then he'd met Walter Wheaton, a sick old man about to lose everything. The rancher had offered him a job when no one else wanted him. As it turned out, they'd needed each other. While he'd gratefully accepted Walt's proposal, Sam had suspected this would be the hardest he'd ever work for anyone, and he'd been right.

But he'd gained so much—a home, a wife, a family. His heart seemed to expand in his chest. He'd given up on love, readily admitting that he'd never understood it or experienced it. Until Molly… This was supposed to be a marriage of convenience, not of love. He and Molly had never said the word to each other, had never discussed how their feelings had changed. It didn't matter. He knew they had.

Sam knew he was in love with Molly.

The attraction between them was only part of it. A pretty fantastic part, to tell the truth. Their lovemaking was the most incredible of his life, and it had nothing to do with technique. It was all about *feeling*. He loved Molly, loved her with an intensity that actually hurt.

He'd never been one to indulge in public displays of affection; such exhibitions embarrassed him. Behind closed doors was another matter entirely.

A month was all it had taken. One month as a married man, and Sam found himself looking for reasons to touch Molly. Reasons to linger in the kitchen after the boys left to catch their school bus—just so he could steal a kiss from her. He enjoyed sneaking up behind her when she was washing dishes and slipping his hands beneath her blouse, filling his palms with her breasts. He loved the scent of her, the feel of her, everything about her. Oh, sure, she put up a token protest, but she enjoyed those times as much as he did.

Other than that first night, they'd never really argued, and he was glad. Sam didn't know if he could bear to have her angry with him. He needed her in his life too damn much to risk endangering their relationship.

He glanced at his watch, wondering if she'd already gone to bed. At the thought a smile curved his lips. He couldn't wait to get into bed...with Molly. He suddenly felt a lot less tired.

Taking the steps two at a time, he hurried into the house. Molly stood at the kitchen counter, packing Tom and Clay's lunches for school.

"Where are the boys?" he asked.

"Upstairs."

He caught a slight coolness in her response, but let it go. She slapped a slice of bread down on top of another with enough force to flatten both pieces. Sam hesitated. "Is something wrong?"

"You tell me."

He sighed and walked slowly toward her. She was still angry about that scene with the sheriff. Okay, so maybe he'd overreacted. It wouldn't have hurt to be a bit friendlier to Maynard. If it would keep the peace, Sam would admit to being at fault.

"Does this have to do with Sheriff Maynard?" he asked, maintaining his composure. He'd made a mistake on their wedding night when he'd allowed her anger to fuel his own. If he didn't let his pride get in the way, maybe they could settle this.

"No."

"No?" Her answer took him by surprise.

She whirled around, and her eyes flashed with indignation and another emotion he couldn't identify.

"You might have told me." Each word was a bitter accusation.

"Told you what?"

"Don't pretend you don't know." She opened the refrigerator and shoved the mayonnaise jar inside. It slammed against the pickle jar and toppled the plastic container of ketchup.

Sam couldn't remember ever seeing her like this. "Molly?"

"How about the truth, Sam? Didn't you think I had a right to know about your prison record? What hurts—what *really* hurts—is that you knew about Daniel and how...how difficult it was for me to tell you my ex-husband was in prison...and you didn't say a word." A sandwich went into the brown paper bag and Sam pitied whichever boy had to eat it.

"I tried to tell you," he argued. "That day we—"

"Don't," she said fiercely. "Don't you dare try to squirm your way out of this."

"It's the truth," he said with enough vehemence to give her pause. "Think back to the day we applied for the wedding license."

She squinted as if deep in thought.

"On the ride into town. I started to tell you, and you stopped me and made this long speech about the past being over and how it'd be best if we both put it behind us and started again."

"I was talking about old lovers!" she flared. "You

can't honestly believe I shouldn't know about a felony record. Second-degree assault, Sam. You tried to kill someone and you just conveniently forgot to tell me that before our wedding.''

"I didn't forget. I—"

"You deliberately chose to hide it from me! Which leads me to wonder what else you haven't told me.''

"You know everything about me—well, not about my time in prison, but everything else.'' Despite his best intentions, he was fast losing ground and with it his patience. Molly had tried and convicted him without so much as asking the particulars. "As far as I'm concerned you *chose* not to hear it.''

Silence throbbed between them. He stood on one side of the kitchen and she on the other, but the distance between them might have been the entire state of Montana.

"I think you should leave,'' she said finally.

"Leave?'' She had to be joking. Apparently she'd failed to remember that they were getting close to roundup. Their entire livelihood was at stake. If ever she'd needed him, it was now. Then there was the matter of the land he owned, deeded to him at the time of their marriage. Land he'd fight to keep.

"Move, then—back to the foreman's house.''

"You *are* joking, right?'' He prayed she was, but one look said otherwise. "Okay, I'll admit you had a right to know. I should've said something before you married me. I meant to tell you, but hell, I'm not proud of having served time, and I'd prefer to put it behind me. If you're waiting for me to apologize, then I'll do it. I'm sorry, Molly.'' It wasn't easy, but he managed to choke out the words, hoping that would satisfy her.

"I feel like such a fool,'' she said miserably. "You

didn't tell Gramps, either, did you? He'd never have let me marry another criminal.'' She turned and leaned heavily against the kitchen counter, bracing her hands on the edge.

Feeling wretched and angry at her unfairness, Sam took one step toward her and stopped. He'd done his damnedest to explain, to apologize, but he wasn't getting down on his knees and begging. If she wanted him gone, then fine, he'd leave—just long enough for her to miss him.

He walked out of the kitchen and slammed the door so she'd know he was going. Half hoping she'd race after him and beg him to stay, Sam climbed into his truck. To be on the safe side, he sat there for a moment or two, just to make sure Molly didn't have a change of heart.

She didn't.

With nowhere else to go, Sam drove to the same tavern he'd gone their wedding night. But he wasn't in the mood to drink. Being stupid enough to think whiskey would solve his problems was exactly what had landed him in jail; that wasn't going to happen again. Sam considered himself a fast learner. Anger and alcohol didn't mix.

Willie's smelled of stale cigarette smoke and beer. He recognized a couple of cowhands who were playing a game of pool in the corner. The music was too loud, the conversation too boisterous. Almost everyone here was looking for a good time.

The only thing Sam wanted was a dark corner to sit in for a while. To think and brood and figure out a way to get Molly to see reason. Dammit all, just when he thought everything was going well, this had to happen.

That bastard Maynard couldn't resist telling her, could he?

He claimed the stool at the farthest end of the bar and let it be known that he wasn't seeking company.

He'd been nursing his beer for an hour or so when he saw her. The hooker who'd talked him into returning to the hotel on his wedding night. It might have saved him a whole lot of heartache if he hadn't gone back; at least, that was the way he felt now. Any other night he might have greeted her and thanked her for the best damn advice anyone had ever given him.

Feeling his attention, she swiveled around and held his look. It took her a moment to recognize him. As soon as she did, her face relaxed into an easy smile. It wasn't a hooker's smile, either, but one of—hell, he didn't know—friendship, he guessed.

When her potential customer didn't pan out, she made her way across the room to where he sat.

"How ya doing, cowboy?"

He shrugged.

"Still married?"

He wasn't sure the marriage would last beyond this night, but for the moment he could answer her honestly. "You might say that."

"How's the missus?"

"Madder'n hops on a griddle."

She cocked one expressive eyebrow. "Don't tell me you had another tiff?"

"Looks that way." He glanced down at his near-empty mug. "My fault this time."

"You gonna tell her that?"

"I already did, but she's really pissed off. I don't blame her. Thought I'd give her time to cool off."

She smiled. "Good idea."

"How're you doing?" he asked just to keep the conversation going. He felt lost and more than a little lonely. Being alone had never bothered him until he married Molly, and now it was as if…as if he wasn't complete without her. "It's Pearl, isn't it?"

She nodded. "I'm doing so-so," she said.

"Business good?"

"Fair." She brushed a strand of bleached blond hair away from her face, and he noticed the dark shadows beneath her eyes. They were prominent enough that makeup couldn't completely disguise them.

"Anything I can do to help?" Maybe he wasn't such a fast learner, after all. It was helping a woman that had landed him in jail that first day in Sweetgrass. But dammit, he *owed* Pearl.

Sam wanted to believe he wouldn't have taken her up on her offer the night of his wedding. He didn't think so, but the mood he'd been in…he just didn't know. What she'd done was a generous thing. He'd never heard of a hooker who'd suggest a client go back to his wife.

"I…" She shook her head. "No, but thanks. It's sweet of you to ask."

The door opened and a couple of rough-looking men, dressed in fatigues, walked in. Pearl's attention flashed to them. Potential clients, Sam guessed, but her reaction said otherwise. She whirled around and Sam noted she'd gone pale beneath her makeup.

"I changed my mind, cowboy," she said, her voice trembling. "If you still want to help me, you can."

Sam set his mug down on the bar. "What do you need?"

She bit her lower lip. "A way out of here. I don't want them to see me."

Sam didn't hesitate. "You got it." He wrapped his arm around her as if they were longtime lovers and, using his body as a shield, escorted her toward the door. The bartender glanced over in surprise, but said nothing. The two men climbed onto bar stools, and if they noticed Sam and the woman leaving, they took no heed.

Not knowing what had given Pearl such a fright, Sam thought it prudent to drop her off somewhere safe.

"Where do you want to go?" he asked. "A friend's house?"

"No." Her short laugh was unexpected. "Call girls don't generally have a lot of friends."

"What about other...you know, other girls like you."

"Not in this town, honey. It's every girl for herself."

This was a world Sam didn't know and had no desire to explore. "Where do you want me to drive you?"

He was all the way down Front Street before she answered. "Home, I guess." She gave him the address, which was directly behind Willie's, so he circled back.

"Are you sure it's safe there?"

"I've got protection," she said, "and they know it."

Sam wanted to do more for her, but he'd learned the hard way that he should just hightail it out of the area before whatever was going down got messy. He'd done his good deed for the night.

He pulled up in front of the address she'd given him. She was about to open the door and climb out when she surprised the hell out of him by throwing her arms around his neck and hugging him tight.

"What was that for?" he asked.

"A thank-you. Now go home to your wife and tell her how sorry you are. If she's smart, she'll forgive you. Decent men aren't all that easy to find, and you're one of them.''

"Thanks.''

She got out of the pickup and he waited until she was safely inside the house and had turned on the lights before he drove off.

She'd given him good advice on his wedding night, and there wasn't any reason to believe her words of wisdom wouldn't work this time. With a renewed sense of hope Sam drove back to the ranch. At least the dogs were glad to see him.

The house was dark and quiet when he entered. Molly must be in bed. Sam was glad; it would be easier to reason with her there. He thought so, anyway. He tiptoed into the bedroom. The moonlight showed Molly's still form, and her slow, even breathing told him she was asleep.

Stripping off his clothes, he lifted the covers and got in beside her.

"I'm home, Molly,'' he whispered, and slid his arms around her waist. His hand crept up, sought her breast. Probably not the wisest move, but holding her like this had become habit.

Molly sighed and snuggled closer.

"Did you miss me, sweetheart?'' he murmured, and gently nibbled at her ear.

Her immediate response gave him a world of hope. Rolling onto her back, Molly wound her arms around his neck. Then she did that thing with her tongue, tickling the hollow of his throat. Goose bumps spread down his arms and legs. "Oh, baby…'' he whispered "I think we should talk, don't you?''

Not answering, she clung to him.

"On second thought we can talk anytime.'' He eased

his leg between hers and was about to kiss her full on the lips when it happened.

The willing pliant woman in his arms went stiff, then bolted up and shoved him away. "Where have you been? Oh, God, you were with another woman! I can smell her all over you!"

Fourteen

Russell Letson's heart stopped cold. He read the head-lines again, certain there'd been some mistake. This couldn't be real! The agony was as fierce as anything physical, perhaps more so.

The paper said that Pearl was dead.

He covered his eyes with one hand in a futile effort to force the fog of pain from his mind. He needed to think, to assimilate what the words said and what he could make himself believe, make himself accept.

Again he read the article, which took up half the front page of the regular Wednesday edition. The *Sweetgrass Weekly* rarely had a murder to write about. Even a murder without a body was big news. The door to Pearl's house had been left open for several days, and when a neighbor had gone to investigate, she dis-covered the place had been ransacked. It was as though a tornado had been let loose inside, she'd said. Blood splattered the walls, and a deep crimson stain was found on the bed, leaking through to the mattress. So much blood. Dear God, had she suffered?

Bile rose in his throat, and thrusting the newspaper aside, he closed his eyes and drew in several deep breaths. To his amazement he felt tears in his eyes. *Sweet Jesus, please, don't let her have suffered.*

He loved her. He'd known it long before he'd seen

her eyes swollen shut and the bruises that marked her upper arms and neck. She'd rejected him, and the pain of that rejection had driven him away, even when he knew she'd lied. Almost everything she'd said to him that Sunday was a lie. What he'd never been able to figure out was why she believed it was necessary.

He'd hoped she'd see reason, but then he'd lost patience and ruined everything. The night he'd gone to her and treated her like a whore had killed any tenderness she might have felt for him.

Ashamed and defeated, Russell hadn't seen Pearl since. But his thoughts had been with her every minute of every day while he tried to sort out what to do next, how to approach her and ask her forgiveness. He'd planned to talk to her, convince her they could make a good life together, if she'd only give them a chance.

But he'd waited too long and now it was too late.

Pearl was dead.

In time someone would find her decomposed body, cast aside like so much garbage on the side of a country road. Perhaps her killer had had the decency to bury her somewhere. He prayed that was the case.

Dear Lord, not Pearl, please not Pearl.

Once he'd composed himself enough to reach for the phone, Russell dialed Sheriff Maynard's office to make a few discreet inquiries.

"Any leads?" he asked in a crisp professional tone, as if a murder case was a routine matter.

Maynard didn't sound pleased to hear from him. "None yet, but we'll eventually find whoever was responsible."

Russell had never felt anything like this need, this all-consuming drive for justice. He'd gone into law for a number of reasons, none of which had much to do with justice, but in the blink of an eye that had all changed. The minute he'd read the headlines, justice—and punishment—took on the utmost importance.

"Then the killer left evidence behind?" Russell pressed, despite the lawman's obvious reluctance to discuss the case. They knew each other well, and Maynard owed him this.

"There's always evidence."

"Who was her pimp?" Russell demanded. If anyone knew, it was the sheriff. He tried to sound as if the matter were one of casual interest. Asking these questions was bound to lead Russell to potential suspects. If he did nothing else in this life, he'd make sure that whoever murdered Pearl paid for his crime.

"Listen, Russell, I can't talk about this case. Not yet. You'll hear the details as soon as I have them. Now stop pestering me. I've got work to do." He paused, then asked, "Why all the curiosity? How well did you know her, anyway?"

The last thing Russell needed was to become a suspect himself. "Every guy in town knew her, didn't he? You did yourself, right?" he asked, making light of his preoccupation with the crime.

The sheriff laughed. "Knew her intimately, you mean," he joked. "Every cowhand in town slept with her at one time or another. Either that or he was a saint. The lady had a body and knew how to use it. That's what makes cases like this so damned difficult. My guess is that her john got a little too rambunctious and things went further than he intended."

Russell stopped breathing to help prevent the mental picture of a man abusing Pearl from forming in his mind. It didn't work, and he was tormented with what her last minutes must have been like.

"I'll say this, though," the sheriff murmured. "I don't think I've ever seen so much blood."

"Is there any chance she could be alive?" He wanted desperately to believe there was a possibility Pearl had survived the beating and like an injured animal had run off to hide.

"I suppose there's a chance," the sheriff admitted after a moment. "But my guess is she's dead. Hard to see how anyone could lose that much blood and survive."

Russell's throat felt like he'd swallowed the cotton in the top of his vitamin bottle. It hurt to breathe. "Why would the killer take away the body?"

Maynard snickered as if to say the question was unworthy of a response. "Think about it. Physical evidence. Anyone with half a brain isn't going to leave a corpse behind at the scene of a crime. Not these days. Why give investigators an edge?"

Russell nodded, surprised he hadn't realized that himself. "Right."

"I'll let you know more when I can."

At this point Russell didn't care how much his curiosity left him exposed. "I want to know everything. Find the bastard. Do whatever it takes, but find the bastard." His hand trembled as badly as his voice by the time he replaced the telephone receiver.

For two days Russell didn't sleep more than a few minutes at a time or eat anything at all. Whenever he closed his eyes, he saw Pearl as he had the last time they'd been together. Her eyes had been bright with unshed tears as she called out to him. Unwilling to listen, he'd turned his back on her and walked away. In those last moments he'd destroyed any hope of reconciliation.

Now he'd have to live with that for the rest of his life, and he didn't know if he could.

Although he made a pretense of working, if anyone had asked him what he'd done, Russell wouldn't have been able to say. He'd been in the office all week, but he'd written no letters, prepared no legal briefs, talked to no clients. He'd had his secretary cancel his appointments. For hours each day he sat and stared into space. His secretary seemed convinced he had the flu. He let her believe what she wanted; it saved him from having to invent excuses.

The buzzer at his desk pulled him out of his reverie. "Yes," he said, resenting the intrusion.

"Mr. Sam Dakota's here to see you. He says it's urgent."

Russell wearily rubbed his face. Instinct told him to send the man home; he was in no shape to offer legal advice. "Tell him I'm already booked solid." A complete lie, but that should let Roberta know how much he wanted her to turn the rancher away.

"I'm sorry, Mr. Letson, but he insists on speaking to you personally. He's very persistent and says it's of the utmost importance."

Russell's head drooped slightly, the weight of the decision almost more than he could bear. "Send him in," he said finally. He'd listen to whatever was troubling Sam, then advise him to hire another attorney.

The door opened and his secretary let Sam into the office.

Russell gestured toward the chair on the other side of his desk, and Sam took a seat. He seemed nervous, sitting on the edge of the cushion and holding his hat with both hands. The first thing Russell noticed was how pale the rancher looked—but then he suspected he wasn't exactly the picture of health himself.

"What can I do for you?" Russell asked when Sam didn't immediately speak. For someone who'd been hell-bent to talk to him, he was taking long enough to get down to it.

"I wasn't sure where else to go or who to call," Sam told him with obvious reluctance. "I don't trust the sheriff, and the bartender and four or five others at Willie's are bound to have seen me and what the hell—" He leaped to his feet and walked over to the window. "I have a feeling deep in my gut that I'm going to end up charged with the murder of that poor woman."

Russell felt his blood stir for the first time since he'd read the newspaper headline. "Murder?"

Sam turned around to face him. "I swear by everything I hold dear that I didn't lay a hand on her."

Russell's blood wasn't only stirring, it was surging in his veins. "You were with Pearl the night she died?" His voice rose with each word, although he spoke slowly and clearly.

"I spent time with her," Sam admitted, "but not the way you think."

"Then explain it to me." His voice was cold, hard, as he stared at the other man, seeing him in a new light.

"Molly and I argued," Sam was saying. "She found out about my prison record." He lowered his head.

Russell's gaze narrowed as he studied the man closely. Maynard had told him about it shortly after Walt hired Dakota, but it surprised him that Molly hadn't known.

"Molly—I should've told her, I know that now. I admit I was wrong to go through with the wedding without disclosing my past." His eyes met Russell's. "I love my wife."

The regret on Sam's face told Russell the truth of his words. "Get back to the part having to do with Pearl," he instructed, not wanting Sam to get side-tracked by his marital problems.

"I met Pearl a couple of months earlier," Sam explained, again with a certain reluctance, "but not, uh, on a professional basis."

Had Pearl entertained other men the way she had him? Russell wondered. A rush of jealousy set his nerves on edge. Loving her the way he had made the thought of anyone else sharing that special closeness intolerable. He'd loved her and she'd loved him. What she'd done with her clients had nothing to do with the feelings between them.

"I met her the night Molly and I got married."

"You were with Pearl on your wedding night?" This was beyond real. Dakota honestly couldn't expect Russell to believe that!

"I met her at Willie's," Sam explained, his expression tightly controlled, revealing none of his thoughts. "Molly and I..." He paused, looking uncomfortable. "Let me just say that Molly and I didn't see eye to eye on a certain issue and I left the hotel in a huff."

"And drowned your sorrows in a bottle of beer at Willie's."

"Something like that," Sam admitted. "That's where I met Pearl."

His gaze roved about the room in an agitated way that might have suggested guilt, but Russell could see that Sam was genuinely distressed. His attorney's instinct told him Sam wasn't the one who'd killed Pearl; if it turned out he was wrong, Russell figured he'd save the courts a lot of trouble and expense and see that justice was carried out himself.

Dakota continued with his story, explaining how Pearl had sent him back to his wife. Russell's heart tightened when he realized what a generous thing she'd done for a stranger.

"You'd never seen her before that night?" he asked.

"Never."

Russell believed him. He stared openly at the rancher; Sam's own gaze didn't waver, which he considered a good sign.

"What did you do with her the night she was killed?"

"I gave her a ride home."

"Why?" He couldn't quite keep the suspicion out of his voice. What man played taxi driver for a hooker unless he had an ulterior motive?

Sam braced himself. "I know it sounds incredible, and I can't think of a single reason for you to believe me, but I swear this is the truth. I met her at Willie's again and she seemed a bit down. So because she'd been kind to me, because I liked her, I asked if there was anything I could do for her, and she asked for a ride home."

"Any particular reason?"

"Two unsavory characters came into the tavern and she didn't want them to know she was there."

"Did you get a good look at either of them?"

Sam shook his head sadly. "The lights were dim, and I paid more attention to shielding Pearl than to studying their faces."

"Did anyone see the two of you leave together?"

"Four, possibly five others."

Russell sat back and tried to absorb what he'd learned. "What about outside the tavern?"

"A couple of guys in the parking lot, but that's about it."

Again Russell paused, mentally picturing the setup at Willie's. He hadn't been in there in months. Willie's was where Pearl had sought out customers, and knowing that, he'd avoided the place. Not that he'd ever gone there much.

"Has Sheriff Maynard questioned you yet?"

"No, but he will," Dakota said with an ironic sort of conviction. "Let's just say the sheriff would be delighted with an opportunity to pin this murder on me."

"And you didn't do it?"

"You're damn right! I didn't have anything to do with it."

In his heart he recognized that the rancher was probably guilty of nothing more than poor judgment.

"What about Molly?" Russell asked.

The look in Sam's eyes when he responded was a familiar one to Russell; he saw it every time he saw his own reflection. Pain. Deep desolate pain. "She only speaks to me when necessary," Sam told him. "I don't know what she believes—then again, maybe I do."

"Have you spoken to her about this?"

He shook his head. "I don't know how... I'm not entirely sure she's made the connection. She smelled Pearl's perfume on me, but she has no way of knowing the woman I was with that night was the woman who was murdered. I've tried to come up with a way of explaining what happened and I can't. You're the only one I've talked to about this."

"You made the right decision in coming to me first," Russell said.

"If worse comes to worst, will you represent me?" Sam asked, and his dark brooding gaze refused to release Russell's.

"I'm not a criminal attorney. You'd be better—"

"You're the only one I trust."

Russell hesitated. Pearl had trusted him, too, and he'd single-handedly destroyed that. Sam Dakota would do well to look elsewhere for legal representation. In his present state of mind, he wouldn't do the man a damn bit of good.

"Will you?" Sam pressed.

Russell avoided eye contact. "God's own truth, I don't know. Let's cross that bridge when we come to it."

Sam hesitated and then nodded. "Be warned. That bridge is well within sight."

The alley behind Willie's was dark and deserted as Monroe waited for Lance. His mind was churning with the recent events involving Pearl Mitchell. Her body hadn't been found, and while he hadn't verbalized his suspicions, he fully suspected Lance was the one responsible. Killing a valuable piece of Loyalist property was just the kind of thing he'd come to expect from that troublemaker.

For once Lance was on time. He opened the car door and slid quickly inside.

"You heard about the fire?" he asked. "At Dakota's?"

"I heard," Monroe confirmed. "Do you have any other brilliant ideas?" It was difficult to keep the sarcasm out of his voice.

"A few."

"Perhaps you'd better clear them with me."

Lance's eyes narrowed. "You don't think I can do the job? Then I suggest you try it yourself. Those two are the stubbornest *luckiest* damn pair I've ever seen."

"I just might." This wasn't the first time Monroe had thought to take matters into his own hands, especially since he was dealing with a man he considered completely incompetent.

The silence between them was strained with tension. "I'm going after their weakest link next," Lance said.

"What's that?" Monroe demanded.

"What it is with any family." Lance was smiling now. "The kids."

"You don't look your normal perky self," Ginny commented when Molly brought her a tall cold glass of lemonade, then joined her at the kitchen table. Ginny had dropped by unexpectedly, taking Molly at her word. Her timing was perfect; if ever Molly needed a friend, it was now.

"I've been feeling a bit under the weather," was all Molly would admit. Pride being what it was, she found it difficult to announce that her marriage of less than two months was a failure. She could barely look at Sam. He'd lied to her, misled her and worst of all cheated on her. It was as though she'd searched out and married Daniel's twin brother, she thought bitterly.

Molly's stomach twisted in a knot of pain. She knew how to choose men, all right. From the frying pan into the fire—that was her. When it came to husbands, she seemed to have a knack for choosing the most-likely-to-hurt-her candidates.

What wounded her most was that Sam hadn't bothered to deny he'd been with another woman. She'd ranted and raved and carried on like a fishwife, but all he'd said was that she could believe what she wanted. Which had made Molly all the more furious. He came home smelling like a whorehouse, and *she* was the one who was supposed to feel guilty?

"Sit down, honey," Ginny advised. "What's wrong?"

To Molly's utter humiliation her eyes filled with tears.

"You want to talk about it?" Ginny asked with a gentleness Molly had rarely heard in the other woman's voice.

She shook her head.

"I suspect you're worried about the price of beef," Ginny murmured, reaching for a cookie. "I'm telling you, it can't get much worse than this."

Molly didn't need any other troubles, but they seemed to come in droves. The cattle were ready for market, and the price per pound was several cents less than it had been the year before. The middlemen were making huge profits and in the process destroying the independent rancher.

As if there weren't enough problems in her life, the current slump in beef prices meant they wouldn't have enough money to meet their accrued expenses. Without a loan or some other way of paying the bills, Molly didn't know what they'd do. It was just one more trouble along with everything else—only the *everything else* seemed more pressing just then.

Ginny leaned over and grabbed her hand. "What's wrong, Molly?" she asked again. "Don't be afraid to tell me. It doesn't take a four-eyed snake to see that something's troubling you real bad."

That was when Ginny's kindness finally reduced Molly to sobs. She covered her face with both hands

and wept as if her entire world had shattered hopelessly.

What amazed Molly was that, as she blubbered out
the sorry tale, Ginny seemed to understand every word.
She told her neighbor about the squabble—but not
what they'd fought over—and how Sam had come
home smelling of expensive French perfume. He'd
been with someone else, Molly was convinced of that.
He'd betrayed her.

"You can't really think Sam would cheat on you,
Molly!"

"I...I don't know what to think anymore," Molly
confessed.

"Hogwash. You married him, didn't you?"

"Yes, but—" She'd married Daniel, too.

Ginny didn't allow her to finish. "That man's so
crazy about you he can't see straight. The minute you
come into view his eyes follow you like a hawk watching a prairie rabbit. He'd no more seek out someone
else than he'd court a rattlesnake."

"But..." Molly hesitated. Ginny didn't know all the
details, and Molly couldn't tell her. "He misled me
about his past." She inhaled a quavering breath and
continued. "It's true I told him this was a fresh start
for us both, but I certainly expected him to tell
me...certain things."

"Certain things?"

Molly twisted the damp tissue in her hands and
looked away. "Sam's...got a prison record."

"Oh, that. I know all about it. Walt told me," Ginny
surprised her by saying.

"Gramps *knew?*"

"Course he did. Do you think he'd let you marry

any man without knowing everything there was to know about him first? You were his only kin.''

"But I assumed… I thought…''

Ginny rubbed her forehead as she mulled over this latest bit of information. "It makes sense, doesn't it?''

"Sense?'' Molly repeated.

"Sam not telling you. The boy was afraid. Figured if you knew he'd done time, you wouldn't have married him. That doesn't sound like a man who'd step out on his wife first chance he got, now does it?''

"Sure he wanted to marry me! Gramps offered him that land and those cattle, and—''

"Fiddlesticks. That land was incentive, all right, and probably got Sam to thinking about marriage, but that *wasn't* the only reason he married you. He was interested in you right off—I could see it and so could Walt. Not having much time left, Walt did the only thing he could. He hurried the two of you along, is all.''

Molly desperately wanted to believe Sam loved her. These past weeks—before the night of the fire—had been the happiest of her adult life. The thought that it had all been a lie hurt more than anything she'd ever faced, including Gramps's death.

Ginny took a long swallow of her drink. "Don't be a fool, Molly Dakota, and make the same mistake as me. I loved your grandfather for longer than I care to admit. We could've enjoyed a few good years together, but we were both too stubborn and set in our ways to let the other know. That was the reason we bickered. We both knew the minute we stopped fighting we'd be making love, and it put the fear of God into us.'' The older woman sniffed loudly, dabbing at her eyes. "Damn allergies,'' she muttered and blew her nose.

"Oh, Ginny.''

"Trust him, Molly. Walt did, and he was the best judge of character I ever knew. I swear to you that you won't be sorry."

Ginny left soon afterward, and as Molly waved her off, she noted that Sam's truck was back. He hadn't told her where he was headed that afternoon, and she hadn't asked. They weren't exactly on speaking terms. He ignored her except for the most basic conversations about ranch or household matters, and she did the same with him.

Still standing in the back doorway, Molly saw Tom and Clay trudging down the long drive, with Clay's half-grown dog trotting beside them; the school bus dropped them off at the end of the quarter-mile ranch road, where Bullwinkle faithfully waited for Clay. Molly had snacks ready and waiting. Both boys acted as if they were half-starved whenever they walked in the door after school.

"You and Sam still fighting?" Clay asked as he grabbed his lemonade and two chocolate-chip cookies.

"We aren't fighting, exactly," she murmured. She'd done her best to hide the tension between her and Sam from the children and was relieved that he'd done his own part to disguise it.

"Well, hurry up and forgive him, would you?" Tom said. "Sam's about as much fun as fried liver and onions these days. How much does he have to suffer before you'll forgive him?"

"Tom!" Molly couldn't believe her son would ask such a question. "What's between Sam and me is none of your business."

"Is this what happens when people get married?" her youngest son wanted to know. "It's great for a little while, and then you fight and everything changes?"

Difficult as it was to admit, her boys were right. This unpleasantness had gone on long enough. Ginny's observations had hit home, and now her own children were saying essentially the same thing.

Running her fingers through her hair, Molly squared her shoulders, took a deep breath and headed out the back door.

"Where you going?" Clay called after her.

"Where do you think, stupid?" his brother taunted. "Leave them be, all right? And if Mom comes back with straw in her hair, don't ask any questions."

Molly turned to glare at her oldest son, but Tom only smiled and winked. Some of the tension eased from her shoulders and she grinned. At the moment a bit of straw in her hair appealed to her. She'd missed Sam. After a decade without lovemaking, it surprised her how easily she'd adjusted to the routine of married life.

Sam was in the barn cleaning tack and barely glanced up when she entered.

"I have something to ask you and I expect the full truth," she announced.

Her statement was met with silence.

"All right?" she asked, feeling suddenly uncertain. It would've been easier if Sam had approached her, instead.

"Fine. Ask away," he muttered.

"Were you or were you not with a woman the other night?"

"That depends on your definition of *with*."

"I didn't realize this was a technical question." She crossed her arms defensively.

"If you're asking if I slept with—as in had sex with—another woman, then the answer is a flat-out no."

"Oh."

"If you're curious as to what I was doing, I'll tell you. A lady asked for a ride home and I gave her one. She was grateful and hugged me, and I swear to you, Molly, that's all it was. A hug, nothing more."

The intensity of his look burned straight through to her heart. She wanted to believe him so very much.

"I've only loved one woman in my life," he continued, methodically polishing the worn leather of her grandfather's saddle. "And that's you."

Molly felt her chest tighten. She wanted it to be true, and while he'd shown her in a hundred ways that he cared, he'd never said the words. Before she could stop herself, she whispered, "I love you, too."

Slowly Sam stood. "Then why are you all the way over there and I'm all the way over here?"

"Can we meet in the middle?"

He grinned for the first time. "You're a stubborn woman, Molly Dakota."

"I had a good teacher," she said, thinking of Gramps.

They didn't walk toward each other, they ran. Sam caught her about the waist and buried his face in the curve of her neck. She threw her arms around him and clung. And all her doubts fled.

"I've been so miserable," she whispered against his shoulder.

"You?" He chuckled, but his amusement was abruptly cut off when his mouth covered hers.

They'd kissed countless times, but Molly couldn't remember any kiss that had meant this much. It was passion, but it was more—giving, taking, holding, sharing. *Trusting.* They both gasped for breath when the kiss ended.

"Do you realize the torment I've been in the past few nights, sleeping beside you?" he whispered.

"You actually slept?"

"You're joking, right?" He kissed her again—and stopped abruptly. "Listen, Molly, there's something…" He hesitated.

"What?" she asked.

"There's going to be trouble."

"What do you mean?"

"The woman I gave the ride to…"

"Yes?"

"It was Pearl Mitchell."

The name blazed itself across Molly's mind, and she pressed her forehead against his shirt. "Oh, God."

No sooner had she said the words than she heard the sound of an approaching car.

"Are you expecting anyone?" Sam asked.

She shook her head.

Before they could make their way outside, the barn door burst open. Sheriff Maynard stood there, looking like an avenging angel.

"Sam Dakota, I'm taking you into town for questioning in the death of Pearl Mitchell."

Fifteen

Sam had lost track of the hours he'd spent in the back room at the sheriff's office. Four? Six? His eyes burned from lack of sleep, but the questions kept coming, some at shotgun speed, others with a slow nasal contempt and the assumption of guilt. His answer was the same to each and every one.

"I refuse to answer any questions until my attorney is present."

According to Sheriff Maynard, he'd been unable to reach Russell Letson. Sam didn't believe him for a second, but said nothing. And wouldn't. Nor did he question the handcuffs, although he hadn't been charged with any crime. It would do no good to demand his rights.

He'd been this route before and had learned the hard way that a uniform didn't guarantee justice, fairness or truth. When he'd been arrested in the barroom brawl that led to his prison sentence, the investigating officer had to rephrase certain questions three or four times to get the answers he needed in order to arrest Sam. Fool that he was, Sam had trusted the man to be unbiased. As a result he'd ended up in jail. Yes, he'd been involved in the fight. Yes, he'd had a knife. Yes, he'd been drinking. Three yeses was all it took to put him behind bars that first time, and Sam had no intention of making a repeat appearance. Not when his life had finally taken a sharp turn for the better. He wasn't going to mess that up.

The ranch was his future, as were Molly and the boys. They'd worked their way deep into his heart. A man didn't walk away from his family, nor did he walk away from his responsibilities. That was a belief he'd shared with Walt. The old man had treated him like a son; he'd loved Sam enough to encourage him to marry Molly, his only granddaughter. And Sam had no intention of letting his friend down now or becoming a victim of circumstances.

"I *demand* to see my husband."

He could hear Molly's determined voice as the young deputy opened and closed the door. Despite the situation, Sam couldn't keep from smiling. It did his heart good to know someone else was butting heads with Molly. He almost felt sorry for the clerk. His wife was a stubborn headstrong woman, which only made Sam love her more. Knowing she was here and on his side gave him the strength to endure another round of questioning, to listen in silence as the sheriff and his men detailed the "evidence" that pointed directly at Sam. Fortunately he was aware of their game plan. Instinct demanded that he argue his case, protest his innocence. But experience had taught him that his declaration would soon be used as "proof" with which to convict him.

An hour later the door opened a second time, and Russell Letson stepped inside. He took one look at the handcuffs on Sam's wrists and demanded, "On what grounds are you holding my client?" His voice suggested Maynard had stepped so far over the line he was lucky not to get tossed into a cell himself.

"Dakota was the last known person to be with Pearl Mitchell."

Russell snorted. "If *that's* all you've got, then I suggest you release him now or become the defendant in a lengthy and very expensive lawsuit for unlawful detainment."

Sam was beginning to believe he'd underestimated the attorney. Mild-mannered Letson was hell wearing shoes when it came to defending his clients. Sam wasn't sure what had persuaded the other man to accept his defense, but he suspected Molly had something to do with it.

Sheriff Maynard's face, double chin and all, was as red as a ripe tomato. Openmouthed, he stared at the attorney as if he couldn't believe what he'd heard. The two were obviously familiar with one another, and they waged a silent battle of wills.

"Now just a minute..." Sheriff Maynard scanned the room as if he felt obliged to make a show in front of his deputies.

"You've gone too far this time," Russell said, more calmly now. "Way too far. You know it, I know it, and so does everyone else in this room. You can stop here or we can pursue this issue in a court of law. The decision is yours."

The two men squared off face-to-face before the sheriff growled something incomprehensible and backed away.

Sam stood up and stretched out his arms for the sheriff to unlock the handcuffs. Maynard did so with undisguised reluctance. When his hands were free, Sam rubbed the soreness out of his wrists. Exhilaration filled him. When he'd walked into this office, he'd been terrified that he might never be free again.

He nearly mowed down two men in his eagerness to get to Molly. She got quickly to her feet when he walked into the waiting area in front of the office. Her beautiful blue eyes met his, and the emotion in them was nearly his undoing.

Without speaking a word, they simply walked into each other's arms. Sam's eyes drifted shut as he wrapped his arms around her and felt her love as profoundly as anything he'd ever known. He gave an audible sigh. Molly was sunshine after a fierce storm. Light after dark. Summer after a harsh winter. His joy. His freedom. His love.

"Are you all right?" she asked, her voice trembling. Her fingers investigated his face, brushed back the hair from his brow.

"I'm fine. There's nothing to worry about." He wasn't entirely sure that was true, but he was hopeful. Thanks to Russell Letson.

Russell was at the counter completing some paperwork, and Sam hurried over to thank him. They spoke for a few minutes and exchanged handshakes. Afterward it seemed to him that when Russell saw Molly standing close to his side, a bit of sadness showed in his eyes, as though he envied them the love they shared. Mentally Sam shook his head; he was growing fanciful.

"I only did what was right," Russell said as they prepared to leave. "I'm sorry it took so long for the message to reach me." He looked slightly embarrassed when Molly stepped forward and kissed his cheek. "Go home, you two, and be happy."

"That's what we intend to do," Sam said, grinning at his wife. The problems hadn't disappeared, and as soon as this crisis was over, there'd be another one, but for the moment nothing was more important than breathing in the fresh air of freedom.

"What time is it?" he asked.

"Three, maybe four," Molly said, and yawned. They'd both been up all night. In a couple of hours the ranch would come alive with activity and Sam would be needed to handle the affairs of the day. But for the next two hours, he planned to make love to his wife.

As soon as they arrived at the house, Molly led the way into their bedroom and didn't bother to turn on the lights. In the dark they removed their clothes, and when Sam got into bed, he held his arms wide. She came to him, unresisting, eager, and sighed openly when he touched her.

"It'll be morning soon," he whispered.

"I know." She let him draw her closer, her breasts nestling against his chest. Then she trailed a series of kisses from his ear and down the underside of his jaw and slid her tongue over the ultrasensitive skin there.

He lifted his head to kiss her with the pent-up longing of all the dark lonely nights of wanting her, of hungering for her. Although he was weary to the bone, he needed her now as he never had before. Needed her as an absolution for the life he'd once lived. Needed her to obliterate the pain of being accused of a crime he didn't commit. As proof that he was alive and capable of feeling and loving and caring. He positioned himself above her and thrust deep inside her welcoming body. A sigh that slipped from the back of her throat told him she needed him, too.

The incredible pleasure drove any other thought from his mind. He gave her everything. His heart, his soul, all he ever hoped to become, all he would ever be. In the aftermath of their lovemaking they clung to each other, holding tight the tenderness and unadulterated joy of being in love. Neither spoke, but the communication between them was stronger, more perfect, than any words they might have said.

Soon afterward, their positions reversed, Molly fell asleep with her head on his shoulder. A wiser man might have followed her into that gentle oblivion, but Sam chose, instead, to hold her as long as he could. To love her consciously a while longer.

Finally, exhausted, he closed his eyes. He couldn't remember the last time he'd slept, really slept, without the weight of innumerable problems bearing down on him. As he felt his mind drifting off to the peaceful state of nothingness, he remembered that Molly wasn't on the birth-control pill yet and that—for the first time since their wedding—they hadn't used any protection. He smiled, despite everything. If Molly became pregnant as a result of this night, he knew he wouldn't regret it, hard as an unplanned pregnancy would be.

"Mr. Wilson would like to see you in his office," Tom's English teacher, Mrs. Kirby, informed him before class.

The principal? Why would the principal want to see him? Tom tried to think what he might have done to get in trouble and could think of nothing. He'd played it safe since starting school. It didn't take a genius to figure out which kids were the troublemakers. Most of them were proud of the havoc they caused. Being bad was their claim to individuality—or so they thought.

When he'd entered the school as a new kid, both sides—the bad-ass guys and the serious ones—made overtures of friendship toward him. The decision had been Tom's as to which side he'd join. Last spring he'd learned his lesson about the consequences of being friends with a troublemaker like Eddie Ries.

At the time Tom had tried to play it cool, but he still felt guilty about that incident. He especially felt guilty about the look he'd seen on his mother's face when she'd come to the school to get him. That was all the lesson he needed. For a mother, his was all right. They didn't always agree, but she was pretty easy to get along with, especially now that she was married to Sam. Tom wanted to make both of them proud, so he'd carefully stayed away from anything that hinted of trouble.

Now this.

"Did Mr. Wilson say what it was about?" Tom asked his teacher. She was older, about the same age as his mother. He liked her. While it was true he wasn't ever going to enjoy reading Shakespeare, she made it tolerable.

Mrs. Kirby's look was sympathetic. "I'm afraid not."

There was a sick feeling in his stomach. To the best of his recollection, he didn't have anything to worry about; still, you didn't get called to the principal's office for the fun of it.

"Should I wait until after class?" Tom asked next.

"If I were you, I'd go now."

Tom reached for his books and walked out of the classroom. It felt like every eye was on him as he walked down the silent hallway toward Mr. Wilson's office.

The secretary, Mrs. Kozar, glanced up when he entered the office. The first thing Tom noticed was that she wasn't smiling. Mrs. Kozar was kind of pretty and she had a funny smile that made anyone who saw it want to smile, too. It started at the edge of her lips with a little quiver and slowly spread across the rest of her mouth. This afternoon there was no quiver and no smile.

Damn, what could he have done?

"Mr. Wilson's waiting for you," Mrs. Kozar said.

Tom wanted to ask her if she knew what this was about, but even if she did, she probably wouldn't tell him. Hell, he hadn't done anything and already he felt guilty!

Tom knocked politely, waited a moment and then walked into Mr. Wilson's office. To his astonishment, he found his mother and Sam sitting there, opposite Mr. Wilson's desk.

His mother cast him a look that spelled *grounded* and worse in one swift eye-meeting glance. It was all Tom could do not to shriek that he'd done nothing wrong, dammit.

"Sit down, Tom," Mr. Wilson invited—no, ordered.

Tom took the chair next to Sam. Although he tried to relax, his body remained stiff. He clutched the chair arms with tense fingers.

"Is something wrong?" he asked, glancing first at Mr. Wilson, then his mother and Sam.

"This morning when I arrived at school," the principal said, "I discovered that someone had spray-painted graffiti on the outside of the gymnasium wall. The north wall."

Everyone focused on Tom. It took him a moment to realize that Mr. Wilson was accusing him of defacing the gym wall.

"Hey, wait a minute!" Tom was on his feet, hardly aware that he'd even moved. "I didn't do it!"

Mr. Wilson sent a sidelong glance at his mother, as if he expected her to leap into the fray.

"Ask anyone," Tom said, gesturing for someone to listen to reason. "I took the school bus this morning, the same as I always do and—"

"What about after school yesterday?" his mother asked.

Tom stared at her because she didn't sound like herself. If he didn't know better, he'd think she was about to cry. Sam and his mother held hands, and that was a good sign because it meant they weren't fighting anymore, but then he noticed that his mother's fingers were white because her grip was so tight.

"I stayed for football practice," Tom said, searching his memory. But that shouldn't be enough to condemn him. He looked at his family and then the principal. "Brian Tucker drove me home, remember?" Brian was the star quarterback and an honor student. Tom made a point of mentioning him, thinking someone would appreciate his wisdom in choosing such a worthwhile friend.

Apparently no one was impressed.

"When you transferred from the San Francisco school district to Sweetgrass," Mr. Wilson said in that prim authoritarian way he had, "we requested and received a copy of your school records."

Good, that ought to show everyone he wasn't a troublemaker. Well, sure there'd been the one incident, but that was it.

"You think because someone spray-painted the gym wall here it was me?" No one had told him *he* was going to be accused every time someone decided to decorate a wall.

"I don't think it could have been anyone else." Mr. Wilson's voice held a frightening certainty.

"I didn't do it." Tom wondered how many times he'd have to say it before someone believed him.

"Your signature's on the graffiti," his mother said, sounding really depressed. It was the same voice he'd heard in the other principal's office. The voice that said he'd failed her and somehow it was her fault. She must be a terrible mother.

"My signature," Tom said, almost relieved now. "That's got to tell you something. I may be a lot of things, but stupid isn't one of them. If I decided to do anything as dumb as spray a wall, I wouldn't sign my name to it." They must think he was some kind of moron!

"Not your name, Tom. Gang symbols."

The blood drained out of his face; Tom could actually feel himself go pale. Even his legs felt weak. He sat back down.

"The identical gang symbols you painted on the wall at your previous school," Mr. Wilson said. "I had your mother look and verify these were the same."

"But I didn't do it!" His words were edged with hysteria.

"Don't lie to me!" his mother cried. "You know how I feel about lies. You've always known. Oh, Tom, how could you do something like this?"

Tom's anger came so fast that it demanded every ounce of self-control not to grab something from Mr. Wilson's desk and hurl it through the window. "Would someone please listen?" he shouted. "I swear to you I didn't do it!"

"You don't expect me to believe that, do you?" Mr. Wilson asked, gazing at him with contempt.

"If you don't mind, I'd like to say something." Sam spoke for the first time, commanding their attention. He was the only one who seemed to be in control. Mr. Wilson was angry and his mother was about to lose it and so was he.

"Please, feel free." Mr. Wilson gestured at Sam.

"I've never known my stepson to lie," he began. "I'm not saying the kid's another George Washington, but in all my dealings with him, he's been honest and fair. If Tom says he isn't responsible for the graffiti, then I feel obliged to believe him."

Tom was so grateful someone trusted him enough to defend him that tears welled in his eyes. It embarrassed him and he looked away and hoped no one noticed when he pressed his sleeve to his face.

"How do you explain the gang symbols then?" Mr. Wilson asked, as if that was all the evidence needed to hang Tom from the nearest tree.

"Tom isn't the only student in the school who knows gang symbols." Again it was Sam who spoke in his defense.

"*California* gang symbols?" the principal said.

"My guess is there are any number of students who have access to that kind of information. Answer me this, Mr. Wilson," Sam said. "Has Tom caused any trouble since the start of school?"

"No, but it's early in the year—"

"In other words, you *expect* me to be a trouble-maker!" Tom shouted, so mad he couldn't sit still.

One sidelong glance from Sam advised him to keep his mouth shut. Seeing that Sam was the only one willing to champion his cause, Tom was willing to follow the unspoken advice.

"What about his friends?"

Mr. Wilson's eyes lowered. "He seems to have made friends with young men who rarely require disciplinary measures."

Like Brian Tucker. Tom nodded profoundly for emphasis, thinking this should be another point in his defense.

"Is there anyone who *saw* Tom do the spray-painting?"

Mr. Wilson cleared his throat. "No."

"Any physical evidence? A can of paint in Tom's locker? Paint on his clothes or shoes the same color as the graffiti?"

Mr. Wilson wasn't making eye contact with them any longer. "None."

Sam paused and glanced over at Tom, giving him a half smile. "Then perhaps it would be best if we decided to forget this unfortunate incident."

"Who's going to repaint the wall?" Mr. Wilson demanded. "I'll have you know that's school property, and it's against policy to deface anything belonging to the school."

"Perhaps you could ask for volunteers?" Sam suggested.

Tom had liked Sam from the first. But even if he'd never gotten along with Sam and resented him for marrying his mother, even if he'd hated the way Sam had become part of their family, everything would have changed this day. Sam was more than his stepfather. He was his friend.

Sam had believed him when no one else did. He'd stuck up for him when his own mother had found him guilty. This was no small thing, and Tom would never forget it.

"Tom," Mr. Wilson said, looking directly into his

eyes. "If I misjudged you, then I apologize. What Mr. Dakota said is true. So far you've proved yourself to be a good student and a fine young man. I hope you'll forgive me for leaping to conclusions. Adults do that sometimes." The principal stood and held out his hand.

Tom shook it and met Mr. Wilson's eyes without flinching. He exchanged a firm handshake with the older man. Sam had taught him about handshakes, too—the importance of meeting the other man's eye and firmly shaking his hand. None of that limp-wristed stuff.

"No problem, Mr. Wilson," Tom said, grateful to be back in good standing with the principal. "We all make mistakes. If I find out who did paint the gym wall, I won't worry about being called a snitch. I'll tell you." Whoever it was had tried to frame him, and Tom wasn't going to let that pass.

"You do that. Now get back to Mrs. Kirby's room."

"Thanks." He was halfway out the door when he stopped and turned around. "Thanks, Sam." His mother's look was forlorn and miserable. He wished she'd stuck up for him, too, but Tom kind of understood. It was because his real father was such a jerk and had lied to her so many times. So he had to forgive her.

"I'll see you tonight, Mom."

She nodded and Tom could see she was close to tears. Good, a little guilt now and again wasn't a bad thing. She'd probably cook his favorite dinners all week to make up for this.

Maybe things weren't so bad, after all.

Molly was an emotional wreck. She'd just been through one of the most traumatic weeks of her life.

First Sam had been arrested, and when she'd finished dealing with that crisis, the school had phoned. The incident with Tom had taught her some valuable lessons. She'd been willing to believe a stranger over her own son. Her heart ached each time she thought about that afternoon. Sam had been the one to stand up for her son.

She knew why he'd done it, too. Sam understood what it was to be falsely accused. She was convinced of Tom's innocence. But not in the beginning, and that she would always regret. She'd let her son down when he'd needed her most.

If that wasn't enough, Sam sold off part of the herd and was forced, along with the other independent ranchers, to accept the lowest price in a decade. The check wasn't enough to cover expenses. They had no choice but to apply for a loan.

Molly rode into town with Sam when he went to the bank to talk to Mr. Burns. There was some consolation in learning that the Broken Arrow wasn't the only ranch in the area experiencing financial difficulties. Sam and Molly had spent most of every night for the past week reviewing the money situation. It didn't look promising.

Although Molly had applied to the school district for work, there hadn't been an opening for a language teacher. She had mixed feelings about this. They needed the money of course—but she actually enjoyed being a stay-at-home wife and mother. For a while, anyway. It was the first time since Clay's birth that she was able to be with her children. In the beginning she'd expected to be bored within a month, but the house needed a lot of work, a lot of maintenance, and she'd been able to provide it with a minimum of expense.

"Do you mind if I don't go in to see Mr. Burns with you?" she asked Sam. He'd parked in front of the bank and didn't look all that thrilled about the appointment himself.

"No problem," he said, and Molly glanced down the street to the pawnshop. Every week without Sam's knowing, she'd taken a little of her grocery money to pay off what was owed on Sam's rodeo buckle. She'd wanted to give it to him as a wedding present, but the cost had been too high.

"Sure you're okay?" Molly asked, her attention returning to the bank. As she recalled, Mr. Burns seemed a decent enough man, sympathetic to the needs of the community. Surely other ranchers had been forced to ask him for assistance.

"I'm not looking forward to this, if that's what you mean," Sam said, and with an exaggerated groan of dread, opened the door on the driver's side.

Molly placed her hand on his forearm, stopping him. "Need a little fortification?" she asked suggestively, then moistened her lips so there'd be no doubt about exactly what she had in mind.

Sam's eyes sparked as he gazed at her lips, and Molly could see he was tempted. "Later, all right?"

She was mildly disappointed, but smiled and nodded.

"Oh, what the hell," he said in an abrupt change of mood. He reached for her, his fingers slipping into her hair as he brought her mouth to his.

The kiss was hot enough to cause a nuclear meltdown, and when they broke apart, Molly sincerely wished they were anywhere but Front Street.

"Does the Sweetgrass Motel rent by the hour?" Sam whispered as his lips hovered close to hers.

"Sam!" Molly giggled and prodded her husband's arm. "Go see Mr. Bank President. Smile real nice and let him know how very grateful little ol' us would be if he sees fit to grant us a loan."

Sam chuckled. "You might be a hell of a lot better at this than me."

"Get in there, cowboy, and do your best." They both avoided talking about what would happen if Mr. Burns refused to advance them credit.

Sam frowned suddenly.

"What is it?" Molly asked.

He shook his head, then looked away. "Someone else once called me cowboy."

"A woman, no doubt." Molly pretended to be jealous.

"As a matter of fact it was. Pearl Mitchell."

"Oh." Pearl's body had yet to be found, but there was plenty of speculation. The matter of Pearl's disappearance might have been forgotten if not for the efforts of Russell Letson. Ginny told her that the attorney spent a lot of time riding Sheriff Maynard about the case. It left Molly wondering what connection Russell might have had with Pearl. Had he been one of her clients? Presumably that wasn't something a man like Russell would want broadcasted. According to Ginny, Pearl was said to have been popular with her customers—but no one seemed to care what had happened to her as much as Russell. Were there personal reasons for his obsession, reasons no one knew? Still, Molly couldn't see the attorney with a woman like Pearl.

"I hope they solve that case." An eerie unreal feeling came over her every time she thought about the murder.

"I hope so, too," Sam added.

Molly's own reasons were mostly selfish. Once the real killer was brought in and tried, no one could point a finger at Sam. Molly believed in her husband's innocence with all her heart, but she wasn't sure everyone else in town did.

"I'll meet you back here in a half hour," Sam said as he headed into the bank.

Molly waited until he was out of sight before walking down to the pawnshop. The bell jingled above the door when she entered. Max Anderson hurried out from the back room and nodded in greeting when he saw her. He was a tall skinny man with a lank ponytail and one gold front tooth.

"Making another payment, are you?" Max asked.

"Please." Molly set her purse on the counter and reached inside for the ten-dollar bill. At this rate it would take her years to buy back Sam's award buckle, but she refused to let him lose it.

"That's an interesting cameo you're wearing," Max said.

Molly's fingers closed around the necklace, surprised he hadn't noticed it before. She wore it every day as a reminder of Gramps and of her grandparents' love. The cameo and the plain gold band around her finger were the only pieces of jewelry that had any real meaning for her.

"Gramps gave it to me years ago after my grandmother died."

"Do you mind if I take a look at it?"

Molly hesitated a moment, but at last slipped the chain from around her neck and gave it to Max.

He held it in the palm of his hand, then turned it over and studied the back. "This is a family piece, isn't it?"

"Gramps bought it during the Second World War, someplace in France, I believe."

"It could have been Italy. Quite a few cameos are made there."

Molly hadn't known that.

"It's lovely."

"Thank you." She held out her hand; Max seemed a little reluctant to let the cameo go.

"You take care of it," he said.

"I will," Molly promised with complete confidence. This cameo, like the ranch, was part of her heritage. Someday she'd give it to Tom's wife or perhaps her own granddaughter. When she did, Molly would tell the story of a young man trapped in a war and the woman he loved who waited half a world away for his safe return.

"I didn't think you'd want to sell it." Max accepted her payment and subtracted that amount from what was owed on the silver buckle. "This is a good thing you're doing," he said with a nod of approval.

"Sam's the generous one."

"He's a good man, I agree with you there," the pawnbroker said.

She and Max exchanged friendly goodbyes. Her business finished, she walked back to where Sam had parked the pickup. Assuming he'd still be a while, she decided to look around the J. C. Penney store. She was about to venture inside when she heard Sam call her.

Surprised he was finished so soon, Molly turned around to see him storm across Front Street.

"Let's get out of here," he said, his mouth tight with anger.

"Already?" He hadn't been with Mr. Burns more than ten minutes, if that.

"No need to discuss the matter of a loan any further," Sam muttered. He turned away, as if he'd failed her.

"What happened?" Molly had to know.

"We aren't going to get any loan, Molly. We're going to have to find another way to hold on to the ranch."

Sixteen

The alarm sounded, and Molly groaned as she climbed out of bed, leaving Sam to sleep while she brewed a pot of coffee. These late-October mornings were crisp and cold, and she reached for her robe and tied it securely about her waist, then made her way, blurry-eyed, into the kitchen. Standing in front of the coffeemaker, she waited for the hot water to filter through for the first cup.

"Mornin'," Sam murmured a couple of minutes later as he moved behind her. He wrapped his arms around her waist and buried his face in her neck. Turning into his arms, Molly hugged her husband, savoring the closeness they shared.

Sam yawned. He was exhausted, Molly realized, and wished he'd stayed in bed awhile longer. She didn't know what time he'd gone to sleep, but it was long after she had, and that had been close to midnight. Sam had wanted to review the accounting books one last time before meeting with the other independent ranchers.

"I've got the Cattlemen's Association meeting this morning," he reminded her.

Molly rested her forehead against his shoulder and swallowed a sigh. With money worries crowding in around them, they clung to each other for emotional support. Their lovemaking had taken on an abandonment, a need, as if proving their love often enough would safeguard their world.

Molly tightened her arms around him. She treasured these moments before the boys paraded down the stairs. The serenity of the morning would shatter as soon as Tom and Clay charged into the kitchen.

The coffeepot gurgled. Reluctantly Molly disentangled herself from her husband's arms and brought down two mugs, filling each one. The aroma, which generally revived her, had the opposite effect this morning. Her stomach heaved, and for a couple of seconds she actually thought she might be sick.

"You okay?" Sam asked. "You don't look so good."

"I'm fine," she lied. It was the strain and worry of their financial situation. Molly knew that stress could manifest itself in all kinds of physical ailments. She didn't want to add health concerns to Sam's already heavy load, so she reassured him with a saucy grin. "If you come back to bed, I'll show you exactly how fine I am."

"Don't tempt me." He took a first tentative sip of his coffee and glanced at his watch. "I've got to get moving." He kissed her cheek and, carrying his mug, disappeared into their bedroom.

Still feeling a bit queasy, she leaned against the counter. She remembered the last time the smell of coffee had bothered her—when she was pregnant with Clay. *Pregnant.* Molly frowned and realized she couldn't recall the date of her last period. She thought she'd been on schedule since Gramps's death, but couldn't be sure. It went without saying that the expense of a pregnancy just then would cripple them. The health insurance they did have was limited, and it paid next to nothing for routine medical conditions. Like pregnancies.

The doctor had told her the emotional upheaval of Gramps's death might upset her cycle, so she'd put off starting her birth-control pills for a month or two. But she and Sam had been so careful! She *couldn't* be pregnant.

At the sound of footsteps pounding down the stairs, Molly removed half a dozen eggs from the refrigerator. One of the pleasures of being an at-home mom was that she could indulge her boys with the luxury of a hot meal on these cool autumn mornings.

"What's for breakfast?" Clay asked as he clumped into the kitchen. The half-grown dog trotted behind him, settling beneath the table. Her son pulled out a chair and immediately reached for the radio. Five minutes of world, national and Montana news was followed by the listing of school lunches, beef prices and the reminder of radio bingo and the local sponsors.

"We get hot dogs today," Clay said cheerfully. "Is it all right if I buy my lunch?"

"Sure." Molly cracked the eggs against the side of a ceramic bowl, then added milk and whipped the mixture with a fork.

"I'll take his lunch if you've already got it packed," Tom said. His voice alternated between two octaves; her oldest son was becoming a man, and the evidence showed every time he spoke.

"You need two lunches?" Molly asked him. He'd grown an inch and a half over the summer, and his appetite had never been better. Must be the country air, Molly concluded.

"I'll eat the second one after school," Tom explained, "before football practice."

Dressed in a pair of freshly laundered jeans, a Western shirt and string tie, Sam joined the others in the kitchen. "Something smells good."

"French toast," Clay informed him.

"You two can set the table," Molly said to the boys.

"Going someplace, Dad?" Tom asked.

Molly smiled every time she heard Tom address Sam as Dad. He'd started shortly after the incident at the school. Sam had never made a big deal of it, but she knew it pleased him. It pleased her, too.

"A meeting with the other cattlemen," Sam answered.

Suddenly the radio announcer had a news flash. Human remains had been discovered along Route 32, about fifteen miles outside town. A couple of hunters had happened upon the decomposed body and reported their find to the sheriff's office.

Molly's hand stilled and her gaze sought Sam's. "Pearl Mitchell?" she asked.

"That would be my guess," he said with a note of sadness.

"Isn't she the lady someone killed?" Clay asked. "I didn't think people got murdered in places like Sweetgrass. That's the kind of stuff that goes on in San Francisco, not Montana."

Molly had believed the same thing. Not once in all the months she'd been in Sweetgrass had she thought to even lock the house. The dogs were protection enough. And as for locking the car—well, according to a crime report she'd heard over the radio, there hadn't been a car stolen in three years.

"How will they know if the remains belong to that missing woman?" Tom wanted to know.

"The sheriff will probably send them to a laboratory in Helena," Sam explained. "With luck, the body could give the authorities enough evidence to locate the murderer."

Molly hoped that was true. Hardly anyone spoke of the killing these days. It had been several weeks now, and with no suspects and few clues, Pearl's murder remained unsolved. Sometimes Molly still worried that the people of Sweetgrass blamed Sam, but that didn't appear to be the case. It was as though the subject of the murdered hooker was forbidden. People felt bad about her death, but she wasn't someone they knew or cared about. The only people who seemed to miss her—besides Russell Letson—were the randy cowhands who came into town looking for a good time. But from what Molly heard, there were plenty of young women willing to take over where Pearl had left off.

The boys grabbed their books and were out the door five minutes before the school bus was due at the end of their drive. Molly carried their syrupy plates to the sink, which she filled with hot sudsy water.

"I'm leaving, too," Sam said, reaching for his Stetson. He paused in the doorway. "Just make dinner for the boys tonight. Something easy."

Molly frowned. "What about us?"

"We're going out to dinner."

They so rarely went out that the idea flustered her. "Where? Why?"

"Dinner and a movie."

Finances didn't allow this sort of thing. "But, Sam—"

"No arguments." He grinned, and any resistance she felt melted away.

"Are we celebrating something special?"

His grin widened. "Yeah, I just don't know what it is yet. How about celebrating the fact that I love you? Is that a good enough reason?"

She nodded, feeling the strangest urge to cry. Sam left then, and in the quiet of the morning, the sun cresting the hill, Molly sat down with a fresh cup of coffee and a piece of toast.

One sip of the coffee and her stomach heaved again. Surprised, she flattened her hand against her abdomen. Her eyes shot to the calendar, pinned to the bulletin board near the phone.

Standing, she took it down. She flipped back to September and studied the notes she'd scribbled—the reminders of meetings and dentist visits, the church women's group, PTA meeting at Clay's school. And there was that terrible night when Sam was arrested. Afterward they'd made love without protection—the one and only time.

Could she possibly be pregnant because they'd been careless just once?

Her stomach was all the answer she needed. She'd enjoyed good health while pregnant with Tom and Clay, but during the first two months she'd suffered frequent bouts of nausea. She'd been forced to give up coffee because the mere smell of it made her retch. Both times.

Molly didn't need a doctor's appointment to confirm what she already knew.

She was pregnant.

Russell sat in the darkness of his cabin, holding a glass of bourbon. The ice had long since melted and diluted the potency of the drink. He wished he was more of a drinking man. That way he might be able to escape this gut-wrenching pain, at least for a little while. All he needed was a few hours' respite so he could sleep.

Since he'd learned of Pearl's death, he hadn't slept an entire night; he woke up frequently, often hourly. Nightmares, grief and tension hounded him the minute he closed his eyes. Once exhaustion dragged him into a troubled sleep, he'd wake abruptly, Pearl's screams echoing in his ears. More likely they were his own.

The sheriff had phoned late the night before to tell him about the most recent discovery. Although Russell had no official connection with the murder investigation, he'd been allowed to visit the site.

Afterward he'd had no doubt left that the remains were Pearl's. The shallow grave had been unearthed by wild animals, and human bones were scattered in a half-mile radius. An hour after he arrived, he'd driven directly to his cabin. He hadn't been there since the murder. Too many memories. Too much pain. He still hadn't been sure he was ready to handle the place, but he'd been so tired and the cabin so close. Here, he wouldn't need to deal with anyone.

If he had it to do over again, there were so many things he'd change. The regrets stacked up till they reached halfway to the heavens. His fingers were numb with cold, and Russell raised the glass to his lips and gulped down the alcohol.

Soon he felt groggy, but not groggy enough. A so-called friend, offering to help him through this difficult time, had given him a handful of sleeping pills. Russell hadn't wanted them, but now he was tempted. He'd been awake all night following Maynard's call about what the hunters had found. This morning, in the woods, he'd watched deputies scoop up Pearl's remains and shove them into a black plastic garbage bag. That had shattered whatever little peace he'd managed to achieve in the weeks since her murder. He withdrew the brown bottle from his coat pocket and spilled two capsules into his palm.

Sleep. He'd sell his soul for a single night's sleep. Without another thought he tossed the pills into his mouth. It didn't take long for the combination of drugs and alcohol to begin having the desired effect.

Moving into the bedroom, he stripped off his clothes and sank onto the mattress, his back to the wall. When he found the energy, he got up, pulled back the covers and climbed between the cool sheets. Almost immediately his bare feet encountered a silky nightgown.

Pearl's. From her last visit.

With a sense of unbearable grief, he reached for the long peach-colored gown and held it against his heart. He closed his eyes, waiting for oblivion.

When he awoke, the room was cold and dark, so dark it was virtually impossible to see. The gown Russell had pressed against his heart was now wrapped around his upper body. He flung it aside and covered his eyes with the back of his hand.

As he lay there, eyes squeezed shut, the scent of roses, the French perfume Pearl had loved, drifted toward him. His need for her was so great his senses had actually invented it, fulfilling his desperate longing for the woman he'd lost.

The lingering aroma of roses grew stronger. Russell knew that the minute he opened his eyes it'd be gone. He was determined to savor it while he could. Fantasy, whatever, he didn't care. Not if it brought him close to Pearl for even a minute.

Pain tightened his chest and he wondered what he'd say to Pearl if he had the opportunity to speak to her one last time. Even though he knew she was dead, he could pretend she was there with him. He wanted her lying at his side as she so often had in the past.

"I'm so sorry," he whispered, his voice shaking with emotion. "We could have made it work...."

The scent of her perfume seemed even more potent. He kept his eyes closed as he struggled to banish from his mind the horror of her last few minutes on earth. These were the thoughts that had tormented him for weeks. She must have been in horrible pain, experienced terrible fear. He hoped with all his heart that she hadn't been bound, that she'd put up a fight. Dear God, he couldn't bear to think about it any longer. Part of him died with her every time he imagined her final minutes.

He must have drifted off to sleep because when he woke up again it was morning. Sun leaked into the bedroom from between the heavy drapes. Pearl's nightgown was next to his pillow where he'd flung it. Sitting up, he reached for it now and brought it to his chest. He wadded up the soft material as he buried his face in it, longing to immerse himself in her perfumed scent. But the beautiful aroma of the roses, like Pearl, was gone.

Sam was definitely pleased.

Money worries had festered in him for nearly a month. Beef prices were at a record low. Ranchers couldn't afford to raise cattle in this current economic climate. At this price, it actually *cost* them to raise beef.

That was what the cattlemen's meeting had been about. As a group, they'd taken their concerns to the bank and Mr. Burns. It seemed the banker was anxious to help when faced with all the ranchers in the county withdrawing their funds en masse.

That morning when he'd left Molly, Sam had impulsively made a dinner date with her. At the time there'd been nothing to celebrate. Now there was. He had the loan, and although the terms weren't the best, it was the first piece of good news in quite a while.

"Are you going to tell me?" Molly asked, sitting across the table from him. She'd barely glanced at the menu.

"All in good time," he said, grinning at her. She looked especially lovely, and he wondered if he could keep his eyes off her long enough to actually eat.

"Sam, I swear, I'll have a perfectly awful evening until you tell me what happened this morning."

There was no help for it. He would've preferred to hold out a bit longer, but... His grin felt like it spread halfway across his face; that was how good he felt. "We got the loan," he announced.

Molly closed her eyes and brought her fingers to her lips. "Oh, Sam."

"The terms aren't that terrific," he felt obliged to tell her.

"But at least we have the money we'll need for now, right?"

Sam nodded and reached across the table for her hand. "First half's due December first."

Her eyes continued to hold his. "So soon?"

"I'm not worried about it, because I'll sell off the last of the herd then. Even if beef prices stay as low as they have been, we'll be able to meet the payment without a problem.''

Molly leaned back in her chair, and the relief he saw in her eyes humbled him. He'd had no idea she'd been this worried. Molly was gutsy and determined, and she'd silently clung to her doubts and fears, rather than place more pressure on him. Sam loved her for it; at the same time he was sorry she hadn't come to him.

Flustered, she brushed her emotion aside. ''I'm sorry—I don't know what came over me.''

''We're going to be all right.'' If nothing else, he wanted to reassure her that no matter what happened, they'd find a way. They'd manage.

''I know. It's just that…'' Sniffling she picked up her purse and sorted through the contents until she found what she wanted. A tissue. She dabbed at both eyes, then stuffed it back inside the purse.

''Did you get a chance to talk to Tom?'' she asked in an obvious effort to change the subject. She blinked furiously to keep back fresh tears.

''He was coming into the house just as I was leaving.''

''He had some good news, too,'' Molly told him.

''About the football team?'' Although thin and wiry, Tom had turned out to be an excellent wide receiver. Brian Tucker had made Tom his favorite pass receiver, and Tom had quickly advanced from junior-varsity level to varsity—something of a rarity for a sophomore. Although he had no right to feel proud of Tom's accomplishments, Sam did. Damn proud.

''By the way, they found the person responsible for the graffiti,'' Molly said.

''Who?'' Sam asked with keen interest.

''Tony Hudson.''

The name meant nothing to Sam. "Another student?"

"A senior. He was caught doing some more spray-painting by Mr. Wilson himself."

"Why'd he do it?" Sam figured someone—this Tony?—had purposely set Tom up. Either that or it was a coincidence, which wasn't too likely in Sam's opinion.

"So many young people are involved in gangs these days," Molly said. "And just as many want to be. It's frightening."

"Even here in Sweetgrass?" That was incomprehensible to Sam.

"Mr. Wilson seems to think so."

Sam mulled that over for a moment. "Did Tony have anything to say in his defense?"

Molly laughed. "This kid needs a good attorney, because his defense is almost ludicrous. He claims someone hired him to do it."

Sam went still. "Who?"

Molly shook her head at the improbability of such a statement. "I think someone ought to contact Russell, don't you?"

Sam grinned, but he wasn't amused. With everything that had happened at the ranch this summer, he wasn't taking such talk lightly. What better way to undermine and discourage a rancher than to attack his children? It was difficult enough to protect his cattle and land. Now Sam knew he had to shield the boys, as well. The best approach would be to sit down and talk with them, man to man.

"You're so serious all at once," Molly said, her happiness shining through her smile. "This is supposed to be a night to set our worries aside and enjoy each other's company, remember?''

"I couldn't have said it better myself."

"Oh, before I forget, I volunteered you for the school Harvest Moon Festival."

Sam groaned in good-humored resignation. All week, Tom and Clay had been joking about whether or not Sam was going to help out at the school festival. Sam wasn't altogether comfortable with the prospect and had half hoped it wouldn't arise. "Okay. What am I supposed to do?"

"Don't you dare look at me like that!"

Sam couldn't keep from laughing, and at Molly's puzzled smile, he explained, "You sound just like a wife."

"I am a wife, as if I needed to remind you."

Sam was still astonished by how much he loved this sense of belonging, of being a part of her and the boys' lives. A family man. A member of the community. A couple of hours stuck behind some booth at the Harvest Moon Festival was a small price to pay.

"Sam."

Dick Arnold approached the table, and Sam got to his feet to shake hands with him. Then he introduced the other rancher to Molly.

"I wanted to thank you for what you said this morning," Dick said. "Hell, if it hadn't been for you, I don't know what we would've done. You sure helped us keep things on track. So thank you, Sam, and I'm saying this for a whole lot of us."

Sam was too shocked to answer. He wasn't accustomed to dealing with compliments. They embarrassed him. He wished Dick had chosen to speak with him privately, rather than in front of Molly.

At last he said, "I'm glad we were able to come up with a workable solution."

"Yeah, but you're the one who convinced us to present a united front. There was some talk after the meeting about nominating you for president next year. Would you consider running? We need someone with a clear head and a sense of direction." He paused, then chuckled. "Look, I didn't mean to interrupt your evening out. Just wanted to stop off, meet the missus and say thanks." Dick touched the brim of his hat. "Nice meeting you," he said to Molly, then turned and walked away.

Knowing his wife was about to hound him with unnecessary questions, Sam reached for the menu. As if on cue, the waitress appeared and they placed their order. He was a little disappointed when Molly declined a glass of wine. It would have gone nicely with their dinner.

"Tell me what you've volunteered me for," he said, steering the conversation back to the Harvest Moon Festival.

"Frying hamburgers between six and seven."

Sam gave an exaggerated groan.

"I'll be working the cotton-candy machine at the same time," Molly added, as if she needed to prove she was doing her part. "Mrs. Mayfield is an expert at getting people to work together for the common good."

"And who, may I ask, is Mrs. Mayfield?"

"Mrs. Mayfield, the choir director from church. She's coordinating the event this year."

Sam grumbled under his breath, but he didn't really object. In fact, he looked forward to slinging a few burgers. Not bad for a man who'd once feared the future.

* * *

A calliope played loudly in the background. The grounds behind the high school had taken on a festive air. Schoolchildren raced in and out of the gymnasium, where they spent their tickets on such wildly popular games as the Balloon Toss and the Jelly Bean Count.

Molly was busy swirling cotton candy around small white tubes. The sticky pink stuff decorated her clothes and tangled in her hair.

Sam dished up hamburgers close by, chatting with their neighbors as if he'd lived in the community all his life. Every now and then she'd look up to see him smiling and exchanging greetings with a fellow rancher. She'd heard from other wives that Sam's speech at the Cattlemen's Association meeting had stirred the ranchers into action. It made her proud to be his wife.

The full yellow moon dominated the evening sky. The air was crisp and cold, but Molly didn't mind. Gaiety and laughter could be heard everywhere, mingled with occasional screams from the Haunted House. Mr. Wilson, the high school principal, strolled past and introduced her to his wife. Mr. Givens, from the supply store, bought cotton candy for his grandchildren. He'd donated two bales of hay and a thousand pennies for the penny search, scheduled at seven.

Tom and Clay had disappeared the minute they arrived, intent on avoiding the embarrassment of being seen with their parents. Sam had given them each enough money to buy their own dinners, but Molly guessed the money had gone for fairground junk food—nothing she would've considered *real* food.

Toward the end of her shift, Russell Letson stopped by and bought some cotton candy, which he presented to a toddler who was begging her mother for a goodie.

Molly had guessed there was a kindness about him, a gentleness. He seemed quiet and more withdrawn than she remembered, but more at peace with himself, too.

"It's good to see you, Molly."

"You, too."

"Are you happy?"

It wasn't a question she would have expected from him. "Very."

"I'm really pleased. Walt was right, you know. Sam's a good man."

"I think so, too."

Russell nodded and with a small wave, walked on to another booth.

"Mom!" Panting, Tom burst onto the scene a few minutes later. "I can't find Clay! Not anywhere."

"I'm sure he's around." Molly scanned the crowd, but to no avail.

"I've looked everywhere! Mom, something's happened to him!"

"Tom—"

"No one's seen him in more than an hour. I've looked. Everyone's looked."

"I'm sure there's a perfectly logical explanation. He's probably sitting in a corner petting a dog or something."

"You didn't believe me before!" Tom shouted, gripping her arm. "Believe me now."

A chill raced down Molly's spine.

"An *hour,* Mom. I've been looking for an hour!"

Tom was close to panic. Molly had never seen him like this. She held his look for an instant, then said, "I'll get Sam."

Seventeen

Sam saw the fear in Molly's eyes even before he heard that Clay was nowhere to be found. "I'm sure he's here somewhere," he said, confident the youngster was just off with friends.

"That's what I thought, too," Tom said, clutching Sam's shirtsleeve. "But I looked everywhere and I've talked to all his friends. No one's seen him. No one. I was holding on to some of his money for him, and we were supposed to meet so I could give it to him. He didn't show up. That was an hour ago."

"Do you think he might have gotten involved in something and lost track of the time?" Sam asked.

"I'd think that, except for one thing. He came after me twice for his money, and I told him he had to wait until seven-thirty like we agreed. He'd been bugging me for it earlier, and then he didn't show."

Sam couldn't pretend he wasn't worried. "So that's when you started asking around?"

"Yeah. No one's seen him."

"I'm sure there's a perfectly logical explanation for this," Molly said again, as if that would make it true. But no one had to remind her that there was a murderer loose in Sweetgrass.

"You're right—I'm sure there's a good reason." Sam slipped his arm around his wife's shoulders. "I suggest we break up and start searching." He glanced at his watch. "We'll go in three different directions and meet back here in fifteen minutes. Okay?"

Both Molly and Tom agreed with a nod. A couple of Clay's friends wanted to help, and Sam asked them to check the gymnasium. Afraid the boy might have been lured into the parking lot, Sam headed in that direction himself. He retrieved a flashlight from the truck and walked slowly down the lanes of parked vehicles.

He called Clay's name repeatedly, and when he'd covered the whole lot with no success, he returned to the rendezvous point. Molly and Tom were waiting for him. He saw by the worry in their eyes that they hadn't found Clay, either. A knot of fear tightened in his stomach. While he didn't want to alarm his family, he was growing more apprehensive by the minute.

This was the worst thing that had happened yet, and it was hard not to believe that everything was connected. He couldn't stand this, couldn't stand the thought of Clay being in danger. If ever he'd needed proof of his feelings for Molly's children, the tension in his gut spelled it out.

"Mom!"

At the sound of Clay's voice, Molly whirled around. The boy ran toward her, legs pumping frantically. He burst into tears and caught her about the waist, clinging as though he never intended to release her.

"Where were you?" Tom demanded, so angry his face was white.

"Someone grabbed me," Clay said, breathless and holding on tightly to his mother. His face was streaked with dirt and tears.

"Who?" Sam asked, squatting down so he was eye

level with the boy. He gripped Clay's upper arms and waited for a response.

"I...don't know. I didn't see who it was, 'cept he wore army boots and one of his shoelaces had broken and was tied short. He threw a gunnysack over my head and carried me away. I couldn't see anything! Then he stuffed me in the trunk of a car and closed it."

"Dear Lord!" Molly gasped.

"I pounded and shouted, but no one came—no one heard me." Clay made a gallant effort not to start sobbing again. "At first I thought it was Tom."

"I'd never do that!" his older brother cried in outrage.

"I know you wouldn't," Clay said. "Then I thought they wanted my money, but I'd already spent it, and besides, he didn't even ask."

"Did you hear his voice?"

"No. But he was big and mean, and—"

"I thought you said you didn't see him," Sam reminded the boy.

"I didn't, but he lifted me up as if I didn't weigh hardly anything and I came high off the ground and when I kicked him, he didn't even grunt."

"How'd you get away?" Molly asked in a shaky voice.

"I...I don't know. Someone opened the trunk, pulled me out and untied my hands, then called me a bunch of dirty names. By the time I got the gunnysack off my head he was gone. I was afraid he'd change his mind and come after me again so I took off running."

"I think we'd better report this to the sheriff," Sam said, more angry than he could remember being in a long time. First the incident with Tom and now this. He placed a protective hand on Clay's shoulder.

"No!" Clay shouted. "I don't like Sheriff Maynard."

Lord knew Sam wasn't keen on the man himself, but he wasn't about to let this incident pass. Someone had tried to kidnap his son, and personal feelings aside, Sam wouldn't put Clay at risk. Not for anything.

"We're talking to the sheriff," Molly countered in a tone that said she wouldn't be persuaded otherwise.

They found Maynard sitting at one of the long rows of picnic tables, eating his hamburger off a paper plate. He didn't look like he wanted to be disturbed, but that didn't deter Sam.

He promptly reported the attempted kidnapping. The sheriff listened intently and wrote down the particulars. "I'd like to speak to Clay myself."

"Fine," Sam said.

The sheriff wiped his hands on a paper napkin and stood. He paused, looking back at Sam. "We got started off on the wrong foot, Dakota. I seem to have jumped to conclusions about you. I haven't seen many guys make turnarounds, but you did. You've proved me wrong. If you're willing, I'd like to put the past behind us."

Sam nodded, astonished by the other man's willingness to let bygones be bygones.

Sheriff Maynard stuck out his hand and Sam shook it.

A ruckus broke out on the far side of the football field, close to where the hay had been spread for the penny toss. The lawman headed in that direction and Sam followed. A group of teenage boys had gathered in a wide circle around a fight in progress. Most were too involved in shouting encouragement to notice the sheriff and Sam approach the outer circle. It didn't take Sam long to recognize the smaller of the two boys.

His first instinct was to jump in and break it up, but he knew Tom wouldn't appreciate his interference, nor did Sam want to embarrass the boy. He expected Sheriff Maynard to do it for him, but to his surprise the lawman stood back for a few minutes and did nothing.

"Sometimes it's best to let them get it out of their systems," he said, chewing on a toothpick. "I'll step in if it gets out of hand."

Sam wasn't sure he agreed, seeing that the other boy had a good thirty pounds on Tom. But what Tom lacked in weight, he more than compensated for with agility. He took a solid hit to the face and Sam flinched, knowing the boy would come away with a shiner. Tom slammed a fist into his opponent's gut, and the kid stumbled backward holding on to his belly. After that, the sheriff stepped into the fray.

He spat out his toothpick. "Okay, okay, that's enough. Let's break it up here." The crowd parted and the lawman grabbed each boy by the scruff of the neck. "You two're finished, understand?"

Tom's nose was bleeding and his right eye had already started to swell.

"Now shake hands and be on your way."

Neither boy was willing to extend a hand.

"Let me put it like this," the sheriff said calmly. "Either shake hands or I'll take you both down to the office, charge you with disturbing the peace and give you a hefty fine. The choice is yours."

Tom and his opponent reluctantly shook hands.

"Good. Now get out of here, and if I see you fighting again, you're going to be in more trouble than you want to even know about. You understand me?"

Tom lowered his head and nodded. As the crowd dispersed, Sam hurried over to him. "Do you want to tell me what that was all about?" he asked, giving Tom his handkerchief.

Tom shook his head.

"Okay. That's up to you. We've talked about fights before, and if you chose to take on someone who's bigger and uglier than you, you must've had a good reason. If you want to leave it at that, then I respect your decision."

Tom held the handkerchief to his bloody nose and looked at Sam through his one good eye. "That's Tony Hudson."

The name sounded vaguely familiar. It took Sam a couple of minutes to remember that Tony Hudson was the boy linked to the graffiti incident.

"I think he might have had something to do with what happened to Clay tonight, too," Tom muttered. "I wouldn't put it past him."

Sam gently squeezed the boy's shoulder. He understood that a man had to protect what was his—and that included his reputation. Tony Hudson had tried to destroy that. Although Sam didn't advocate fighting, he wasn't going to lecture Tom. He grimaced; no need to guess what Molly's reaction would be when she saw her son's swollen face.

His wife took one look at Tom, covered her mouth and promptly exploded with questions. "Are you all right, Tom? How's your eye? Who started the fight?" She paused for breath. "What's the matter with you?" she cried, then turned disgustedly to Sam, as if he was somehow personally responsible for the fight.

"Molly—"

"Stay out of this, Sam. How could you have stood

by and let this happen?'' she snapped. ''I saw you—
standing there, encouraging him.'' Whirling back
around, she caught Tom's chin and angled his head
upward, none too gently. ''Let me see that eye.'' She
gasped when she saw how swollen it was and glared
again at Sam.

''I'm ashamed of you, Thomas. Ashamed.''

''Ah, Mom. Sam's cool about it. Why can't you
be?''

Molly tossed Sam a look that could have turned a
man to stone. She steered both boys toward the car and
left Sam to follow or remain at the festival and find his
own way home.

He had the feeling this evening wouldn't be ending
the way he'd planned—making love to his wife. At the
rate things were going he'd be lucky if she so much as
kissed him good-night.

After the doctor confirmed what Molly already
knew, she realized the next step was to tell Sam. She'd
planned to do it the night of the Harvest Moon Festival,
but then everything had gone so wrong. First Clay's
disappearance, followed by Tom's fistfight. Molly had
been furious with Sam, claiming it was his influence
on her son that had induced Tom to settle a disagree-
ment with his fists. His eye had swollen so badly that
by the time they arrived home he could no longer see
out of it.

Molly hated violence. Every time she looked at
Tom's poor eye, she had to resist the urge to weep.
She'd cried that night, and her tears had come as a
shock—but this had happened with her first two pregnancies, as well. The minute she was pregnant, her
emotions seemed to go askew, and she found herself

weeping at the most inappropriate times. Television commercials for greeting cards and dog food. Movies. Even when she won at radio bingo. It was a wonder her husband hadn't already guessed, but experience told her men were obtuse about these things.

Matters being what they were the night of the festival, Molly couldn't very well announce she was pregnant. Nor on the days that followed. Troubles were said to come in threes, and they certainly did with them.

First Sam's truck broke down and he learned he needed a new transmission. While he was able to do the repair work himself, the parts came to more than a thousand dollars. Money they could ill afford, but Sam needed the truck.

Then the roof of the house sprang a huge leak, ruining the ceiling over Clay's bedroom. Sam had to climb onto the steeply pitched roof in the middle of a horrendous downpour. The plastic tarp was a stopgap measure. The whole thing needed to be replaced, and the job couldn't be delayed much longer. The work they'd done earlier in the year had only been a temporary fix.

"I'll go into town and see about the price of shingles," Sam had said when he climbed down from the roof, drenched to the skin.

It went without saying that a new roof wouldn't be cheap. Shivering with cold, he'd showered, then sat at the kitchen table hugging a cup of coffee while he went over their finances. So *that* wasn't the time to tell him she was pregnant.

Finally, with all the rain, it seemed unlikely their well would go dry—but that was what happened the following week. Sam looked like he'd been punched in the gut when he learned the price of having a new well dug. Again, this wasn't something they could put off.

Molly simply didn't have the heart to add to his troubles by telling him about the pregnancy. She calculated the costs, and with doctor's fees and hospital estimates, having this baby would cost several thousand dollars. Not including baby furniture, clothes and supplies. So Molly kept the news to herself, struggling to hide her morning sickness and lack of appetite. Her emotions were something else entirely. Sam assumed her mood swings were due to financial worries, and she let him believe it.

Ginny was the one who guessed first.

"Sam doesn't know," Molly told her neighbor over hot chocolate the first week of November.

"You've seen Dr. Shaver?"

Molly nodded. "He's got me on vitamins big enough to choke a horse. They don't come cheap, either." Her grocery money would only stretch so far.

"You take them, understand?" Ginny insisted.

"Of course." Molly didn't quibble over doing whatever was necessary for a safe pregnancy. "It's just that Sam doesn't need another financial burden right now," she explained.

"You're looking at this all wrong," Ginny said gruffly, patting Molly's hand. "This is *exactly* the kind of news he needs. That man of yours is carrying the weight of the world on his shoulders. I bet you the first calf of spring he'll be so excited when you tell him I'll hear him all the way over at my place. He's gonna be so proud, Molly. Just you wait and see."

Molly nibbled on her lower lip, wanting to believe Ginny. "You really think so?"

The older woman didn't express the least hesitation. "I know so."

Taking her friend's advice, Molly planned the perfect evening. She arranged for Tom and Clay to spend the following Friday night with friends, thawed out a rib roast and planned the menu right down to a small bottle of champagne. One glass wouldn't hurt the baby, she decided, and it would do the mother a whole lot of good.

The champagne was on ice and dinner in the oven when Sam walked in the back door, looking exhausted. He didn't notice that she'd set the table in the dining room with china normally reserved for holidays and special occasions. Nor did he appear to realize that the boys were away and it was just the two of them.

"What's for dinner?" he asked, appreciatively sniffing the kitchen as he made his way toward the shower.

"Roast," she said, eager to please him with a special meal.

"Smells great."

Molly waited until he'd gone into the shower before she boldly opened the door and stepped in to join him. He sent her a shocked look, almost as though he'd never seen her naked. His astonishment quickly turned to a smiling welcome, and he made room for her under the warming spray.

"I thought I'd wash your back for you," Molly said, reaching for the washcloth and bar of soap.

He hesitated. "What about dinner?"

She sighed; the man knew nothing about romance. "It's in the oven."

"But the boys..."

"Are spending the night with their friends. We're alone, sweetheart. Just the two of us."

A smile lit his face. "Why didn't you say so earlier?"

With the water pelting down on them, Sam backed her into a corner of the stall and his lips grazed hers. Molly wound her arms around his neck, and his hand slipped between their bodies to capture her breast.

This was heaven, Molly thought. This playful time with her husband. They exchanged small nibbling kisses that became more erotic, more intense. She barely noticed that the water had turned lukewarm. The soap and washcloth dropped to the floor, and she could deny him nothing.

Molly had planned a long slow seduction, but Sam wasn't interested in any of that. He soon had her pinned against the tile wall, her legs anchored around his waist, ready to receive him.

But raised as she was, the water hit her directly in the face and she was all but drowning. "Sam," she sputtered, trying to twist away, fighting for each breath.

Once he realized her dilemma, he quickly reversed their positions so that he was the one with his back to the wall.

"I don't think this was such a good idea," she said with some regret. They were both slippery and wet, and she found herself slipping out of his grasp.

"It's a wonderful idea," he insisted, shifting the burden of her weight and holding her thighs more firmly. But it didn't work, and she started slipping again, banging her ankle against the shower door.

"Dammit," she muttered irritably. This did *not* feel sexy.

He grumbled something about her gaining weight, but she decided to ignore the comment or, more appropriately, forgive him. Sam refused to give up and eventually they managed to arrange their bodies and adjust to each other for the optimum lovemaking position. Sam braced his shoulder against the wall, while holding on to her. Molly's back was to the water, with her knees against the sides of the shower stall for leverage.

Just when everything seemed to be working, the water went abruptly from warm to ice cold.

Molly let out a scream, but because her body blocked his, Sam obviously hadn't noticed the change in temperature yet.

"That's it, honey. That's it." His eyes remained closed, but not for long as she squirmed and bucked in an effort to escape the freezing water. Her movements, however, did wonders for Sam, who closed his eyes, breathing fast. Finally she was able to move in a way that allowed the blast of cold water to hit him full in the face.

He let out a yelp of surprise, lost his balance and promptly dropped her. Molly landed in a heap on the shower floor while Sam reached for the controls and turned off the water.

Her dignity was hurt far more than her derriere; nevertheless, she wasn't pleased.

"Sweetheart, are you all right?" He had the grace to look embarrassed.

"I guess so." Because the soap had melted and the floor was slippery, she had difficulty getting back on her feet.

He opened the shower door, stepped out and handed her a towel. No sooner had she wrapped it around her than he took the smaller hand towel and began to dry her hair.

The towel obstructed her vision, but apparently that

didn't worry Sam as he led her out of the bathroom. "Sam," she said, swatting at the towel. "Where in the name of heaven are we going?"

He paused as if the question confused him. "Going? Honey, we're gonna finish what we started."

"But—"

"You don't want to stop, do you?"

"It's just that I'm a little cold," she said, shivering.

"I'll warm you, I promise. You game?" The hopeful need she heard in him was her undoing.

"I'm always game for you," she told him softly, "and you know it."

He rewarded her willingness by lifting her in his arms and carrying her into the bedroom. He groaned as he approached the bed. "You *have* gained weight, haven't you?"

"Sam." She tried to kick herself free, but he wouldn't allow it.

"That was a joke," he whispered, and kissed away any protest she might have voiced. His tongue stroked the curve of her ear as he pressed her against the bed. "Oh, baby," he whispered, "this is the best idea you've had in a long time." He stroked her hip and thigh and peeled open the towel. Taking a moment to smile down at her in the dim light, he gently kissed each nipple before his mouth sought hers. Again and again he kissed her, and in almost no time Molly had completely given herself over to the heat of their love-making.

Sam held her for a few minutes afterward, then brushed his lips across her brow. "Meet you in the kitchen," he said.

Molly got dressed and, after combing the tangles out

of her wet hair, she joined him. "This is a very special night," she said, wanting to set the mood for her news.

"You can say that again," he murmured, scooping some frosting off the carrot cake she'd made and licking his finger. "You certainly didn't need to go to all this trouble."

"It's no trouble."

He froze, and she noticed that he stole a glance at the calendar. "I haven't forgotten anything, have I?"

"No, of course not."

"It isn't your birthday?"

"No!"

"Our anniversary's in June, right?"

"Sam, would you kindly stop?" She pulled the roast out of the oven and set it on the stove. "If you like, you can open the champagne."

"Champagne?"

"On the table. And the crystal flutes are in the dining room."

He picked up the bottle and seemed to be looking for the price. "This is real nice, sweetheart, but we can't afford champagne."

"It wasn't any more expensive than a bottle of wine."

He nodded. "Yeah, that's true. And it's not like we do this every night."

He sliced the roast while she carried the dishes out to the table and lit the candles, then he brought out the meat platter and put it carefully in the center. "This is great." He slipped his arm around her waist and kissed her neck.

"Thank you. I wanted tonight to be memorable."

"It's already been memorable." He pulled out his chair and reached for the platter of roast beef before she'd had a chance to sit down herself. Molly cast him a look she normally saved for the boys, and with an apologetic grin, he put the platter back down. When she'd spread the linen napkin on her lap, they smiled at each other. Sam poured the champagne, then helped himself to the meat, the potatoes and squash, the salad.

Throughout the meal, Molly waited for the right moment. She'd planned what she wanted to say, hoping against hope that Ginny was right. She had his reaction all worked out in her mind, too.

In her romantic fantasy Sam would fall quiet and look at her with adoring eyes. Then he'd clasp her hands and say something charming about how her love had forever changed him. That was certainly the way she *wanted* it to happen, but their evening had gotten off to a less than romantic start with their comedy of errors in the shower. True, things had improved later on, and the meal was going well. But this was too important an announcement; the timing had to be perfect.

Sam expressed his appreciation for the dinner over and over. He made every effort to show her how much he enjoyed her cooking, accepting a second piece of carrot cake for dessert.

He helped her clear off the table, and while she put on a pot of decaf coffee, he turned the radio on softly and sat in the living room to wait for her. Starting at nine o'clock in the evenings, the local station played light classics, fifties jazz, instrumental versions of popular songs—music that soothed.

"There's something I need to tell you," Molly said, growing concerned the night would slip away before she completed her mission. That could happen easily enough, considering how nervous she was about it. She reminded herself that a new life was reason to celebrate, and that she and Sam loved each other. He'd be happy; she knew he would.

She carried in the tray of coffee and set it on the table. "Actually this probably won't come as a surprise." Her back was to him as she poured them each a cup, adding a splash of cream.

"Sam?"

"Hmm?"

"What I wanted to tell you…"

Silence.

She turned around and found him sitting in the recliner with his eyes closed, humming quietly along to the music.

"Sam," she said again.

Seeing this might well be the moment she'd waited for all night, she set the coffee aside and nestled in his lap. His arms automatically came around her and he reached over to turn off the lamp, casting the room into a welcoming dimness. It wasn't hard to imagine her grandparents sharing a special moment in this room, the same way she was with Sam.

Pressing her head to his shoulder, she kissed the underside of his jaw. This was nice. Really nice.

"I love you so much," she whispered.

"Me, too."

"Do you remember how eager we were to make love—"

A smile cracked his mouth. "What do you mean *were*? You can tempt me any minute of any day. What happened in the shower should prove that."

She stroked his chest, loving his solid muscular warmth. His head leaned against the back of the chair and his eyes closed.

"These have been a hellish couple of weeks," he murmured.

"But we're doing okay, aren't we?" She continued to kiss his throat, then moved her lips along his jawline.

"It wasn't you on that roof in a pounding rainstorm."

"True." She unbuttoned his shirt and slipped her hand inside. "You know, sometimes things that seem disastrous are really blessings in disguise."

"Next time I'll let *you* crawl under the chassis and discover the transmission's shot."

"I wasn't talking about the truck repairs."

"Obviously."

"There's something else."

He went very still.

"But it's not bad news," she added.

"Good, because I've had more of that than I can handle."

With her head resting against his shoulder, Molly worried her lower lip, uncertain now. She wanted to believe he'd be pleased, but feared he'd look on the pregnancy as just another burden. As it turned out, she waited too long, because the next thing she knew, he was snoring in her ear.

The next morning, Sam knew something was wrong with Molly the minute he awoke. It probably had to do with that dinner scene the night before, but God's honest truth, he'd had one bitch of a day and was dead on his feet. Not wanting to disappoint her, he'd gone along with her romantic charade, and to be fair, he'd been surprised and delighted when she joined him in the shower. Never having made love in an upright position, he'd been required to improvise—admittedly without total success. But all in all it had worked out rather nicely once he got her into bed. He was too much of a tradionalist to be very experimental when it came to making love with his wife. But he was willing to try if she was.

Dinner was wonderful, and it was clear that Molly had gone to a lot of trouble. But now he knew he'd committed some terrible faux pas. Molly was curled up on the far side of the bed, as near the edge as she could possibly get.

"Morning, sweetheart," he whispered, wriggling across the bed to get closer to her.

He knew it probably hadn't been good form to fall asleep in the chair so soon after dinner, but he'd been exhausted. He didn't even remember getting into bed.

Silently Molly tossed aside the covers and climbed out of bed.

"Is something wrong, sweetheart?" he asked.

"Oh, Sam, sometimes you make things so difficult."

He sighed, wondering how often he'd be obliged to apologize for falling asleep in the middle of her romantic evening. He did feel bad about it, but she *could* be a bit more understanding.

"Just tell me what's wrong, okay?"

"Nothing's wrong," she whispered.

He'd swear she was crying. "Molly, for heaven's sake, tell me!"

"You don't know, do you?" She shook her head, her expression hopeless. "You honestly don't know." Sniffling, she grabbed a tissue from the dresser.

"Uh..."

"Think about it, Sam. Just think. I had a wonderful night planned for us and... I don't know why I should have to tell you anything! You should be able to figure this out yourself. You were the one who noticed I've gained weight.''

''Honey, a few pounds. Don't worry about it. You look great. You *are* great. It's just a little more of you to love.'' He reached out to her, planning to pull her into his arms.

She slapped his hands away and blinked hard. ''Sam, there's a reason I've gained a few pounds.''

''Sure, it's all the desserts you've been baking lately, but I don't want you to worry about it.''

She released a soft groan and left the bedroom.

Sam didn't know what her problem was, but he had work to do. The way he figured, she'd tell him when she was ready. Right now he needed to get over to Lonesome Creek to check on the herd.

Molly had coffee and toast waiting for him when he joined her in the kitchen.

''I gotta go.''

''I know.'' She'd wiped all traces of tears from her cheeks and kissed him. ''Think about what I said, all right?'' she murmured.

She looked so small and pitiful that Sam held her longer than necessary before he headed for the barn to saddle up Thunder.

As he rode toward Lonesome Creek, it hit him.

Molly was pregnant.

Pregnant!

His heart felt like it would explode with excitement. With happiness. His instinct was to turn around and ride back, kiss her senseless, tell her how thrilled he was. He would have, too, but he heard voices just then, and the sound of a truck. This was *his* land and anyone on it would be up to no good.

Without considering the fact that he was alone and

unarmed, he charged for the hill and crested it in time to see four men dressed in fatigues loading up his cattle.

They saw him, too.

What happened next seemed unreal, like something out of a flickering scene in a silent movie. He heard a shout and watched transfixed as one of the men raised a rifle to his shoulder and took aim. It was a moment before Sam realized the man was aiming at *him*.

With a cry of outrage, Sam pulled back on Thunder's reins to reverse the gelding's direction. Bending low over the horse's sleek neck, he made for the ranch, knowing that even the slightest hesitation could cost him his life.

The sound of the rifle blast reached him at the precise moment he experienced the searing pain of the hit. The sheer force of it flung his arms wildly into the air. With his weight off center, he slid from the saddle, just managing to free his feet from the stirrups. The gelding's thundering hoofs echoed like cannon shots as he fell. His last conscious thought before he slammed against the hard ground was a simple prayer. He asked for only one thing. To live long enough to tell Molly how happy he was about the baby.

Eighteen

This wasn't going down the way Monroe had planned. The Loyalists needed the Wheaton land, but the old man had been too damn stubborn. Wouldn't listen to reason. Okay, he'd expected that. Walt Wheaton had been a cantankerous fool most of his life. Monroe had considered it a godsend when his granddaughter arrived, but he'd been wrong. The situation had quickly gone from bad to worse.

Sam Dakota had thrown a monkey wrench into the entire scheme. Without him Molly would've been forced to sell the property, and she'd have been glad to be rid of it. Dakota was as stubborn as the old man, and it was clear he intended to fight for the land with the same unshakable determination.

Monroe leaned forward and planted his elbows on his desk. The situation had taken a sharp turn south starting with Pearl Mitchell's murder. He'd confronted Lance, who claimed he'd had nothing to do with it and offered an alibi. When Monroe checked, he was surprised to learn Lance had been telling the truth. Yeah, he'd come to town that night, but Lance had been at Willie's playing pool with that hothead Travis. The bartender confirmed it.

It would have been convenient if they'd been able to pin the murder on Dakota, but that hadn't panned out. Monroe could deal with Molly, persuade her it'd be wise to sell—if he could get her husband out of the picture. What shocked him was that his cousin, his own flesh and blood, was the one responsible for seeing the man set free. It angered him every time he thought about it. Damn attorneys weren't to be trusted. Even when they were part of the family.

He wished the hell he knew what Russell's angle was with Pearl. The way his cousin had hounded the sheriff's office for information led him to believe there might have been something between them. That was enough to make him laugh. His cousin falling for a hooker!

Monroe felt bad about Pearl's murder, too, but she was the one who chose to live this life. She knew the risks. If he found out who'd killed her, he'd make the son of a bitch pay, if for no other reason than the lost income she'd provided. The freebies Pearl threw in every other week or so would be sorely missed, but he'd convince one of the other girls to be just as accommodating.

The girls had gotten nervous after Pearl's death, and profits had dropped by thirty percent. He'd been against setting up this prostitution ring in the first place, afraid someone would trace it back to him. But it was the least of his worries now. Lately there'd been any number of problems developing.

Tightening the screws on Dakota had been downright fun, but the bastard had refused to break. Messing around with his stepsons hadn't done it, either. Hiring the Hudson kid to paint the wall had been Lance's idea. He snorted. Lance was a fool and not to be trusted. He was sure Lance's friend was the one who'd set the Cogan boy free. Travis was a good man and a capable soldier, but he couldn't stand seeing anything happen to kids. They were his weakness. Damn fool.

Burns had turned on him, too. Without ready cash Dakota would've been at their mercy, but the bank president had stepped in and rescued him. Monroe understood that Burns had to put business first, but it complicated an already complicated situation. Once Monroe heard the terms of the loan, though, he'd realized what had to be done. Dakota had to be prevented from getting his cattle to market.

The door opened and Lance walked into his office.

Monroe's anger flared like a match to a blowtorch. "I told you never to come here." He was on his feet, prepared to personally drag Lance's sorry ass onto the street. Talk about stupid!

"It went wrong," the other man muttered.

This wasn't what Monroe wanted to hear. "Meet me behind Willie's at midnight."

"Travis shot him."

"Shot who?" he demanded. Forced as he was to deal with incompetence and insubordination, it amazed him the organization had held together this long.

"Dakota," Lance said. "There was nothing we could do."

Monroe gave a slow satisfied smile. So Dakota was a goner. No great loss. And who better to comfort the grieving widow than Monroe himself?

Grumbling to herself about how obtuse men could be, Molly set about her busy day. There never seemed to be any shortage of projects needing attention. She had a list of chores for the boys, as well.

Humming as she sorted laundry on the back porch, she heard the unmistakable sound of a horse galloping into the yard. It didn't seem possible that Sam could be back already—but maybe he'd figured out what she'd been trying to tell him. She felt a bit queasy this morning, and she pressed her palm over her stomach, loving her unborn child with the same fierceness as she loved her boys.

Molly peeked outside to see Thunder prancing about in front of the barn door, snorting and jerking his head.

Riderless.

Molly stared at the horse. Where was Sam? Grabbing her sweater from the peg, she raced onto the porch.

"Sam?" she called. She stopped suddenly. She *knew* something was wrong. Terribly wrong.

With her breath coming in short frantic gasps, she stormed back into the house for the truck keys. Her fingers trembled so badly she had trouble inserting the key in the ignition, and she cursed under her breath. Taking a moment to calm herself, she pushed in the clutch, revved the cold engine and headed in the direction she'd seen Sam ride.

The pasture was anything but smooth, and she was hurled, jarred and jolted as she sped across the uneven terrain. All the while she prayed frantically, fear gnawing at her insides. She had no idea what she'd find. If Thunder had thrown Sam, there was a possibility he'd reinjured his back. He'd been forced to give up the rodeo because of a spinal injury; any further damage could leave him paralyzed for life.

Dread roared through her like wildfire. So intent was she on her worries that she nearly drove right past Sam. When she did see him staggering across the pasture, holding his head, she stomped on the brakes.

Leaping out of the cab, she raced toward him. When

he saw her, Sam sank to his knees. Blood oozed between his fingers and flowed onto his face and into his eyes.

Molly gasped.

"It's not as bad as it looks," he assured her, his voice barely audible.

"Sam, oh, Sam."

"We got troubles, sweetheart."

His eyes fluttered and she knew he was going to pass out.

"Rustlers got our herd." With that he toppled over, face first.

Sam awoke and groaned at the hammering in his skull. Pinpoint lasers pierced his brain, blinding him with light. He raised his hand to protect his vision and tried to figure out where he was.

He recognized nothing.

"Sam?"

Molly was with him; that was promising, anyway.

"Where am I?" Each word demanded tremendous effort.

"Home. Dr. Shaver just left. Ginny's here, too. I don't know what I would've done without her and Fred. They helped me carry you into the house. Can you tell us what happened?"

"Rustlers...got the herd."

"I know." He caught the way her voice trembled, but doubted she fully understood the magnitude of what this meant. "The loan, Molly. We have to make a five-thousand-dollar payment in three weeks."

She grasped his hand tightly. "Don't worry about that now. We'll find a way."

"But..." He half lifted himself from the bed, not sure why, but knowing he had to do something. Everything around him had an unreal quality, as though it were all part of a bad dream. The worst nightmare of his life. If so, he wanted to wake up soon.

Dear God, what were they going to do?

"It's all right," she insisted gently. She placed her hands on his shoulders and eased him back against the mattress. He felt her lips on his cheek and for a moment welcomed her comfort and her love. But comfort couldn't last, not when they'd been robbed of every hope for their future.

"Sheriff Maynard." He struggled to speak and clutched her arm, wanting her to know the importance of his request. He needed to talk to the lawman, and the sooner the better.

"I called him already," Molly answered calmly. "He wants to talk to you as soon as you're a bit better."

"Now."

"Soon, I promise. But for now, please rest." Her voice trembled again, and he did as she asked, rather than upset her further.

The pain in his head was vicious. Unable to fight it any longer, he closed his eyes. "Tell Maynard...I can identify one...if I saw him again." The one with the rifle. Sam had gotten a good look at him. Unfortunately it wasn't someone he recognized. A stranger. In another sense, however, the fact that he *was* a stranger brought Sam a measure of relief. It would be difficult to accept that any of his neighbors would involve themselves in something so criminal.

Who? Why? The questions pounded in his brain, as painful as the physical agony.

Although his eyes remained closed, Sam was awake,

at least partially so. Bits and pieces of conversation drifted his way.

"Dr. Shaver said another inch to the left and the bullet would have gone directly into his brain," Molly said. "As it is, it gouged a path across the top of his skull."

"Were they trying to kill him?" The voice belonged to Tom, and from his tone Sam knew the boy was fighting mad. "Who would do something like this? Who? If I ever find out—"

"Tom, we don't know," Molly responded. "No one does."

"What are we going to do if we can't make the first payment?" Tom asked. Sam wondered the same thing, and the weight of that burden was heavier than anything he'd ever experienced, including the prison sentence. It crushed him with fear.

Molly hesitated. "I don't know what'll happen, but we don't need to deal with it now."

"Won't the bank give us more time?"

"I already called and explained the situation," Molly said. "And while Mr. Burns is sympathetic, he said he couldn't make allowances."

"We aren't going to lose the ranch, are we?"

Molly hesitated and her voice shook ever so slightly when she answered. "I...don't know."

"Will we move back to San Francisco?"

Sam wanted to protest, reassure Tom and Clay that he'd do everything in his power to see that didn't happen. They belonged in Montana now, as much as he did himself.

"What about Sam? If we have to move, will he go with us?"

Sam living in a big city. Not likely. He nearly snickered out loud. He wouldn't last a day.

"Of course he will," Molly said. "Sam's my husband."

Although his head hurt like a son of a bitch, Sam almost smiled. Molly loved him, and by God he couldn't, wouldn't, let her down now. Walt had brought them together, and the old man knew exactly what he was doing. He and Molly might not have started their marriage in the traditional way, but they were going to make it work.

In his thirty-six years Sam had committed more than his share of sins. In all that time, he'd never asked for much. Mostly he hadn't given a damn about anything or anyone, including himself. Then he'd met Walt Wheaton and fallen in love with Molly.

He cared now. Cared about his family—Molly, the boys, his unborn son or daughter. Cared about his own life. Cared more than he'd ever thought possible. Somehow, some way, he'd get that money.

Russell sat in his office and read over the faxed report a second time. He'd had to pull a number of strings and call in several favors to obtain this information. Now that it was in his hands, right here in black and white, he was even more confused. He knew more about militia groups and domestic terrorists than he'd ever expected to learn. He'd made contact with the FBI and could negotiate the Internet like a pro. And he'd discovered that the paper trail led directly back to the Loyalists in Sweetgrass. To a member of his own family.

Countless hours had gone into his research. It had all started with Pearl's murder. Every time her name passed through his mind he experienced a deep sense of loss. The weeks hadn't eased it. Nothing had, and he suspected nothing ever would.

There'd been little comfort for him, except that one night he'd spent in the cabin. Often he'd close his eyes and bask in the memory, feeling again the cool silk of her nightgown, smelling her rose-scented perfume. Remembering her. It made him more determined than ever to find the man responsible for her death and see that justice was served.

That promise had led him to the papers that lay before him now. The print blurred and he pinched the bridge of his nose, weary in body and mind. It'd been a long day, and if this contract said what he thought it did, Pearl's death hadn't come at the hands of an overzealous john. She'd been a tool used by the Loyalists; he believed she'd been killed because she knew too much. Perhaps she'd threatened to tell what she knew.... For the first time he understood why she'd rejected his marriage proposals. Had she died trying to free herself from the Loyalists in order to marry him? It didn't bear considering. He understood now who was responsible for her death. His cousin. And the irony was that it'd been through his cousin that he first met Pearl.

With this realization came a renewed sense of guilt. Indirectly *he* was responsible for putting her in danger. He'd been the one who taught her to read. Lovely, generous Pearl had been like a child, tasting life for the first time, soaking up everything she learned, each sound, each new word. Her joy had been his own.

Who would have guessed this newly acquired skill would get her killed? Russell was ninety-nine percent sure that was what had happened. She'd read something she shouldn't have and gotten caught. Or perhaps she'd inadvertently let the information slip. Whichever, it had cost Pearl her life.

He'd never be the same without her. He wasn't sure he could continue living the way he had before he loved her. Once this was over he didn't think he could stay in Sweetgrass.

Rubbing his eyes, he studied the paper one last time, then tucked it into a file, which he locked inside the cabinet.

He turned off the light as he left the office and started for the parking lot. The cold was like a physical shock when he stepped outside. Snow was predicted that night.

Climbing into his car, he warmed up the engine and headed home. On impulse he drove past Pearl's house. New renters had moved in a month earlier, apparently unaware or unconcerned that a murder had taken place there.

He stopped off at the minimart and bought himself a sandwich, then drove home and ate it in front of the television while he watched CNN.

"I'm closer," he whispered to Pearl before he got into bed that night. "It won't be long now. I'll know why. You won't have died in vain, my love. Whoever killed you will pay. Whatever you found out—he'll answer for it."

This was his promise, and he fully intended to keep it.

The alarm buzzed in Molly's ear, and blindly stretching out one arm, she fumbled with the knob until the irritating sound ceased. Not wanting to leave the warm comfort of the bed, she cuddled close to Sam and absorbed his body heat for a few extra moments before quietly getting up. Sam had been in such a bad mood since his injury, extra sleep could only do him good.

It was a week ago that he'd spoken to Sheriff Maynard. Because Sam had been unable to name any of the men and because the sheriff had found no concrete evidence, there was little hope the cattle would be recovered. Since then Sam had been listless and cranky. She knew he was physically and emotionally drained. Although Doc Shaver had insisted he remain in bed for at least two days, Sam had simply refused. Molly had done her best, but the man defined stubbornness.

They didn't discuss the loan payment again. Really, what was there to say? Sam couldn't make the money appear out of thin air, and she was no magician, either. And so they didn't speak of it.

Some nights the tension in the house was so oppressive, Molly wanted to shriek. The boys had been restless and ill-tempered, too.

"It snowed!" Clay yelled as he flew down the stairs for breakfast. He said it as though no one else had noticed a thing.

Molly smiled at his enthusiasm, pleased to hear something other than whining or complaints.

"It's beautiful, isn't it?" she said, gazing out the kitchen window. The sun rose over the horizon, casting a pinkish glow on the white perfection.

"It's stupid," Tom said. He'd followed his younger brother down the stairs. Molly set a plate of hotcakes in the middle of the table and Tom helped himself. He poured on enough syrup for the pancakes to float.

"Hey," Clay protested, jerking the plastic container out of his brother's hand. "I want some, too."

A tug of war ensued, and soon the two boys were at

each other's throats. Molly quickly broke it up, but the bickering continued until the boys grabbed their schoolbags and headed out the door to meet the bus.

Still angry, Clay stood in the open doorway and glared at Molly as though the fight with his brother was all her fault. "I hate Montana."

Molly sighed and shook her head. "Clay, that isn't true and you know it."

"I don't care if we lose this stupid ranch. The only thing I like is Bullwinkle. I want to move back to California." Having said that, he ran out, slamming the door.

Defeated, Molly slumped into the chair and raised her hands to her face. The boys' constant quarreling depleted her energy. It didn't help that Sam had been sullen and pessimistic all week.

"What was that about?" Sam asked. She hadn't heard him come into the kitchen.

Whenever Molly looked at the bandage on his head, she experienced a twinge of pain herself. The head wound was only a small part of what he'd suffered. For reasons as yet unclear to Molly, he blamed himself for the loss of the cattle. He'd never come right out and said so, but she hadn't lived with him and loved him all these months without being able to figure that out.

"The boys got into a fight," she explained. "No one's in a good mood."

"Maybe Clay can have his wish," Sam said without emotion.

"What do you mean?"

"Maybe it isn't too late for you and the boys to move back to California."

Her heart seemed to lurch to a sudden stop. He had to be joking, but one look told Molly he was serious.

"Is that what you want?" she asked, barely able to say the words.

He shrugged as if her returning to California or not was of little consequence to him.

"That's a perfectly rotten thing to say, Sam Dakota! It's obvious that you don't understand what marriage really means. I committed myself to you when I said my vows. No ands, ifs or buts. Love isn't just a feeling. It isn't hormones, either. It's commitment, standing beside each other, facing problems together. It's holding on to what's really important." When she finished, her eyes had filled with tears.

"To my way of thinking, you got the short end of the stick in this marriage," he said.

"I could say the same thing about you. I came into this relationship with two children and a complete set of emotional baggage. But we're married now, and no one's keeping score of who got the short end of what stick—or anything else!"

He turned his back and walked out of the kitchen.

Molly heard the radio come on and knew he'd settled down in the living room. He'd gone there in order to avoid her. Well, she wouldn't *force* him to speak to his own wife!

Unable to stay in the house, Molly dressed, fighting back tears and nausea, and drove to Ginny's place. The older woman stepped onto the porch when she heard Molly's car.

"More troubles?" Ginny called out, concern evident on her face.

Molly shook her head. "I came for coffee and a few words of encouragement."

"Encouragement I got, but my coffee tastes like cow piss." She chuckled. "That's what Walt used to tell me, but you know he had more than his share of my coffee and he wasn't too proud to down a slice or two of my apple pie while he was at it."

Molly smiled at the reference to her grandfather. She missed Gramps more than ever. He'd always been there for her; he'd always been willing to look at a problem straight on. She understood now how much courage that took. And he'd had a way of coming up with solutions....

"It's a bit early in the day for pie," Molly said, "but I'll gladly accept a cup of that coffee."

"Great." Ginny led the way into the house.

The warm homey kitchen was where Ginny and Fred spent most of their time. The radio rested on the kitchen counter, and a stack of mail and books and magazines took up at least half the table, along with a deck of cards and an old cribbage board.

"Walt and me used to play cribbage and two-handed pinochle now and again," Ginny explained. "Not often, just enough for me to think of him every time I look at that old board. Can't seem to bring myself to put it away. Sometimes Fred and I play a bit in the evenings, but it's not the same...."

Molly touched the older woman's hand. "I miss him, too."

Ginny sniffled and dabbed at her nose with her hankie. "How's Sam this fine morning?"

Molly looked away, not meeting Ginny's eyes. "He...he suggested I move back to California with the kids."

"You didn't believe him, did you?"

Molly didn't know what to believe any longer.

"What that husband of yours needs is someone to read him the riot act," Ginny said, frowning darkly. "If he feels sorry for himself now, just wait till I get through with him. He should be shot for saying something like that."

"Someone already tried," Molly reminded her.

"From the way Sam's acting, you'd almost think he's disappointed the guy's aim was off."

Molly held on to her mug with both hands and stared into the steaming coffee. "He blames himself for what happened."

"That's ridiculous. It could've been my herd just as easily."

Molly pushed her hair off her forehead. "I don't know what we're going to do, and Sam refuses to talk about it. Now it seems as if he's given up and wants out of the marriage."

"Don't you take him seriously," Ginny chastised. "Not for a moment. Maybe you should tell him about the baby now. It'd give him something else to think about."

"No." Molly was adamant about that. "If he doesn't love me enough to ride out the troubled times, then a baby isn't going to change things." Thinking about the many difficult times her grandparents had faced, Molly gripped the cameo dangling from the gold chain. Somehow it helped her feel closer to them both.

"That cameo's lovely," Ginny said. "Have you ever thought about selling it?"

"No." Molly was horrified Ginny would even suggest such a thing.

"It might be valuable. When was the last time you had it appraised?"

Appraised? Molly had never even given appraisal a

thought. She'd always assumed its commercial value wasn't more than a couple of hundred dollars. The sentimental value, however, made it priceless.

"I seem to remember Walt telling me once it was a collector's piece," Ginny murmured. "I know how you feel about it, but it wouldn't hurt to have a jeweler take a look."

Molly held the cameo more tightly as she recalled the pawn broker's interest. She'd figured it was because he considered the cameo so unusual, not because of its monetary value.

Over the past few days she'd given ample thought to what assets they could sell to raise money. One problem was the fact that they had so little time. As for selling equipment or one of their vehicles, no one in Sweetgrass had money to spare or to spend. Her car, while paid for, wasn't worth five grand, and Sam's pickup was pretty old. Besides, he needed it on the ranch. Walt's old truck was worthless, and everything else they owned was mortgaged to the hilt.

"You're right," Molly said, finding a new resolve. "It wouldn't hurt to have a jeweler look at it."

"You want me to come along? On our way we can stop off at your place and I can beat the crap out of Sam. If he wants to feel sorry for himself, then I'll be sure and give him plenty of reason."

Molly laughed, for probably the first time in a week. "Oh, Ginny," she said, "I'm so glad we're friends." Impulsively she hugged the older woman. "But I can deal with Sam."

Immeasurably cheered, Molly returned home, hoping Sam's mood had improved.

"Sam," she called as she walked into the kitchen. Silence.

"Sam?" She checked the living room and glanced into the bedroom, thinking he might have gone back to bed for a nap.

He was as familiar with the doctor's orders as she was—in bed for two days, and then quiet and rest for the following week. She knew he was feeling better, but not well enough to leave the house.

Checking outside, she noticed that his truck was missing.

"Sam Dakota, where did you go?" Her instinctive reaction was anger that he'd defied the doctor's orders.

She searched for a note in the kitchen and found none.

Then she noticed that the hall-closet door was ajar, and she understood. That was where they stored the suitcases. She crossed again to the bedroom door, looked in and noticed that each one of the drawers on his side of the dresser had been left open.

Molly's legs felt like they were about to give out on her. She clutched the door frame with both hands as she took it all in.

Sam had left her. Unable to deal with their problems, he'd packed his bags and driven off. Without even saying goodbye.

Nineteen

Paul Harden, the jeweler, gently turned the cameo over in the palm of his hand. "Ginny was right. This piece is a rare collector's item. I couldn't begin to give you an accurate appraisal without making a couple of phone calls first."

"Could you guess?" Molly urged. "Maybe...a thousand?" she asked, hardly daring to believe in the possibility.

Unable to deal with Sam's abandonment, she'd driven into town. With all the problems crashing down around her shoulders, she'd decided to deal with the most pressing one first—the loan payment. She might be able to talk Mr. Burns into accepting a partial payment until they could get back on their feet financially and regroup after the loss of the herd.

"Much more than that. I'd say it was closer to five or six."

"Five or six thousand!" Molly's voice echoed in her ears, and she felt slightly dizzy. "You're not joking, are you?"

"Not about something like this," Paul told her. He was a jovial man in his early sixties with dark brown eyes that twinkled when he laughed. He'd sold Molly and Sam their wedding bands the day before the cer-

emony, and as a favor to Gramps had sized them overnight.

"Oh, my…"

"Are you interested in selling?" he asked.

"I…I don't know. I mean, no, I don't want to, but
I imagine I'm not going to have any choice."

Paul frowned. "I swear Burns is squeezing every
rancher in the area. If you want, I'll make a few calls
and ask around, see what I can do to get you the best
price."

"I'd appreciate it." Molly couldn't believe her good
fortune. Once again, even after his death, Gramps had
supplied the solution to her troubles. But giving up the
cameo would be so very difficult. She'd worn it all
these years and it held such meaning for her.

"Give me a call in the next couple of days," Paul
said, "and I'll let you know what I've found out."

Molly nodded, pinching her lips to keep from crying.
She'd rather sell her right arm than her grandmother's
cameo, but if worse came to worst, there'd be no help
for it.

"Don't worry," Paul said, patting her hand. "These
things often have a way of working out for the best."

"Thanks," she murmured, and turned away before
he saw the tears in her eyes.

This wasn't easy for Molly, but it was either take
matters into her own hands or become an emotional
casualty. Since Sam had seen fit to abandon her, she
had no choice but to do what she could to secure the
future for herself and her children. If that meant selling
a family heirloom, then so be it.

Molly arrived home thirty minutes before the boys
were due back from school. She dreaded telling them

Sam was gone. But it wasn't something she'd be able to hide. Tom, especially, would take the news hard.

From past experience she knew her children would look to her for their emotional cues. If she was strong and brave, they would be, too. For their sake, as well as her own, Molly prayed she'd be able to pull it off. While the breakup of her first marriage had devastated her, it didn't compare to the numbed sense of disbelief she felt now.

The phone rang, and Molly stared at it, not sure if she should answer or not. Part of her wanted it to be Sam; at the same time she didn't know if she could talk to him.

She answered on the third ring.

"This is Patrick Sparks from the Butte Rodeo returning Mr. Dakota's phone call."

Molly didn't understand why Sam would be calling Butte. "I'm sorry, he isn't here."

"Would you take a message and let him know I'm sorry I wasn't here to talk to him personally? Naturally I've heard of Sam." He paused and laughed briefly. "Best damn bull rider I've ever had the privilege to watch. I'd heard he was forced into retirement some years ago—but if he wants to ride again, we'd be more than happy to have him in Butte. In fact, we'd consider it an honor."

"Sam called you?" Molly asked, barely able to get the question out.

"Yes. Early this morning. Unfortunately I was out of the office at the time. I would've enjoyed talking to a rodeo legend like Sam Dakota."

"Are...there any other rodeos going on now?" Molly asked, thinking quickly.

"The season's winding down, but Missoula's putting on a big one this weekend."

"Thank you," Molly said. "Thank you so much."

Racing into the bedroom, she yanked the top drawer on Sam's side of the dresser all the way open. Sure enough, his clothes were there; only the top layer of T-shirts and briefs was missing. Molly berated herself for jumping to conclusions, for assuming the worst. For not trusting Sam. He hadn't left her at all! He'd packed up and gone to compete in a rodeo, hoping to collect the prize money.

Her husband was risking his life for her and the boys in order to make the payment on the ranch.

"Oh, Sam," she whispered, relieved and furious with him at once. "You're an idiot." What he didn't know was that this wasn't necessary, not any longer. She could sell the cameo. *Would* sell it.

The back door opened and the boys wandered in, their faces red from the cold and the long trek down the driveway.

"Each of you, pack an overnight bag," she instructed them, clapping her hands to get them moving.

"Are we going somewhere?" Tom asked, eyes wide with surprise.

"To the rodeo," she said, and because the relief overwhelmed her, she cupped his cold face between her hands and kissed both his cheeks. "First I'm going to phone Ginny—ask if Fred can stop by here to see to the horses and dogs...."

"Rodeo?" Tom ardently scrubbed her kiss from his cheeks. "Mom, have you lost it?"

Laughing and crying at the same time, she nodded. "No. I've *found* it. Found something wonderful."

"What?"

"Love," she whispered, then repeated. "Love."

It amazed Sam that anyone remembered him. He certainly didn't feel entitled to the hero's welcome he'd received when he paid his entry fee. All he cared about was the purse, a hefty five grand, which was exactly the amount needed to make the first payment.

He was the last entrant, the last man to ride. Exactly eight seconds—that was how long he needed to stay on. Eight seconds to win five thousand dollars. He stared down into the chute at the snorting bull, and his blood fired to life. It'd been a long time, and the adrenaline surged through his system. He was ready. He missed the old life—but not enough to trade it for what he had now. Sweetgrass was where he belonged. No, he belonged wherever Molly was, Molly and their family. She'd taught him that with her gentle love.

The bull snorted again, eager to be released from the constraining chute. In a couple of minutes Sam would ease his weight onto the beast's back and the door would open.

He was in top physical condition—strong, fit and agile. Working the ranch had done that for him. He'd recovered from his head injury; if he hadn't, the ride would have been a suicide mission, and he had no intention of dying. Nor did he intend to spend the remainder of his days crippled. He was a man with a lot of reasons to live. The time had come to start counting his blessings, instead of keeping tabs on what he'd lost.

Given the nod, Sam climbed over the top of the chute and settled himself on the bull's massive body. The animal's head reared back, and he slammed from side to side in a futile attempt to unseat his rider. The old boy would have eight seconds to do that once the chute door opened. From what Sam had seen so far, the bull was determined to give him a ride he'd feel all the way to his back molars.

Sam wrapped the bull rope around his hand. His blood roared in his ears, and he focused on the memory of Molly's face. The announcer's voice boomed over the public address system, and Sam heard his name and the cheers that followed. The other riders weren't the only ones who remembered him; apparently the audience did, too.

When the announcer finished, Sam gave the signal and the chute opened. The bull charged out of the pen, and Sam's right arm instinctively went up to maintain his balance.

Colors blurred as he was jerked and yanked and spun about. Yet despite the blurred images, he thought he saw Molly standing on the sidelines with the boys.

Here? How was it possible? He'd gone mad, Sam concluded. He'd tried to reach her at Ginny's and discovered she'd already left. Fred had promised to let her know, but Sam hadn't mentioned *which* rodeo for exactly this reason: he hadn't wanted Molly to come.

It felt as though every bone in his body had been jarred from its sockets before the buzzer finally went off. Spectators leaped to their feet and the applause was deafening. He'd done it. He'd stayed on the bull for eight seconds, the longest eight seconds of his life. He had the purse.

Soon Sam was behind the stands, out of the limelight. He felt weak enough to faint, but exhilaration kept him on his feet. His throat was parched; he accepted a drink of water and gulped it down. As he set the cup aside, he saw her.

Molly stood no more than five feet away. It hadn't

been his imagination—she'd been there. She'd watched him ride, had screamed and cheered for him.

"Hello, sweetheart," he whispered, holding out his arms to her. His arms and his heart.

She seemed unsure which to do first: kiss him or give him the lecture of his life. He looked at his oldest son, but Tom shrugged as if to say Sam was on his own.

The lecture won. "Sam Dakota, how could you leave me like that and without so much as a note?" she demanded.

"Fred was supposed to tell you." Unwilling to wait for her to come to him, he covered the distance separating them and gathered her in his arms. The feel of her filled his heart. He'd briefly feared that old life would tempt him once he was back; it hadn't happened. Instead, he'd realized something. The injury that ended his rodeo career had really been a gift, because it had brought him Molly and the boys. Neither fame nor glory could replace the contentment he'd felt since his marriage.

"I didn't talk to Fred—just Ginny." Molly shook her head. "Oh, Sam, how could you have taken such a risk?" she whispered, sounding close to tears.

"That was easy, my love. I did it for us."

"You could've been killed!" she cried, fighting back tears.

"I wasn't."

"Or badly hurt."

"I'm none the worse for wear." He kissed the tip of her nose and she buried her face in his neck. Then he rubbed the side of his face against her hair, loving the fresh scent of it.

"Dad! Dad!" Clay tugged hard at his sleeve, and

Sam placed his arm around the boy's shoulders. Clay tugged harder. "That man over there," he said urgently. "He's got a broken shoelace."

"He should be wearing cowboy boots like the rest of us," Sam teased. For a moment he was amused by the things kids noticed. Then he made the connection—just as Clay said, "But he's got those combat boots, exactly like the guy who grabbed me."

"Where?" Sam demanded, releasing Molly.

"Over there." Clay pointed to a tall man dressed in fatigues who stood by the corral, talking to another man.

Sam recognized him immediately as one of the two unsavory characters who'd walked into Willie's the night Pearl was killed. The men she'd wanted to avoid.

Without hesitation Sam started across the yard, anger driving his steps. "Why don't we ask him about it right now?" he said between gritted teeth. He had every intention of finding out why a grown man would want to terrify a boy and his family.

"I'll get the authorities," Molly said, and before Sam could assure her he wouldn't need anything other than his fists to get the answers he wanted, she was gone.

"We need to talk," Sam said, interrupting the two men.

The first man barely glanced at him, but the second one stared back as though he'd seen a ghost. He recovered quickly, however, and asked, "What do we need to talk about?"

"My son."

"I didn't know they let jailbirds like you—" As soon as Sam was within striking distance, the man attacked, hitting him square in the jaw with a powerful right hook.

Sam didn't see it coming and the punch caught him off balance and sent him sprawling to the ground. His jaw hurt, but not nearly as much as his pride. He half rose and hurled himself at the other man, hitting him just above the knees. The force made him topple backward, but Sam wasn't able to pin him down. Dust clogged the air as they rolled around in the dirt.

"Sam, Sam…" Molly's voice drifted toward him. He wanted to tell her to stand clear, but he dared not divert his attention.

"Give it to him, Lance," the man's friend shouted.

Lance outweighed him by some pounds, and Sam was stiff and sore from the recent bull-ride. He guessed from Lance's technique that he'd been trained by the military.

"Sam…Sam!" Molly screamed in warning as he blocked a punch. He turned to tell her to get out of the way and saw that she'd picked up a shovel.

Unfortunately her aim was slightly off and when she slammed it down, it missed Lance entirely and hit Sam on the shoulder instead. Pain shot down his arm and he crumpled to the ground. He must have briefly lost consciousness when his head hit the ground because the next thing he knew two sheriff's deputies were standing beside Molly. Somehow she'd managed to corner Lance with the shovel. His friend was nowhere to be seen.

"What's going on here?" one of the lawmen asked, moving between the two men.

Molly and Sam both started talking at once. Molly stopped and signaled Sam to continue. He explained what had happened with Clay.

"Someone stole our winter herd last week and shot my husband," Molly threw out. "Ask him about *that* while you're at it." She pointed at Lance, her face a study in contempt.

"Hey, you're not pinning that on me." Lance wiped away blood at the corner of his mouth. He glared at Sam. "If you want to ask anyone questions, you can ask Mr. Hero over there about a certain woman who disappeared. He knows a lot more than he's saying."

Sam tensed at the mention of Pearl's murder. "You're the one she was hiding from," he accused, vividly remembering the fear on Pearl's face when she saw Lance.

"My husband had nothing to do with the poor woman's death," Molly said righteously. "Now arrest that man." She pointed in Lance's direction. "On kidnapping charges."

"Is there a problem here?" Sheriff Maynard stepped through the crowd of curious onlookers and presented his badge to the deputies.

"Sheriff Maynard." Molly sounded relieved, and truth be known, Sam was pleased to see the other man, too. Surely now he could count on the sheriff of Sweetgrass to clear his name.

"I have a warrant for that man's arrest. He's charged with the murder of Pearl Mitchell," Maynard announced. As everyone watched openmouthed, he slapped handcuffs on Lance's wrists and led him away.

"You're an idiot," Sheriff Gene Maynard—alias Monroe—shouted at Lance.

The younger man sat in the back of the patrol car. "Come on, Monroe," he whined. "This is a joke, right?"

Monroe could sense Lance's resentment—and frankly it felt good to put handcuffs on that bastard. It was what he deserved for all the screwups. The incompetence Monroe was left to deal with was like an aching tooth. The pain never seemed to lessen nor was it likely to go away. You'd have a bad tooth pulled, he thought. You'd get rid of it. Lance was a disgrace to the Loyalists. A hothead. Insubordinate.

"You're the one who killed her, aren't you?" he muttered as he drove toward Sweetgrass. Despite the so-called alibi provided by the bartender, Monroe believed that Lance was responsible for Pearl's death. It was the only scenario that made sense.

"How many times do I have to tell you I didn't do it?" Lance growled from the back seat.

Monroe felt such a blinding flash of anger he had trouble keeping the car on the road.

"Where you takin' me?" Lance demanded.

Monroe wasn't sure until precisely that moment. "I'm hauling your sorry ass to jail where it belongs."

"Oh, no, you don't," Lance squawked. "You can't! You wouldn't!"

Monroe experienced a deep sense of satisfaction on informing him otherwise. "Just watch me."

Lance fell into a sulk. As they neared Sweetgrass, Monroe asked him, "How'd the kid know it was you?" His gaze met the other man's in the rearview mirror.

Lance shrugged. "No idea."

"You should've stayed away from the rodeo."

"Couldn't help myself. I like rodeos. How was I supposed to know Dakota was riding? His name wasn't on the program."

"Good thing for you that you didn't know."

"Whaddaya mean?"

Monroe sighed. The question was another example of the man's incompetence. "Well, if you'd known, you might've been able to keep him from picking up the prize money, right?"

"Oh, yeah. Right."

"So at least you have an excuse for screwing up—again." Monroe's hands tightened around the steering wheel. Burns and the others weren't going to be pleased when they learned Sam and Molly had managed to come up with the first payment. Damn stubborn fools, Dakota and his wife. They would have saved themselves a lot of grief if they'd given up the ranch sooner. Now Monroe had no choice. The Loyalists needed that land and they intended to get it, but the matter was in Monroe's hands now. He couldn't trust Lance; the man was useless. Besides, freeing him would raise too many questions. Monroe grinned. He couldn't deny he relished this assignment. Sam Dakota needed to be taught a lesson, set down a peg or two. And he was just the man to do it.

Sam was tired but happy. He had his family around him and, at least for the moment, all was right with the world. They were home, and the ranch house had never looked more inviting. Especially now that they'd be able to make the loan payment. Sam suppressed the sudden urge to laugh. It was a ticklish sort of feeling, one that bubbled up from the soles of his feet and touched every part of him. The crushing burden of this financial worry had been lifted from his shoulders. And that was only part of the good news.

Lance Elkins had been arrested, and judging by the anger brewing in Sheriff Maynard, Sam guessed that

Lance would be making a few more confessions. Perhaps they'd finally be able to get to the bottom of the freak "accidents." If anyone could persuade Lance to talk, it was the sheriff. Sam almost felt sorry for Lance.

"Sam?"

Then there was Molly. His love, his wife. His pregnant wife. They hadn't spoken about it yet and it had taken him long enough to figure out, but he was sure. So sure. "In here." He sat in the living room, his feet propped on the ottoman, more tired than he'd ever been in his life. His head ached, his back throbbed, and there didn't seem to be a single muscle in his body unwilling to raise a protest over his return to bull-riding. The fist fight with Elkins hadn't helped.

"Oh." Molly walked into the room and stopped abruptly.

He opened his eyes. "Oh, what?"

"You...you look tired."

"That depends," he said, grinning up at her. "I'm certainly not too tired to make love to my wife."

"Sam!" She chastised him in a whisper and glanced over her shoulder to make sure the boys weren't listening in.

"They're upstairs," Sam assured her.

"We need to talk," she said, and then, as if the subject distressed her, she looked away. "I realize now isn't the best time for me to get pregnant but—"

"Why isn't it?" he asked. He'd given this more than a little thought in the past week, and try as he might, he couldn't make himself regret the fact that they'd been careless. His heart felt as though it might burst with joy, and all because Molly was carrying his child. Burst with joy. He'd heard that expression before; he'd never understood it till now.

"Our insurance only covers a small portion of the cost."

"Then we'll make payments to the doctor," he said with complete confidence.

"You never said how you felt about us having a baby…" She clamped her teeth on her lower lip.

Holding back a smile would have been impossible just then. "I don't think I've ever been happier in my life."

He held out his arms to her and she'd just started toward him when there was a loud crack of sound against the wall. Sam knew a rifle when he heard one. Grabbing Molly's arm, he leaped out of the chair and jerked her forward, pulling her down.

Together they hit the floor. Sam took the brunt of the impact and yelped at the flash of pain.

"What is it?" Molly asked, her eyes wide with terror.

"Someone's shooting at us."

"No—that's impossible!"

The dogs started barking frantically and Clay raced into the living room. Sam yelled, "Get down!"

The boy dropped to the carpet just as a bullet whizzed by where his head had been a second earlier.

"That does it." Sam crawled on his hands and knees into the kitchen. "Nobody move." Just then a blaze of bullets ripped a line in the wall directly across from him.

Molly's cry of alarm intensified his anger and his fear. She covered her head with both hands and buried her face in the carpet.

Clay screamed as a window exploded, spraying glass about the room.

"Sam! Sam!" Tom shouted from upstairs. "What should I do? Tell me what to do."

"Stay where you are," he instructed. "Don't move."

Molly raised her head enough to reach for Clay and drag him to her side where she could protect him.

Sam didn't know what the hell was happening, but he wasn't going to sit still and let his family be used for target practice. All that he held dear was in this house, and whoever was shooting had best make peace with his maker, because Sam wasn't going to wait around for answers.

Slipping into the master bedroom, he opened the bottom dresser drawer and removed a handgun. Exiting the house undetected was no easy matter, but the safest room from which to leave was the bathroom. He climbed over the window ledge and fell into the darkness, landing hard.

Once outside, he crouched low and headed in the direction he'd seen the first round of bullets. His advantage was his knowledge of the land. The horses moved restlessly in their stalls; their tension strong and pungent.

Carefully he made his way along the wall to the corner of the barn.

"That's far enough, Dakota. Drop your weapon."

Sam stopped abruptly. A chill ran down his spine when he recognized the voice.

"Do it *now*, or you're a dead man."

Sam's fingers relaxed as he bent forward and cautiously dropped the pistol on the ground. "Maynard?" Slowly he turned around to face the other man.

"I can see you're surprised."

Sam didn't bother to deny it. "Why?"

Sheriff Maynard continued as if he hadn't heard. "It's a real shame, seeing how you managed to make good and all. Just when it looked like you'd done a turnaround, an unknown assailant attacked the family. In your effort to see to their safety, you were shot and killed. Then a few weeks after you're buried, the town will learn how you swindled old man Wheaton and duped Molly into marrying you. She won't be able to hold her head up in public, and she'll sell out at a lower price than originally offered."

"What's so important about this land?" Sam demanded, his hands doubled into fists.

"Me and my friends, we need it."

"Friends?"

A slow grin twisted the lawman's face. "The Loyalists."

Sam had heard of the militia group and knew they were active in the area, but he didn't know much about them. None of this made sense.

"This country's losing everything it stands for," Gene Maynard explained. "That's what we believe. The only way to hold on to our freedom is to overthrow the government. It just so happens this land is perfect for training purposes. We knew Wheaton was on his way out, so we had the plans drawn up and we aren't going to change things now." His mouth thinned. "You threw a wrench into our plans when you arrived."

Sam realized that his appearance on the scene was one thing, but his marriage to Molly another. No wonder the lawman had had it in for him.

"It's a shame to kill you, Dakota. You've kind of grown on me. But I could see a long time ago that you don't share our views, and that's unfortunate because you could've done us good. You've got guts."

"Why'd you kill Pearl?"

Maynard ignored the question. "Not long after you're dead, the town will discover you were the one responsible for her death."

"But he isn't the one who killed her, is he, Gene?" Russell Letson's voice rang out from behind the sheriff.

Maynard froze.

"Drop the gun."

"Russell, get out of here," Maynard said, glancing over his shoulder. "Go before I forget we're related."

"I know who killed Pearl."

"Great. You can tell me all about it later. Now, for your own sake, leave, and forget you ever saw me here with Dakota."

"That's one difference between you and me, cousin," Russell murmured sarcastically. "I have a very long memory. I'm not going to forget anything I heard or saw tonight."

"This has nothing to do with you."

"That's where you're wrong. Did she suffer, Gene? Did she beg you to let her live? Did she plead for mercy?"

"For the love of God, man, it wasn't me! Now drop the gun."

"You beat her." The words were full of anger and accusation.

"All right, all right, I beat her," Maynard confessed, "but I wasn't the one who killed her, I swear it." As he spoke, he swung around toward Russell.

Instinctively Sam knew what Maynard intended and with a wild cry leaped toward him, wanting to knock him off balance before he could fire. But a gun exploded before Sam was two inches off the ground.

Gene Maynard slumped down. Rearing back, he aimed at his cousin, but Sam used the momentum of his leap to kick the gun out of his hand.

Slowly Russell walked toward the moaning sheriff. His eyes burned with hatred as he leveled his weapon at the man's chest.

Whimpering for mercy, the sheriff twitched and tried to crawl away.

"Don't do it, Russell," Sam said. "He isn't worth spending the rest of your life in prison. Let *him* rot there, not you. The inmates will have a field day with him. Let them dole out the punishment."

Russell blinked and Sam knew his words had found their way through his hatred and into his mind. "I want him to suffer."

"He will," Sam promised.

"No!" Maynard shouted. "I didn't kill Pearl. I swear it." Blood flowed from his wound as he stared up at them with glazed eyes. Russell hesitated for the first time. "Why'd you want the Broken Arrow Ranch?"

"It was for the militia—the Loyalists. We were going to use it ourselves, build our training grounds here. This place and the one next to it. Two old people about to die…"

"Burns is involved, as well, isn't he?" Russell asked, and it was clear from Maynard's reaction that he was surprised the attorney knew it.

"Yes," he moaned.

"He's losing a lot of blood," Sam warned.

"Let him. I want him to rot in hell."

"She was a hooker, man! Why do you care?" Maynard asked, clutching his wounded shoulder.

"I cared," Russell said slowly. "I cared."

"Sam...Sam!" The lights went on and Molly raced across the yard. He caught her in his arms and hugged her fiercely.

"Tom," Sam said to the older boy, who'd followed his mother out, "call for an ambulance. After that I'll contact the authorities in Missoula."

Molly continued to hug him, as if she was afraid to let him go. "It's all right, sweetheart, not to worry," he murmured. "I'm fine."

"Sheriff Maynard?"

"I'm afraid so."

"But why?"

"It's a long story." He kissed her, then removed the pistol from Russell's fingers. "How'd you know it was Maynard?"

Russell's smile was infinitely sad. "You might say Pearl told me." His face darkened with pain and he looked from Molly to Sam. "I hope the two of you will be very happy."

"We already are," Molly said gently, and smiled up at her husband. "And that's not going to change."

Epilogue

Molly gave birth to a healthy baby girl the afternoon Gene Maynard, alias Monroe, Lance Elkins and David Burns were sentenced. They were convicted on a number of federal charges and would spend the rest of their natural lives in prison.

Sam had gone into the delivery room with Molly and coached her through the final stage of labor. When the baby was born, the physician had placed her in his arms for the first time. As Sam held his daughter and stared awestruck at her beautiful face, his eyes filled with tears.

The emotion he felt today far surpassed what he'd felt when he won the silver buckle—his rodeo triumph. *This* triumph, the birth of his child, made his rodeo accomplishments seem hollow. The buckle had attained a new meaning for him, though—because Molly had given it back to him. When he looked at it now, what he thought of was her love.

"She's perfect," he whispered, his voice hoarse with emotion. "Just like her mother."

Exhausted by the long hours of labor, Molly smiled contentedly.

"Welcome to the world, Cassie Marie Dakota." Sam gently kissed her brow. "You have two older brothers who're gonna spoil you something terrible."

"And a daddy, too."

"Oh, Molly," Sam said, gazing at his wife. "How did a saddle bum like me ever get so lucky? I have you, Tom, Clay and now Cassie. My heart's so full it feels like it's about to jump out of my chest." He stroked the baby's face. "Hey, Cassie. Your Grandma Dakota's gonna love you. And your aunts and uncles..." Sam had called his family Christmas Day; they'd come to visit a week later, just in time for New Year's. Another new beginning. They'd be back, all of them, once Molly and the baby had settled into a routine.

Molly's eyes drifted shut.

"I love you so damn much," Sam added.

"I love you, too, sweetheart...but right now I have to sleep...."

While she was wheeled into the recovery room, Sam took Cassie into the nursery and handed her to a nurse.

When Molly woke up, she was in her hospital bed, and Sam was asleep in the chair beside her. Clay and Tom tiptoed silently into the room. "How'd you feel, Mom?"

"Wonderful," she assured them.

"We just went to see Cassie. For a girl she's not bad-looking," Clay said, then gave a small sigh just so she'd know he was only a *little* disappointed she hadn't given him the brother he'd requested.

Tom claimed he'd wanted a sister all along and beamed her a proud smile as if she'd purposely ordered a girl on his behalf. "The way I figure it, she'll need an older brother to look out for her."

"Hey, she's going to need two older brothers," Clay said. "You're not her only brother, you know."

"What about changing her diapers? Will her older brothers be willing to do that?" Molly asked.

"Sure," Tom said, sending Clay a sidelong glance. "*He'll* be more than happy to help change poopy diapers."

Molly laughed, and Sam opened his eyes. Stretching his arms high above his head, he looked around the room. "I'm certainly glad you boys gave me a little practice in this fathering business," he said with a grin.

"Hey, glad to do it," Tom teased. "Cassie will thank us later."

"You willing to do this again?" Clay asked. "Next time, get me a little brother, all right?"

"Anything you say, son." Sam reached for Molly's hand. He brought it to his lips and gently kissed her palm. His eyes were bright with love. "I wish your grandfather were here."

"He's here, Sam," she assured him. "I'm as sure of that as I am of your love for me. Both my grandparents." She closed her eyes and could almost hear her grandmother whisper to her beloved husband.

"Walter, you chose well for our Molly. You chose well."

As Russell sat in his office reading, the door opened and two men dressed in dark suits stepped inside.

"I'm sorry," he said, "we're already closed for the day."

"Come with us," the first man said without explanation.

Russell stood. "I beg your pardon?"

"You're to come with us."

The second man pulled out a badge and flashed it, but Russell wasn't able to read the identification card.

All he knew was that these two men worked for the federal government.

"Where are we going?" he asked as he followed them out the door. Neither one answered. "Should I call someone?"

"That wouldn't be advisable."

Not that there was anyone to call. His mother had died that past Thanksgiving, and the only close friend he had these days was Sam Dakota. Molly had come home from the hospital the day before, and he'd been out to visit her and hold Cassie. The infant had immediately charmed him; he'd found it difficult to leave.

One man drove and the other sat in the back seat with him. They'd been on the road twenty minutes, still refusing to answer his questions, when Russell realized where they were headed. His cabin. This puzzled him even more.

A little later they pulled into the driveway and parked in his usual spot. A second car was already there.

"We'll wait for you here," one of the men told him.

"I'm to go inside?"

"That's right." This was said as if it should have been obvious.

Not knowing what to expect, Russell walked into the house. A woman stood at the far side of the living room, at the window that overlooked the valley. The first thing he noticed was how familiar she seemed.

"Hello, Russell."

Not until she spoke did he recognize her. His voice nearly failed him. *"Pearl?"*

"It's a shock, isn't it?" she asked softly.

Her hair was different and she'd gained a few pounds; the hollowed places in her face were filled out.

She'd been pretty before, but there was a gentle beauty about her now, a serenity.

His knees were too weak to hold him and he sank into the first available seat.

"I'm sorry to do this to you," she said. "I didn't think I'd ever see you again, but now that the trial's over, they said I was free to contact you." Her voice wavered a bit and she stopped.

"The trial?" His head buzzed with questions.

"I was the one who got in touch with the FBI," she explained. "They staged my death.... I couldn't tell you, Russell. I couldn't get you involved."

"But all that blood?"

"It wasn't mine."

"The body? They found the body."

"That was...fortuitous. Some poor murdered woman—I feel terrible about that. She still hasn't been identified...." Her voice trailed off.

Anger propelled him to his feet. "You let me believe you were dead!"

"I didn't have any choice."

He whirled around, away from her, while he thought this through.

"Monroe...Gene didn't know I could read," she whispered. "He...he left information around without any fear that I'd read it and understand. But then you taught me and I was able to tell the authorities the Loyalists' plans. I remember almost everything I've read—I have a good memory. Please, oh, please, don't be angry with me."

What was the matter with him? Russell mused. He had Pearl back. It was far more than he'd dared hope, more than he'd dared dream.

"I love you," she whispered, tears shining from her

eyes. "Now you know why I did what I did." After an awkward silence she bowed her head. "You can go now if you want—the agents will take you back to town."

"I'm not going anywhere without you," Russell said, walking toward her. He wrapped his arms around her and she clung to him, weeping softly. "Not ever again."

"You'll have to give up your life as you know it. Take on a new identity. Become part of the Witness Protection program."

"Done."

"And love me for the rest of your life."

"Done," he whispered brokenly. "For the rest of my life."

"And mine," Pearl said, smiling up at him, her eyes bright with tears.